The Youngest

A Tale of Manitoba

Bessie Marchant

Alpha Editions

This edition published in 2024

ISBN : 9789362991577

Design and Setting By
Alpha Editions
www.alphaedis.com
Email - info@alphaedis.com

As per information held with us this book is in Public Domain.
This book is a reproduction of an important historical work. Alpha Editions uses the best technology to reproduce historical work in the same manner it was first published to preserve its original nature. Any marks or number seen are left intentionally to preserve its true form.

Contents

CHAPTER I The Wonder of It ....- 1 -
CHAPTER II Concerning the Doynes ....- 8 -
CHAPTER III Tremulous Beginnings ....- 15 -
CHAPTER IV A Series of Shocks ....- 21 -
CHAPTER V Against her Will ....- 27 -
CHAPTER VI A Wild Journey ....- 34 -
CHAPTER VII Worse than Her Fears ....- 41 -
CHAPTER VIII Great Expectations ....- 47 -
CHAPTER IX A Dreadful Blow ....- 53 -
CHAPTER X The Worst ....- 61 -
CHAPTER XI A Wild Revolt ....- 67 -
CHAPTER XII The Glory of the Wheat ....- 72 -
CHAPTER XIII A Trick of Memory ....- 80 -
CHAPTER XIV In the Rush ....- 87 -
CHAPTER XV Temptation ....- 94 -
CHAPTER XVI A Blow of Fate ....- 101 -
CHAPTER XVII Black Ruin ....- 108 -
CHAPTER XVIII Standing in the Breach ....- 115 -
CHAPTER XIX A Disquieting Rumour ....- 122 -
CHAPTER XX An Impossible Favour ....- 129 -
CHAPTER XXI Out of the Silence ....- 136 -
CHAPTER XXII The Errand is Done ....- 143 -
CHAPTER XXIII Something of a Mistake ....- 150 -
CHAPTER XXIV A Revelation for Bertha ....- 157 -
CHAPTER XXV Disappointment ....- 164 -
CHAPTER XXVI En Route ....- 172 -

CHAPTER XXVII A Weird Night ....- 179 -
CHAPTER XXVIII Consternation ....- 188 -
CHAPTER XXIX A Great Embarrassment ....- 193 -
CHAPTER XXX Bad News ....- 201 -
CHAPTER XXXI The Tidings Confirmed ....- 208 -
CHAPTER XXXII The Man at Last ....- 215 -
CHAPTER XXXIII The Mystery Clears ....- 221 -
CHAPTER XXXIV The End ....- 230 -

CHAPTER I
The Wonder of It

BERTHA heard the commotion as she came round the bend, where the road from Paston led out on to the cliffs. It was a very quiet day, although there was a heavy swell on outside, which meant danger to any small craft that got among the rocks. She was very tired, and there was a horrible stitch in her side from walking so fast. But she was anxious to get home in time to cook supper for Anne, and she had simply raced along the level bit of the road.

Old Jan Saunders, with his wife and the fat German who kept the little store at the bottom of the hill, were standing in an excited group at the edge of the roadway and pointing out to the upstanding rocks called the Shark's Teeth, which showed grim and deadly a few yards out from the shore.

"What is the matter? What is wrong?" she gasped, panting still, and pressing her hand against her side to quiet the pain of the stitch.

"Ach! Ach!" sobbed the fat German, wringing his pudgy hands, while the tears rolled down his cheeks. "It is a man; he is caught on the Shark's Teeth, and he will be drowned."

"Oh, how very, very dreadful!" exclaimed Bertha, turning pale, and wishing that she had gone the other way, although it was so much longer, and she would certainly not have been home in time to get the supper ready.

"We haven't got a boat," piped old Jan in his thin, wavering voice. "Nowt but a rope. Our Mestlebury fleet went out on the morning tide, there ain't a boat nearer than Paston, and with such a sea it would take four hours to row round."

"He'll be drowned afoor then, poor chap, he will; for the tide is flowing in fast, and his boat won't lift more than another foot!" cried Mrs. Saunders, who was weeping like the German.

Bertha turned sick and faint. If only, only she had gone the other way, instead of stumbling on a scene like this! Suddenly old Jan turned upon her with an almost fierce expression on his kindly old face. "You can swim, missie. Tak' a roop oot to that poor chap yonder, and we will tow you back safe enough, boat and all."

"Oh, I am afraid, I am afraid!" she cried, covering her face with her hands to shut out the sight of the grey, heaving sea, the little boat wedged in under the rocks, and the man who sat there waiting for death to take him, because he could not swim, and his boat was caught too fast for any effort of his to push it off.

"He will drown! Ah, what a cruel fate it is, and my three boys gone just the same! Dear Lord, when shall it be that the sea will give up its dead?" wailed Mrs. Saunders.

"Ach! Ach! And such a proper man too! Dear Gott in Heaven, don't let him die before our eyes," sobbed the German, sinking on his knees in the roadway with his hands clasped in supplication.

"I will run for Anne; she can swim, and she is so brave!" cried Bertha, whose breath was coming in lumpy gasps of excitement.

"No use at all; he would be drowned before school-marm could get here, if she ran every step of the way," said old Jan hoarsely. "See, the boat bumped that time, and he got a nasty knock, poor chap! It is your chance, missie, and only yours; and it is a man's life that is hanging on your hands, to save or to throw away."

Bertha felt as if her brain would burst. A man's life to hang on her feeble, incapable hands! And it was the wonder of it that roused her to prompt, decided action.

"Fetch the rope!" she said curtly, as she wrenched off her coat and stooped to the buttons of her boots.

A chill dismay came over her then as her hand touched her heavy serge skirt. It would have to come off, and she had nothing underneath but a grey underskirt patched with green. How her sisters had laughed at those two patches with the contrast of colour! But she had been too indolent to alter them. Yet now she winced as she stood before the three, erect and slim, with those two patches of vivid green upon her knees.

"God speed you, missie!" muttered old Jan, as he knotted the rope about her waist. "Swim east when you start, and the current will drift you right down on the boat."

A man's life on her futile hands!

What was it Hilda had said to Anne only that morning at breakfast when the porridge was burned and the coffee was half-cold? "Bertha is hopeless; she dreams all day, and wastes every atom of her strength in building castles in the air, while we have to work and to bear all the discomforts of her incompetence."

And now she, Bertha, the incompetent one, had to save a man's life or to see him drown!

"Oh, I would rather die myself than see him drown!" she sobbed, and then she took the water with a motion so swift and graceful that the three on the steep, rocky shore gave a wavering cheer of encouragement.

The man in the boat called out something too, but it was a warning to her not to risk her life for him. This she did not hear, however, and would not have heeded if she had.

She was swimming steadily, gliding through the water with quick, curving strokes, which Anne had taught her on the holiday afternoons in summer, when they had gone to bathe from the little strip of sand in front of Seal Cove. Anne held a silver medal for swimming, but Bertha had never even thought of competing.

The water was cold, so cold; for autumn was far advanced. The great storm of yesterday was still leaving its effect upon the sea. Bertha felt the heave and throb of it even in that sheltered little bay, and before she was halfway across to the Shark's Teeth she knew that it would be an awful struggle to get there. But now there was no thought of turning back. If she had to die she must, but she could not—oh, she could not!—fail that man out yonder whose life depended upon her. Panting heavily, she was swimming almost blindly, struggling forward, yet knowing all the time that the drift of the current had her in its grip, and she was powerless to fight against it.

She could not go much farther, she could not. She would have to fail after all, and her sisters would say, "Bertha is always so ineffectual, poor little girl!"

But she did not want to be pitied, she just hated it. She wanted to do something that was worth the doing; so she struggled and struggled, until it seemed to her that she had been in the water for weeks and weeks.

Then suddenly a strong hand gripped at her shoulder and a voice said in her ears, "Downright plucky you are, and you have saved me from an uncommonly tight corner!"

She had reached the boat, and it was the man whom she had come to save who was helping her to scramble on board. She was fearfully exhausted, but that did not matter. What troubled her most was to think of those bright green patches which were absolutely vivid now because of the wet. She had tumbled into the boat anyhow, vigorously helped by the man, who had at least strong arms, even though he could not swim nor yet extricate himself from a plight into which no prudent person should have fallen.

Whew! How cold she was! She was shivering violently, and her teeth were chattering. The man dived under the seat upon which he was sitting and dragged out a coat. "Here, put this on; it may help a little," he said, holding it out so that she might slip her arms into it.

The coat was long and roomy, and Bertha dragged it round her dripping underwear, feeling that it was a comfort unspeakable to have it, and then she sat and watched while the three on the shore tugged at the rope, and the man in the boat used the oar as a lever to do his part in getting out of his tight corner.

How the fat German tugged and strove! A gurgle of irrepressible laughter escaped from Bertha when the boat suddenly gave, and the three on the shore tumbled all in a heap.

"I am glad that you are able to get some amusement out of it," said the man rather curtly, for he too had also fallen with the jerk of the boat and had banged his elbow on the side.

"Please forgive me; I did not mean to make fun, but they did look so comical," murmured Bertha contritely; and the man, who had supposed that she was laughing at him, was instantly mollified.

The boat was going through the water now by leaps and jerks. The zeal of the fat German was without discretion, and as he was the strongest of the three, he naturally set the pace.

"Hold, hold; careful there; mind the rocks, or you will upset her!" cried old Jan warningly.

The two in the boat were quite at the mercy of the tow-rope, for the man had broken one oar in trying to lever his boat out from the grip of the Shark's Teeth, and the other had been torn from his hand and lost in that sudden jerk which had upset the three on the shore.

"Oh, the rocks!" cried Bertha, with a gasp of dismay, realizing that unless the towing were very steady, they must be upset when nearing the shore.

Then she thought of Anne, who would be coming home from school to find no supper ready, most likely the fire out, and a general air of discomfort everywhere.

"Oh dear, oh dear, she will think that I did it on purpose!" said Bertha to herself, repressing a sob with difficulty. She had meant so honestly to be all ready for Anne this evening, so it was fearfully disappointing to have failed.

"Mind the rocks! Pull in slowly!" she shouted, reaching out one arm in a roomy coatsleeve, and fending the boat away from a half-submerged rock. But at that moment the German gave a wild tug at the rope, and the boat jerked up against a rock on the other side. The two were pitched violently against each other, and then, before they could sort themselves out at all, they were flung headfirst into the water.

Fortunately they were so near the shore, that old Jan waded in and, with the help of the German, dragged out the man, who had knocked his head against the rock in falling, and seemed helpless, while Bertha scrambled ashore as best she could, terribly encumbered by the big coat, and fearfully worn out with all that she had gone through.

But she had done what was expected of her, and nothing else seemed to matter in the least. The others could look after the man. She did not even stop to see if he were rallying from that desperate blow on the head which he got when the boat was overturned. Thrusting her wet feet into her boots, and gathering her coat, skirt, and hat in her arms, she fled along the road as fast as she could go. If only she could get home before Anne, and slip into dry clothes, it would still be possible perhaps to have some sort of supper ready for the tired eldest sister.

There was a wonderful elation stirring in Bertha's heart. It was as if something had broken away and set her free. She had saved a man's life at the risk of her own, and the very thought of it thrilled her into new life and vigour. Her limbs were shaking still, and her breath came in sobbing gasps as she fled along the road; but she was happier than she had ever been in all her life before.

Flip, flap, flop! Flip, flap, flop! Her unbuttoned boots squelched up and down over her wet stockings, and she looked wildly dishevelled as she dashed along Mestlebury Main Street. One or two women standing at the doors of their wooden houses called out to know what was the matter, but she paid no heed at all, and so at length came in sight of the little drab-painted house with green shutters where she lived with her sisters.

She was in time, for the door was still fast shut—sure sign that Anne was not home yet. Thrusting her hand into the place where the key was always hidden when they all chanced to be out together, she drew it out, and, unlocking the door, passed hurriedly in to see if there were any fire still left in the stove. It took but a minute to thrust a handful of dry kindlings among the embers, which were still hot; then, filling the kettle and standing it on the stove to boil, she darted into her own room to shed her wet garments.

The chamber, a small one, was in the wildest confusion. Sheets of manuscript were strewn on table, chair, and bed. Garments of all sorts lay about in the wildest disorder. The bed was unmade, and a liberal coating of grey dust showed on such of the furniture as was not covered with papers or clothes. She gave a groan of dismay at the sight. It was as if the eyes of her mind had been opened at once to see all her defects and shortcomings.

"I can't stop to tidy it now. But I will do differently to-morrow—oh, I will!" she said, with a fervent outburst, as she dragged on dry garments and twisted her wet hair into an untidy knot at the top of her head.

The wet clothes were all left in a heap in one corner of the room, for her sole idea was to have supper ready for Anne—the very nicest supper which could be managed in the time.

This was one of the nights when Hilda did not come home to sleep, and it was a secret satisfaction to Bertha that she would be able to get her small reforms well under way, before her sharp-tongued second sister appeared on the scene again.

"It will have to be white monkey on toast, I think; that is the quickest thing that I can do," she muttered, as she darted to and fro collecting the milk, flour, butter, egg, and other ingredients which went to the making of the dish known as white monkey; then, while the milk was getting hot in the double saucepan, she grated the cheese and toasted generous slices of bread, on which the white monkey was to be spread.

There was such a glow of triumph in her heart, and such a sense of elation in her bearing, that for a time it over-mastered her weariness. She had done a brave thing, a really plucky deed, and although she had been in a manner forced into the doing, nothing could take the joy of it from her.

Oh, it was good, it was good to be of use in the world—to do something which but for her must have been left undone. And Jan Saunders had said that the man's life hung upon her hands!

"My dear Bertha, what have you been doing to yourself?" cried a voice from the door, in a tone of shocked surprise, and Bertha, who had been too busy to notice the sound of approaching steps, turned quickly, to see her eldest sister standing on the threshold, while just behind was a gentleman who was a stranger to her.

Then it flashed upon poor Bertha what an awful object she must look, with her wet hair screwed into a tight knot on the top of her head, and her garments simply pitch-forked on to her person.

And Anne was as neat and trim as if fresh from making a toilet, although in reality she had been teaching the township school all day.

"Is this the musical sister?" asked the stranger, advancing upon Bertha with outstretched hand and a manner glowing with kindness.

A gurgle of irrepressible laughter shook Anne as she thought of what Hilda's feelings would have been if she could have heard the question, and then she answered hastily, "No, indeed; Hilda is not at home this evening. This is only Bertha, my youngest sister."

"SHE HAD REACHED THE BOAT"

CHAPTER II
Concerning the Doynes

ANNE DOYNE was a really striking personality. Had she been born in a different class of society, she might have been a reigning beauty, so perfectly moulded were face and figure, so beautiful her colouring, and so regal the manner in which she carried herself. But she was only the orphan of a Nova Scotian clergyman, with two younger sisters more or less dependent on her, and if sometimes the sense of her overwhelming responsibilities made her a trifle dictatorial, she was surely to be forgiven.

The mother of the three girls had died when Anne was twelve and Bertha only six years old. But then Cousin Grace had been there to mother them, and life had been fairly easy until the death of their father, just five years ago, had thrown the three girls upon their own resources, and this time without any Cousin Grace to bear the heaviest end of the troubles, for she had married and gone west two years before the death of Mr. Doyne. Since then Anne had been the head of the family—father, mother, and breadwinner rolled into one.

Hilda, the middle sister, was bright, keen, and clever. She lacked the beauty of Anne, but she made up for it by a sparkling wit, which, if sometimes a trifle caustic in its tone, was at least always meant good-naturedly.

The two sisters were a really fine pair, and they had made a splendid fight against narrow means, uncongenial surroundings, and those other evils which vex the hearts of girls who, having lost their natural defenders, must face the world and make the best of it for themselves.

Anne taught the township school, earning enough to keep home together, and out of school hours she made their frocks, and did all sorts of things to make the little income go as far as possible. Hilda, on her part, worked away at scales, exercises, and fugues on the little old piano, which had been a wedding present to their dead mother. Then, when by sheer pluck and perseverance she had pulled through sufficient exams to give her a teaching certificate, she had hunted round for pupils. There had been few enough to be found in Mestlebury, which was on the northern coast of Nova Scotia, but she had gone inland among the farmers who were well-to-do, and so had gathered a little teaching connection, the fees from which were added to the family funds.

But Hilda knew very well that she had touched only the barest fringe of musical knowledge, even though she was the best player and the best teacher for many miles round. It was the dream of her life to go to Europe, to get at least a year of study in Germany, and to hear some really good musicians.

The dream seemed very far off realization, however, and meanwhile she was travelling long distances, getting cheap pupils, and struggling to keep herself in the public eye, which, after all, is the only way to get on as a travelling music teacher. This she had long since discovered, and she was astute enough to take the utmost advantage of every opportunity which presented itself for making her way.

Bertha was the disappointment of the family, for she was only a dreamer, while the other two were workers, and very hard workers, their lot being all the more toilsome because she did so little. She wrote little poems, in which heart rhymed with part, and that contained many references to soulful yearnings which stayed unsatisfied. Sometimes she even attempted short stories; but these were so morbid in sentiment, that Anne would have turned sick at such mawkish rubbish, while Hilda would have gone into fits of laughter and made fun of them for months afterwards.

But neither sister ever did see them, and Bertha wasted precious hours over her futile scribbling which had been much more usefully employed in looking after the comfort of the two elder sisters, who worked so hard and had no time to waste in dreaming at all.

Poor child! she believed herself to be a genius, and secretly she looked forward to the time when she should burst upon the world with a full-blown literary reputation, without any preliminary preparation of climbing and falling, only to climb again. If anyone had told her that genius was only an infinite capacity for hard work in any given direction, it is to be feared that she would not have believed it, but would have still dreamed on, expecting to wake some day to find herself famous.

If there had been anyone in her little world of whom she could have made a confidante, her eyes might have been the sooner opened to her mistakes; but the three girls kept very much to themselves, and Bertha would just as soon have thought of standing on her head in Mestlebury Main Street, as of confiding any of her aspirations to her sisters.

So she emerged slowly from girlhood, growing more dreamy and futile with every month that passed over her head, until that day in the autumn when she had walked to Paston in the morning with Hilda to help carry some music to the train depot, and had come back by way of the shore, to find the man on the Shark's Teeth. It was old Jan Saunders who had torn the veil from her eyes and had made her see that it is a finer thing to be up and doing, ready to help where help is needed, than to spend one's time in thinking noble thoughts, which never by any chance developed into works of practical kindness and utility.

And the firstfruits of her awakening had been an intense but wholly salutary disgust of herself and all her previous doings. It was this feeling which had sent her scurrying along Mestlebury Main Street half-clad, and dripping with water from her swim, in order that she might be home in time to get supper ready for Anne.

But she had not reckoned upon a visitor, and when Anne appeared with the stranger, who was introduced as Mr. Roger Mortimer, from Adelaide, Australia, Bertha was so upset by the thought of what she must look like, that she would thankfully have run away if she could.

There was no chance of this, however, for Mr. Mortimer at once proceeded to make himself so much at home and to engross her attention, that presently she even forgot how frightfully untidy she was. He toasted more bread while she buttered the slices and spread the white monkey upon them; he even made the coffee while she finished setting the table, and by the time that Anne came out of her bedroom ready for supper, Bertha felt as if she had known the genial Australian for quite a long time.

Indeed, as it turned out, he was not a stranger, for he had been an old friend of the Doynes many years before, and he had, as he declared, carried Bertha on his back more times than he could count.

"Do you remember the day we went sleighing to Micmac Cove, Anne, and how the sleigh came to grief, and we had to carry the kids home between us?" he asked, looking across the table at Anne, who appeared to have blossomed into a greater beauty than ever, as she presided over the humble little supper table, with a sweet dignity and graciousness that would not have been out of place in a mansion.

"Oh yes, I remember it perfectly," replied Anne, with a merry laugh. "But it was Hilda whom you carried then, for she had a bad foot and could not walk; so I stumbled along under the weight of Bertha, and my arms ached more or less for a whole week afterwards, although I do not think that she could have been very heavy, because she was always so small and thin for her age."

"She is small and thin now, and her face is so white. Don't you feel well, Miss Bertha?" asked the visitor abruptly.

Bertha, who was conscious of feeling extremely queer, roused herself with an effort, declaring that there was nothing the matter with her except that she was rather tired.

"Girls like you ought never to be tired, not until bedtime, that is, and then they ought to sleep like logs until morning. What have you been doing to get tired?" he asked.

It was Anne who answered, for Bertha was struggling with a desire to laugh or to cry, it did not seem to matter which, so long as she could make a noise or a fuss over something.

"Oh, Bertha never does very much; she has not begun to take life very seriously yet, you see. But she walked to Paston to-day to help Hilda carry some music, and I expect the extra exertion has knocked her up a little."

Bertha clenched her hands so tightly that the nails entered into the flesh. A little extra exertion—what a joke it was! She wondered what Anne would have said to have seen the struggle to reach the Shark's Teeth, with the rope that was to save the life of a man. A little extra exertion, indeed! Well, it was quite true it was extra, and then the funny thing was that she suddenly seemed to be in the water again, and doing battle for her own life and for the life of the man whom she was trying so hard to save. She seemed to be crying and laughing all in a breath, then there was more confusion, the sound of many waters in her ears; and then she came to herself to find that Mr. Mortimer was holding her in his arms at the open door, while Anne bent over her with a face full of concern.

"Bertha, darling, what is the matter? Are you ill, dear? You have given us such a shock!" cried Anne, whose eyes were swimming in tears.

Somehow it was the sight of the tears which helped Bertha to rally her flagging powers, and to keep from slipping back into that gulf from which she had but just emerged. It was so rarely that Anne showed any sign of tears, and surely it must be something very much out of the common to induce them.

"Oh, I am all right," said Bertha slowly. "I was tired, you know, and I was so afraid that I should not have supper ready in time for you."

A cloud crept over the face of Anne. To her there seemed no reason why Bertha should have been overdone by the walk to Paston and back, while supper had not called for very active preparation. But Bertha always took so long to do the simplest thing, and even then the doing was mostly unsatisfactory.

"She looks clean worn out; I should put her to bed," said the visitor, with such a clear understanding of just how Bertha felt, that she blessed him in her heart and wondered that he should be so wise.

"Yes, I should like to go to bed," she murmured faintly, and then suddenly remembering all those new resolutions that she had made, she said hurriedly, as she tried to free herself from the arms which held her, "But I will wait and wash the supper dishes first, for Anne must be so tired with working all day."

There was a note of derisive laughter from the man, but which was promptly checked as Anne exclaimed, in very real concern, "Oh, I am sure that she is ill, poor darling, because she does not trouble about the supper dishes as a rule!"

"Wait until the morning before making up your mind that she is bad," said Roger Mortimer. "She may be quite all right when she has had a night of sleep. I will carry her to her room now, then you can put her to bed, and afterwards we will wash up the supper dishes together, you and I; it will be like old times."

Bertha was drifting again, but she roused at this speech to make quite a vigorous protest—she could not, and would not, be carried to her room by this man, who was a stranger, or almost a stranger. The thought of the awful muddle—the unmade bed and the wild disorder which reigned there—seemed to give her a momentary spurt of strength. She must walk to her bed on her own feet—she must, she must!

But Anne broke in upon her gasping, half-incoherent protests with a quick word of common sense. "Bring her into my room, please. I must have her with me to-night, and mine is the only double bed in the house."

Bertha dropped quiet with a sigh of relief. If there was no danger of her room being seen, she would just as soon be carried as walk, for her limbs seemed to have lost all power, and she felt quite stupid.

Mr. Mortimer carried her into Anne's room, which was just a picture of neatness, and laid her on the bed. But Bertha would not let Anne stay for any work of undressing, declaring that as she was so tired, it was too much trouble to take her clothes off yet awhile.

Perhaps Anne did not require much persuading, for sounds from the outer room seemed to point to the fact of the visitor being engaged in very active clearing of the supper table. But she left the door ajar, and Bertha lay for a time in a state of dreamy content, listening to the voices in the next room.

Presently she drifted into slumber, and she must have been sleeping for some time, for the room was quite dark when she awoke, while a gleam of lamplight showed faintly from the room beyond. It was the sound of voices that roused her, a woman's tones, eager and agitated, while Anne's voice replied in surprised, almost unbelieving, query.

"But, Mrs. Saunders, Bertha did not say anything about it, and she cannot swim very much, certainly not well enough to take the risk of swimming out to the Shark's Teeth with a rope in a sea like this, for there has been a heavy swell on all day from the storm of yesterday."

"Well, Miss Doyne, she did it—as true as I am sitting here, she did it—and we towed the boat ashore with the gentleman in it, though I'm sorry to say the boat fouled the rocks just as we were drawing her inshore, and he got a nasty knock on the head which, he said, made him feel downright stupid. But he was so upset because your sister went away without his having so much as a chance to say thank you to her, so I said that I would just come along and see how she was after getting such a chill and a wetting, for the water is real cold to-day," replied the voice of Mrs. Saunders in very real concern.

"Then, of course, it was the shock and the excitement which upset her and gave us such a bad scare at supper, when she was first hysterical and then fainted," said Anne. "I was afraid that she was going to have a bad illness, poor child!"

The voice of Mrs. Saunders took a lower key, and presently Bertha fell asleep again.

It was later still when she roused once more, to find this time that Anne was kneeling beside the bed sobbing, and sobbing in a fashion more stormy than Bertha had ever heard before.

"What is the matter, Anne?" asked Bertha in alarm, in that first moment of confused awakening. She had forgotten all about her brave deed of the afternoon, and only wondered why it was that every bone in her body seemed to be aching with a separate and individual pain.

"My darling, my baby, why did you not tell me how brave you had been, and how you had saved that poor man's life?" cried Anne, with so much keen reproach in her tone that Bertha was roused to fresh wonder, though the pain of her limbs demanded so much in the way of endurance, that she had little attention to bestow on anything else.

"Mr. Mortimer was here—I could not tell you in front of him; besides, it would not have made any difference," replied Bertha languidly, not liking to admit that she would hardly have screwed her courage to the pitch necessary to the telling, even if Anne had been alone.

"It would have made a difference—it would have made all the difference!" cried Anne sharply, and her arms, which were round Bertha, tightened their clasp.

"How?" There was a dreamy wonder in Bertha's tone, but she was so tired, and her limbs ached so badly, that she was only about half-conscious of what was going on, or what Anne was saying.

"Because I have done something to-night that I do not think I should have done, if I had even dreamed that you were going to wake up like this!" said Anne, her voice breaking in another sob. "Don't blame me, dear, for I was so tired of my heavy responsibility, so I took the easiest way out; but I never would have done it if I had known."

"It does not matter, things happen so sometimes," said Bertha vaguely, and then she went to sleep again.

CHAPTER III
Tremulous Beginnings

IT was a whole fortnight before Bertha was able to leave her bed and creep about the little drab-painted house again. An anxious fortnight it was for the two elder sisters, who had their own work to do and to nurse Bertha in between whiles. Sometimes Bertha was conscious and sometimes she was not, but always, always, whether sensible or insensible, there was pressing upon her the shadow of a deep disgrace. She had set her hand to do a brave thing, moved thereto by the feeling that she could not stand by and see a fellow creature die whom she might have saved. But the price she had to pay for having saved him was that she herself had to be the most awful nuisance to her two sisters, who worked so hard and had the living to earn.

A little while ago this would hardly have troubled her at all. But now, just as her eyes had been opened to her own very serious shortcomings, and she had made up her mind to set about a wholesale reformation of herself without delay, it was nothing short of tragic that she should have been taken ill. It did not even comfort her to remember that but for that act of daring, which had taken her so completely out of herself, she might still have gone on in the old aimless fashion, remaining futile and incapable to the end of the chapter.

The worry of it was likely to retard her recovery. It seemed to her, in the new mood which had taken possession of her, that she could never do enough to repay her sisters for the nights of broken sleep and the days of worry and hard work which they endured on her account. Then a grain of common sense came to her rescue, and she remembered that the sooner she was well and able to take up her accustomed duties, the sooner they would be able to get some rest and relaxation.

When she arrived at this wholesome state of mind, convalescence set in steadily, and in a very short time she was creeping about the house, making pathetic attempts to be useful, when both Anne and Hilda would much rather that she would sit still and get a little stronger.

They were very kind to her, and never once in those two anxious weeks did she hear one word of complaint from either of them because of the hardness of their lives. There was a difference, too, in their manner of treating her. Bertha thought at first it was a sort of respect such as they might show to one who was their equal at last, and no longer a child to be chidden for indolent ways and careless habits. But as the days went by it began to dawn upon her that the manner of both was tinged with pity—just unmistakable pity!

This first irritated and then frightened her. Did they think she was going into a decline, she wondered? And although she had written yards of feeble poetry about the joys of dying young, the mere prospect of such a thing occurring put her into such a condition of fume, that she made quite extraordinary efforts at getting better, and succeeded even beyond her expectations.

Then Hilda was able to go her long-distance journeys again, and Anne went off to school, and stayed away the whole morning without running back between classes to see how it fared with the invalid.

The first morning that this happened was a cold grey day, when there was a feeling of snow in the air, and Bertha was ordered to take life as easily as possible, and not to burden herself with any duties beyond keeping the fire in. But Bertha had her own ideas on the subject of what she was going to do, and prepared to carry them out to the best of her ability.

There had been no proper meals cooked since she had been ill. Broth, beef tea, and gruel had been prepared for her as she had needed, or the things had been offerings from kindly neighbours as hard-working as the two Miss Doynes, and the girls had just lived on bread and butter, because they lacked the time to do any cooking for themselves. But this sort of thing was coming to an end now, so Bertha told herself with great decision, as she got up out of the rocking chair as soon as Anne had passed out of sight on her way to school.

"I am going to be useful somehow, or perish in the attempt," she said to herself, with a laugh which somehow ended in a sob. She was so weak still, and everything demanded such a desperate effort to accomplish. But she was thinking of that night when she was first taken ill, and Anne had knelt sobbing beside her bed. Somehow Bertha just hated to think of that night, and she hated to remember the words which her sister had uttered. Indeed, she had tried her very best to forget them, but it seemed as if the more she tried the more vividly they came back to her. There was an uneasy feeling in her heart that somehow, that had been a day of fate in more senses than one. Sometimes she wondered if her sister's sobbing words had had anything to do with the visit of Roger Mortimer; but she had dismissed the idea as ridiculous, for she had not seen him since, and she had never once heard Anne mention him since, except yesterday, when she herself had asked Anne when he was coming to see them again, and Anne had replied that he was away in Halifax just now, but that he might return next week or the week after.

Anne had gone on to speak of other things immediately, as if the subject of Mr. Mortimer were not interesting enough for discussion. But she had blushed in a vivid and glorious fashion right up to the roots of her hair, and it was the memory of that blush which worried Bertha so much as she moved feebly about, cooking the early dinner.

Oh, how truly awful it would be if one of them were to fall in love and get married just now, when she so badly wanted to show them what a good sister she could be! Indeed, the thought was so much too bad to be borne, that she put it from her, resolved to think no more about it, but to confine herself entirely to the business in hand.

When the cooking was well under way, she set about tidying up the sitting-room, which had to be kitchen, dining-room, and drawing-room combined. The house did really boast two sitting-rooms, but the second one had been taken by Anne for a bedroom. For it seemed so much more desirable to the three girls to have a room each for their private use than to be crowded together at night, to have the doubtful advantage of another sitting-room for use in the day.

Very tired was Bertha when she had done, in fact she had to stop far short of her intentions in the matter of tidying, because her strength gave out so much before her energy. But at least it was a beginning, and she sat down for a brief half-hour of rest before Anne came home, feeling as if her feet were set at last on the steep ladder which had to be climbed to capability and usefulness. It was then, as she sat resting, that she thought of her own room, and the awful confusion awaiting her there.

"I will start on clearing it up when Anne has gone back to school this afternoon," she said to herself, as she crouched by the stove. The house was very quiet, but outside there was constant sound and commotion, as long streams of migratory birds passed overhead on their way from the cold, rock-bound shores of Labrador and the land round Baffin's Bay. They were bound for the warm and sunny south, and the air echoed with the plaintive "hawnk, honk" of the geese as they flew in single streams or wedge-like masses.

So quiet was the house, and Bertha was so very tired, that presently she fell asleep, and was still dozing when Anne came in, all blown about, and sweetly fresh with autumn winds and raindrops, for the weather was getting more stormy as the day wore on.

"Oh, Bertha, why did you trouble to cook?" cried Anne, with a little dismay in her tone. The savoury smells resulting from Bertha's labours were filling the house, and saluted her as she burst in at the door, hungry and tired with her long morning of work in the school.

"It was not any trouble," said Bertha, starting up and rubbing her eyes with much the same guilty feeling which came to her, when she overslept herself in the mornings, "and it is so long since you have had anything better than roast potatoes and butter for your dinner."

"Roast potatoes and butter are not to be despised, I can tell you," laughed Anne, as she sat down at the table to enjoy the unwonted luxury of being waited upon; "but a real stew properly made is something of a luxury, I can assure you."

What was there in those words to make Bertha wince as if someone had struck her a blow? There would have been nothing, less than nothing, but for that awakened conscience of hers, which reminded her of the many times her sisters had had to sit down to badly prepared and insufficient meals, just because she had been too indolent to bestir herself for the cooking.

"I am sorry it storms so. Hilda will have quite a dreadful journey across to the Sudeleys," she said presently, as she sat watching Anne, getting a lot of enjoyment out of her sister's zest for the meal, but eating very little herself.

"Hilda won't mind that, I fancy," laughed Anne. "Mrs. Nelson is to be at the Sudeleys to-day, and Hilda is very keen on meeting her, you know."

"No, I don't know. I do not believe that I have ever heard of her before. Who is she? The mother of a likely pupil?" asked Bertha, with no lack of interest now; for another pupil, of course, meant more money, and where the means are so straitened every little sum becomes of vital importance.

Anne laughed. "Of course you do not know. I keep forgetting that you have been out of everything for the last fortnight. But we had to keep you as quiet as possible, because you would go off your head every minute that you got a chance for doing it. But when Hilda comes home to-morrow she will tell you herself all about her hopes and fears, and what her chances are. Now I am going to make haste and wash the dishes, because I must be back at school very early this afternoon."

"You will do nothing of the sort," said Bertha, giving her a gentle push back into the chair from which she had just risen. "You will sit down and read a book, or go to sleep, or do what you like for as long as it would take you to wash the dishes, then when you have gone I will wash the dishes myself, if you please."

"Are you going to develop into a domestic tyrant?" asked Anne, with a laugh, as she went over to the rocking chair by the stove and sat gently swaying to and fro, very much at ease.

"I can't say what I may develop into," replied Bertha, with a shake of her head, and then, with a great shrinking upon her, she was just going to confide in Anne something of the purposes and resolves that were stirring in her heart, when there was a knock at the door, and a shock-headed boy very much out of breath with running appeared on the threshold, saying that one of the children had burned herself at the school stove, and would teacher please come at once.

Of course Anne had to rush away in a great hurry then, and Bertha's chance was gone for the time. When the dishes were washed and put away, Bertha turned her steps to her little bedroom, which had scarcely been entered since she was taken sick. At least she could take a look round and decide where to begin the work of clearing up to-morrow.

The window was shut, and the room had a close, musty feeling. Her first move would have been to the window to fling it wide open, but for the moment she could not get there; for a chair laden with papers and clothes had somehow been upset in the middle of the open space, and she had to pick them up and sort them over before she could get across the floor to the window. Naturally she paused to read some of the lines written on those fluttering sheets of paper, and she winced again to think that she could ever have written such mawkish rubbish.

"Oh dear, and it was only two weeks ago; why, it might have been two years!" she exclaimed, as she gathered up the sheets and laid them aside. It was strange how that swim to the Shark's Teeth had altered her outlook. She had gone to save a man's life because there was nobody else to do it. But it was her own self that she had discovered when she performed her little act of courage and daring.

The wet garments she had shed in such a hurry, when she came home to get supper for Anne, still lay in a heap in the corner just as she had cast them off, and she lifted them up with a rueful air. One's clothes are never improved by lying for a whole fortnight in a wet heap on a dusty bedroom floor. But no one was to be blamed—the two elder girls had far too much to do to be able to think of anything outside, and she herself had been too ill to remember. She shook the garments out one by one and hung them from pegs on the wall, meaning to take them out to the other room and dry them one by one at the stove. But the last garment of all puzzled her not a little, for it was a man's coat of a very roomy description.

"Why, how did that get here?" she exclaimed, and then suddenly remembered that the man whom she had gone to save had dragged a coat out from under the seat of his boat, and had told her to wrap herself in it because she shivered so.

"And of course I came home in it. I remember now how it flapped about as I ran. But I wonder that he did not come for it, or ask Mrs. Saunders to get it for him," she said, as she picked the water-logged garment up from the floor and shook it out.

Something dropped on to the floor with a thud, and she laid the coat over a chair while she went painfully down on her knees to pick it up. Those two weeks had been so full of rheumatism and similar afflictions, that moving from one position to another still took some time, and also entailed something in the way of endurance. The something was a little morocco case bound with silver at the corners, and looking very much as if it were intended for cigars. There was a spring at one side, and Bertha pressed it to see if the case would open. She had her full share of curiosity, and the little case seemed very heavy. "Perhaps it is money," she said to herself, with a little shiver of dread; for she was wondering what the stranger must think of her, if it were indeed money that made the case so heavy.

"He might even think that I had found it, and meant to keep it!" she muttered, as she wrestled with the spring, which was rather hard to move.

Presently it flew open with a jerk, and she saw to her relief that it contained not money, but twelve dull grey stones of slightly varying sizes. Pebbles they looked like, and her first thought was that they were geological specimens. Perhaps the man was a scientist, stones being his particular ology.

"He might even have been looking for stones of sorts when he got into such a dangerous place," she muttered, and for ten minutes or so she tried to make herself believe that these dull grey pebbles were just specimens and nothing more.

But at the end of that time she had thrust the little case right at the back of her one lock-up drawer, and turning the key upon them she went out to the other room, which was warm and pleasant from the glow of the stove. Marching straight to the bookcase, she hunted until she found a little dictionary of common things which belonged to Anne, and turning the pages over hastily she hunted up "Diamonds".

"Colourless or dull grey stones of exceeding hardness," she read aloud, and a look of care and perplexity dropped on to her face. If those stones in the case were uncut diamonds, why was the man carrying them in the pocket of his loose outer coat? and why, oh why, had he not sent to enquire for that same coat?

CHAPTER IV
A Series of Shocks

A FIT of shivering seized Bertha. Of course she was weak and unstrung still, or the incident would not have struck her as being of such magnitude. As it was, she felt as if she were up against the greatest trouble of her life. Was the man a thief? Had he stolen the diamonds, and so when he lost them was afraid to make enquiries about them through fear of being found out? But that seemed hardly probable, because, of course, he might have come to enquire for his coat. The question which troubled her most was whether he would think that she was a thief. Indeed, her fertile imagination immediately sketched a pretty but wholly improbable piece of fiction, as to how the man had missed his diamonds, but would not enquire for them, being willing to sit down under the loss because she had saved his life.

"Oh dear, oh dear, what shocking nonsense, and I don't even know that they are diamonds!" she exclaimed, putting the book back into the bookcase, and turning her attention resolutely from the affair because it worried her so.

To-morrow she would go as far as the little house where Jan Saunders lived, and ask for the address of the man she had helped. Then she would send him a letter, telling him what she had found, and ask him to fetch his property or tell her how to send it to him, and so she would be quit of this tiresome responsibility.

That evening was full of petty worries. Anne came home from school very late, because she had been out to a farm which lay far back in the woods, to take home the little girl who had burned herself in the dinner hour. And when she did get home she was most dreadfully depressed, for the mother of the child, instead of being decently grateful for the care and kindness bestowed upon the little girl, chose to consider herself aggrieved, because the children were left to themselves in the noon spell.

"She said that I was paid to look after them, and I ought never to leave them. Just fancy what a hateful time I should have of it if I had to stay in that pokey, horrible schoolhouse for the dinner hour!" said Anne, with more heat than she usually displayed; for she was blessed with an evenly balanced temperament, and was not easily ruffled.

"But no one would expect you to stay, would they?" asked Bertha, opening her eyes very wide. "No reasonable person, I mean."

"School committee-men are not always the most reasonable of creatures, and as Mrs. Scott declares that she will lodge a formal complaint and ask that the teacher be requested to stay at the school for the noon spell, it is quite probable that I may find myself with a little extra duty tacked on to what I already have," replied Anne, with a short laugh that had very little mirth in it.

"If it comes to that, I will take the noon-spell duty for you. The committee won't be particular who it is, provided there is some responsible person there," said Bertha, with intent to console.

"My dear, you could not manage that rabble," said Anne impatiently. "They would be quite equal to turning you out of the school and locking the door upon you if you chanced to offend them, or they might take the other course of locking you in. It takes every bit of will power that I possess to master them, I can tell you, and I was born to rule, which you never were."

"No, I'm afraid I wasn't," admitted Bertha meekly, but she felt keenly mortified notwithstanding, because Anne had not seemed more grateful for her offer of help.

Even her request to help in the preparation of the needlework for the class next day met with a refusal, for Anne was irritated with her reception from Mrs. Scott, and she was not sufficiently alert to see how much Bertha wanted to be of service.

So the evening, which might have been so restful and pleasant, was spoiled for both of them, and they were thankful when bedtime came.

"I shall go back to my own room to-morrow, and then you can have your bed to yourself again," said Bertha, as the two prepared for slumber.

"Yes, that will be better, now that you are quite well again," Anne answered, in an absent-minded fashion. And she was so silent and absorbed that Bertha chafed in miserable discomfort, wishing she had put her own room straight and aired the bed to-day, then Anne could have had her own room free from disturbance. With this sort of mood upon her, it was not wonderful that Bertha said nothing of what she had found in the pocket of that wonderfully roomy overcoat. Anne might be angry because the coat had been forgotten so long, or she might feel hurt because of the appearance of neglect on her part, in not having hunted round Bertha's little bedroom to find the wet garments which had lain unheeded so long.

Next morning the sun shone, and although the wind was keen with the breath of coming winter, the air was so pleasant that everything looked easier. Even the prospect of having to stay in school for the noon spell was not so dreadful as it had seemed last night, and Anne set off for her day of work in quite good spirits, just her own serene self, with all the petulance of the previous night quite gone.

Then Bertha brought the coat to the fire, and, drying it carefully, folded it into a neat parcel ready for sending away. When this was done she put on her hat and coat, and, taking a stick, because she felt so waggly on her feet, she set out for the little cottage where Jan Saunders lived. But she did not take the coat with her, for she knew very well that, being a useful garment, it would probably get no farther, as Mrs. Saunders had very stretchable ideas on the rights of property.

Oh, it was good to be out again, even though her feet were not all they should be in the matter of steadiness, and Bertha walked slowly along Mestlebury Main Street, noting all the differences which had come over the face of the gardens and orchards during the time in which she had been shut up in the house.

Mrs. Saunders was out on the cliff as usual, and as usual she was doing nothing but gaze out to sea, while old Jan smoked a pipe in calm content at her side. They both fell upon Bertha with a greeting that was fairly rapturous, and the old woman, with a tear in her bleared old eye, said fervently, "My dear, my dear, you look that delicate that a puff of wind might blow you away!"

"It would have to be a very strong puff—something that was first cousin to a whirlwind or a tornado, I fancy," replied Bertha, with a laugh, and then she turned to Jan, who might be trusted to tell the truth if he knew it.

"Can you tell me where the man lives whose boat got stuck on the Shark's Teeth?" she asked.

"Furrin parts somewhere, ain't it, Mother?" asked the old man, taking his pipe from his mouth and looking across at his wife.

Mrs. Saunders pursed up her mouth in a disapproving pucker and slowly shook her head. "He said something about Peru, but it might have been Australia, or somewhere round that way. Anyhow, he was in a mighty hurry to be off again that night, when we had pulled him out of the water and dried him up so beautiful. Downright ungrateful I called it, for I had arranged for him to sleep with Herr Schmudcht, and I had lent a pair of nearly clean sheets to put on the bed, and then the gentleman would not stay, and Herr Schmudcht has slept in those sheets ever since, so now I expect they will want washing before ever I can lend them to anyone else; it is really downright vexing, so it is," and Mrs. Saunders heaved a windy sigh over her misplaced kindness, which was meeting such a poor return, but Bertha burst out laughing.

"I should insist on Herr Schmudcht washing the sheets himself; I am sure that he is stronger than you are," she said, and then becoming suddenly grave, she asked again, and this time with a ring of real anxiety in her tone, "But where did the man go to on that night when he left here, and what was his name?"

"My dear, he wasn't a man, he was a gentleman," said Mrs. Saunders, with quite crushing emphasis, and then she went on, "It wasn't for us to be asking him all sorts of personal questions. I never was one for poking into business what did not concern me, I am thankful to say."

"But you surely must know something about him; and I want to write to him," said Bertha impatiently, and then she was surprised to see a flicker of fear in the old woman's blear eyes.

"Well, I guess that the writing will have to wait a bit. Perhaps he will happen along this way again some day, and then you can say what you want to—a much better fashion than putting things in black and white, so that they can be sweared to in a court of justice," said Mrs. Saunders, with a toss of her head, and not another bit of information could Bertha get out of her.

"I shall have to ask the girls what I had better do," she said to herself, as she went slowly back to her home to start on her belated morning's work.

Even that short walk had tired her so much, that it needed the entire stock of her lately acquired resolution to keep from sitting down and letting things go anyhow. But by a great effort she stuck to her task, and was all ready for Anne, who came rushing home about a quarter past twelve, snatched a hasty meal, and rushed back again, uneasy all the time lest her turbulent charges should get up to serious mischief in her absence.

Then Bertha was left with the long afternoon before her, for Hilda could not be home much before six o'clock. However, there was the house to put tidy, and the work she could not accomplish in the morning was cleared out of the way in the afternoon, and she found herself with an hour of rest before the girls came home.

She was tremendously proud of the tidy rooms, and she kept walking backwards and forwards admiring her handiwork, until some undarned stockings poking from an over-full drawer in Hilda's room suggested a fresh outlet for her new-found energy, and taking them out to the kitchen, she sat down by the stove and began to darn them. It was the work that she hated most of all, so the voluntary doing of it was the most real self-sacrifice that she could have shown. However, Hilda had been forced to do all sorts of things for her when she was ill, and so it was up to her to make what amends were in her power. Anne was in, and supper was ready, when Hilda came back from Paston, rushing into the house like a whirlwind, and shouting in great excitement—

"Girls! girls! I have got some of the most wonderful news for you. What do you think is going to happen?"

"How should we know?" cried Anne, standing erect and staring at Hilda in amazement; for the second sister usually hugged her dignity too closely for exhibitions like these.

"I am going to Europe!" cried Hilda, stopping in the middle of the floor, and dropping the words out one by one with tremendous emphasis and solemnity.

"You are going to Europe—when?" cried Anne, who was the first to recover the power of speech, while Bertha caught at a chair to steady herself, because the room would keep swinging round at such a rate.

"We start next month, just four weeks to-day. I am to take Mrs. Nelson's two daughters to Germany for a year. Oh, Anne, Anne, don't say that I can't go! It is the chance of my life; I can never hope to get such another opportunity," said Hilda, casting herself upon her elder sister and hugging her frantically, as if to squeeze a consent out of her in that way.

"It is not for me to say that you may not take a chance when it comes," said Anne, turning suddenly pale, as pale as Bertha, who still clung trembling to the chair. "Especially I could not say anything to you now, when I have just decided to take my own chance of an easier life. Only it does seem hard for poor Bertha that we should both be going away at the same time."

"I was afraid you would say that," said Hilda; and now there was a mutinous look on her face. "But why, oh why, should I have to lose my chance in life because of Bertha? She can surely be boarded out somewhere for a year; I can spare a part of my salary to help pay for it, and we can sell this furniture. Oh, let us be willing to make any sacrifice to meet an emergency like this. I did not venture to put one straw of protest in your way, Anne, when you said that Mr. Mortimer wanted to marry you, so it is hardly fair that you should begrudge me my chance, now that it has come to me."

"My dear, I do not grudge it to you," said Anne, with keen distress on her beautiful face. "I was only thinking of poor Bertha, and how hard it would be for her."

"What is it all about?" asked Bertha, finding her tongue for the first time; but speaking with horrible difficulty, because her heart was beating so fast. "Are you going to marry Mr. Mortimer, Anne? And when?"

Anne came closer, and put her arms round Bertha's trembling figure, holding her sister in a tight embrace.

"Bertha, darling, I would have told you before, only you have been so ill, and I did not like to worry you until you were quite strong. Mr. Mortimer came all the way from Australia to ask me to marry him, and I said yes, for I was so tired of this awful driving life; but I have been afraid ever since that I put my own happiness and comfort before your welfare, and it has seemed so dreadfully selfish of me. This is why I flew out at Hilda just now."

"There is no need to worry about me," said Bertha, in a dazed sort of tone, "only it has all come so suddenly, that I do not seem able to take it in."

"Of course it looks like trouble to begin with," burst in Hilda, and her voice was just a wee bit patronizing, or so poor Bertha, in her new sensitiveness, judged it to be. "But next year, when I come back from Europe, as Mrs. Nelson says, I shall be able to charge almost what I like for lessons, and then we can set up house together."

"Here in Mestlebury?" asked Bertha, not because she particularly wanted to know, but because she must say something, just to keep herself from sobbing like a baby.

"I should sincerely hope not," laughed Hilda. "I would have left this out-of-the-way corner of the country ever so long ago if it had depended upon me only. But there was Anne's school to be considered. We could not afford to keep this house on if I lived in lodgings, and so I have had to put up with it, and fearfully wearing work it has been. Think of the miles I have had to travel to earn a dollar, and all the fag, and the wear and tear of my life. Oh, no more of Mestlebury for me, thank you, not when once Anne is married."

"Where will you live, when—when you are married?" demanded Bertha sharply, as she faced round upon Anne. A sudden dread had assailed her that Anne would have to go right away, and the thought was unbearable.

Anne's face fell. By instinct she guessed what was in the mind of Bertha, and it seemed such horrible cruelty to take one's own happiness when it brought so much pain to the others, or at least to Bertha; for Hilda, with her own career in front of her, could not be expected to care so much about the parting.

"Dear, Roger has a big sheep run fifty miles from Adelaide, and that is where our home will be."

Anne's tone was low and soft; then, when she had finished, a deep hush fell on the group. Bertha stood white and rigid, like a figure carved in stone, and the other two were afraid to disturb her.

It was shock upon shock, blow upon blow, and it was small wonder that she was left, as it were, battered and breathless, trying to realize all that these changes would mean to her, yet, in spite of it, too dull and numbed with the pain to take it in.

CHAPTER V
Against her Will

IT was a week later, and the first snow had fallen, just a thin white coating on the hills and the plains, while the wind moaned with a new mournfulness through the forests of pine and of hemlock, stirring the fluttering pennons of black moss, as in the days when Evangeline's people, the simple Acadian peasantry, tilled the land and lived upon the products of their industry. But the face of the countryside was changed since the driving forth of the village lovers to the long exile of separation and suffering. Where had stood the forest primeval, the ground was covered with fat orchards, with fruitful fields, and with bustling townships, which had "Progress" for their watchword.

Bertha had lived through the week in a kind of dream. Anne and Hilda discussed the various schemes they were making for her benefit, but at present she was too dazed to take much interest in them herself. It did not seem to matter in the least what became of her, and she found herself wishing sometimes that when she was ill she had been a little more ill, just enough to have carried her through the dark portal, and settled the question of her future once and for all. Of course this was very wrong. It was also very unnatural. But then Bertha at this time was scarcely normal, and so was to be forgiven and pitied, instead of being held up to censure or severe criticism.

Then at the end of the week the mail came in, bringing with it a letter which effectually settled the question of Bertha's destiny, and that without any chance of appeal. The letter was from Cousin Grace, now Mrs. Ellis, who had been so good to the girls when their own mother died.

> "So Anne is going to be married, and is to live in Australia. What a piece of luck for me! Now, girls, what you had better do is to break up your home, let Hilda take a teaching post in a school, where she will have a regular salary to fall back upon, and then I can have Bertha. Oh, you can't think what it will mean to me to have someone that I can depend upon in the home! Life is really a terror sometimes with so many babies to look after, to clothe and feed, and only my one pair of hands to do it all."

Anne read so much of the letter aloud, and then she stopped short, with a quiver of breakdown in her voice.

"Why, what a charming idea!" cried Hilda, looking up from a great heap of theory exercises through which she had been laboriously wading. "I wonder that it never occurred to either of us to ask Grace to take Bertha. Why, the arrangement will be perfectly ideal!"

Bertha, who was kneading a batch of bread at the table at the far end of the room, jerked up her head with a quick motion of protest, but before she could utter the words which rose to her lips, Anne, who was sitting back to her, began to speak—

"If I had asked Grace to take Bertha, I do not think that I should have felt so sure that it was the right thing to do. But seeing that the settlement of her future has been, as it were, taken right out of my hands and all arranged for me, I am sure that it must be right. With Grace, Bertha will be as safe as if she were with you or me, and she will be as kindly cared for. Oh, I am too thankful for words!"

"Poor old Anne!" muttered Hilda, and then, sweeping the pile of exercises on one side, she jumped up, and flinging her arms about Anne, she gave her a sounding kiss.

Bertha clenched her fists hard and punched the bread with quite unnecessary vigour, while she winked and winked to keep back the tears she was too proud to shed.

Oh, it hurt her! No one could even guess how it hurt her to think that her sisters had so much trouble to dispose of her. She knew that Hilda had asked Mrs. Sudeley to have her as a sort of mother's help, but because she was not musical Mrs. Sudeley would have nothing to do with her. Bertha knew that she might have been musical if only she had tried hard enough. It was never any trouble to her to learn anything, but she had never worked at scales and exercises as Hilda had; indeed, she had never worked at anything, and now this was the price she had to pay, that when a home was needed for her no one wanted to be burdened with her.

Mrs. Sudeley's refusal to have her had been a bitter mortification, although she had said no word about it. Once, nearly a year ago, she had paid a visit to the Sudeley homestead, and had been charmed with all the comfort, and even luxury, which the house contained. It was in most romantic country, too, and Bertha, who was always most strongly influenced by her surroundings, had been filled ever since with the longing to go there again. So it had not made her disappointment easier to bear to know that it was entirely her own fault that she could not teach elementary music and look after the piano practice of the elder children.

And now she would have to go thousands of miles away, right out on to the prairie, away from the sea, away from the forests, into a house crowded with little children, whose mother was overdone with work, and wanted someone to help her drudge through the monotonous, unlovely days!

"Bertha, Bertha, do you hear? Cousin Grace wants you to go and live with her. Do you think that you will like it?" called Anne, holding out her hand with the letter in it.

"It is very kind of Grace, but won't it be a very expensive journey?" asked Bertha dubiously. She could not say outright that she simply hated the thought of going to Grace, and that if she had to be left with strangers she would much rather they were real strangers. Her memories of Grace were not very vivid, and Mr. Ellis she had only seen twice, and it was dreadful to think of being pitch-forked into a household and in a manner forced to remain there whether she liked it or not.

"Of course it will be an expensive journey," replied Anne; "but, my dear, think of the comfort of it! Why, I shall be able to take my happiness now with a clear conscience, which so far I have not been able to do. Oh, Bertha, you do not know how bad I have felt about it!" and, to the surprise and dismay of both the girls, Anne, the brisk, brave, and capable, put her head down upon her hands and burst into a passion of tears.

In a moment Bertha had crossed the floor, and was sliding a pair of hands well caked with dough round her sister's neck.

"Anne, dear Anne, don't cry like this. Of course it is most awfully good of Cousin Grace to want me, and I expect that we shall get on most beautifully together," said Bertha, making up her mind that in any case Anne would not be told about it, however unhappy she might be.

"Poor old Anne! you have been overdoing it lately," put in Hilda, in a tone of pitying common sense, and it restored Anne to composure quicker than anything else could have done.

Somehow Hilda never could bear anything that even verged on emotional display, and Anne was careful not to upset her in this direction. Bertha was quite different; indeed she was a regular bundle of nerves and emotions, with a strong dash of sentimentality thrown in. And when later in that same day Hilda told her that once before Mr. Mortimer had written from Adelaide, asking Anne to marry him, and she had refused because of the two younger girls, for whom she must make a home, that little bit of confidence, joined to the sight of Anne's breakdown, settled the future for Bertha without any hope of appeal. If her lot in the Ellis household were to be ever so hard or uncongenial, Anne must never know of it. There was something of the spirit of the martyr about Bertha, and she set herself to endure this hard thing which had come into her life with a Spartan disregard for pain.

But oh, the relentless heartache of those next few weeks! There were things in after-life which she could never see nor touch without it coming back to her in waves of pain and homesickness.

There was another letter from Grace, directly she heard of Hilda's good fortune, and in this second epistle she gave all the necessary directions for Bertha's journey westward, and with great generosity even enclosed the money to pay for her ticket through to the nearest railway station, which was thirty miles from the farm.

But she wanted Bertha to go at once, before the snow became so very deep. Sometimes in winter even sledges could not get through to the railway for weeks at the stretch, and it would be so very trying if Bertha were to be held up *en route* in this fashion. Moreover, if the home were to be broken up, there seemed to be no sense in delaying the upheaval.

"That is just what I think!" exclaimed Hilda, when she read the letter. "And if Bertha starts before I do, I can take her to Halifax and put her on the cars myself, then she will be all right until she gets to Winnipeg. I wish that Mr. Ellis could have met her there, but I suppose that is too much to expect. But anyhow, it will be a great relief to be able to start her on the journey myself."

"Oh, I could manage somehow; I am not a baby, you see," said Bertha, with a nervous laugh. As a matter of fact, she dreaded the journey horribly, but she was not going to upset Anne's peace of mind if she could help it.

"It will be better for Bertha to go before the sale of the furniture. Let me see, that is next Wednesday; then Bertha had better go on Tuesday," said Anne, who was up to her eyes in work of all sorts, arranging for the break-up of the only home they had ever known, making plans for her wedding, which was to take place almost directly; for Mr. Mortimer, having waited so long, was not disposed to wait any longer.

"But that will mean that I shall have to go before you are married," said Bertha, with a note of protest in her tone.

"It cannot be helped, dear, and, after all, you will be spared a little more sadness," Anne replied gently. "Weddings are harrowing things at the best of times, and mine must be sadder than ordinary, since it means so much parting for us all."

Bertha turned away. Of course it was best that she should go away before Anne was married. But it was just horrible, like everything else. And because no one wanted her in the house just then, she thrust her arms into her coat, and, dragging her hat on, she set out through the snow to that part of the shore where the road from Paston came out on to the rocks.

She had only been there once since that day when she swam out to the rescue of the man, who had gone away without saying thank you, or even claiming the coat which was his. The thought of the coat came into her head now as she plunged along the snowy road, where the drifts were not yet packed hard enough to make walking a very pleasant exercise.

Of choice, she would have sent, or taken, the coat along to old Jan Saunders, and had no more responsibility in the matter. But she knew that it would not do to trust Mrs. Saunders even with the coat, and, of course, there was the morocco case with those grubby-looking pebbles which might be diamonds, or might be only the commonest stones of the roadside for aught she knew.

Oh no, it would never do to let Mrs. Saunders know anything about that case. Indeed, Bertha did not feel inclined to trust her in the matter of the coat either, so she had decided that the best thing that she could do would be to give the old people her address, and then they could write to her if the man wrote to them, or even came to interview them on the subject of his missing property.

A moaning wind swept round the headland, and Bertha shivered, for it was as if the wind were voicing her lament at leaving the sea and the rocks and the trees, with all the other beautiful things to which she had been accustomed all her life.

"Oh, I cannot bear it, I cannot!" she muttered between her set teeth; yet she knew all the time that she would have to bear it, and many a hard thing besides, since to bear and to endure is the lot of the human family.

"But I will come back some day. I will not stay all my life buried away on the prairie," she said, as she turned from the sea towards the little house where old Jan Saunders lived.

It was the woman who opened the door to her to-day, and the old creature said that Jan was ill in bed, and that he had just fallen into a quiet sleep—the first rest that he had had for two days and nights.

"Then, of course, you must not disturb him on my account," said Bertha, although she would much rather have done her errand to the old man, who at least meant to be honest.

"It would be a sin and a shame to disturb him, missie," said the old woman. "But if you will tell me what it is that you wanted to see him for, I can let him know when he wakes up."

"I am going away from Mestlebury, and my home now will be a long way off in the west, and so I thought that I had better bring you my new address, so that you might write to me if you hear anything of the man whose boat we pulled off the Shark's Teeth. I must write to him as soon as I can, as I have something of his which I want to give back to him," said Bertha, and then she produced a stamped and addressed envelope, which she gave to Mrs. Saunders.

"Something belonging to the gentleman? Now—why didn't you say so when you was here before?" asked the old woman in a whining tone, as she shook her head disapprovingly.

"But it would have been no use if I had," replied Bertha, with a laugh. "Don't you remember that you told me you did not know who he was or where he had gone?"

"Still, I might have found out," objected the old woman.

"Just so. And it is because I want you to find out now that I have told you this. Of course, I cannot make any promises for another person, but I should not be at all surprised if the man were to give you some small reward, if you could put me in communication with him," said Bertha, hoping to raise the old woman's curiosity, and to stimulate her endeavours by this suggestion of profit to be gained.

But again there was a look of something like dread on the face of Mrs. Saunders, and although she promised to do what she could towards the furthering of Bertha's wishes, there did not appear much prospect of ultimate success in that direction.

Bertha was turning her steps homeward again, feeling that she had not achieved much beyond a little extra heartache by her outing, when, as she was passing the little store kept by the fat German, she heard her name called, and, looking round, she saw him beckoning to her to come nearer.

For a moment she hesitated, half-disposed to go on her way without heeding a summons of such a sort. But reflecting that his manners were, after all, made in Germany, and hence their limitations, she crossed over the patch of trodden snow to the door of the little store and asked the fat man, what it was that he wished to say to her.

"*Ach, himmel,* it is the bad manners of me to call you so, but it is the bad foot on me which will let me only stand and not walk," said the German, pointing downward to a bandaged foot, whereupon Bertha promptly forgave him for the lack of courtesy that he had displayed.

"You have a bad foot? I am very sorry," she said gravely.

"It has been bad, very bad, ever since the day when the stranger's boat got stuck on the Shark's Teeth," explained the fat man, puffing and snorting and spreading his pudgy hands out as if his feelings were too much for him, and then, suddenly leaning forward, he asked, in a confidential whisper: "Has the old woman given you your share yet?"

"What do you mean?" asked Bertha, drawing herself up with an offended air.

"The man we saved left money with the old woman to be given to you. I heard him say so myself. He thought that you were poor, and he sent the money to you with his best thanks. Has she given it to you?" said the German anxiously.

Bertha drew herself up, looking more haughty than ever. "No, indeed; and I should not think of taking money for doing a thing like that!" she said indignantly.

The German laughed in a deprecating fashion as he said, in his deep, rumbling tones: "That may be all very well for you, but she has kept the money that was meant for me also, and this I do not approve."

CHAPTER VI
A Wild Journey

It was over at last, and Bertha was on board the train which was to take her through to Winnipeg. In a certain sense it was a huge relief when the last goodbye was said and the long train of westward-bound cars drew away from the depot, leaving Hilda standing white-faced on the platform, while Bertha, with a smile which seemed frozen on her face, stood at the rear end of the car, watching until there was nothing more to be seen.

But the parting with Hilda, bad though it was, could not be compared with the pain of saying goodbye to Anne, who had been the head of the family and the mainstay of the home for so long. If Bertha had been the ordinary sort of girl, who looks upon change and upheaval as a welcome sort of diversion, she might not have suffered so keenly at this breaking up of home. Being cast in a different mould, and hating change as much as the domestic cat, she had to endure an exquisite torture of regret and longing in those last days at Mestlebury.

She had never even anticipated change, nor even supposed that any of them would marry. There were not very many educated young men in Mestlebury, and both Anne and Hilda had a trick of looking down upon the men with whom they came in contact as rather inferior sort of creatures; so it is not wonderful that Bertha had not taken their getting married into serious consideration. But Roger Mortimer was so different from any of the men she had been in the habit of meeting, that she did not wonder Anne liked him well enough to give up her sisters for his sake.

"But I—oh, I really believe that I hate him!" said Bertha to herself, with a little vindictive snap of her jaws, as the cars bore her out of sight of Hilda standing white and rigid on the platform, and the wide, wide world yawned to take her in.

"Hush, my dear, it ain't right to hate anyone, specially when you are so young," said a motherly body, who sat in the seat opposite, and who reached out a comforting hand to pat Bertha's arm, as the poor girl dropped in a limp heap now that the strain of parting was over.

"Did I speak aloud? Oh, I am sorry; and you are quite right, I ought not to hate anyone, especially a good, kind man, but it is so horrid to say goodbye," faltered Bertha, her lips quivering piteously, for she had much ado to keep from breaking down in childish crying.

"Ah, that it is!" The voice of the woman was wholly sympathetic, for she too had known what it was to suffer in similar fashion, and during the three days and nights they were together on the cars no one could have been kinder than she was to poor Bertha.

It was after Winnipeg was past, and she had changed into the cars that were to take her out to Rownton, which was the nearest point of railway to Mr. Ellis's place, when the real loneliness began. The cars into which she had changed were not so comfortable as those she had left, the people were not so kindly, while, chiefest discomfort of all, a blizzard had set in which threatened to snow them up before they reached Rownton.

It was prairie now—a limitless stretch of snow as far as the eye could see on every side. But when the blizzard began it was not possible to see anything beyond the white smother which shut them in, while their progress was so slow that sometimes they hardly appeared to be moving at all. They had passed the Gilbert Plains Junction, and another three hours should have found Bertha at Rownton, when the train came to a standstill. A great buzz of talk broke out then, and everyone had some story to tell of snowed-up trains and the sufferings incidental to such a condition. But the conductor came along presently to give them what comfort he could, telling them that the engine had been taken off to drive the snow-plough, and that probably three or four hours would see them on the move again. There was an old man in the cars who aroused Bertha's compassion; he was so very frail and feeble, and he looked so unfit to be travelling alone. He had a topcoat, but no scarf, and the keen wind which would penetrate the cars, despite red-hot stoves and shut windows, seemed to wither the poor old fellow with its rigours.

"Won't you take this scarf of mine? I do not need it in the least, and you look so cold," she said, with gentle pity in her tone, as she held a big woollen scarf towards him.

"You are very kind, but I could not deprive you of your wraps," he answered, with a little bow.

"But please, I do not want it," said Bertha, pressing the gaudy woollen thing upon him. She had knitted it herself last winter for a sofa blanket, but, like most of her undertakings in the direction of fancy-work, it had turned out quite different from what she had intended it to be, and as it was much too narrow and twice too long for a sofa blanket, it had been laid aside to come in useful some day. Then, when the long cold journey west had to be undertaken, there certainly seemed a chance of its finding a use at last. But so far she had not been sufficiently cold to make her willing to wind those shades of blue, yellow, grey, and brown wools round her throat.

"Are you sure?" His voice was wistful, and she could see that he was trembling with cold.

"Quite sure." As she spoke Bertha got up, and, taking the scarf, she wound it round and round his neck and shoulders, so getting for the first time a little satisfaction out of that sorely bungled piece of fancy-work which ought to have turned out so different in shape and size.

The man was so old and frail, that it became a sort of duty to look after him. Moreover, he reminded her a little of poor old Jan Saunders, whom she liked as much as she disliked Mrs. Saunders. The reminder was only that of association, for whereas Jan was a rough, uneducated man, this individual whom she was befriending spoke like a person of culture and refinement.

"Are you going far in this direction?" the old man asked presently, when he had thanked her for her goodness to him.

"Only to Rownton by rail, but I have a cross-country journey of about thirty miles after that," she answered, giving a glance at the whirling snow atoms outside, and wondering however that journey would be accomplished in this sort of weather.

"And I have come wrong, and shall have to take the next cars back to Gilbert Plains Junction, for I took a west fork cars instead of going for an east fork train. These trunk lines are very bewildering to a stranger," he remarked, with a little petulance in his tone.

"Yes; indeed I think that I should have gone wrong several times if I had not had my directions written out so very plainly for me," answered Bertha, with a laugh.

"You are fortunate to have someone to do it for you. But there, it is only the old who are alone; the young can always find friends," he said bitterly.

"Are you alone? I am so very sorry!"

There was so much sympathy in Bertha's tone, that the old fellow looked at her in surprise.

"Why should you be so kind to an old man? Have you a father of your own?" he asked gruffly.

"No; my father is dead, and my mother too. But you said that you were alone, and because I also am alone I felt sorry for you," replied Bertha simply.

He nodded, but did not say anything more for a long time, and she thought he was asleep, as most of the other passengers were. The slow hours dragged on, the blizzard raged outside, and presently darkness settled down; but the engine had not come back, and people began to wake up, telling each other in low tones of anxiety that it could not get back. Then the conductor came back, and they at once fell upon him with their questioning, but he could not tell them more than they knew already—the engine had gone ahead with the snow-plough to clear the track. It had not yet come back, probably could not get back, in which case they were stuck fast until such time as something came along to help them out of their fix.

Most of the passengers took the ill fortune quietly, since after all it was of no use to rail at what could not be helped. But there were a few, and Bertha's old man was among them, who abused the railway company in no measured terms for not taking more care to keep their roads clear.

"I shall lose money heavily from the delay, and I can ill afford to add loss to loss in this fashion," he said querulously, when he came back to sit with Bertha, after he had spent himself in his utterly useless complaints.

"Perhaps it will not be so bad as you fear. We may not be delayed very long after all," she said, trying to speak courageously, although she was dreadfully depressed by the existing state of things, which was so much worse than anything that she had expected to encounter in her journey.

"It could not very well be much worse. The fact that I got on the wrong cars at all means a delay that will stand me in to lose two thousand dollars, while a few weeks ago I was robbed to the tune of about two hundred thousand dollars," he said angrily, taking off his gloves and beating his poor wrinkled old hands together to warm them a little.

A great pity came into the heart of Bertha. Not for one moment did she believe this story of the old man's losses, but it was plain that he believed it himself. The poor shabby clothes which he was wearing would not lead anyone to suppose that he had ever had any money to lose; but one must be kind to the old and the frail, especially when there is poverty behind. So Bertha soothed and quieted him; she even bought him hot coffee and other comforts of the kind all the time there was anything on the cars left for anyone to buy, and he received her little attentions with so much gratitude, that her pity for him grew stronger every hour—she even forgot her own discomforts in trying to mitigate the hardship for him.

The long night wore to an end, as the longest must do; but when the tardy daylight came again, the cars were completely buried, snowed right over, and frozen in until it was like being entombed in an ice cave. The men formed themselves into a party of volunteers, and, armed with coal shovels, iron bars, or anything else which came handy, set to work to dig themselves out. The exercise warmed them, certainly, but it did not accomplish much else; for where was the use of digging the cars out and letting the cold in when they had no engine to drag them forward or put them back to Gilbert Plains Junction? They tried to get on to the telegraph wires to let their plight be known; but the wires were broken with the weight of the snow, so that attempt failed also.

Then some of the more adventurous spirits were for starting across the snow to find some settler's house where food and firing might be purchased. There was such grave danger about such an undertaking, however, as the party had no snow-shoes, that the brakeman and conductor refused, in the name of the railway company, to allow anyone to take the risk.

"But we can't sit here and die!" exclaimed a fat man with a very red face, who seemed the very embodiment of restless energy, and could not keep still for five minutes at the stretch.

"You don't seem in any immediate danger of passing away from starvation," said the conductor, with so much ironic emphasis that the others burst out laughing, and the fat man subsided into the background, quashed for the time being.

"Help will reach us before night," the officials said confidently, as they went through the cars comforting the women and children and saying encouraging things to the men. They were heroes in their way, and all through that long dreary time of waiting no one heard an impatient word from them or a murmur of any sort.

The fuel had run so low that the stoves had all to be let out save one in the middle car, and into this car all the passengers were gathered, a fearful crowd, of course, but it was better to be crowded than to freeze in solitude. The engine having gone, they were entirely dependent on the stoves for warmth, and if help did not come by the time the ordinary fuel was exhausted, it would be necessary to break up some of the fixings of the cars for firewood; but that had been done before, and could be done again if need be. What a long, long day it was! And before it came to an end Bertha realized that the poor old man who had talked so much about his losses was very ill.

"Is he a friend of yours, miss?" asked the conductor.

"No; I had never seen him until I boarded the train at Gilbert Plains Junction," replied Bertha.

"There isn't a doctor on the cars nor a nurse either, and what we are to do I'm sure I don't know," said the official, permitting himself to look really worried now, for the situation was getting serious.

Then suddenly the shout was raised that men were approaching on snow-shoes, drawing sledges behind them. Half the passengers turned out to meet them, and the conductor was left alone at the end of the car with Bertha and the poor old man, who was plainly so very ill.

"Can you stay with him, miss, while I go to see if a doctor can be got here somehow? or shall I call one of those ladies yonder?" asked the man.

Bertha looked across at the group of women cowering round the stove. Most of them had small children with them. The exceptions were a fat old lady with a peevish voice, who seemed to have a great difficulty in moving about; two girls of about her own age who were travelling with their father; and a young woman with a pleasant, sensible face, but a bandaged arm, which showed her plainly unfit for anything beyond taking care of herself.

"I will do my best for him," she said quietly. "But come back as soon as you can, for he seems very ill."

"Yes, and I'm afraid by the looks of him that he is going to be worse before the night is out," said the conductor, as he hurried away.

He was back inside of ten minutes with the cheering news that the snow-ploughs were within six miles, and that they hoped to get the line clear by midnight.

"So we may hope to draw into the depot at Three Crowns by nine o'clock to-morrow morning at the latest," he said.

"And shall we have to manage until then without help?" asked Bertha, in dismay.

"I am afraid so, miss, but we can clear them all out of this car and make the poor old fellow a little more comfortable," replied the conductor.

"Is anything wrong? Can I help?" asked the girl with the bandaged arm, coming up to Bertha.

"An old man is ill—he seems so very ill—and we cannot get to Three Crowns until nine o'clock to-morrow morning. I am wondering whatever we can do for all the night," said Bertha, with more dismay in her tone than she knew.

"And you have got him to look after? Oh, I am sorry for you! Shall I come and help? Not that I can do much because of my arm; but, anyhow, I can be a little company, and most of the other women here have got children to look after, poor things," said the young woman, who was not so very young after all.

"Oh, I shall be glad!" cried Bertha. "He is such a poor old man, and he seems so frail. I have thought all day how ill he looks, but for the last hour he has been so very much worse, and now he does not seem to know where he is."

"Ah, he is light-headed—old people get like that very quickly; but he may be very much better in the morning. Draw those curtains at the back of him; yes, like that. Now we will make him up a bed on that long seat, and when the conductor comes back he will lift the old man on to it for us; no, you must not try to do it yourself, you are not strong enough."

The girl was so brisk and alert in her ways, that her presence was an infinite consolation to Bertha, on whom was dumped the responsibility of being nurse-in-chief. But it was a night long to be remembered; neither Bertha nor the girl with the bandaged arm had time to even doze, for the poor old man tossed and raved, talking of all sorts of wild and impossible things, or he would break into grievous lamenting about some boy whom he had wronged. He was moaning now for someone whom he called Tom, and a minute later he would burst into bitter invective against some other person, name unknown, who had robbed him of property of great value.

Just about midnight there was a jar and a bang when the engine reached them and was fastened on once more; then they went slowly forward on the journey that had suffered so much delay. At Three Crowns depot, a wooden shed planted by the side of the track in company with half a dozen houses and a tin-roofed store, the old man was carried from the cars, and Bertha had to go with him, because he had hold of her hand, and was crying pitifully that he could not be taken among strangers, who would be sure to rob him. So the cars had to be kept waiting while the short journey to the house of the doctor was accomplished.

"Tell me your name—please tell me," pleaded the poor old fellow, when he had been taken into the house of the doctor, and Bertha had told him that she must go.

"My name is Bertha Doyne, and I am going to the house of Mr. Ellis at Duck Flats," said Bertha, and then the doctor laid a firm but kindly hand on the wrist of the poor old fellow to set Bertha free—for the train could not wait indefinitely—and she was hurried away.

CHAPTER VII
Worse than Her Fears

A TIMBER house, a barn, two sheds, and a fenced enclosure, that was all, and they stood black specks on the vast snowfield, visible for miles before they were reached.

"There you are, that is home!" exclaimed Tom Ellis, pointing away to the dots on the horizon, and at the same moment the pair of horses quickened their pace, as if they too had seen and understood that yonder was the end of the journey.

Bertha thrust her head a little forward and peered and peered; but she was so nearly blinded with the glare of the snow, that dots on the horizon were quite invisible to her.

"It is home, sweet home," chanted Tom Ellis, in a musical baritone. He was a cheerful soul, with strong faith but little imagination, and those black dots on the distant horizon encompassed his world. "Cousin Bertha, I hope you are going to be very happy with us at Duck Flats."

"Thank you," replied Bertha, in a strictly non-committal tone. But all her heart was crying out against the monotonous ugliness of a landscape that had no hidden things, no mystery—which, after all, is the charm of nature—and nothing that appealed to the imagination in the slightest degree.

"It is a great land," said Tom, with a sweep of his arm that included the whole horizon from sky to sky.

"It is certainly very big," said Bertha, wondering if that were the right thing to say, and then she ventured a question: "What do you grow? I mean, what is there under the snow—grass?"

"Wheat is what I grow," replied Tom, with a thrill of pride in his tone; for to him the man who grew wheat was a public benefactor. It was not his own profit that was secured merely, but the good of the world at large, since everyone needed wheat in some form or other.

"And is it all one big field?" she asked, "or are there fences under the snow?"

"Except for the fence round the house, there is not a fence for ten miles. The land is not all mine, of course; but we all grow wheat in this district, and a ridge thrown up with the plough is boundary enough," he answered serenely.

"I should have thought that mixed farming would have paid better. I don't think that I should like to put all my eggs in one basket," said Bertha, with a little shrug of her shoulders under her wraps. "Suppose the wheat should fail for one year?"

"Then I should fail too, and pretty quickly, I can tell you. But don't talk about it; the bare idea of such a thing gets on my nerves sometimes, and then I can't sleep in the nights," he answered.

"But if you feel like that, why do you take such a risk?" persisted Bertha, who could not understand this sort of vicarious tribulation.

"Because the profits are greater, and there is less outlay in proportion," he replied. "I grow wheat, and I grow nothing else. Very well, then, I only need the implements for wheat-growing, and most of them I can hire at reasonable rates, which pays me, don't you see. Then, when my wheat is harvested and thrashed, my cares for the year are over, and I have nothing to do but to plough for next year's crop. Of course, the thing can't go on for always, for it stands to reason that you can't grow the same crop year after year without the ground becoming impoverished. When that time comes, however, I shall sell the land and move on into a new district, where I can start afresh. That is the way that money is made, little cousin. There is risk in it, I grant you, but that is half the fun; it takes from the dead-level monotony of the affair."

"And does Grace like that sort of thing—the risk, I mean, and being dragged up by the roots, and dumped down in a fresh place when the impoverished land makes a move necessary?" asked Bertha, with some curiosity. She was thinking that if it were herself she should just hate it all.

Tom Ellis shook his head with a merry laugh. "I am afraid that my wife got some very stodgy, old-fashioned notions from living so long in Nova Scotia. Why, she was even saying the other day that she meant to have a flower garden next summer, an awful waste of ground, really, but you can't get women to be practical. And she insists on my keeping a cow!"

"But why shouldn't you keep a cow?" asked Bertha, in a puzzled tone, quite unable to see where the enormity of such a course came in.

He laughed again, and told her that she would understand the situation better when she had lived eight or nine years on the prairies.

"Which I never, never will, if by any means in my power I can get away!" said Bertha; but she said it to herself, being too sensitive regarding the feelings of other people to let one word of her deep discontent show itself as yet.

The door was flung open as the horses drew up with a flourish before the house, and Mrs. Ellis appeared on the threshold, her arms stretched out in eager welcome.

"Oh, Bertha, little Bertha, can it really be you! My dear, my dear, it is almost too good to be true!" she cried, and there was so much of downright breakdown in the voice of Grace, that Bertha caught her breath sharply, and at the same moment looked anxiously round, hoping that Tom Ellis did not hear.

But he was hauling the baggage out of the sledge, and was much too busy to notice how near to breakdown his wife had come.

"Oh, what a lot of children! I mean, what a lot they look altogether," said Bertha, as she was half-led, half-dragged into a room which seemed to be full of babies.

"Yes, are they not darlings? This is Dicky, my eldest, a very bad boy mostly, at other times very good indeed; then comes Molly, who always reminds me of you when you were a baby. After her there are Jimmy, Sue, and Baby Noll, who will be a year old on Christmas Day. Now, children, just give Auntie Bertha the very nicest welcome that you can manage."

But the small people were much too shy to make any demonstration of welcome. Dicky and Molly stared at her from solemn eyes, which to Bertha seemed to have a disapproving stare; while the twins, Jimmy and Sue, who were two years old, burst into howls of protest when she wanted to kiss them, and the fat baby swelled the chorus.

Bertha's heart grew heavy with secret dismay. She had so little first-hand knowledge of children, and she wondered how it would be possible to endure the long months of winter shut into a small house with so many crying babies. Perhaps if she had not been so very tired with her long journey, and the wearing strain of the time when they were snowed-up on the western fork, things would not have seemed quite so dreary or so hopelessly hard to bear.

"Oh, my dear, my dear, you cannot think what joy it is to have you here!" cried Grace again. "I had no idea how much I loved you all until I came away, and you cannot think how much I have longed for a sight of some of the dear home faces. But you have altered so much that I should not have known you, and you look so quiet, though you were such a restless, fidgety child, never content to sit still for more than two minutes at the stretch. Your father used to call you 'Little Quicksilver', and that is what you were."

"I am afraid that I must have outgrown the character, then, with my flapper frocks, for I am not a bit quick at anything now, and the girls would tell you the same," replied Bertha ruefully.

"Oh, what nonsense! You cannot really expect me to believe that a Doyne could be slow at anything, except in the matter of thinking evil of one's neighbour," said Grace, with a laugh. "And you are only a flapper still, for the matter of that. How old are you—seventeen?"

"Almost eighteen, but I feel quite thirty," Bertha answered, with a serious air.

"Wait until you are thirty, then the chances are that you will feel only about thirteen. Oh, I know what girls are like, especially girls with brains, and you were due to be the genius of the family!" said Mrs. Ellis, as she swept the crying twins up from the floor with one arm, and picked up the baby with the other, upon which ensued a great calm, for even a stranger was tolerable when viewed from the safe vantage-ground of mother's arms. Little Dick and Molly had retired into private life behind her chair, and so the whole family watched Bertha take off her wraps, very much enjoying the spectacle.

"It is Hilda who is the clever one," said Bertha modestly, "and Anne is very nice-looking, but I have neither beauty nor brains."

Mrs. Ellis leaned back with her armful of babies and surveyed her young cousin critically. Then she said, with her head held a little on one side: "You are certainly not plain, or, in other words, ugly; and I should say that in a year or two you will probably be rather nice-looking in a quiet, distinguished sort of way. Anne, of course, is downright handsome, but she was always good-looking, even as a child. Hilda is smart and clever, but she is not a genius, though she will make her way in the world, because she is careful and painstaking. She has also a great deal of tact, which, after all, goes further than genius."

"How well you know them both!" cried Bertha, and half against her will, for at this stage she did not even want to be happy. A feeling of home peace stole into her heart, and she felt that however much she might detest the flat monotony of the prairie, or feel the irksomeness of that little house packed with noisy, crying babies, she could not be wholly unhappy where Grace was.

"Of course, I know them well. Think how your home was my home, and your people were my people," said Mrs. Ellis. "It was a very dear home, too. But here am I talking and talking, while I have never showed you your room. I am so very sorry, dear, that we could not give you a room to yourself, and I have made Tom promise that he will build a room on at one end next summer, between seeding and harvest, so that you may have a little spot quite to yourself; but until then I am afraid that you will have to put up with Dicky and Molly as room mates."

Bertha's heart went right down into her boots as she followed Grace into the smaller of the two bedrooms, which was all that the house contained. She had expected, at the very least, to have a room to herself, and to know that never for one hour in the twenty-four could she be sure of uninvaded privacy was a blow indeed. But it had to be borne, and for the sake of the kind eyes that were on her she bravely hid the trouble, so that Grace, shrewd though she was, did not guess it.

Bertha had not expected Grace to be so kind. It was almost disappointing, in fact, for she had strung herself up to the pitch of heroic self-sacrifice, and lo! there was nothing in the way of sacrifice demanded of her, except perhaps in the matter of not having a bedroom to herself. Even that was rather an advantage than otherwise, if she had but known it, for she was thus unconsciously put upon her honour in the matter of keeping the little chamber tidy, and since habit stands for so much, she was effectually cured of the shocking untidiness which had been such a bone of contention in the old days between herself and her sisters.

But she suffered in those long weeks of winter as she had never suffered in her life before. The bare ugliness of the house and barn was a positive pain to her eyes, which simply ached to look on things of beauty. Then there was nothing in the dead level of the prairie to rest the eyes. From the time she arrived at Duck Flats, in early November, until late in April, it was white from one horizon to the other, and she was forced into the continual wearing of tinted glasses to save herself from going blind with the glare. She grew to hate the snow as she had never hated it before, and one day she broke down in childish crying over a little branch of an evergreen shrub which Tom Ellis had brought from Rownton.

"Oh, please forgive me; I did not mean to be so silly!" she exclaimed, when Grace chanced to find her in tears.

"My dear, I have cried over the bare ugliness of it all too often not to be able to sympathize with anyone else. But it is strange how that passes off, and one grows to find a beauty even in the flat monotony, at least I have found it so," said Mrs. Ellis, with a rapt look, which poor Bertha could not understand or in any way appreciate.

"That is because you are content with your home and your children; they are your world, and you do not want anything else!" she cried. "But with me it is different, and I feel as if I would give almost everything that I possess for the sight of a tree, or a hill, or a bit of rock-bound shore. I have loved beautiful things all my life, and especially have I loved beautiful scenery, and this is worse—far worse—than I ever dreamed it would be."

"Poor little girl!" murmured Grace, patting her in a soothing fashion; then she said hopefully, "Do you know, Bertha, I should not be at all surprised if this yearning of yours for beautiful things wakes up the sleeping soul that is in you."

"What do you mean?" demanded Bertha, in wide-eyed astonishment. She had always imagined that her soul was extremely wideawake; indeed, it had always seemed too much awake for her to do the practical things which everyday life demanded of her.

"I mean that no one has seen the best of you yet, and that you do not even know yourself what is in you. I believe that you are going to surprise us all some day, and the very thing to bring out the best that is in you is this same horrid monotony, as you call it."

"In what way do you expect me to surprise you?" asked Bertha, pausing in the sewing she was doing but indifferently well and looking at Grace, while a thrill of hope quivered in her heart, for when people expected anything of her, she mostly found that she could rise to it.

"Would it be a surprise if we knew?" demanded Grace, with a laugh. "I expect that it will be a surprise to you when it comes."

CHAPTER VIII
Great Expectations

SPRING was coming. The feel of it was in the air, and though howling winds and driving rains swept over the plain, while the earth was like a quag on Duck Flats, everyone remarked how fine the weather was, which meant what a welcome change it was after months on months of snow, of frost, and of winds so keen that they seemed to scorch and sear the skin. Bertha sang about her work in the mornings now; it was sheer gladness of heart, because the white covering had gone from the ground and the brown earth was showing once again. The day that the first plough was put into the ground was like a festival, and then followed weeks of such strenuous labour, that there was scarcely time to get through the allotted toil between sunrise and sunset, and they all went to bed to fall at once into dreamless sleep until morning came again.

She had a salary now, just the money that Grace would have paid to a hired help, and the feeling of independence which it gave her ministered not a little to her happiness and content. But the real fount and spring of her happiness lay in the fact that she had begun to write, and that already, young though she was, the sweet of a tiny success had come to her.

By the advice of Grace she had let poetry severely alone. There was no demand for it, and however fond of writing poetry people might be, they rarely cared to read much of it; there was not absorbing interest enough in it. So Bertha had tried her prentice hand upon a short story, and then had gone almost delirious with joy when it was accepted and paid for. But not a word did she say in her letters to Hilda or to Anne of the good thing which had come into her life. It would be time enough for that when she had done something bigger, and all her hopes were centred now on having a book published. If only she could manage that, it would serve as something to show for her labour. So she thought of it by day and dreamed of it at night, while little by little, like the building of a house, the story took on form and shape in her brain.

It was so strange to her to have someone to whom she could talk of her hopes and aspirations. She would never have dreamed of talking to her own sisters as she talked to Grace. They would have laughed at her, and would have said to each other in pitying tones, "If only Bertha were more practical and did not dream so much, what a good thing it would be!"

But Grace seemed always to understand that dreams were the great factor in Bertha's happiness, and that she could not be happy without them. It was that power to understand which gave Grace the influence on her young cousin's life. Bertha had not been at Duck Flats for a week before it had seemed quite possible to her to tell Grace everything that was in her heart. She had even confided in Mrs. Ellis the story of that one brave deed of hers which had brought so much discomfort to the three girls, and incidentally had left so much mortification behind it.

Bertha had never been able to tell Anne of what the German had told her, about how the stranger had left money with old Mrs. Saunders to be given to her for saving his life, but which the old woman had kept for her own private use.

"And I have always felt quite certain that the old woman could have told me of his whereabouts if she had liked, only she was afraid that he would find out about her keeping the money," said Bertha. "But what I never could understand was why he never came to see what had become of his coat and his diamonds."

"Diamonds?" echoed Grace, in amazement. "My dear Bertha, what are you talking about?"

"They may not be diamonds at all, nothing, in fact, but pebbles from the Micmac shoals," laughed Bertha. "But you shall see them, and then you will be able to tell me, perhaps."

She went off to her room and unearthed the coat and the little case from among her belongings, and then told Grace how the man had thrown the coat round her because she shivered so; she had run home in it, and then it had lain in a corner of her room until she was well.

"They are diamonds, I am sure of it," said Mrs. Ellis, in a tone of conviction. "Tom had an uncle, an old Welshman, who had some choice uncut diamonds in his possession, and Tom has often told me that they looked just like dirty pebbles, only they were so very, very hard, that they could not possibly be mistaken by anyone who had any knowledge of such things. Do you mind if I tell Tom about these, and ask him to look at them?"

"Of course not. But it does make me so fearfully uncomfortable to have the things in my possession like this. I feel as if I had stolen them," said Bertha, who was very much relieved because at last the story was off her mind, and the knowledge shared by someone else.

Grace laughed. "Oh, you poor little Bertha, you are the sort of child that it takes a mother to understand. I expect that Anne and Hilda would about cry themselves blind if they thought they had in any way failed in their duty to you, and yet, poor girls, they could never get at the heart of you, while you have opened out to me like the rosebuds to the sun."

Bertha shuffled uneasily. "It was my fault, of course," she said stiffly. "But I had a downright morbid dislike of being laughed at or criticised, so I mostly kept things to myself."

"Well, I shall laugh at you and criticise you, and when you shut yourself up like an oyster I shall worm things out of you somehow, so be prepared," said Grace, and she had been true to her word.

Mr. Ellis had looked at the diamonds which were in the case, and he had declared them to be very valuable indeed. "There is no mistaking them, and they are worth many thousands of dollars. I wish you had not got them, Bertha; it is horrid to think of your being bothered with valuable stuff like that."

"Put them into the bank," suggested Grace.

But Bertha shook her head. "I don't think I will," she said slowly. "It would only cause comment and speculation, perhaps; for how could a girl as poor as I am become possessed of diamonds like these in an ordinary way? Besides, I may some day encounter the man to whom they belong, and then I can restore them without any fuss, don't you see? If no one knows that I have them, there is no danger of their being stolen."

"The house might burn down," suggested Grace.

"That would not matter at all so far as the diamonds are concerned, for I keep them in my tin trunk, and there is little danger of a diamond robbery right out in the heart of the prairie," said Bertha; and then she carried the little morocco case back to her room and put it, with the coat, in the bottom of the tin trunk, after which they sat and talked of Tom's old uncle, the Welshman, who had brought him up, then quarrelled with him, and cast him off in his young manhood just when most he needed a friend to help him.

"But I have got on in spite of being left to my own devices," said Tom, with pardonable pride in his own achievements, and then he went on more soberly. "But it upsets me to think that the old man would persist in believing that I wanted his money. I was a great deal more keen on having someone to care for. Perhaps I ought to have been more patient with him. But when he was always flinging it at me that I was hanging round for the chance of what I could get out of him, it riled me so badly that I just cleared out and came west."

"How hard it must have been for you!" murmured Bertha, who already knew Tom Ellis well enough to understand that his loneliness must have been frightful.

"It was about as rough as I cared for," he answered. "When I got off the cars at Winnipeg I had only half a dollar left, so I had to go to work sharp, and not stand too fine as to what sort of job I got. I did anything I could get for two years, and then, as I had saved a little money, I pre-empted on a quarter section of land out here, lived on it for six months in each year to fulfil requirements, and the other six months I went east and earned enough to keep me going."

"And that is where Grace came in, I suppose?" There was keen interest in Bertha's tone. She was remembering that Anne and Hilda had always maintained that Grace had married beneath her, but surely a man who could carve his way through difficulties like these was well worth caring for. It was far more to his credit that he had carved his own way, than if he had still hung on with his uncle, bearing all sorts of abuse meekly for the sake of the gain which might come to him later.

The coming of the spring made a vast difference to the comfort of the little house on the prairie. There seemed so much more room to move now, for the children were out from morning to night, not even coming indoors to eat if they could only get their food given to them out-of-doors. The work of the house could much of it be done outside also. Tom Ellis had fitted up a bench and a table on the veranda, and here the washing of dishes and the washing of clothes, with many other similar activities, could be carried on—which lessened the work in no small degree.

Another horse had been bought to help with the spring ploughing and seeding, and when the corn was all in, Tom bought a side-saddle from a man who had no further use for it, and insisted on Grace going out for rides with him. He would have taken Bertha also, but she was not good at that sort of locomotion, and greatly preferred being left at home to look after the house and the children in the long quiet evenings, while Tom and Grace went for long expeditions among their own crops or those of their widely scattered neighbours. Then, with the cares of the day all done, and the children asleep or at play, Bertha enjoyed herself in her own way, working at the book which was to make her famous, as she fondly hoped, or merely dreaming dreams.

She was sitting so one evening, when the twins and Noll were safe in bed, while Dicky and Molly worked hard at making a flower garden in one corner of the paddock, which they had dug up and were planting with wild columbine, common blue violets, early milk vetch, and silver weed, which she had helped them to dig up and bring home earlier in the evening. It was getting late, but Bertha had not noticed it; indeed, she was oblivious to most things just then, except the very pleasant dreams in which she was indulging, of being able to earn enough money by literature to keep her from the necessity of doing anything else. Her arms ached with breadmaking, washing, and ironing, and all the other activities of the prairie day, where, if one does not do the work with one's own hands, it has to go undone. Then up sauntered Dicky, his spade over his shoulder, while Molly trailed limply along behind.

"We're about done, Bertha, put us to bed," said the small boy, dropping in a heap on the floor, because he was quite too tired to stand up any longer.

"Very well, I will bath Molly while you eat some supper, and then you can bath yourself, because you are a man, or soon will be," said Bertha, coming out of her dreams with an effort, and thinking how delightful it would be for her when these minor worries such as bathing children and that sort of thing were lifted from her.

"Oh, I had rather go to bed as I am to-night, and I can't be very dirty, for I had a dreadful big wash yesterday," sighed Dicky, who had rolled over on to his back, and was surveying the rising moon with a very sleepy gaze.

Bertha laughed. "I wonder what the sheets would be like to-morrow if you went to bed as you are," she said, as she picked up Molly—that being the quickest way of getting the little girl into the house. "Suppose you get your buttons all undone while you are waiting, and then it won't take you so long."

By the time Molly's bedtime toilet was complete, the little evening prayer said, and the child had trotted off to bed, Dicky was fast asleep on the veranda floor, and Bertha had to undress him and put him into the water before he roused at all; even then he was almost asleep again before she could get him into bed.

"Oh dear, why could he not have kept awake a little longer!" she exclaimed, going back to her dreaming, only to find the spell broken, and that a strange restlessness had taken possession of her which would not let her even sit still.

"I wonder when Grace and Tom are coming home?" she said to herself, as the twilight, grey and mysterious, crept over the prairie. A flock of birds flew shrilling overhead, and then there was silence unbroken and profound.

Unable to bear the oppression of the quiet, Bertha went into the house, looked at the sleeping children, lighted a lamp, but remembering that the petroleum was getting low, she put it out again and went out-of-doors, because, after all, the silence and the waiting were more bearable out there than inside the close little house. Then a great sigh close at hand startled her almost into a fit, until the sound of a subdued munching reached her ears, and she realized that it was only the third horse which was feeding with the cow in the paddock that had frightened her so badly.

"Oh dear, how silly it is to be afraid!" she cried, pressing her hand over her fluttering heart. "I don't suppose there is a creature within three miles of the place, unless, indeed, Tom and Grace are nearly home. But we shall be fearfully tired to-morrow if we are so late going to bed to-night."

Her panic passed off presently. It was really very pleasant sitting out there in the cool darkness, and, almost without knowing it, she began to get drowsy. But she must not go to sleep, oh, that would never do! Shaking herself vigorously, she sat erect for about five minutes, and then—

But it must have been hours later, and the night was growing very cold, when she awoke with a start to hear a long sobbing breath close beside her.

CHAPTER IX
A Dreadful Blow

"WHAT is it, oh, what is it?" cried Bertha, not really wideawake even now, and so bewildered by the strangeness of her waking as scarcely to know what she was about.

"Berfa, Berfa, I'm so fwightened, and I want mummy," said the voice of Molly close beside her, and then instantly Bertha's power of self-control returned. She had been afraid of she knew not what. But when it was only Molly in trouble who was sobbing at her side, she could be brave again, or at least she could soothe the child and keep her fears to herself.

"My poor darling, did you come out here on your bare toes?" she exclaimed, picking the child up in her arms and groping her way back into the house, where she lighted the lamp, for the night was now at its darkest.

"I waked, and it was dark, and I couldn't find no uns," explained Molly, with a whimper—she was addicted to becoming incoherent under stress of emotion—then she asked, in a plaintive tone, "Where is mummy, Berfa? I wants her."

"Mummy has not come back yet, darling; but I will put you into bed, and then you will shut your eyes and go fast to sleep again," said Bertha, soothing the frightened child with loving words and caresses, though she was not a little anxious and dismayed herself; for the clock in the kitchen pointed to half-past one, and she knew that something dreadful must have happened to the two who had gone out riding; because they would never have left her alone in this fashion if they could have helped it.

"Will mummy be home when I wakes?" demanded Molly tearfully; and Bertha made haste to be as soothing as possible, for as a rule Molly could not enjoy being miserable unless all the others were miserable too, so a shower with her stood commonly for a downpour all round, and Bertha felt that she simply could not bear having all those children crying together just now.

"Yes, I expect mummy will be here by that time," she said cheerfully. "But she will not like it if she comes home in the dark and finds you awake, so you had better make haste and go to sleep again."

"Me will," replied Molly, struggling with her sobs and suppressing them with a great effort, for the stroll out-of-doors into the big dark to find Bertha had tried her small nerves considerably.

When Molly was safely asleep again, Bertha went back to the door, but this time she did not put out the light. If they were coming home now they would need the light to guide them, maybe; in any case, she was glad to have the company of it as she stood on the dark threshold straining her eyes and her ears to the night.

What was that? Surely it was a cry away in the distance!

Panting and trembling she clung to the doorpost, her head bent forward so that she might hear the quicker, but for a time she heard nothing more. The hands of the clock were pointing to past two; in another hour it would be daylight, but what, oh what would the new day bring?

Ah, there it was again! A real cry, and no mistake about it. She left off trembling then. It was no use to shake and shiver when there was something to do, and Bertha was quite sure by this time that there was need of her help, only first she must find out from which direction the cry had come.

Leaving the door wide open, so that the light of the lamp might shine out, she went away from the house, right out to the darkness of the paddock, and then stood listening again. She thought that she would hear better out here, and when that cry came again she meant to answer it, for all thought of fear was gone from her heart now, and only the desire to help remained.

"Ber-tha, Ber-tha!"

It was Tom's voice that called, so it was Grace that was hurt, she told herself, with a quick understanding of the situation. Then she lifted up her voice in a ringing shout and began to run. Oh, how she ran! Slipping through the rails of the paddock fence, she took a bee line across the brown earth from which the green blades of wheat were already strongly springing.

It was getting lighter—what a mercy that the night was past! Even in her sharp anxiety she had time for this bit of thankfulness. Then she paused, wondering whether she were running wide or going straight, for as yet she could see nothing but the unending stretch of brown earth, with the dim shadows of the springing wheat.

"Where are you?" she called, straining her eyes and her ears anew.

"I am here; you are coming straight," answered the voice; but it was so exhausted, and so filled with anguish, that Bertha caught her breath in a sob, realizing that the trouble might be even worse than anything which she had feared.

On and on she ran, until it seemed to her that she had been running for hours, and she thought with dismay of the five sleeping babies which she had left in the little lonely house with the door wide open. But it could not be helped, and after all they might not wake.

Ah, there was Tom! She saw him now; he was staggering along under a burden which seemed to weigh him down.

He was carrying Grace! Then where were the horses?

But Bertha had no time for speculation just then, for just as she picked him out in the pale light she saw him lurch and stumble, try to recover himself, but failing, pitch forward on to the ground. Surely she had never run so fast before! She could hear herself panting as she sped along. But before she could reach him he was on his feet again and was gathering his wife up in his arms afresh.

"She isn't dead, Bertha, she isn't dead, for I heard her groan, poor dear, when I fell with her. I am afraid I must have hurt her dreadfully. But it is good to know that there is a little life left in her. For the last two hours I have thought she had really gone."

The poor fellow was sobbing from sheer relief and thankfulness, but Bertha thrust him aside and tried to take Grace in her own arms.

"I am sure that I can carry her for a little way, just to let you get your breath," she said, and at the first was more shocked by the awful haggard look on his face than she was by the white insensibility of Grace.

"No, you can't, for you are smaller than she is. But you can help me, and I am nearly spun out," he said faintly, and again she was startled at the look on his face.

Clasping their hands under the insensible form, they went slowly forward in the growing light of the dawn. Neither spoke a word—they had no breath left for speech—and Bertha was too appalled even to want to ask a question as to how the calamity had come about.

Slowly, slowly, slowly went on that dreadful progress. Bertha felt as if her arms were being dragged out of her body; it was a horrible, intolerable pain. There was a tightening of the muscles at her throat which bade fair to choke her; she felt as if she were going blind as she stumbled forward on that interminable walk—her very senses were reeling—and then suddenly Tom's voice called out sharply: "Mind the gate, Bertha!"

They had reached the paddock. Oh, the blessed relief of it! She made a great effort, took on a fresh spurt of strength, and fairly counted the steps across the paddock to the open door of the house where the light was still burning. Into the kitchen they carried the poor unconscious Grace, and then Tom lurched forward on to the floor and lay there, while Bertha turned swiftly to the pantry for the jug of water which she had put there last night, which already seemed so far away. Pouring some of it into a basin, she dipped her handkerchief into it and bathed his face and hands. She must get him better somehow, for she was afraid to touch Grace, who lay exactly as if she were dead. For a few dreadful moments Tom lay as apparently lifeless as his wife, then he drew a long breath and faintly asked for water. Bertha lifted his head and held the glass to his lips, for he seemed incapable of doing even so much for himself. But when he had gulped down a glassful his strength came slowly back to him, and at the end of ten minutes or so he was able to sit up again.

"There is brandy on the top shelf of the cupboard; get it down; we must try to make her swallow some," he said, pointing to the cupboard which stood in the corner.

Bertha hastened to obey. The sight of the white-faced rigid figure on the couch filled her with awe, for there appeared to be no life there at all; but Tom seemed so sure that his wife still lived, and now he was saying over and over again:

"She really groaned when I fell with her, Bertha; she really groaned, I tell you."

"Yes, yes, she will be better soon," panted Bertha, scarcely knowing what it was that she said, yet realizing the tremendous need there was for keeping his courage up at this most critical time. Then she got a teaspoon, and when Tom lifted the poor unconscious head, she gently trickled a few drops of the spirit through the clenched teeth.

"Give her more, give her more; there is plenty in the bottle," he said hoarsely; a terrible fear had struck him that she was gone too far for any restorative to bring back.

"I dare not put in more than a few drops at the time; it might choke her," whispered Bertha, who was listening anxiously for the sound of a drawn breath.

There were long, awful moments of waiting, then Bertha tried again. Her face was almost as white now as the face of Grace, but there was a sort of desperate courage in her heart; she must do her best and wisest, she must, for it was upon her that the poor distracted husband was leaning for help, and she had never felt so ignorant in her life, never.

"Ah, she swallowed then! I am sure of it!" cried Tom, in a tone of ecstasy, as the muscles of Grace's throat contracted in a little spasmodic jerk.

More moments of waiting, Bertha had tried again, and again there was distinct response. Grace was alive, she could swallow, and they could hear her breathe; but she did not open her eyes or in any way recover consciousness, and they were sure that she must be terribly injured.

"I must go for the doctor," said Tom thickly; but he looked so exhausted, that Bertha took a sudden desperate resolution.

"I shall go myself," she said sharply. "You are not fit to sit a horse after what you have gone through, and it will take longer to get the doctor here if you can't ride fast."

"I can't trust you out alone on horseback; you are not enough used to riding," objected Tom.

Bertha's face whitened. Only too well did she know her limitations with regard to horseflesh; but it did not weaken her resolution, rather it strengthened it.

"God will take care of me," she said simply, reaching down a wide-brimmed hat that hung on a peg just inside the door. The sun would be high before she got home, so the hat would be a necessity.

"There is only my old saddle, and you will have to ride Pucker, for I turned the other horses loose, and they may not be home until to-morrow, if then, for Grace's horse was dead lame," said Tom, getting on to his feet again with difficulty, for he had been kneeling by the side of his wife.

"I shall ride cross-saddle, I don't care what I look like, and I shall be safer that way," said Bertha. "If I catch Pucker and bring him up to the door, will you help me fix the saddle on? I am not quite sure that I know how it ought to go."

"I will saddle for you if you can bring the old horse up," he said, and Bertha hurried off to catch Pucker, which was fairly easy, as the old horse was rather of a nuisance than otherwise, for it was in the habit of hanging about the house to get little scraps of food and dainties of sorts not usually appreciated by horses.

In about five minutes Bertha was back again, leading Pucker by the forelock, while Tom had fetched his old saddle from the barn and was tying it up with string.

"Will you be able to milk at six o'clock?" asked Bertha. "I can do it before I go, if you like, only it will hinder, and we ought to get the doctor here as soon as possible."

"I can do it, and give the children their breakfast too. What are they to have?" he asked, as he slipped the saddle on to the quiet old horse and fastened the girths.

"Oh, give them as much milk as they like, and there is some bread in the pan; they will not hurt until I come home. But, Tom, can you tell me how it happened?" she asked, in a hesitating tone, with a nod of her head in the direction of the silent figure which was lying on the couch in the kitchen. "I hate to worry you; only, the doctor will want to know."

"Of course he will; but I thought I had told you," he said, as he helped her on to the back of Pucker. "Her horse put its foot into a hole and fell, shooting her over its head. When I picked her up I thought she had a broken neck, and that is what I am afraid of still."

"Oh, but that could not be!" she exclaimed, with a quick instinct to comfort. "For remember, she is alive."

"Only just; but while there is life there is hope. God bless you, Bertha, for all the help and comfort you have been to me to-night," he said brokenly, and then, as she rode away, he called out: "Tell the doctor that it happened between eight and nine o'clock last night, and I was all that time getting her home."

Bertha gasped. No wonder that he had seemed so fearfully exhausted, if he had been toiling along with such a burden for so many hours!

Pucker had done no work for three days beyond carrying Dicky and Molly round and round the paddock whenever it pleased them to take a ride, so the old horse was able and willing to go. It was not the thirty miles to Rownton that Bertha had to ride. There was, fortunately for her, a doctor living at Pentland Broads, fifteen miles away, where they went to church on Sundays, and where was the nearest store and post office.

A thought came into her mind that she might ride across to Blow End, where their nearest neighbour lived, and ask her to go over to Duck Flats and stay with poor Tom until she got back again. But second thoughts decided her against it. Mrs. Smith was a dreadfully nervous woman; moreover, she had a young baby, and would naturally find it very difficult to leave home in the morning. Besides, it would mean half an hour's delay in getting to Pentland Broads, and that would be serious.

Pucker was not the easiest of horses to ride, for the creature gambolled along with a difficult sideway motion which always made Bertha feel as if she were pitching off. But the cross-saddle fashion in which she was riding made her feel safer; she had so much better chance of sticking on than when she sat upon a side-saddle.

She had no whip, but when the first mile or so had been got over at a horrible shaking trot, she managed to cuff her steed into a lumbering gallop, and then she got forward at a great pace. She had no chance of guiding the horse, every faculty being absorbed in the effort to hold on. But Pucker was more used to going to Pentland Broads than anywhere else, and having once had his nose set in that direction, there was not much danger of his going any other road.

"Oh dear, oh dear! I do really believe that I shall be shaken to bits if this sort of thing keeps on much longer!" she muttered to herself, as the sun grew hotter and hotter, and the shaking, racking experience of Pucker's very best foot foremost made her ache in every limb. Then a long way ahead she saw the houses at Pentland Broads standing out clear against the sunshine, and knew that the long, dreadful ride was nearly at an end.

She could not think what would happen if the doctor should chance to be out. But it was so early in the day, that such a thing would not be very likely, unless indeed he had been away all night.

Cloppety, cloppety, clop! Cloppety, cloppety, clop! Poor old Pucker was entering into the spirit of things with praiseworthy energy; but the worst of it was that the poor old creature had its limitations, and could not understand that its rider would want to go anywhere but to the post office. So it tore past the doctor's house just as if it were doing the most colt-like bolt imaginable, then it came to a sudden stop before the post office, and stood there as if it were planted, while Bertha sat still on its back, and dared not try to turn the creature round through fear lest it should start off again, like John Gilpin's horse of immortal fame, and take her straight home again with her errand unaccomplished.

She knew that she could not get off unassisted either, unless indeed she rolled off; but in that case she might sustain some sort of damage, and that risk must not be run, in view of the urgent need there was for her most active assistance now in that stricken household at Duck Flats.

Presently a woman poked her head out from the door of the post office to see why the old horse with the girl on its back had halted so long just outside.

"There ain't no letters from yesterday's mail for you, Miss Doyne, and to-day's mail isn't in yet," she said.

"I have not come for letters; I have ridden in for the doctor, but my horse brought me past his house, and I dare not turn the creature round for fear that it will carry me back home without stopping at the doctor's house. I am not used to riding, you see, and I am not very good at managing horses either. Could you help me get down? Then I will hitch my horse up here and go back for the doctor," said Bertha, hoping that the woman would not laugh at her for being so helpless.

But nothing was further than laughter from the thoughts of Eunice Long at the mention of riding for the doctor. It takes a person dwelling in those remote places of the earth rightly to understand what sickness means in such widely scattered communities.

"Oh dear, oh dear! Come for the doctor, have you? Who is bad—one of the children? I am downright sorry for you," said the little woman, with such kindly sympathy that it nearly broke down Bertha's self-control.

"Mrs. Ellis has had an accident out riding; I am afraid that she is very badly hurt indeed," said Bertha, and then she rolled off into the arms of Eunice Long. But as she was more heavy, or perhaps more awkward, than the little woman expected, the result was that they both rolled over in the dust together, and it was a man who was passing that picked them up and set them on their feet again.

Staying for only a brief word of apology, Bertha set off running along the road to the doctor's house. She was horribly stiff and cramped with her long ride, and her progress was neither swift nor graceful; but the urgency of the case drove her along, and soon she was knocking at the green-painted door which carried Dr. Benson's modest brass plate.

But, to her intense dismay, the woman who opened the door to her said that the doctor was not at home, that he had been away all night, and might not be home until the next day.

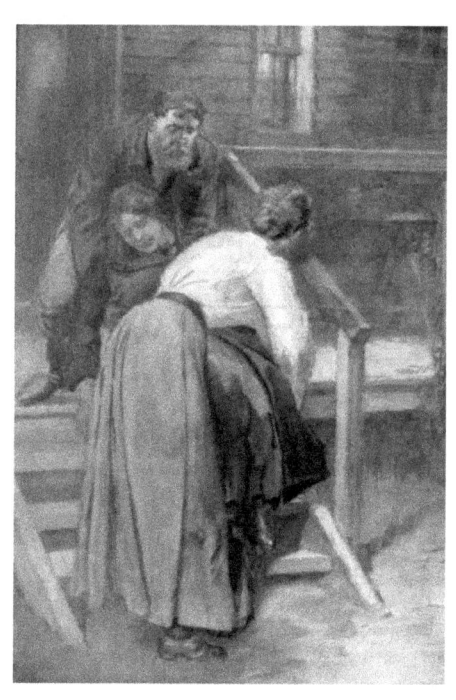

GRACE MEETS WITH AN ACCIDENT

CHAPTER X
The Worst

"Oh, what shall I do? What shall I do?" cried Bertha; and now, under pressure of this new calamity, her overstrained nerves gave way, and, sitting down on the doorstep, she burst into a passion of weeping.

"Good gracious! Is it anything very bad the matter?" asked the doctor's housekeeper in great concern.

"Yes, yes, there has been a bad accident. Mrs. Ellis has been hurt, and she may die if we can't get a doctor to her quickly," sobbed Bertha, wondering however she would dare to go back and face poor distracted Tom if she did not take the doctor with her.

"Well, well, whatever is to be done!" cried the woman, holding up her hands in consternation, but not able to suggest any way out of the trouble. It was the quiet voice of Eunice Long, who had followed Bertha along the road to the doctor's house, that settled the question of what would have to be done.

"Where has the doctor gone, Hester?" she asked, reaching out her hand to give Bertha a comforting pat on the shoulder.

"He is away to Pottle's Bent. A man there has broke a leg, and doctor said as there was nothing pressing he'd stay over there to give him a bit of attention, because he is such a big man that his wife can't move him, and it is so wearing to the horses to do that journey very often," replied the woman.

"Someone must ride out to Pottle's Bent and fetch him back at once. Twenty miles, isn't it? Now, I wonder who has got the best horse?"

Eunice Long had taken command of the situation, and poor harassed Bertha sat on the doorstep and listened, thankful to have the dreadful responsibility lifted from her shoulders.

"Why, Silas Ford has got the best cattle in Pentland Broads; trust him for that. But whether he will be willing to ride so far for the doctor is quite another question. Myself, I should be inclined to doubt it," said the doctor's housekeeper in a dogmatic tone.

But Eunice Long smiled, as she said softly: "He will go, I feel sure of it. That would be a hard-hearted person who would not help a neighbour in such distress. Besides, Tom Ellis has done us good turns all round, so we are bound to do our best for him to-day. Just step over to Mr. Ford, will you, and ask him to set off at once. Tell him that Mrs. Ellis may die if the doctor is not fetched as quickly as possible."

"Hadn't you better go yourself? You are a deal cleverer than I am at making folks do things they don't want to do," said the woman.

"I can't. I am going to take this child back to the post office and give her some breakfast, and then I am going to get Bill Humphries to drive us both out to Duck Flats in his wagon. I could not ride out there if I tried, and I guess that Miss Doyne has had enough of it for one day," replied Eunice, in her quiet, determined fashion.

"Oh, how kind you are; you think of everything!" exclaimed Bertha, as she limped back to the post office, there to snatch a hasty breakfast, while Bill Humphries, who kept the forge, hitched a pair of particularly mettlesome horses to his wagon, in obedience to the softly uttered command of Miss Long.

"We are bound to do our best for each other," said Eunice. "It is you that need it to-day, but it may be me to-morrow, don't you see, and if we don't do a good part for each other, who is going to put themselves out for us?"

"How can you leave the post office?" asked Bertha, for she knew that David Long, the brother of Eunice, was away, and Government servants cannot do as other people.

"Oh, Kitty Humphries will watch the instruments, and her mother will stand sponsor for her, and will keep the key of the safe," answered Eunice. "I would not like to promise that Kitty won't read all the post cards; but that is not a serious matter, because people should not put private business on post cards, and what is already public does not matter."

At this moment Bill Humphries drove his skittish pair up to the door, and the two made haste to clamber into the wagon, while Bill's eldest boy hung on to the heads of the horses to keep them from bolting.

"Oh, what shall I do with Pucker? Shall he be tied on behind?" asked Bertha, suddenly remembering her horse, which still stood as if it were planted in front of the post office.

"Better not; the poor old creature can't travel as fast as my colts. I'll send my Jim out with him this evening; he can bring over the doctor's stuff," said Bill Humphries; then he shouted an order to Jim to look after Pucker, and to give the old horse a good feed, to which Jim responded with a yell, as he sprang clear of the horses, which immediately started off at a tearing gallop.

"Has the other man gone for the doctor yet?" asked Bertha in a low tone, as Eunice tucked a cushion at her back to rest her a little and save her some of the jolting of the wagon.

"Silas Ford? Yes, he started before we did," said Eunice, and Bill Humphries rumbled out a low laugh of amusement, which even the solemnity of the occasion could not prevent.

"He was mad about it, though, and he said downright flat that he wouldn't budge, for he is behind with his seeding, and looked to about finish it to-day; but the doctor's housekeeper told him as how Miss Long had said that he had got to go, and then he gave in as mild as a calf—ha, ha, ha!"

Bertha wondered where the joke came in, and then was amazed to find that the face of Eunice Long was scarlet with hot, distressful blushes. She turned her head quickly then, for it did not seem right to spy into matters which did not concern her, and she could not bear for Eunice to know that she had seen. How those horses did go! And with what skill Bill guided them along the rough trail through those endless stretches of ploughed land, where the green wheat was springing in straight furrows which seemed to have no end. But Bertha hardly saw the wheat. She was wondering what was happening at that lonely little house at Duck Flats. Had Grace shown any sign of consciousness yet? And how was Tom bearing the weary waiting for the help which was so long in coming?

Bill had lapsed into a sort of shamed silence after his burst of laughter about the way in which Silas Ford had been made to do his duty, while Eunice spoke no word at all, only once or twice reached out a comforting hand to pat Bertha on the arm, as if to show a sympathy that was too deep for words. Presently the house with its barns and sheds came in sight.

"She is still alive," announced Bill suddenly, with so much relief in his tone that Bertha instantly forgave him that unseemly burst of laughter.

"How do you know?" she asked.

He pointed with his whip to two small figures scuttling to and fro before the house, which were plainly Dicky and Molly feeding the chickens and doing small chores to the best of their ability.

"See the children running out and in. Do you think Tom Ellis would let them do that if the poor mother had gone? Don't you fret, Miss Doyne, I guess if the poor thing has lived so long she is going to get better," he said, with the cheery optimism that was a part of his nature.

"Yes, please God, she is going to get better," breathed Eunice; and Bertha was comforted in spite of her fears, for faith is somehow infectious, and one could not utterly despair in such company.

Tom was at the door to meet them when the wagon drew up at the house; such an unkempt, dishevelled figure he looked. "Where is the doctor?" he demanded, with fierce impatience, as his eye swept the little group in the wagon.

"On his way here by this time, if I know anything about Silas Ford and the ways of his cattle," said Bill Humphries, as he leaped off the front of the wagon and held out his arms to lift Eunice down first. He reckoned that she was of the most use at this juncture, having had more experience in sickness than Bertha, so he put her in readiness for action first.

Tom groaned. It was dreadful to think of having to wait longer, after having waited so long already; but it was something to see Eunice Long on the scene, for it was well known that she was more clever and capable than most in sickness and trouble of all kinds.

"How is she?" asked Eunice, putting Tom aside with one hand, and stepping across the threshold, followed by Bertha.

"She is alive, and that is all I can say about it," answered Tom, following them into the kitchen, where Grace still lay on the couch just as he had lain her down with the help of Bertha in the dawning.

Eunice stooped over her, deftly touching her here and there, while the other two looked on, and then she said, with a look at Bertha: "I think we ought to get her to bed. Is it ready for her?"

"The bed is, but the children have not been dressed yet. I will get them out of the room," said Bertha, turning towards the bedroom, where Noll and the twins, still in a state of undress, were having a great time at a pillow fight.

She swept up an armful of little garments, seized Noll in the other arm, and, calling to the twins to follow, took them out on to the veranda, and there set Molly and Dicky to the task of clothing the three small children, active assistance being rendered by Bill Humphries, who, having a large family of his own, had learned many things by experience, although he confessed that the buttons and tapes were to the last degree bewildering to a mere man.

Inside the house Eunice and Bertha, with some help from Tom, carried Grace and laid her on her bed, then, sending him away, Eunice removed the garments one by one and anxiously searched for possible injuries. But there was not one to be seen. Grace did not even seem to have been bruised by the terrible fall, although she lay so still and motionless.

"What is it? What are you afraid of?" asked Bertha sharply, seeing the gravity had become deeper on the face of Eunice.

"It is her brain or her spine which has been injured, I fear, perhaps both," said Eunice softly, although she might have shouted and Grace would still not have heard or understood.

"Will she get better?" asked Bertha, her parched tongue rattling against the roof of her mouth.

"If the Lord wills," replied Eunice, in a solemn tone; but there was no ring of hopefulness in her tone now, and Bertha turned away wondering, yet did not dare to ask another question.

It was noon before the doctor came. Bill Humphries had put his horses in the barn and was doing such things about the house as Tom would have done in happier circumstances; but Tom himself was lying on the bed in the little room where Bertha slept, in such a state of collapse, that it looked as if they were going to have two invalids to care for instead of one.

A long half-hour the doctor was shut in with Grace, with only Eunice for a helper, and when he came out his face was as grave as that of Eunice had been when the injured woman was undressed. Tom was asleep, too worn out and exhausted to keep awake for the news which was like life or death to him, so there was only Bertha to hear the verdict of the doctor.

"There is some concussion of the brain, but that will probably pass off in a few hours, and Mrs. Ellis will become conscious again," said the doctor.

Bertha's face lightened with a flash of radiant hope. "Then do you think that she will soon be better?" she asked, with such bounding relief at her heart that she longed to shout or sing.

"That I cannot say yet," replied the doctor, and his manner was so very grave that the riotous hope in Bertha's heart died suddenly.

"What is it that you are afraid of? Tell me quick; I can bear it," she said sharply; but she turned so very white that the doctor had his doubts about her ability to stand up under any more trouble just then, so he said that he would be glad of a meal if she could get him something to eat, then he would go out and lie on the straw in the barn for a couple of hours, after which he would see Mrs. Ellis again before he went away.

"But why the barn?" asked Bertha; then remembering that Tom was lying asleep in the other room, she said quickly, "I will rouse my cousin; he would not like you to be turned into the barn, I am sure."

"I should be very angry if you did rouse him," said the doctor, looking so fierce that Bertha quailed before him. "We have got quite enough trouble to face in this house just now without having Tom Ellis for a patient as well as his wife. It is this sleep that may save him from collapse, but he will need to sleep for hours and hours if it is going to do him any good. I have had to rest in a good many places not half so comfortable as that barn yonder, so you need not worry about me. Only, if I am not back in the house again by three o'clock, I shall be glad if you will come and call me."

"I will do it, certainly," she answered; then, plucking up courage, she said timidly, "but will you please tell me what is the matter with Mrs. Ellis? I have got to know sometime, and there is nothing so wearing as suspense."

The doctor went suddenly silent, stirred his coffee with an air of impatience, as if angry at being bothered, although in reality he hated to give pain, then he said gruffly: "There is injury to the spine, and I am afraid, I am very much afraid, that she will be a helpless invalid for the remainder of her days."

CHAPTER XI
A Wild Revolt

BERTHA stared at the doctor in speechless horror, but he was stirring his coffee again and frowning at the tablecloth as if it had offended him. Then she turned and walked out-of-doors, feeling her way with her hands because she could not see.

It was awful, too awful for words! Busy, active Grace, with her tribe of little children, a hopeless, helpless invalid! Why, surely sudden death would have been kinder! What would they do? Who would nurse Grace and mother the children, wash, cook, and mend for the household? Who would do all these things?

"I shall have to do them myself," she groaned, then realizing all that it would mean to her cherished prospects and the tremendous giving up that it would involve, she muttered between her set teeth as she clutched at the post of the veranda to keep herself from falling, "I can't do it, and I won't! Oh, I won't!"

How long she stood there she had no idea. She knew that the doctor went past her on his way to the barn; she heard Eunice come to the door and call softly to Bill Humphries and then go back again. But mercifully no one took the slightest notice of her, so she clung fast to her post, while the whirling revolt in her heart grew blacker and wilder, until she felt as if she would go off her head.

It was the cry of a child which brought her to her senses again. Baby Noll had come to grief again, and was yelling in the whole-hearted fashion in which he always voiced his woes. Tom must not hear him, and the crying of the child would be sure to rouse him. Bertha remembered how Grace had often said that Tom always heard the children cry at night long before they roused her.

Moving slowly, because she felt so weak and spent, Bertha went to pick up the crying child, and comforted him, as she had often done before, until he was soon laughing again; for happily his griefs did not last long. Then she went back to the house. It was all very well to make up her mind that she would accept no responsibility with regard to this distressful family in the immediate future, but to save her own self-respect, and because her heart was kinder than she believed it to be, she had got to do her duty by them at the present. She was clearing up the kitchen, moving in a dull, mechanical fashion because of her dreadful weariness, when Eunice came out of the bedroom and laid forcible hands upon her.

"You must have some rest or you will break down, and you have been such a dear, brave child," said the little woman kindly.

"I can't rest yet; I have to call the doctor at three o'clock, and this muddle must be cleared up," said Bertha, stoutly resisting any attempt to make her rest, but secretly wincing at the words of praise from Eunice, because she knew herself unworthy of them.

"I can call the doctor, or I can rouse you to go and do it at the proper time. Come in with me and lie on the children's bed for a little rest, then you will feel so much better, more fit to help everyone who needs you," said the little woman in her gentle, persuasive fashion.

Bertha yielded then because she had no more strength to hold out, only when she went into the room where Grace lay unconscious she glanced fearfully at the still white face, as if fearing that the mute lips would upbraid her for the wild revolt which was tearing at her heart. Then she dropped on to the little bed where the twins slept at night, and for a brief spell her troubles were forgotten in the slumber which comes so easily when one is young.

It was Eunice who called the doctor, for Bertha was so very fast asleep. Then he came stealing into the room, looked at Grace, gave a curt order or two under his breath, and then rode away. He would come again to-morrow. Meanwhile, there was nothing to be done but to watch and wait.

It was six o'clock when Bertha woke, and she was dreadfully ashamed of herself for having slept so long. She went out to get supper then and to bring in the tired children, who had played out-of-doors the whole day long. Bill Humphries wanted her to say that he might take Dicky and Molly back with him for a while, so that they should be off her hands, but Bertha, remembering how useful those two had been in looking after the three babies that day, said that she could not spare them. It was a little puzzling to know where to put them to bed that night, but finally the three youngest were put into their mother's room as usual, and if their father did not rouse later on, Dicky and Molly would have to sleep on the sofa which stood in the kitchen. But she and Eunice would watch in the sickroom; for who could say what the turn of the night might bring to the white-faced woman on the bed?

Young Humphries rode Pucker home in the evening. He brought medicine from the doctor with him, and he had also discovered the two horses feeding by the side of the trail through the wheatfields, had managed to catch them, and had brought them along also. He told Eunice that her brother had come home, so that the post office need not trouble her, and that someone would come out next morning to relieve her as nurse for a few hours. Then he helped his father hitch the frisky horses to the wagon, and the two drove away in the twilight, and darkness dropped softly over the wide stretches of wheat and over the little house with its burden of pain.

Tom Ellis was still asleep, and the two elder children, to their great delight, were put to bed on the couch, where they lay in rapturous enjoyment of the novelty of the situation, giggling ecstatically until they went to sleep.

It was at the turn of the night, that weird hour between one day and another, when so many sufferers slip their fetters, that the eyes of Grace came open, and in a tone of surprise she asked: "Where am I?"

"At home in bed," replied Bertha, making her voice sound as natural as she could, though she was trembling in every limb.

"Was it a bad dream that I have been having, then?" Grace asked. "I thought that I was hurt, or was it Tom? Oh, Bertha, where is Tom?"

"He is asleep on the bed in the other room," said Bertha soothingly, while Eunice sank farther back in the shadows, fearing to excite Grace with her presence just then.

"Bertha, there was an accident then, and he was hurt! Is he still alive, oh, tell me, quick, quick?" she panted, her eyes moving with an expression of the keenest distress; but she did not lift a finger or attempt to move herself in any way.

Bertha stooped over her and gently stroked her face. "He is not hurt at all, dear, only he is very, very tired, for he brought you home in his arms. It took hours; he was fearfully exhausted, and the doctor said that we were not to wake him on any account."

"The doctor? Then he is hurt? Oh, Bertha, Bertha, it is cruel, cruel to tell me falsehoods even in kindness!" exclaimed Grace, and there was such a pathos in her voice that Bertha shrank back affrighted, looking at Eunice for help.

The little woman stepped forward out of the shadows and gently thrust Bertha to one side.

"She is quite right, Mrs. Ellis, your husband was not hurt. It was you that were thrown, pitched on to your head, and it has made you dazed for a time. Mr. Ellis had to carry you so far that he was really knocked up, though I think it was his worry on your account that upset him as much as anything."

"Why, it is Miss Long!" said Grace, in great surprise.

"Yes, I came over when I heard that you had had a fall. Bertha is not very much used to sickness, you see, and I knew that you would come to me if I were bad and needed you. Now, suppose you take this stuff the doctor left for you and then try to sleep, you will feel better when you wake again," said Eunice, a kind of mesmeric soothing in her voice, as she held the medicine to the lips of Grace.

"I can't move, and I can't feel what is the matter with me. Shall I be better when I wake?" asked Grace, with such a look of terror in her face, that Eunice swallowed a sob and kept her voice steady with a great difficulty.

"You will be stronger when you wake. Go to sleep now, dear, go to sleep," said the little woman gently, and then, under the influence of the medicine, which was a sleeping draught, Grace was speedily unconscious again.

"Her brain is all right, thank God!" said Eunice, in a low moved tone, as the two stood looking at the quiet figure in her deep slumber.

"But her body! Oh, Miss Long, did you hear what she said?" cried Bertha, with a sob.

"Yes; but the body is such a small matter compared with the brain, and in time who can say but what she may be quite well again. Stranger things have happened, and doctors are human and likely to make mistakes like the rest of us," said Eunice, in a cheerful tone; then she added, with a graver note in her voice, "Meanwhile, she has you, and what a blessing you will be in the house! It will be your chance of paying back to your cousin the care she gave to you and your sisters when your mother died."

Bertha drew a sharp breath and turned away without answering. This was a side of the question she had not looked at before. She had entirely ignored her own responsibility in the matter in that night's wild revolt, and the recollection of it was like a fetter to bind her to the life from which she was so anxious to escape.

Tom did not wake until daylight, and then he was himself again, at least it was a comfort to know there was no fear of having him for an invalid also; and Bertha tried to rally her drooping spirits as the day wore on, telling herself that most probably things would not be so bad or so black as at first they had threatened.

It was late in the afternoon when the doctor came, and Grace was just rousing out of her deep, drug-induced sleep. Again it was Eunice and the doctor who were shut up with her, while Bertha waited in anxious dread outside the closed door, and Tom, who did not know that there was anything to dread, hovered round, so glad and thankful that his wife was still alive, that it made Bertha's heart ache to watch him.

Why, oh why had Eunice not warned him of what might be in store? It seemed so cruel to let him hope when perhaps there was no hope.

"What a long time the doctor is in there! Was he as long yesterday?" Tom asked, coming restlessly into the kitchen and standing by the table where Bertha was busy breadmaking. To her it was like the grimmest irony of things that daily work had to be done, whatever issues were at stake. But she only nodded her head in reply, for at that moment the doctor came out of the room, and, crossing to the outer door, beckoned to Tom to follow him. Bertha heaved a great sigh of relief. At least she had been spared the heavy task of letting him know of the trouble which might be in store for him.

In about ten minutes he was back again with such a look on his face as she had never seen there before, and she caught her breath in a little gasp of amazement. It was a glorified expression that he wore, and it lifted him above the commonplace.

"Can I go in?" he asked, as Eunice at this moment appeared on the threshold of the inner room; and when the little woman nodded her head, he passed in and shut the door behind him.

If trouble could make a plain man look like that, surely it could not be unmixed disaster! That was the thought in Bertha's mind for the remainder of the day, and though she tried to escape it she could not. All her life she had worshipped beauty wherever she could find it. Tom Ellis had seemed hitherto to be only a struggling unlettered farmer, more intent on making money than improving his intellectual standing; but the blow which might have felled a less noble soul had left him standing erect and strong, so surely the disaster had wrought him only good.

The question was, What would it do for her? Could she, too, rise above this crushing blow of fate and watch all her bright ambitions smitten to the dust, while only the satisfaction of duty done remained to her? Could she rise above it? Could she?

But meanwhile there was bread to bake, five little children to care for and feed, the housework to do, and all the thousand-and-one things that come to tax the strength and patience of the prairie housekeeper, so Bertha went straight on, leaving the question of what she could really do and bear to settle itself.

CHAPTER XII
The Glory of the Wheat

THE magic of Manitoba was laying hold of Bertha. There was a vigour and a stir in the wild, solitary life of the prairie which was like new life to the girl who had been so pale and listless when she lived at home, sheltered and cared for by the two hard-working elder sisters. There was not much sheltering or carefulness on her account in these glowing summer days while the wheat was ripening and the busy farmers were preparing to deal with a record crop.

Grace lay in the same helpless condition in which she had been brought home. She could move one hand a little, her face and speech were just the same as when she was well, but the rest of her was as if it were dead so far as her feeling went.

Regardless of the expense, Tom had had a specialist out from Winnipeg; but the great man could only endorse the opinion of Dr. Benson, who had said that Mrs. Ellis might recover after some years, when the paralyzing effects of the fall had worn off, or she might all her life remain a helpless invalid. The cost of the specialist's visit would leave Tom Ellis a poor man until after he had reaped his harvest, and the worst of it was no good had come from it save that little ray of hope for the future, which, after all, might not be hope. But husband and wife accepted the inevitable with the resignation and patience born of a great faith and trust, making the best of things so far as a best could be made.

Friends and neighbours were as kind as kind could be, but it was on Bertha that the heavy load of the household burden fell. It was she who had to mother the children now, to make the bread, and cook the dinners. It was her sorely incapable hands which, when the cooking and cleaning were done, had to fashion the little garments for the children. Only in this matter of sewing Grace, though helpless, was of the greatest assistance, because she knew just how it ought to be done, and she could direct the cutting out, the putting together, and all the planning and fixing which goes to work of that kind.

Bertha's revolt was over. No one had even guessed the time of struggle through which she had gone, unless indeed Eunice Long had read what was in her heart during those black hours when the disaster was new. But Bertha felt that never again would she be able to respect herself because of the manner in which she had fallen in her self-esteem that day, when first she had been told that Grace would probably be helpless. She hated the thought of her bondage as much as ever, but she knew that there was no escaping it, and so accepted her fate with the best grace she could.

Perhaps it was that most wholesome disgust of herself which helped her most at this time, because she forced herself to perform all her manifold duties with the quickness and thoroughness she would have put into work that was a joy, and if in the morning her soul revolted at the thought of the long, toilsome day ahead of her, no one knew it but herself.

The children grew and throve in the sunshine, they lived in the fields from morning to night, and the narrow little house was strangely quiet and peaceful in the long summer noons when Bertha came to sit by the couch, and learn the unspoken lessons of patience which Grace was teaching her day by day.

From the window of the kitchen, which was sitting-room, dining-room, and kitchen all combined, there was nothing to be seen save the wide stretches of waving wheat, varied here and there by low grassy knolls covered with golden rod in full bloom, a mauve chrysanthemum and the bright purple thistle common to the prairie. Bertha's eyes ached for the cool green of tree foliage, but the only green leaves to be seen were from the pumpkin vines, which she herself had planted by the veranda in the springtime, and which had flourished and spread until they made a shade of greenery most welcome to the eye.

"Another month and all will be bare stubble. Of what a relief it will be!" said Grace one hot afternoon, as her eager gaze wandered out through the open door to the landscape bathed in sunshine, where the waving wheat was already turning to gold in readiness for harvest.

"It will be a very busy time, but we shall get through somehow; don't worry about it," replied Bertha soothingly; for she thought that Grace was wondering how the harvest rush of work would go through without her hands to help.

"It was not the thought of the work which made me so anxious to have it over," went on Grace, with a far-away look in her eyes, as if she were seeing more than the waving stretch of wheat. "I am afraid that my faith is of very poor stuff, because it gets so feeble in times of strain. But sometimes I can hardly sleep at night, wondering what would happen to us if tempest ruined the crop now."

"A tempest might damage it, but surely, surely it would not entirely ruin it now," said Bertha, who found it difficult to realize all that was involved by this system of specializing in agriculture.

"Sometimes a thousand acres of corn are destroyed in a night on these prairie lands, and if it is fate—our fate—who can stay it?" said Grace, as her gaze travelled to and fro along the little stretch of horizon that could be seen from where she lay. Then she cried out, with an anguish of fear in her tone: "Bertha! Bertha! What is that out yonder?"

Bertha sprang to her feet, startled by the terror in the tone of the invalid. But she could see nothing at all to rouse a fear; it was just a stretch of golden-floored space, with the blue sky above, and a dim white cloud on the edge of the horizon.

"There is nothing wrong, dear, that I can see, nothing," she said, but all the same she went to the window, which gave a different view to that spread out before the open door; for she wanted to make sure that there was really no cause for alarm.

"It is smoke! It is smoke!" cried Grace hoarsely. "Don't you see that white cloud on the edge of the horizon? It was not there ten minutes ago, and it is not a real cloud, I am sure of it. Something has set fire to the wheat, and the wind is driving this way. Oh, Bertha, what shall we do? What shall we do?"

"There may be nothing wrong," said Bertha quietly, although her heart was beating furiously. "I will run across to the barn and climb the ladder. Tom left it there this morning when he was mending the shingle at the corner. There was not enough wood to finish the job, so he said that it would have to wait until to-morrow."

"Take the glass, you will see farther; it stands on the shelf in my bedroom. Only, make haste, make haste!" panted Grace.

Bertha flew to obey. She was growing alarmed herself, for certainly this was like no cloud that she had ever seen before, and already the whole horizon was streaked with filmy haze.

Slipping the field glass into her apron pocket, so that she might have both hands free for climbing the ladder, she swarmed upwards as fast as she could go. Reaching the ridge, she steadied herself with one hand, and, pulling the glass from her pocket with the other, she tried to see what it was which made that dreadful murky haze away to the west, where the stretch of corn reached to the horizon.

Her hand was shaking so badly that the glass wobbled up and down, and she could get no focus at all. But alas! alas! she did not need the evidence of her eyes to tell her what it was, for the west wind was bringing on its breath the smell of smoke. Grace was right; it was the wheat that was on fire, and the wind was blowing it straight on to their section. Tom was away. He had gone over to Pottle's Bent with two horses to bring home a reaper, in readiness to start cutting on the next day but one. But if the fire had its way there would be no cutting to do, and the golden plenty which waited for harvesting would be nothing but a blackened ruin.

"What can I do?" she wailed, as she slid down the ladder, and then with unerring instinct ran indoors to ask Grace what was the wisest thing to do.

"If the reaper were here, you might ride up and down a swath until you had cut enough to stop the fire. But the reaper isn't here, and so that is out of the question, and there is nothing to be done but to beat it out," said Grace, her nimble mind taking in the best way to meet the danger and overcome it.

"I'll go and hitch Pucker to the wagon and put a barrel into it; I shall have to fill it with water afterwards, and it will take time, but I will be as fast as I can," panted Bertha, and then she rushed away in a great hurry, bidding Grace remember all that she would want to take with her.

The wagon stood outside the barn, and it did not take many minutes to roll an empty barrel towards it, and then by sheer strength of arm get it up into the wagon, where she wedged it tight to keep it from spilling the water. Pucker came up to see what was going forward, and she caught him promptly, hitching him to the wagon with a dexterity born of much practice, then, driving up to the house, she proceeded to fill her barrel rather more than half full of water. Luckily she had that morning drawn up from the well the water she would want the next day for the family wash, and this saved her much time.

"Throw half a dozen sacks into the wagon, some pieces of string, and two or three brooms—you will be able to fight the fire quicker with a bag on a broom," said Grace, then she bade her prop the doors open and go.

"Say Godspeed to me, dear; I am so horribly afraid!" panted Bertha, halting for a moment by the couch, her face white and drawn, and all the old cowardice of her nature rising up to mock her, now that she so badly needed to be brave and strong.

"Godspeed you, dear, and make your arms strong to save our harvest for us," said Grace, and there was such a thrill in her tones, that Bertha was stirred by it into forgetting the miserable tremors which made her shrink from the task before her.

Scrambling into the wagon, she drove across the paddock to the gate leading out to the westward trail. The children were playing behind the barn, where there was a thin strip of shade, and she called to them to go back to the house to look after their mother. She would have liked to take Dicky with her, because he was quite able to help her fight the fire. But he was the eldest, and must be left to look after the smaller children; for Molly was a feckless mite, and the twins were mostly in mischief.

When once the paddock gate was shut, and she had mounted the wagon again, she drove along the trail a hard gallop. The old horse doubtless wondered why so much stick was his portion, but he rose to the occasion, and did his level best to get over the ground. Grace had told her to put a cover on the barrel so that the water should not be spilled, and although a little washed over and wet her frock, it did more good than harm, since if she were wet there would be less danger of her clothing taking fire.

Once before, when she and Hilda were staying at a farm, she had helped to fight a fire which broke out in a hayfield, but it had been comparatively easy for half a score of people to tramp out the sparks and flames in a field of burning grass. But now she had to wrestle singlehanded with a stretch of fire that threatened a vast area of wheat which was more than waist high.

"But someone else will see it, and if I am the first there I shall be sure to have help soon," she said to herself, as the wagon bumped, bounced, and swayed over the roughness of the trail. She was getting nearer now; the flames were visible, shooting out like red tongues through the thick smoke, while she could hear the soft rustle and rush of the flames.

Luckily the trail led along one side of the burning area, and so she was able to get quite near with the wagon before plunging into the waist-high wheat. Her great trouble was with Pucker. The poor old horse was afraid of the fire, and she was so much in dread that he would bolt. To prevent a catastrophe of this sort, she dismounted and, tilting her hat over the eyes of the animal, led it forward right up to the edge of the burning corn.

Before she could begin to fight the fire she had to unhitch Pucker from the wagon and tie him so that he could not stampede. When this was done she set to work knocking out the fire, but it was awful toil. Every time she wanted to wet her broom afresh she had to swing up into the wagon, dip the broom and the sack into the barrel, and swing down again, rush across the patch of blackened, smouldering stubble, and dab away at the fire until her weapon was dry again. Her boots were singed; her short skirt would have been blazing long ago, if she had not taken the precaution of dipping it in the barrel, so that it hung limp and soaked about her feet.

Would no help ever come? She was making no headway in putting out the fire, though it was not gaining as it would have done if she had not been there to check it. There was a great terror on her lest her water should be exhausted before help came. If this happened, she would have to go back to the house for more, and she would have to draw it up from the well; and oh! the very thought of it almost broke her down, while there was a noise of many waters in her head, the sun scorched her with a fierce heat, the fire burned her shoes, and she was so nearly exhausted that she was afraid that she would roll into the burning wheat, and so come by a terrible death in her efforts to put out the fire.

Slowly she swung herself into the wagon for the last time—it must be the last time, for there was hardly enough water left to damp her sack. What was the use of even trying to keep on any longer, when she could only keep the fire in check and could not succeed in putting it out?

Squelch! Squelch! Down into the bottom of the barrel went the singed and smouldering broom. Surely there was more water left than she had supposed! She could keep on a little longer yet, and, yes—really she was sure that the stretch of fire was no greater than it had been.

But hark! What was that?

A strained shout reached her ears, but as yet she could not see anyone coming. Her eyes were smarting so with dust and steam that everything was misty and indistinct; but it was a shout that she had heard, and—ah, yes, there was another!

Joy! Joy! The wheat might be saved after all! Down from the wagon she sprang, the black, dirty water splashing into her face, which was blacker still; but no one thought of looks in times of stress like these. She was stronger now that her hope had revived, and she fled across the blackened space to fight with renewed energy, while the shouts came nearer and nearer. She could hear horses galloping, and knew for a certainty that help was at hand.

"Look out; you are afire!" yelled a voice, too hoarse and strained for recognition, and at the same moment Bertha felt a swirling hot blast strike her on the side, and, to her horror, a tongue of flame shot up the sleeve of her blouse. There was no time to think, she could only act, and, dropping promptly on the ground, she rolled and rolled, fighting the terrible danger that menaced her. Then suddenly something wet and cold dropped upon her, there was more vigorous rolling, only now it was someone else who did it, and then, when she tried to get up, a woman's voice said in her ears:

"Lie still a few minutes; you will feel better then. But I must go and help them put the fire out."

For a little while Bertha lay still, trying to get rid of that horrible fluttering at her heart which had seized her when she saw the fire creeping up her arm; then, remembering the dire need there was for her to be up and helping, she struggled to her feet again. At first she swayed dizzily, but by dint of leaning on her broom handle she managed to get across to where several people were working with frantic haste at the line of fire.

"Better, are you?" panted the woman, whom Bertha now recognized as Mrs. Smith, from Blow End, their nearest neighbour.

"I am all right, thank you," Bertha answered, and then, dipping her broom into a barrel of water, which the two men who were also fighting the fire had placed on the ground, she went to work with a will again. It was easier now—the terrible sense of responsibility was lifted. Moreover, it was so much easier with the water on the ground: one could dip and run, dabbing and beating with a dripping sack, and so quenching out a much longer area of fire with the same amount of labour.

Neither of the men spoke to Bertha, except that once Mr. Smith shouted to her to be careful and wet her frock, or she would be on fire again. At the end of half an hour the danger was over, and the four blackened, exhausted firefighters gathered in a group to discuss the ruin which had been so narrowly averted, and to rest their aching arms after the trial of strength and endurance through which they had passed.

"We were drawing up the water for washing to-morrow," said Mrs. Smith, a young and pretty woman with two little children, "then a traveller from Brown & Smedley's Implement Factory at Gilbert Plains rode up and said he'd seen smoke over this way. I guess we acted on that hint pretty smart. His horses were fresh, and ours wanted catching, so we just filled three barrels with water, and I shut the children into the bedroom. They were both asleep, luckily, and then away we came. But I guess we should have been too late to have done much good if it had not been for you. My word, but you were plucky to tackle it alone, and you must have worked like a nigger!"

"Is there much wheat burned?" asked Bertha, miserably conscious now of her most awful appearance, as the traveller from Messrs. Brown & Smedley turned to look at her with what she deemed a calm and critical gaze. He was black and dusty himself, but nothing compared to her.

"Not more than two acres, I should say," replied Mr. Smith. "But that is thanks to you, Miss Bertha. It would have been touch and go with a hundred acres if you had not kept it from crossing the Rownton trail."

"I am afraid that I should never have been brave enough to face it alone. But Mrs. Ellis told me that I must come, and so I just had to do my best," replied Bertha. "And oh, can you do without me now, for I have left her alone except for the children?"

"Yes, go by all means; the men can do without any more help now. I am going myself, too, for I tremble to think what may be happening to my babies," said Mrs. Smith; and then she called out: "Here comes someone else—what a blessed relief! Now I shall be able to be driven home instead of having to walk."

The someone else was Bill Humphries, who had been driving back to Pentland Broads from the depot at Rownton, but, seeing the smoke, had driven as hard as his horses could travel to reach the place.

While these explanations had been going on, Bertha went off to hitch up Pucker, and she was quite unreasonably annoyed because the strange young man, who was a traveller from Messrs. Brown & Smedley, came to help in the hitching-up process.

"I do not need help, thank you," she said, in a frosty tone.

"I can quite believe that you do not, still it is a pleasure to do something, all the same," said the unknown, who did not appear to be easily rebuffed; for he had calmly taken the business into his own hands, and Bertha found herself relegated to the position of mere onlooker, which made her more vexed than before. She told herself it was like cool impertinence to thrust her on one side in this fashion.

So she stood silent and ungracious, then, when the wagon was ready, she mounted with a brief word of thanks and drove off, glad to get away from those calmly scrutinizing eyes.

CHAPTER XIII
A Trick of Memory

POOR old Pucker had a good deal of stick on the return journey also, but he was a horse that mostly needed considerable encouragement of this kind. Moreover, Bertha was sick with anxiety on account of Grace, who had never been left alone since the accident. She had not had time to think about her before, the need had been too desperate, but now—well, Pucker had to do his very best in the matter of speed, that was all, while the empty wagon bounced and bumped, threatening to overturn at least half a dozen times, yet never quite managing to do it.

What a relief it was when the house and barn came in sight! What a still greater relief when she drove up to the gate of the paddock, to find Dicky running to open it for her! And when she had driven through, and the gate was shut again, she stopped the horse and reached down to help the adventurous Dicky to climb up beside her.

"Have you taken good care of Mummy?" she asked, letting Pucker cross the paddock at a walk, because she felt that she could not bear any more bumping just then.

"Of coorse I has," replied Dicky, with a great deal of swagger. "But I just wish that I had been able to come and help you fight the fire, Bertha. Wasn't it fine?"

"No, it was not—it was horrible!" she exclaimed, with a shudder, thinking of some of the moments when she was almost at the point of despair before help came.

"I shouldn't have been afraid, at least not much," said the small boy, with a sigh; and then he burst out: "I say, Bertha, a man has been here since you went away."

"What man?" asked Bertha sharply, thinking that if it were a stranger, Grace must have been dreadfully upset.

"I don't know, and I don't like him either, though he gave me half a dollar, and he gave Molly another," said Dicky, frowning heavily. In his estimation people who could bestow largess to that amount ought to be in every way satisfactory, which made it disappointing when they were not.

Bertha drove up to the house with very active wonder stirring in her mind, and, jumping down, she lifted Dicky out also, and then hurried indoors to see how it fared with Grace. One look at the face on the pillow was enough to show Bertha that the excitement of the afternoon had been far too much for the invalid, and, letting everything else go, she set herself to the task of making poor Grace quiet and composed once more.

"Is the fire under?" asked Grace, who was wild-eyed with fear and agitation.

"Yes, it is quite out; but Mr. Smith and Mr. Humphries are both there, and one of them will stay until there is no more fear of it lighting up again, though it looks as if it might rain, in which case there will not be any danger at all," said Bertha. And then she refused to talk, or to let Grace talk, finally succeeding in getting the invalid off to sleep for a short time. Not a word had Grace said of any person having been at the house, and Bertha might have been inclined to think that Dicky had dreamed it but for those two half-dollars, which he and Molly displayed so proudly when she went out to them in the paddock after their mother had dropped into a doze.

Having unhitched Pucker and turned the old animal loose to feed, she went indoors to change her singed and dirty garments, and incidentally to wash her face.

"Oh! oh! what an unutterable fright I look!" she gasped, staring at herself in the glass, and reflecting ruefully that Mrs. Smith had not looked bad at all; there had not been the shadow of a smudge across her face, and her hair, although a little loosened by the wind and the hard work, had been quite passably tidy.

But Bertha's heavy masses of hair were hanging down her back, her face was streaked and smudged with dust and blacks, her blouse was torn open at the neck and slit up the arm where it had taken fire, and her skirt was a ruin.

"It is my fate to look a most awful guy when I am forced to do anything out of the common," she muttered to herself, as she washed her face with tremendous zeal and energy, and then, as she did her hair, she recalled that time when she had been forced to swim out to the Shark's Teeth at Mestlebury in that dreadful garment with the patches of vivid green.

Suddenly she dropped her comb with a clatter, and stood before the glass with her hands tightly clasped. She was recalling the face of the man whose life she had saved. He reminded her of—of—of whom?

"Why, why, I do believe that the man with the Smiths to-day was the very same individual!" she gasped. "But surely, surely the coincidence is too ridiculous!" and she laughed nervously as she stooped to pick up the comb; then she twisted up her hair in a great hurry, clothed herself in tidy garments, and went out to get supper.

There was little room in her busy days for dreaming now, and to-night she seemed more driven than ever. Grace was decidedly unwell from the strain and excitement of the afternoon, while the children were tired, hungry, and, truth to tell, rather cross; for the day had been fiercely hot, and they had been running about since early morning.

For a time her one pair of hands were more than full, but when the little ones had been fed, washed, and put to bed, there was a brief half-hour of respite in which she could sit still and think. And the more she thought the more sure she was that the man with the Smiths to-day and the individual whom she had saved from the Shark's Teeth rocks were one and the same person. To-morrow she would go over to Mrs. Smith and ask for the name of the unknown. Then she would write to him and tell him that she was the girl who had saved him, and she would remind him that she had his coat still, if he wished to claim it again.

Would she write to him?

She was remembering what the fat German had told her about the man having left money to be given to her, which old Mrs. Saunders had appropriated. Well, what of that? Surely she could tell him that she had never had the money, and did not want it. But it would be a horribly difficult task. If she told him that she had never had a reward for what she had done, it would seem, it must seem, as if she were asking for something, and all her pride was up in arms at the mere suggestion. But there were the diamonds! If she kept them and said nothing at all, how much better would she be than a thief?

Then again came the old question, why had the man never made exhaustive enquiries for his valuables, which he surely must have missed long ago? If he had come by them honestly, he of course must have made a fuss, and that he had made no move at all made it look very much as if he did not dare to make a stir. Oh, it was altogether a most worrying business! If it had not been for the valuables in her possession, she would not have minded so much. Indeed, she would not have minded at all. But these, of course, made all the difference.

Tom was late in getting back with the reaper and binder which he had gone to fetch, and Bertha knew that Grace was uneasy about him. She was just going indoors to see what could be done by way of cheering the invalid up, when she heard the clank of machinery in the distance, and guessed that he was coming along the trail. Calling to Grace that she was going to open the paddock gate, she set off across the sun-dried pasture at a run, and had the gate open before the horses reached the place. But instead of driving on to the house and leaving her to come slowly after him, Tom jumped off the machinery and came up to her, seizing her hand and nearly wringing it off.

"Bertha, you are a brick, a downright brick!" he said, and his voice was so unsteady, that to her alarm she saw he was on the verge of breakdown.

"It is of no use to call me nice things," she said, and her voice was more harsh than she knew. "I am afraid that I should have been too much of a coward to have stirred half a dozen steps to fight that fire alone. It was Grace who spurred me on to do it, so the credit does not belong to me."

"The town thinks differently, I can tell you," said Tom heartily. "And, my word, you were plucky! Smith said that your clothes were burning on you when they drove up."

"Yes, they were, and the pathetic part of it was that I had come to the end of my water, so what would have happened to me if they had not come along just then, I cannot imagine. I rolled frantically, but the ground was so hot that I could not quench the fire," said Bertha, with a nervous laugh that was very near to being a sob.

"Were you badly hurt?" asked Tom, with an air of concern, realizing what a grave risk she had run to save his wheat and that of his neighbours from destruction.

"I was not hurt at all; that is the incredible part of it," said Bertha. "But I think that what saved me was the fact that I had torn the sleeve of my blouse badly in swarming up and down to get the water from the wagon, so when my sleeve caught fire it did not touch my arm. Does anyone know what started the blaze?"

"Smith said that he found a piece of a glass bottle lying to windward of the burned patch, so doubtless it was the focusing of the sun's rays on the glass which set the corn on fire. It might have been a very serious matter for me, and would have about spelled ruin, I am afraid," Tom replied gravely.

Bertha nodded in complete understanding, and then she offered to unhitch the horses for him while he went in to talk to Grace.

But this he would not hear of, declaring that she must be far more tired than he was, which was most likely true. So leaving her to hold the horses for a minute, while he went in to assure his wife that he had reached home safe and sound, he came out again and unharnessed, while Bertha put his supper ready and did those other things which were necessary. Then she went away to her bed, leaving husband and wife together. Bedtime was one of the hardest parts of her hard days just now, for that was when regrets rose up and assailed her, and she had neither the strength nor the philosophy to keep them at bay. And to-night the struggle bade fair to be harder than common, for in her hurried dressing, when she came back from fighting the fire, she had come across the package containing the story which she had been writing on the evening when Grace had her bad fall.

To be shut back from the life she loved and longed for, and forced into a round of drudgery which led to nothing, was surely the hardest discipline that any girl ever had to face. But there was no help for it. She knew very well that no one could have taken her place in the little house at Duck Flats and filled it as she was filling it now. There was nothing heroic in Bertha's nature, or at least she thought that there was not, so she got no satisfaction from the fact of her self-sacrifice, and indeed did not consider it in the light of self-sacrifice at all; it was merely that she had to do the work, that there was no way out of it, and no one else to do it.

Poor girl! Her mood was very bitter to-night. She was too ignorant to know that she could not write words that would live until she had been taught by that hardest of taskmasters—experience. Her idea of life hitherto had been to dream the precious days away, to spend hours in analysing her own moods, and then to write feeble verse upon the results. Then Grace, knowing the commercial valuelessness of that sort of poetry, had directed her attention to stories, but these could have been in the end no better than the poetry, seeing how deficient her education had been and how narrow her outlook was.

But it was hard, so very hard, to grub when one wanted to soar. And it was small wonder that when she laid her head on her pillow that night, Bertha yielded to the weakness of tears and cried herself to sleep, which perhaps had a beneficial effect upon her by relieving the strain of her nerves and making her rest more profound.

She was in a whirl of domestic work the next morning, washing up dishes on the veranda, where she did every bit of the housework that it was possible to carry out-of-doors, when Tom came along and, seizing the dish-towel, started to wipe a great pile of plates and basins while he talked, which is a little way they have of economizing in time on the prairies, where time is of more value than money, especially in harvest.

"Did you know that Uncle Joe came here yesterday?" he asked, his voice a little lower than usual, as if he did not want what he said to reach the ears of Grace, who had not yet been brought out of her bedroom.

"Do you mean the uncle that cast you off?" she asked, staring at him in a dazed fashion, and then, suddenly remembering the children's talk of the man who had come and had given them half a dollar each, she said, "I really thought that the children must have dreamed it, because Grace did not say anything about it to me."

"Grace is badly upset, poor girl, for I do not think that the old man was any too kind in the things he said to her. She won't tell me everything, but she is quite transparent enough for me to be able to read between the lines, as it were, and she forgets how well I know the old man. But I guess that if I had come along yesterday and heard him telling her that an invalid wife and a houseful of little children were enough to take the spirit out of any man, that even his grey hairs would not have saved him from the thrashing he so jolly well deserved," said Tom, in a wrathful tone, putting the basin he was wiping down with such a bang that it was quite wonderful that it was not damaged by the treatment.

"But I don't understand." Bertha looked at Tom in a puzzled fashion. "I thought that you had quite lost sight of your uncle, that he did not know where you lived or anything about you. So how did he know where to find you out here?"

"That is the funny part of it." Tom started on another basin as he talked, and this one being rather badly cracked, he handled it in a gingerly fashion. "It seems that the old man knows you, and it is through that he found out where I lived."

"Well, I haven't the pleasure of his acquaintance, so it is a rather one-sided sort of knowledge," said Bertha, poking a pile of plates into the dish pan and using the mop vigorously.

"Just so, but there are similar cases on record," answered Tom. "For instance, you and I know the German Emperor, the President of the United States, not to speak of the King of England, yet none of these gentlemen have the slightest knowledge of us. It is the penalty of greatness to be known and not to know."

"Don't you think it would be quicker to tell me plain out what you mean, instead of talking in riddles?" asked Bertha, with an air of exasperation; then she said, with a little jump of amazement which made the dishes rattle, "Was that old man who was taken ill in the train when I was coming here your Uncle Joe? What an astonishing coincidence!"

"Just what I thought," remarked Tom dryly. "But it is the sort of coincidence that I could do without, seeing how the old fellow contrived to upset Grace, who has enough to bear without stings of this sort being added on to her load. It is rather curious, though, the old man was always taunting me with wanting his money when I lived with him, and now that he has lost it all, or nearly all, he takes the trouble to look me up to see if I can help him."

"But why did he not stay to see you, or at least wait until I came back?" asked Bertha.

"I expect he thought there was not enough chance of getting what he wanted," said Tom, "though Grace said that he told her he might give us a look in on his way back from Rotten Edge. He asked Grace if I could lend him five hundred dollars for six months, but she told him that the visit of the specialist had made us so poor that we should have our hands full to keep out of debt until the wheat was sold."

"Does Grace know how much that cost? Oh, I thought that you did not mean to tell her!" cried Bertha, in a reproachful tone.

Tom shrugged his shoulders and wiped away energetically, then remarked, "Grace always could turn me inside out. You see, I am no match for her in point of cleverness, and when she wants to know a thing she mostly gets her own way. I told her that it did not matter to her, and that if it had cost twice as much, I would still have had the specialist."

"What did she say to that?" asked Bertha, laughing a little; for well she knew that Tom was quite right when he said that he was no match for Grace, who always seemed to twist him round her little finger.

"Oh, she was very cross, and declared that she would have to make haste and get better, if only to save me the expense of a funeral," said Tom; but he winced as he spoke, for Grace was everything to him, and the bare mention of her dying was more than he could endure.

"SHE WAS MAKING NO HEADWAY"

CHAPTER XIV
In the Rush

"OH, if the days were a little longer, what a comfort it would be!" sighed Bertha, as she hurried to and fro setting out a supper for the harvest helpers on the veranda.

"So far as you are concerned, I think that it is a pity that they are quite so long," said Grace, who could do no more to help in the rush of work than to tell Bertha when a saucepan was going to boil over. Yet even that was a help, and Bertha toiled through the hard days all the more easily for knowing how genuinely sorry for her Grace was.

The wheat was almost all cut. For a week past the binder had been driven round and round the waving squares of wheat, until now it stood in stooks ripening in the sun. But to-night a threshing machine had puffed and panted its way across the uneven trails from Pentland Broads, drawing behind the engine the various parts of machinery necessary for sacking the grain and disposing of the straw. While it was at Duck Flats the men who came with it would have to be boarded, and hence the extra work which made Bertha long for the days to be more stretchable in the matter of time.

From morning to night no one thought or talked of anything but wheat, how it was coming down, how it was ripening in the stooks, and how it would thresh out. Bertha went even a little further than this, and dreamed of wheatfields night after night; but they were always covered with snow in her dreams, just as they had been when she first came to Manitoba. She had keyed herself up for the extra work of the harvest time, while Grace from her couch, like a good general, planned the campaign. Both of them knew that, when the threshing was over, and the grain had been drawn to the depot at Rownton, the days would be long and silent, and to a certain extent full of leisure; but if only a few hours of that future leisure could have been mortgaged for the needs of the present, how glad they would both have been.

Then one morning Bertha got up with one of the worst headaches that she had ever known, and was wondering however she would manage to get through the long, hard day of baking, boiling, and stewing for the hungry men who were working so hard afield. The numbers were to be reinforced to-day by a party of neighbours from Pentland Broads and another engine; so there would be double the number to provide for, and meals would have to be duplicated, as the men would feed in relays.

"But I must get through, I must," she said to herself, as she leaned over a basin of the coldest water she could get, and tried what bathing her head would do towards lessening the pain.

But the headache was due to overstrain, and it was not a matter of cold water that was going to cure it. She was still slopping the cold water on to her face, when she heard a wagon drive past the window and stop before the door.

"The Pentland Broads lot, I expect," she said to herself in a languid tone, and, wiping her face with a towel, she went out to receive them; for she was not quite sure where Tom was just then, and the second engine was to work over on the farther section of the Duck Flats land. Then she saw that there was a little woman seated among the men, and she gave a glad cry as she recognized Eunice Long.

"Oh, I wonder if you can even faintly guess how glad I am to see you!" she cried, and suddenly the long, hard day looked as if it might be not only bearable, but to a certain sense enjoyable.

"That is good hearing. I like to be sure of my welcome when I go anywhere," said Eunice, with a laugh, as she submitted to the vigorous hugging which Bertha bestowed upon her. "But you look about tired out before the day begins, child! What have you been doing to yourself?"

"I don't know," said Bertha, radiant content in her tone. "My head was aching pretty badly awhile ago, but it is going to get better now that you have come."

"I suppose that you were a bit daunted by having so many to feed; but it is wonderful how easy it is to provide for hungry men. They are certain to appreciate everything that is set before them, and they are not very particular, as a rule, provided there is no shortage. What is to do first? Have you enough bread?" asked Eunice, who was tying on a businesslike apron.

"I did a big baking of cakes and pies yesterday, as well as bread," replied Bertha, opening the pantry door and proudly displaying the stores within. "In fact, I was making and baking the whole day long; but there are all the vegetables to get ready, and they will want a great lot, because it is so hot that they will not be able to eat so much meat."

"Then I will set to work on the vegetables straight away," said Eunice. "And look here, Bertha, don't you think that it would be a good thing if I cooked some of them now, so that there are dishes of cold vegetables as well as hot? The poor fellows do love cold things when they are working in the heat and the dust at threshing times."

"That would be a good idea," said Bertha, sighing with relief to think how it would lessen the rush of work later on to have some of the things cooked now. "I will come and help you, and we can soon have a lot of them on to boil."

"No, you won't," said Eunice, with decision. "You will just drop everything and lie down on your bed for an hour and half. I can do without you for so long, and it will make all the difference to the comfort with which you can get through the day. Don't worry about the time to get up; I will call you, I promise, so you can go to sleep with a clear conscience."

"Oh, but it seems too bad to do that when you are here! I want to be with you all the time," said Bertha; but her objections to resting were only half-hearted, and five minutes after she had put her head on the pillow of her unmade bed she was fast asleep, and did not wake until she roused to see Eunice standing beside her holding a steaming cup of coffee just ready for drinking.

"Have I slept too long?" asked Bertha, in alarm, for it seemed to her that she had been lying there for a very long time.

"No, dear, the time I gave you is barely up yet; but Mrs. Ellis wanted you to go into her room when you did wake, so I thought that you would be easier in your mind to be wakened in good time," said Eunice, who looked very warm from her active exertions at the stove.

"Isn't she so well?" asked Bertha, in alarm. Grace stayed in her room this morning, because that would leave the kitchen a little freer for all the bustle of feeding that had to be got ready there.

"I think that she is all right; but she had a letter that she wanted you to see, and you need not hurry her if she wants to talk it out with you, for I can manage very well for a little longer," said Eunice, in the unflurried tone which always made her seem such a restful person.

Bertha jerked her head in token that she understood, but she was scalding herself too badly with the coffee for speech just then.

Grace had a twinkle of fun in her eyes, for even the tragedy of her condition could not wholly dim the brightness of her spirit. There was an open letter fixed in one of her helpless hands, and she was looking at it when Bertha came in at the door.

"Are you better, poor thing?" asked Grace, who found it so much more natural to be sorry for other people than for herself.

"Yes, thank you; I feel much more fit now that I have been to sleep. What have you there? Something that you wish me to read to you?" asked Bertha, pointing to the letter.

"I think that you had better read it to yourself and tell me what you make of it," said Grace, with a low laugh. "It is from your old man, Tom's beautiful Uncle Joe."

Bertha took the letter, but at first was troubled to understand the queer, crabbed handwriting, which was plainly characteristic of the writer, then finally this is what she made it out to be—

"Dear Nephew Tom,

"I am sorry that I could not wait to see you on the day a little while ago when I called at your house. I should doubtless have made time to come if your wife had held out to me any reasonable hope that you would be able to lend me money. I will admit that she offered for me to share your home if my funds would not keep me in food and shelter. But happily I am not quite penniless yet, though there is no saying how soon I may be, unless my luck soon turns. My greatest trouble has been that I have been openly robbed of some extremely valuable property that, in view of some recent losses, I had determined to raise money upon. For months I was unable to track the thief, but, to my amazement, I came face to face with him a few days ago, and although he promptly disappeared, I have every hope of running him down before very long. If I succeed in recovering my property, I may come to see you some time during the winter or the spring, for I rather like your wife, although she must be a very heavy burden to you in your struggle to get on.

—Your affec. uncle,

J. Ellis."

"What a horrid letter!" cried Bertha, a wrathful light coming into her eyes, when she thought how it must have cut Grace.

"Do you think so?" said the invalid, and again there was a twinkle in her eyes. "Now, I have been lying here pluming myself on the conquest that I have made; for, just reflect, the poor old fellow says that he rather likes me, and think what an admission that is, seeing that I am plainly not a good investment from a money point of view."

"Is he poor?" asked Bertha, whose lip curled at the thought of the pity and the care she had lavished on the frail old man who had seemed so lonely and so friendless. But if he were lonely he had only himself to thank for it, and a man who would have friends must himself show a friendly spirit.

"Tom thinks not, although of course he cannot be sure. He says that perhaps this great loss which seems to be preying on the old man's mind may be nothing after all, while, on the other hand, he may have flung away almost everything that he has got in foolish speculation," replied Grace.

"What is he, or what was he? I mean, what was his trade when he was in business?" asked Bertha.

"Nothing very dignified, I am sorry to say," answered Grace, smiling broadly. "He bought old clothes, old furniture, or anything else that seemed to offer a fair chance of being turned into money again very quickly. One of his grievances against Tom was that my poor dear refused to wear secondhand garments just as soon as he could earn the money to buy something brand new. Have you not noticed how fond Tom is of things that are quite new?"

"That is not wonderful under the circumstances," said Bertha, with a laugh, and then she put the letter back into the fingers of Grace and hurried out to the kitchen, where Eunice was doing valiant battle with a great rush of work.

Bowls of peas and beans, great dishes of carrots, turnips, marrows stood cooling on a side table, while a second lot were steaming away on the stove, and outside on the veranda the table was already being laid for the first lot of hungry men to come in and feed.

"I feel so much better, that work is quite a pleasure now," said Bertha, as she darted to and fro, filling jugs with lemonade and mint tea, cutting bread into chunks and piling into little baskets which were handy to pass about, and seeing that plates and knives and forks were all in readiness.

"That is good hearing, especially seeing that the work has got to be done somehow," said Eunice, who was cutting pies into neat sections, so that the busy workers should not be delayed by any work of carving the food. Then she said quietly, "Have you noticed the change in Mrs. Ellis?"

"What change?" Bertha dropped a whole handful of knives in her alarm and agitation.

"Nothing to be frightened at, but rather something to rejoice in. She is going to get better, Bertha, I am sure of it; and if she does, it will be largely your doing. And oh, my dear, I think that you are to be envied!" said Eunice, in a moved tone.

"What do you mean? I have done nothing, not for Grace, I mean," said Bertha, in a bewildered manner. She was thinking of massage and all the elaborate rubbings and poundings which Dr. Benson had said would be done to Grace if she were in hospital, but which the specialist had said were of no use at the present time.

"My dear, you have done everything for her, for you have given her hope. She sees you taking hold of things and running the house as well as she could do it herself, so she gets rest of mind, and nature has a chance, don't you see," said Eunice.

"But what makes you think that she is getting better?" asked Bertha, who had seen no improvement.

"Her hands are not quite so helpless as they were, and she can move her head a little. Oh, there is a decided improvement, and though it may take a couple of years for the paralysis to wear off, just think how the knowledge that she is getting better will help her."

Bertha drew a long breath. "It seems too good to be true. Why, to see Grace getting better would be like—like——"

"Like seeing the prison door come open at the end of a long term of imprisonment, I think you mean," said Eunice, with that rare sympathy which seemed to divine the thoughts without any necessity for words.

"I am afraid that it has been dreadfully wicked to feel like that," said Bertha ruefully.

"I think it is very human. After all, we are human at the bottom, you know, and what is in us will show out under stress of circumstances," Eunice answered, with a little laugh, and then the first batch of men came trooping in for a meal, and for the next two hours there seemed to be work enough for four people.

The men were desperately hungry, and they fed with the same zest of endeavour with which they did their work, while Eunice and Bertha flitted to and fro waiting upon them, filling jugs, dishing vegetables, and bringing fresh provisions from the pantry, until they could eat no more. Then in came another batch, the same process was repeated, and so the long day went on.

The next day brought almost as great a rush, but with no Eunice to help with the heavy end of the burden. Bertha, however, had got a tiny germ of hope in her heart now, and it proved a plant of vigorous growth too. If there was any likelihood of Grace recovering, why, immediately there was a time limit to her bondage, and she could cheer her heart with looking forward.

The third day brought Eunice over again, to the great relief of all concerned; for there was another thresher at work, which meant another set of hungry men to feed. Then Mrs. Smith, with real neighbourly kindness, drove over from Blow End and carried off the five children, a huge relief to Bertha, as with two threshing machines at work it was extraordinarily difficult to keep the children out of danger.

While Mrs. Smith was loading up the children into her little one-horse wagon, Bertha put the question which had been on her mind ever since the day when the standing corn fired and they had to work so hard to put it out.

"Who was that man you brought over to help fight the fire, Mrs. Smith?"

"Oh, that traveller from Brown & Smedley's place? I don't know his name, but I understood him to say that he was leaving them next day. Nice fellow, wasn't he? I liked the way he took hold and did things; there was no nonsense about him," replied Mrs. Smith; then, having wedged the last child in so that it could not possibly fall out, she clambered up to the driving seat and started with her load, leaving Bertha standing looking after the wagon.

"Whatever can I do?" she muttered. "How I wish that I had never seen those horrible stones!"

CHAPTER XV
Temptation

THE rush of harvest work was over. The threshing machines had gone, and all the men were busy on some other farmer's holding. Even Tom was away most days helping his neighbours, as they had helped him. When all the corn in that neighbourhood was threshed out, then would begin the task of carrying it to Rownton for storage in the grain elevator there, until the cars could distribute it to the markets of the world.

At first Bertha was so thankful for the cessation from driving toil and release from the constant preparation of meals, that she just sat still and enjoyed the quiet. Then, alas! it began to pall, and she would have given a great deal just for the privilege of driving off in the mornings to help some sorely pressed housewife, as Eunice had come to help her. But this was not possible, because someone must be at home to take care of poor helpless Grace, and all that Bertha could do in the way of returning or passing on the kindness which had been shown to her was to send for the Smith babies from Blow End, and keep them for the whole four days that the engines were at the Smiths' place, which was a very real help indeed; for little children not old enough to know where danger lies are apt to be a considerable care at threshing times, when no one has a moment to spare for keeping them out of danger.

Even the babies had gone home now, and there were only their own five small people to look after, and with no machinery about to excite their curiosity, they required so little taking care of, that Bertha had no worries on their account. She sat out on the veranda every day when her housework was done, professedly sewing, but half the time with her hands at rest, whilst her hungry gaze roamed the wide stretches of dun-coloured stubble in search of something, anything, which would break the monotony of those level sweeps of land, reaching on every side to the horizon, from which the wheat had been harvested.

"Oh, what would it be to see a grove of trees, a hill, and a waterfall!" she murmured, with such a wave of homesickness for the dear old life at Mestlebury, that her eyes grew blurred with tears, and she had to sit winking her eyes very hard to keep them from falling. Grace could see through the open door to the place where Bertha was sitting, and it would have been cruel exceedingly to let the poor thing even guess the riot of misery which was going on in the heart of Bertha at that moment. Suddenly she stood up and shaded her eyes with her hands, flicking away the tears with her fingers as she did so.

"What can you see?" enquired Grace from her couch.

"There is a man riding along the trail from Pentland Broads. I wonder who he can be?" Bertha answered.

"It would not be likely to be Tom, because he has gone in the other direction," replied Grace. "It may be someone coming this way on business, or perhaps it is a visitor. Don't worry about it, Bertha; the creature shall not disturb your peace. Just plant him, or her—if it is a woman—on a chair within reach of my tongue, and I will exert my conversational powers to the utmost until I tire the visitor into going away or until it is supper-time, just whichever comes first."

"It is not a woman, that is certain, unless indeed it is a woman in rational dress and riding astride," said Bertha, laughing. "So you will have to hold forth to a man until Tom comes home to relieve you. I never can talk to men—I do not know what to say; and as they never by any chance know what to say either, the result is decidedly embarrassing."

"You may get over that some day, if you ever chance upon a congenial spirit, that is," replied Grace, and then she dropped into silence, while Bertha got up and moved about in a restless fashion as the horseman came nearer and nearer.

She felt that she could not sit still and watch him coming nearer and nearer, for some strange instinct was telling her that he was a messenger of fate, but whether of good or bad she could not tell. She stirred up the embers in the stove and made the kettle boil. The arrival might like a cup of tea, and certainly Grace would be glad of one, for the hot weather wore her so much.

"Why, it is Mr. Long!" said Bertha, in surprise, as the horseman rode up the paddock. "I wonder what he can have come for?"

"Have patience and you shall know," replied Grace, with a smile, and then a minute later the brother of Eunice Long drew rein before the house and greeted them with western heartiness.

"I had to ride through to Sussex Gap with a telegram that was paid right through to Jim Ford's door, and as there were letters for you, I thought it would just be neighbourly to ride round this way and deliver them," he said, with so much meaning in his manner as he looked at Bertha as to make her blush an uncomfortable red, for Mr. Long's intentions were always quite painfully obvious.

But Grace came to the rescue with ready tact, calling out from her sofa, "Oh, Mr. Long, how nice of you to come! Why, it is ages since we have had a visitor, and now that Tom is away so much helping other people, it is downright lonesome. Come right in and sit down; you can talk to me while Bertha makes us a cup of tea. There are heaps of things I want to ask about."

Mr. Long went in as he was invited, although, truth to tell, he would much rather have stayed outside talking to Bertha; but pity for poor Mrs. Ellis would not allow him even to seem to neglect her. And Grace displayed such an amazing thirst for information, that the poor man had no chance to talk to Bertha at all, which was just what Bertha wanted; for Mr. Long's attempts at love-making were to the last degree embarrassing, while no amount of civil snubbing had the least effect upon him. He had brought two letters for Bertha, for which she was bound to feel grateful, as otherwise she would have had to wait until the next day or even the day after before getting them. One was from Hilda, and the other, a thick one, from Anne.

As she had not heard by the last two mails she was very eager to open them and read, so it was rather trying to be obliged to stay and make tea for Mr. Long and Grace, when she was aching to shut herself up in her room and tear open the envelopes. But there are limits to most things, and Mr. Long had to bring his visit to a close much sooner than he had intended, because that stupid Jim Ford had chosen to send a reply telegram, which he had to put on the wires without too much loss of time. However, he could come again soon, for now that harvest was almost at an end, it would be possible to think of something besides the eternal wheat theme, which, of course, had been the staple of thought and conversation for the last five months or so.

"Oh, I thought that he would never be done drinking tea!" sighed Bertha, when at last the visitor had mounted his horse and was riding away across the paddock. "Grace, do you want me to read any of your letters to you?" said Bertha, holding them one by one before her, so that she could see the addresses.

"No, thanks, they will all keep until Tom comes back; meanwhile, I will just lie and imagine what is in them, which is very good fun when one has nothing better to do. Run along, dearie, and enjoy yourself."

Bertha needed no second bidding. Hurrying into her room, she shut her door and sat down by the window. She would be sure to cry—she always did when letters came from the girls—and it did not seem right to let Grace see the tears.

Hilda's letter was not very long, and it was so packed with glowing accounts of her own doings, of the lovely time she was having, and how her music was improving under German teaching, that there was no room at all for enquiries as to how Bertha was getting on, or how the burden of work and responsibility was being carried.

"Anyone would think that she had not had my letter telling her about poor Grace," said Bertha, with a little sigh of dissatisfaction, as she turned the sheet over, thinking that she had read it all. Then a short sentence crammed into a corner of one of the margins caught her eye, and she twisted the sheet round so that she could read it.

> "Very sorry that Grace has had such a nasty accident. I hope that she is quite well by this time. What a good thing that you are with her to be a little help. I dare say that you cannot do much, but every little counts, especially when there is sickness in a house."

Bertha laughed aloud, only the merriment had a hollow ring. She wondered what Hilda would think if she could see her wrestling with the work of every day—washing, cooking, mending, nursing, and, not least by any means, mothering the five little ones whose mother could no longer do it herself.

"I think that I will show it to Grace, and yet—no, I don't think that I will. If I were Grace I should want more fuss than that to be made over my bad accident," murmured Bertha, shaking her head in a dubious fashion, and then, laying it on one side, she reached for the envelope from Anne. When her sisters' letters came together she always read the one from Anne last, because it had always more affection in it, and surely no one ever hungered for love more than Bertha.

Anne's letter was long, and very serious in its tone. After commenting at length on the disaster which had overtaken poor Grace, she went on—

> "Now comes the question of what to do about you. My husband and I are both of one mind in the matter, and we want you to come out to us here. This is a sparsely settled district, and you may find it very dull, but it will be better for you than staying with the Ellises now that poor Grace is so helpless. They may even be glad not to have you, as you say the house is so small. I suppose that Tom has had to get a housekeeper. I hope, for all your sakes, that she is a capable body. Of course, dear, I know that you would do anything you could for Grace and Tom, but it is not as if you were able to take hold of work and do it. I know how our little housekeeping at Mestlebury used to bother you, and I am afraid that you must be very uncomfortable indeed in such a muddled life as you must be living now. I am afraid that I was sometimes not very patient with you, but oh, I have regretted it so sorely since, and I fear that I must often have judged you hardly in my ignorance and rude strength. But I will do my best to atone when I get you here, and you shall have the very easiest life that we can make for you. Ask Tom to advance you the money for your journey, which we will at once repay when we know how much it is, or if it is not convenient to him to do this, cable to us and we will get the money sent to you as quickly as possible. Poor little Bertha! It seemed to me at the time that I was doing my very best

for you, but if I had known what was going to happen to Grace, of course I should never have dreamed of sending you West. I suppose that what I really ought to have done was to bring you out here with me. But I have always so stoutly maintained that it is not fair to a man that he should have to be hampered with his wife's relations, and I tried to live up to my theory. Although if I had known my husband then as well as I know him now, I should have understood how little difference it would have made. He is so good and kind, that he would welcome not merely you, but Hilda also. Therefore, little sister, have no doubts about your welcome, but come to us as soon as you can."

There was more of the same sort, and when she had read it a wave of the most terrible homesickness swept over Bertha. It seemed to her that she simply could not bear the hard life that she was living for another day. She must get out of it somehow, oh, she must, she must! Grace and Tom had no right to expect so much of her; it was not fair. Her sisters never expected her to be capable and efficient, and why should other people put such heavy burdens upon her?

It was true that Tom had generously increased her salary, and would have given her still more, only, knowing the struggle he was having, she would not accept it. But if he could pay her, of course he could pay someone else instead, and then she might slip the burden of this distressful family from her shoulders. Then she would go out to Australia and settle down to the old life of irresponsible ease, with nothing to do but to dream dreams and think noble thoughts. She might even attain to fame as a story-writer, although she was a little dubious about this, as a farm in the back-blocks of Australia did not seem exactly the place for acquiring knowledge.

"And it is knowledge that I need most of all," murmured Bertha to herself, as she sat with the letter tightly clasped in her hand.

It was her only bit of wisdom to know that before she could write with any sort of power she must have knowledge, far more knowledge than at present she possessed. But her one idea of knowledge was that it must be gained from books, whereas by far the most valuable knowledge is gained at first hand by experience and observation.

"They must find a housekeeper and let me go; oh, they must let me go!" she muttered, standing up and stretching out her arms towards that point of the compass where she imagined Australia to be. "Oh, Anne, Anne, why didn't you take me with you at the first?"

But she had inadvertently spoken aloud, and it was the sound of her own voice which aroused her to an understanding of her own selfishness. It was then that she realized it was more a desire for her own ease than from such a sick desire to see her sister that she was so anxious to go to Australia.

"Oh, what a horrible, low-down sort of nature mine must be, for it is only my own ease that I am thinking about!" she exclaimed, with an impatient shrug, and, springing to her feet, she bustled about her room for a few moments, just to get rid of those telltale marks of tears on her face, the sight of which would be sure to make poor Grace uncomfortable. Then presently she went out to the other room, to find Grace with an open letter in her hand.

"Why, why, however did you manage that?" demanded Bertha, for none of the children were in the house, and the letter had not been opened when she went to her room.

"I did it myself," said Grace, with a sob of pure happiness. "Oh, Bertha, darling Bertha, I do believe that I am going to get better, for see, I can hold that finger and thumb quite close together, and I managed to scratch the envelope across that spike in the wall. I reached out to it, do you understand?"

"Hush, hush, you must not excite yourself so much or you may do yourself an injury," said Bertha soothingly, for she was fairly frightened by the blaze in the eyes of Grace; then she said quietly, "I have noticed that you were getting more power. Eunice Long pointed it out to me when she was here helping at harvest time. But we did not say anything, because we did not know whether the improvement would go on, and it seemed so cruel to raise hopes that were not going to be realized."

"But they are going to be realized now, oh, I am sure of it! Oh, to think that there is a ray of hope for me after all these weeks and weeks of black despair! Bertha, Bertha, do you know what it will mean to me and to my poor dear Tom?" and she burst into a fit of sobbing, her brave self-control breaking down at this tiny ray of hope, as it had never broken down since her hard fate overtook her.

Bertha dropped on her knees beside the couch, soothing Grace as she would have soothed one of the children. Such stormy emotion must surely be bad for the invalid, and it would shake the feeble spark of life in the helpless body, might indeed even shake it out, or so in her ignorance she feared. But Grace was soon quiet again, only there was a deep glow of happiness in her eyes, and the radiance of hope on the face which had grown so wan from the weeks of hopeless helplessness.

"Often and often I would have prayed to die, if it had not been for Tom," said Grace, after a while, when she had grown calm enough to speak of this wonderful hope which had come to her. "But he said to me, on that first day when I realized that I was as helpless as a log, that he would rather have me like that than not have me at all, and that I should be ten times more his inspiration than I had been. So for his sake I had to keep hold of life for a little while, at least, until he and the children could do without me. But I don't think that my courage for the effort would have held out if it had not been for you, dear. If I had seen the children neglected, or Tom bowed down with more worries than he could stagger under, I should have turned coward, and asked the good, kind Father in Heaven to take me out of this evil world, and spare me the sight of misery that I had no power to relieve. If I get better I shall owe it to you, for you have kept the hope alive in my heart."

Bertha got on to her feet in a scrambling, unsteady fashion and rushed out on to the veranda. She was afraid that Grace would be able to read all the miserable selfish thoughts and desires that were in her heart, and she did not want to be despised at this the very sweetest moment in all her life.

No, she would not go to Australia, she could not. Anne and Hilda must think what they liked about her incapacity and general helplessness. She must be of some use in the world, for she had given Grace the courage to keep alive. It was a joy that more than repaid her for the hard toil, the monotony, and the unloveliness of her life. But the trouble was that the temptation would keep coming back, and for weeks afterwards, while the shortening days crept down to winter, and the sting of bitter cold came into the little house on the prairie, Bertha was fighting her longings for a life of leisured ease.

CHAPTER XVI
A Blow of Fate

IT was summer again, and for more than a year Bertha had borne the burden of the household on her shoulders. They were stronger shoulders from the strain, which had not broken her down, but in some mysterious manner had seemed to build her up and bring out the very best that was in her.

It had been a hard winter. The weather had been so fearfully cold, that it had been almost impossible to keep Grace warm at all. Then the children had all sickened with measles at once, and followed this with a bout of whooping cough. But that was happily all over now, and five stronger or more mischievous children it would surely have been hard to find. Grace had not improved so fast as Bertha had hoped or expected; indeed, to a casual observer it would seem as if she hardly improved at all. She could certainly use her hands a little, but her other limbs were as helpless as ever.

"It will take me ten years before I am able to stand on my feet at this rate, and I expect that you will want to be married before then," Grace would say to Bertha, with a rueful pucker on her face.

And Bertha would always reply with a merry shake of her head and a laugh that matched, "Oh, don't worry on that score, all my instincts are towards single blessedness; but if I did happen to want to get married, I am quite sure that Molly will be able to keep house by the time she is twelve years old."

They always laughed together at this statement, for it would surely have been difficult to find a more irresponsible, feckless bit of goods than Miss Molly aged five. The twins were marvels of usefulness compared with her, and even Noll was more to be trusted in the matter of shutting the gate or looking for eggs than his eldest sister. But it was good for Grace and Bertha to have something to laugh over when the days were extra dreary, and nerves were strained almost to the point of breakdown.

There had been one of those times in the dead of winter when Anne had written straight to Tom, and had said that the life was too hard for Bertha, and she must be sent to Australia forthwith. As the letter had been accompanied by a banker's draft containing money to cover her passage out, it really seemed as if Bertha would have to go. But the old yearning for a life of ease seemed to die then, and it was Bertha who decided what the others would not venture to decide for her.

"I shall not go," she had said quietly, as she stood confronting Tom, who looked almost wild with anxiety. "You and Grace are kind enough to consider that I earn my living, and so I am independent. If I went to Anne and her husband, they would probably not let me do this, and so I should be dependent on the charity of my brother-in-law, and that I should not care for at all, now I have once tasted the sweets of independence."

"Are you sure that you won't repent?" asked Tom hoarsely, for he knew very well that if Bertha did go, it would be almost impossible to fill her place.

"I went through all that back in the fall, just after harvest was over, when the first letter came," Bertha answered steadily, though her lips trembled a little as she thought of the many times when the strangled temptation had come to life again to torment her with fresh vigour, for, after all, she was very human, and her present life was harder than most.

"But you did not say anything about it; at least, I never heard of it," said Tom.

"No, and you would not have heard now if Anne had not written to you," replied Bertha. "You see, the trouble is that neither Anne nor Hilda think that I am good for much in the matter of work. I used to be most fearfully lazy in the old days, and they both had to suffer a great deal in consequence, so it is not wonderful that they do not think that I am fit to run this house alone, and I expect that both of them pity you and Grace from the bottom of their hearts."

"They need not, at least not on the score of your housekeeping," interposed Tom hastily, and then he said in a worried tone, "But what am I to say to this letter? Or will you take it and answer it yourself?"

"No, I think that you will have to do it, because you have to send that money back, you see," answered Bertha, who felt that she would not be easy until that banker's draft was on its way back to Australia. "You can tell Anne, if you like, that I am a paid employee, and it would not be fair to ask me to resign unless I misbehave myself; and as I have not given you notice, and do not intend to, yours is rather a delicate position."

"Ha, ha, ha!" laughed Tom, in sheer relief and joy. "But I am afraid that she will see through that; anyhow, she will be downright mad with me."

"Never mind, you are far enough away to be secure from bodily apprehension, and the other thing will not matter," said Bertha, and then she went on with a laugh that was meant as a cloak for a good deal of feeling which was under the surface and must be kept there. "Are we not a widely separated family, just three sisters, and we each live in a different continent?"

"Some people get on better the wider apart they are; anyhow, I am glad that Anne does not live within visiting distance of us at this present time," said Tom, and again he heaved a great sigh of relief to think that Bertha would not leave them in their present difficult circumstances.

But Bertha was secretly uneasy until that banker's draft had been sent back to Anne. She had a miserable distrust of herself, and it seemed to her that at any moment her courage might give way, and she would take the chance of escape which lay ready to her hand. There had been no weak looking back, however, for she was stronger in purpose than she believed herself to be, and she was gaining in power every day; so that what had tried her so sorely at the first was now only a very bearable sort of activity.

It was even possible to enjoy life a little this summer, and, as she had learned to drive, she took turns with Tom in driving to meeting on Sundays. One Sunday she went with all the children packed into the wagon beside her, and the other Sunday she took care of Grace while he went. There were weekdays also when it was possible to get away from work this year, even though the outing might only be to the house of a neighbour, where there was about the same amount of work to be done as she had left behind her; yet it was a change of a sort, and she had come to that happy frame of mind when she could be satisfied with a very little. Of course the talk was all of wheat, just as it had been last year, only perhaps it was a little more so, for last year had been a very successful time, and the farmers had done extremely well in that district.

At last came the Sunday immediately before the starting of cutting. A lovely, peaceful day it was, although so intensely hot that it made Bertha feel as if she were passing through a furnace when she drove the children to meeting in the morning. It was not her turn to go, really, but Tom was going to Rownton the next day, and he might even have to go as far as Gilbert Plains if he did not find his new binder waiting for him at the depot, and so, as he was very tired, he had decided in favour of staying with his wife, while Bertha took the children to Pentland Broads to church. Just outside the door of the meeting-house she encountered Eunice, who looked ghastly pale.

"You are not well; what is the matter?" asked Bertha, with quick sympathy, for of all the acquaintances and friends that she had made in the West she loved Eunice Long the best.

"I feel rather bad," said Eunice, speaking slowly and with a very apparent effort; then she asked abruptly, "Do you believe in visions or dreams?"

"I might if I had them, but I sleep so soundly now that I can't get in time for anything of the sort," Bertha answered, with a laugh, as her mind went back to the old days when sleep was often a terror of weird dreams.

"Neither do I, as a rule, and that is why I am disposed to think that it was a warning from Heaven that was sent to me last night," said Eunice, with a little gasping breath. "Oh, Bertha, I dreamed that the wheat was all destroyed!"

A cold chill of apprehension crept over Bertha. Had they not, all of them, been living at a terrible rate of tension for the last six weeks or so? She thought of Grace, and the wistful looks the invalid cast out over the plains of waving grain, and of the tension on the face of Tom, which grew more strained with every day that passed; and again the old impatience seized her. Why did these men sow all their ground with wheat and nothing but wheat? Suppose something dreadful happened to the crop before it could be harvested. There had very nearly been disaster last year, and this year it was hotter still; there had been no rain for weeks, and oh, what an awful thing it would be if something happened now when harvest was so near! But, after all, there was no sense in being frightened out of one's senses by a dream, so she rallied her courage and said cheerfully, "You are out of sorts this morning, dear, or you would not be so scared by a simple dream. Have a sleep this afternoon, if you can, and then you will feel better."

Eunice shook her head, and her lips took a straighter curve, betraying the emotion she was so carefully keeping down. "It was midnight when my dream woke me, and so sure am I that it was sent as a warning, that I have not slept since—no, nor have I tasted food."

"But surely that was a mistake, dear," said Bertha, her tone reproachful now; for how could a person who had taken no breakfast keep an evenly balanced mind?

"I could not sleep nor eat for thinking how they would suffer, all these poor people here," and the little postmistress moved her hand towards the groups of people who were passing into the church. "Do you realize it, Bertha? If the crop failed now, every one of these comfortable men and women would be ruined, just ruined!" and Eunice began to sob with hysterical violence.

Bertha acted promptly then. Asking Mrs. Smith to look after the children until she herself could get back, she bundled Eunice back home with more haste than ceremony, and insisted on putting her to bed.

"You are ill and worn out," she said, with kindly severity. "To-morrow you will feel better, and then you will say that you were wrong to be so faithless. Can you not believe that if God permitted a disaster like the ruin of the wheat crop to fall on the district, He would give men strength to bear the trial—yes, and the women too?"

"He might do, and yet, why should He?" said Eunice, looking at Bertha with a strange intensity of expression. "Have you ever reflected that if the Almighty gives brains and judgment to the sons of men, He expects them to use these things?"

"Of course, or why should they be given?" queried Bertha.

"Very well. Then, to apply the theory to practice, every man who farms in this township knows that while wheat is by far the most paying crop, it is also more liable to disaster than many others, and yet in ten thousand acres of land in this district there is only of about a bare three hundred acres, that are not sown with wheat. So if disaster comes, men must know that they have only their own unwisdom to thank for their ruin."

"Go to sleep now and leave it," said Bertha soothingly. "After all, there is no sense in meeting trouble halfway, and if we get through safely this time, you shall go round the country next winter preaching a crusade in favour of mixed farming."

"I don't think that I can sleep, but it is good to lie still," replied Eunice, who looked fearfully exhausted as if from severe mental struggle. Then she lay back on her pillow and closed her eyes. Bertha watched by her for a little while, then finding that she was quiet, she stole away and hurried off to church; for she was not at all sure that the twins and Molly would behave with any sort of propriety if left to their own devices.

But she was haunted by a dread and apprehension which effectually banished her Sunday peace, and she was more thankful than she could express when the service came to an end and the congregation poured out into the sunshine once more.

It was hotter than ever. The sun, like a ball of fire, scorched down from a sky that was like brass. There was something in the day now that was overpowering. People spoke of the likelihood of a storm, and Bertha hurried to start on the long drive back to Duck Flats; for what could she do with her wagon load of little ones if a storm were to come up suddenly?

The journey home was a painful drag. The horse streamed with sweat, and could hardly make a pace that was better than a walk, while she and the children were bathed in perspiration. Noll lay at the bottom of the wagon crying in a dreary fashion for the most of the journey, while the twins sat beside him fanning him vigorously with the broad-leaved weeds that grew at the soft spot, which was just halfway between Pentland Broads and Duck Flats. But Dicky and Molly took turns at holding an umbrella over the head of Bertha, which would keep wobbling into her face or catching in the trimmings of her hat. Tom was at the paddock gate, anxiously on the lookout for them.

"I am more glad than I can say to see you safe home again, Bertha. I've been downright worried about you, for there is weather coming," he said, and there was a sound of endurance in his tone which made that ominous chill come over her again.

"They said when we came out of church that it looked like a storm, and so I got away as quickly as I could; but it has been so hot that we could hardly get along at all," she replied.

"It will be a storm of the very worst description, I am afraid. Look out there," said Tom, pointing back by the way she had come.

Bertha turned to look, and saw the clouds gathering in billows of blackness.

"How fast it is coming!" she exclaimed, thankful indeed that her journey was over.

"Yes, and when they come up from that quarter, we mostly find that they are about as bad as they can be," he said briefly.

When the house was reached, the children were taken out of the wagon and hurried indoors, but Bertha stood watching in a fascination of fear the gathering blackness which was spreading so rapidly over the sky. There was no thunder yet, the heat seemed to grow more intense every minute, and from the unclouded part of the sky the sun poured down with a lurid glow which made one think of fire.

"Here it comes; get indoors, Bertha!" cried Tom sharply. But he was not quite quick enough, for before Bertha could turn and run, a blast of wind took her, which whirled her round and round, taking her breath and battering the sense out of her.

She was conscious that Tom seized her by the arm and dragged her inside the house; but if it had not been for his timely grip of her, she must have been whirled away on that terrible blast, for she had no strength to stand against it.

Bruised and battered to an incredible soreness from that moment of conflict with the tempest wind, Bertha crept across the floor to the side of Grace, and, gathering the terrified children in her arms, cowered there in shrinking dread. Doors and windows were rattling and banging. She was aghast at the riot all around her. Then there was a sudden crash as a whirling something dashed against the window and stove it inwards, the glass flying in a shower over the heads of the children and herself. Even Grace was struck on the face by a flying fragment, which cut her cheek, making it bleed.

"Come and help, Bertha, come quick!" shouted Tom, who was trying vainly to barricade the broken window.

She sprang up to his assistance, and then was suddenly beaten back by what seemed a solid blast of icy cold. At first she was almost choked, for it had come full in her face, taking her breath and her strength too. But the next moment she had rallied her forces, and was struggling across the room to help him turn the big table up against the window, which had been blown in as if driven with a battering ram.

"Is it rain?" she gasped, marvelling that drops of water could be so cold and cut like knives.

"No, it is hail," he answered, in the wrung tone of one who realizes that the very worst has happened that by any possibility could happen.

Then the full force of the disaster made itself clear to Bertha, as she stood beside Tom, helping to keep the table steady against the broken window. Speech was not possible now, for no shouting could have pierced the noise of the tempest. Even the crashing of the thunder came to their ears only as a distant, far-away sound, for the roar of the hail filled all space, and it was the most terrible sound that she had ever heard. The lightning flashed in and out, but no one heeded it, for a greater force than the swift darting flashes was abroad, and the terror of it was too dreadful to be borne.

The children gathered closer and closer to their mother, and if they cried with fear, neither Tom nor Bertha could hear, nor could they leave their post for a single moment; for if once the tornado wind got into the room, the whole house might be wrecked. So they stuck at their post, and it seemed to Bertha that she had been holding on with her whole force to that table, pressing it against the aperture of the broken window, when the voice of Tom reached her as from a great distance:

"You can leave it now, Bertha; I think the hail is over."

How quiet he was! Bertha drew a sharp breath, and was tempted for a moment to think that it had all been a horrible nightmare. But it was only for a moment, and then the table was lifted down and all the hideous ruin was revealed. The sun was shining again beyond the storm, and where the waving stretches of golden wheat had been, was now a seared and twisted desolation.

" 'The Lord gave, and the Lord hath taken away!' " said Tom hoarsely.

And the voice of Grace added softly: " 'Blessed be the name of the Lord!' "

CHAPTER XVII
Black Ruin

IT was not the Ellises alone who suffered on that disastrous Sunday before harvest. Every man whose land was within the area of the storm had his wheat beaten flat, twisted, cut, and riddled, until there was nothing left that was fit for gathering in. It was black ruin for most, and it had come as suddenly as a bolt from heaven might have done. The hailstorm had raged over a district about five miles broad and sixty long, spending itself finally over a stretch of swamp away in the wilderness.

In Pentland Broads half the houses had been unroofed, some of them, indeed, were entirely wrecked; but its force was weakening somewhat by the time it reached Duck Flats, or doubtless the house there must have gone also. As it was, it escaped with the slight damage of the window, which had been battered in by flying fragments from a little shed outside which was blown entirely to bits, some of the scattered wreckage being found afterwards half a mile away in the ruined wheatfields.

There was another heavy storm on the following day, only then it was rain and not hail which fell, but it finished the tale of disaster for the poor people, many of whom were practically homeless.

The post office had been more sorely damaged than any other building, Eunice Long and her brother barely escaping with their lives. But when Bertha drove over to Pentland Broads, two days later, to see how it fared with her friend, she was amazed at the steadfast light and the hopeful trust which shone on the face of the little postmistress.

"The worst has come that could come, and although it is ruin for a time, we shall get over it; and think what a blessing it is that not a single life has been lost anywhere—not even a horse killed. A dog is supposed to have died of fright at Blow End, but even that rumour has not been verified yet," said Eunice, smiling bravely up at Bertha, who was so much the taller.

"You are wonderful, just wonderful!" cried Bertha, choking back a sob. "But then, so is Tom, poor fellow. I have not heard one word of murmuring from him, or from Grace either."

"Murmuring is of no use, and only a waste of breath. What we have got to do is to learn the lesson the disaster was sent to teach, and try to manage our affairs more wisely next time," said Eunice briskly; then she asked abruptly, "What will Mr. Ellis do? Will he go away to work next winter, do you expect?"

"I don't know," said Bertha, and there was surprise and dismay in her tone. "But how could he go away with Grace in such a condition?"

"Very easily, seeing that he has you for an understudy," answered Eunice, with a laugh. "My dear Bertha, how truly modest you are! I don't believe you have the slightest idea of the power there is in you, or how really capable you are. Why don't you get a better opinion of yourself?"

"I don't know," answered Bertha ruefully. "I never seem to be able to do things unless I am pushed into them, and I never want to be pushed either."

Again Eunice laughed softly, and then she said: "I expect you are one of those people who unconsciously always measure their own capacity by what other people think that they can do. You have lived with two elder sisters who could never be brought to realize that you were grown up and able to do anything properly, and so it has come about that you feel you cannot do things unless you are absolutely forced into the work or endeavour, or whatever it is that wants doing."

"I expect that you are right. But oh, dear, I am always sighing for a quiet life—I mean one that runs on peaceful lines and has no upheavals in it—but somehow I do not seem able to get what I want," said Bertha, with a sigh; for she saw very plainly that this disaster which had overtaken Grace and Tom would be sure to involve her in heavier responsibility. Happily for her peace of mind, however, she had not the dimmest idea as yet how heavy her burden was likely to prove.

"Then plainly a peaceful life, as you call it, would not be good for you," said Eunice. "But I wish that you would ask Mr. Ellis to come over to-morrow if he has nothing very important to do. Tell him to be here by noon, for a man is coming over from Rownton to see my brother, and it might be useful for Mr. Ellis to meet him."

"I will tell him," said Bertha, and then she went out and mounted the wagon, to drive back along the trail through those ruined stretches of wheat which not a week ago had promised such a bountiful harvest.

Oh, how dreadfully sad it was! And because of the terrible suffering and misery which had overtaken so many people whom she knew and cared for, Bertha gave way to a fit of bitter crying, which, of course, was very silly, although she felt better when the tears were dried.

"I must do my very best for poor Grace and Tom now," she said softly to herself, as she hurried the leisurely trot of old Pucker, as she was anxious to get back to start on doing some of the many things which were occurring to her as ways in which she might help to tide over this time of trouble.

"I shall take no salary for a whole year, at least," she said to herself, "and if Grace insists, why, I shall just use it in the housekeeping, and she will be none the wiser. But, oh dear, I do wonder how we shall manage to get through the winter without any ready money. And it will be such a long time until next harvest."

The question of ways and means was a problem that she could get no light on, and she had to give it up and try to look as cheerful as possible when she reached Duck Flats.

The children and Tom were all out on the battered, twisted wheat trying to glean something from the ruin which might help out the food supplies for the long barren months stretching ahead of them. Tom had said that morning that he believed they might pick up a few bushels if only they worked hard enough, but it would have to be done at once, for already the district was black with birds which seemed to have scented the feast from afar, and had come in legions to partake.

"If Tom goes to Pentland Broads to-morrow, I will go out gleaning with the children," Bertha said to herself, as she drove in at the open gate of the paddock and proceeded to unhitch old Pucker.

Grace was quite alone in the house, and the pathetic patience of her face stirred Bertha up to fresh courage. She dared not show the white feather herself with such an example before her, inspiring her to do the very best that was in her.

"Are you tired of being alone, dear? Would you like me to stay with you, or shall I go and put in a couple of hours in the fields helping the others?" Bertha asked, coming to stoop over the couch.

"Go and help them, if you feel you can," replied Grace. "Tom sent Dicky in to see how I was getting on about half an hour ago, and the small boy said that they were picking up bushels and bushels, but I suppose one must allow something for youthful exaggeration. Still, every bushel saved is one bushel less to buy; for we can grind it in the little handmill for porridge, and we can rear a lot of chickens next spring. You see, there are so many ways of making the most of things, if one only sets about looking for them."

Bertha nodded, and, slinging a pillow-case in front of her, she went off in a great hurry to take her share in the work that was going forward. Hearts were too full for much speech in these days of difficulty, and she and Grace had a trick of understanding each other without many words on either side.

The children hailed her coming with shouts of glee, for it would certainly give a zest to this rather monotonous sort of play if only Bertha were on hand to make things lively for them.

Grace and Tom had at first tried hard to make the small people call Bertha aunt, but somehow the title had never seemed to fit her, and so, at her own wish, she was only Bertha to them, and they loved her with a fervency that they might have given to an elder sister. She was just one of themselves, only a little bigger and a good bit wiser; for she could tell the most thrilling stories that surely anyone had ever heard, and they all eagerly demanded a story now to relieve their toil in picking up the wheat.

Of course it was simply awful to have to stoop in the hot sun and talk all the time as well; but she compromised as best she could by going down on her knees, which was much easier than stooping, and then in a slow, mysterious tone she began a story, which she manufactured as she went along, about some people in Russia.

It was characteristic of the Ellis children that they rarely cared for stories about their own country, but they devoured with avidity every bit of information which she gave them of other countries, especially countries of the old world, and so they had already learned a considerable lot about Europe.

"I know all about Russia," said Molly, with a toss of her pert little head. "It is the country where the king cuts off people's heads himself and then sends them to Siberia."

Bertha laughed, in spite of herself, at the fancy picture of the Czar of all the Russias cutting off the heads of criminals and sending the headless bodies to walk in procession to Siberia. But it helped out the story, and she weaved a wonderful romance about a poor Russian noble who, for his sins, was sent to Siberia, and how he got lost in a great forest, which bordered a wheatfield so big that it would take a man three days to walk across it.

The forest had to be explained to the children, who had scarcely seen a tree as high as a house, and the story being of the stretchable kind, which could go on almost for ever, it was still only in its first stages when Bertha had to leave off wheat-picking and go back to the house to get supper. But the children had worked all the time; even small Noll had filled his little sack three times, while the twins had beaten Molly, which was just what they intended to do, and so they were radiantly happy.

Bertha herself was so tired with her double exertion, that she went back to the house in a rather depressed frame of mind. She had no time to indulge her mood, however, for Grace had been alone so long that it was just dreadful to be moody and silent now; so she had to chatter away all the time that she was preparing the evening meal, and then when Tom and the children came in it was still more necessary to be bright in her manner, so that there was no space for self-indulgence. And when the long day was done, she laid her head on the pillow, to fall asleep at once, which is the reward of hard and self-denying labour.

Tom went over to Pentland Broads on the next day, as Eunice Long had asked that he would. He grumbled at having to leave the wheat, since every handful saved was some small gain in the middle of their great loss. But Bertha had begged him to take his gun early in the morning and shoot some of the birds which swarmed over the hailed-out fields, and he had provided the household with meat enough for a week, so there was another gain. Then he drove off, and Bertha arranged a mosquito muslin over Grace to keep off the flies, then started with the children on that new employment of wheat-picking, which, alas! would have to be the main work for every day so long as they could find any corn to pick up.

There would be no seeding next year. It being so close to harvest when the disaster took place, the grain was ripe enough to grow, and so the farmers would plough their land as soon as they could and hope for a bumper crop next year. Only the pity of it was that next year was so far away, and they had to get through until next harvest as best they could.

Bertha was still afield when Tom came home, and when he came out to put in some more time at picking up corn, she had to go back to the house to get supper. The look on the face of Grace startled her when she crossed the threshold, for the invalid looked as if she had had a great shock, and yet her eyes were shining with a light that had not been there since the hail came to dash their hopes of harvest.

"What is the matter? Are you ill?" breathed Bertha, and then called herself foolish, for there was no appearance of bodily discomfort in Grace, whose expression was more rapt than suffering.

"No, but I have heard something which has startled me," Grace answered. "How brave do you feel at this moment, Bertha?"

"I don't know; I don't think that I am ever brave," said Bertha slowly; then, suddenly remembering what Eunice had said about her being able to do anything that was required of her, she said, "But I expect that I can muster up as much courage as you require me to have."

"Good girl! Always be ready to meet the demands upon you, and then you will do," replied Grace, with a laugh which was unsteady in spite of herself.

"But what is it?" asked Bertha. "What am I required to do that is likely to make me quail, in spite of myself?"

"Tom has had a good offer, a very good offer indeed, of six months' employment, but it will take him right away from home, and he cannot go unless you are willing to take care of me and the children," said Grace, and her eyes were very anxious as she waited for the other's reply.

"Six months? Why, that is nearly all the winter!" cried Bertha, in dismay, for however solitary Duck Flats might appear in summer, it was as nothing to what it was in winter, when sometimes for a week at the stretch they saw no one at all but themselves.

"Yes, dear, but it is eighty dollars a month and all found. Think what it will mean to us this year! Why, it is like a plain interposition of Providence on our behalf, only it depends upon you whether we can get it," said Grace, in a wistful tone.

Bertha gasped, and for one moment she seemed to be back in Mestlebury, and it was old Jan Saunders who was telling her that on her depended the safety of the man whose boat had been caught on the Shark's Teeth. Why, oh why did people always thrust such hard things upon her?

Then suddenly she remembered that however hard the things had been she had always managed to do them, although at the first they had seemed quite impossible.

There was quite a big silence, which Grace did not dare to break, and then Bertha said slowly: "I suppose that I shall be able to do all right; anyhow, I will do my best, and, as you say, it is a most wonderful chance, and the money will make all the difference. Why, it will keep us round to next harvest, won't it?"

"I think so, that is, we must make it keep us, and be very, very thankful that we have got it. Tom will sell all the horses except old Pucker, and then we can get Mr. Smith to plough for us, and so we shall get through. Oh, my dear Bertha, what a huge comfort you are to us! For Tom would never have been able to go if it had not been for you; but he says that he can trust us to you, and I would rather be left with you than with anyone," said Grace, with a long sigh, which suggested, although it did not reveal, all the emotion which lay underneath the surface.

"What is it that Tom will have to do?" asked Bertha.

"There is some prospecting work to be done, just what for I cannot tell you. It is a private venture, and that, I suppose, is why the pay is so good," said Grace. "There is a Mr. Brown, from Winnipeg, who has come over to arrange for a party of men to go. It seems that they want to start at once, only the difficulty was to find men in harvest. Then, when Mr. Brown was at Rownton, he heard of this district having been hailed out, and at once came on, guessing rightly that he would find men here who would be glad of employment. Eunice Long's brother is going, and one or two more. It was very good of Eunice to send for Tom, as otherwise he might not have heard anything about it until it was too late."

"What do you mean by at once?" asked Bertha, starting up in alarm, for she had done the family wash that morning, and Tom's shirts were still on the line, as dry as bones, doubtless, but not ironed yet.

"The day after to-morrow," replied Grace, with a swift intake of her breath, as if the near prospect of parting was more than she could bear.

"Never mind, the sooner he goes the sooner he will come back. And what a meeting that will be!" said Bertha cheerily.

Then she went out to the line and brought in the clothes, which she damped and folded in the pauses of getting supper ready. When the meal was over and the children had been put to bed, she sat darning by the light of a kerosene lamp. They did not allow themselves the luxury of a light at night at this time of the year in an ordinary way, but to-night Tom had gone back to Pentland Broads to let Mr. Brown know that he would be ready by the next day but one, and as there was a good deal to be done to get him ready, Bertha decided that she was justified in the lamplight, although she was so sleepy that she could hardly see to sew at all.

It was bright moonlight outside, a typical harvest night, only, alas! the harvest was destroyed, twisted, mangled, cut, and battered until it was no good at all—a ruin to weep over—and yet, bad as it was, it might have been worse, for the people were only impoverished and not destroyed, while out of the ashes of this year's hopes western energy would most certainly kindle some light for the future. But meanwhile there was the parting to be faced, and the helpless woman on the couch looked out to-night at a prospect which to her was as bitter as death.

CHAPTER XVIII
Standing in the Breach

A WEEK slipped away; the dreadful parting was over. Tom had gone, and the little household had settled down to make the best of the six months of solitude, narrow means, and general monotony.

Just at present Bertha was much too busy to notice the monotony. The days were only about half long enough for all that she had to do in them, and the nights seemed only about half long enough either for the amount of sleeping that she desired to get through.

Housework had scanty attention just now. Other things were so much more important, and so the things which mattered least had to go. She had discovered that she could shoot birds, and although she simply hated to do it, the birds were such a valuable addition to the food supply, that she forced herself to the necessary hardness of heart. Of course, if she did not shoot them somebody else would, or the poor creatures would die of want when the snow came, or a dozen evil fates might befall them, and, comforting herself with these reflections, she took out Tom's gun every morning and did such execution among the prairie chicken, that the little household was well supplied still, even though the master of the house was far away.

Bill Humphries had brought her over a dog, and already the creature was of the utmost value in retrieving the chicken, so that she was spared the horror of having to dispatch the birds which she had only winged. The children always prepared the birds for cooking, and were by this time quite expert at the task, which would certainly have taken away Bertha's appetite if she had had it to do.

In the middle of the second week after Tom went away there came a letter from him, the last that they could receive, so they believed, until his party made their way back to civilization once more. It was written from a place beyond Porcupine Mountains, where the expedition had halted for a week of exploring in a wild district into which, so far as they could discover, no white man had ever penetrated before.

Tom was in his element. There was a great love of primitive life in him, and very often during his days at Duck Flats the call of the wild had been almost too strong to resist, would have been quite too strong, probably, had not his duty bound him with fetters of steel. So now that it was his duty to go forth, he could enjoy the adventurous days to the full, and indulge his bent for prospecting as he had never been able to do before.

So far he had not discovered the real intentions of the expedition. Sometimes he was disposed to think that they were merely out on a general survey in the interests probably of some syndicate, formed for the purpose of buying up land, but there were indications in plenty that they were keeping their eyes very widely open for everything else which was there to be seen. The men were promised bonuses on certain finds, in addition to their pay, and this had the effect of making everyone exceedingly alert; for who should say what riches the wilderness might not reveal to those who had eyes to see them?

"Poor Tom! this will seem like a real holiday to him after his hard years of homesteading," said Grace, with a sigh of content for her husband, when she had read and re-read the letter which had come to her from the edge of the unknown.

Bertha looked at her and marvelled anew at her patience. Surely it must have needed a tremendous amount of courage to consent to his going, seeing how helpless Grace was, yet she had never, by word or look, tried to hold him back, but had sent him forth with a heroic cheerfulness which had been a credit even to a strong woman.

"I suppose that he will have to work pretty hard there. They would hardly pay so well if they did not expect some adequate return for their money," Bertha remarked as, by dint of much pushing and tugging, she got Grace on to the wheeled chair and dragged it into the bedroom, where, by dint of more pushing and tugging, she got her on to the bed, which was all the change of place and position the invalid could have.

"Oh yes, there will be awful work to be done," answered Grace. "Those poor fellows will have to stagger along under burdens that will make their shoulders raw, they will be footsore and thirsty, they will be scorched with heat, devoured by mosquitoes, and, later on, they will be nearly starved from the lowness of their food supplies, and frozen by the bitter cold. And yet, if I know them, it will seem like one long picnic, and they will go on from day to day with the zest of school-boys out on holiday. I should love it myself, I know. Why, when I was a child I was always wishing that I had lived about a hundred years ago, so that I could have been carried off by Micmacs or had adventures of sorts. And really, you know, life nowadays is very tame indeed."

Bertha laughed, although in truth she could just as easily have cried, to hear the poor helpless woman talking of adventures with such incredible zest. What a fine plucky spirit it was that was caged in that prison-house of clay! And the difference between Grace and herself struck her more forcibly than ever.

"I wish you could give me some of your love of enterprise," she said wistfully. "I always feel more or less of a fraud when people are kind enough to say nice things to me, because I know that underneath I am a most awful coward."

"What matters about what is underneath if you can but succeed in keeping it there?" laughed Grace. "If you come to bed-rock personalities, I guess that you would find we are all more or less cowards, and the best thing to be done is not to admit it, even to ourselves, lest in an unwary moment our bottom nature should rise up and gain the mastery over us. Now, get off to bed, you dear, plucky Bertha, and let us have no more talk of secret quailings."

And Bertha was so glad to go to her well-earned rest, that it seemed too much trouble to undress. It was always an effort to get Grace from couch to bed, and to-night the task seemed harder than usual. But it was done, and now there was nothing more for tired limbs until morning. Oh, how beautiful it was to rest!

She had flung herself on the bed, all dressed as she was, intending to just lie there for a few moments, and then get up and undress before going to bed properly. But alas for good intentions! In about a minute she was sound asleep, and not even the twins in the little truckle bed in the corner lay in profounder repose. How long she had slept she had no idea, but suddenly, for no reason at all, she became quite dreadfully wide-awake. What was the matter? Something must be wrong, she was sure of it, for she had not waked up like that for months.

Sitting up in bed, or rather on the bed, she strained her ears in listening for some faintest sound which might seem to indicate anything gone wrong. Her heart was thumping at a tremendous rate, there was a creeping, crawling sensation all over her, and she would have been thankful for the privilege of screaming in a wild hysterical fashion. But it would never do to upset Grace and the children in such a fashion, so she must control herself and keep down that impulse for screaming. Then the dog whined, and, with a sudden access of courage, Bertha slid off the bed and opened the door.

"Bertha, what is wrong?" asked the voice of Grace from the other room.

"I don't know, dear, but I came awake suddenly, and so I thought that there must be some reason for it, and I got up to see," replied Bertha, more thankful than she could express to find that Grace was awake, for it seemed to take away half the loneliness and the horrid weird fear which had gripped her.

"Bouncer has whined once or twice, but he often does that, because the poor old fellow feels as if he would like to have his liberty on these fine nights," said Grace, in a tone which was devoid of the least shadow of fear.

"Shall I go out and see what is wrong?" asked Bertha, who was feeling quite valiant now.

"I should not trouble if I were you; it will only wake you up and spoil your chances of going to sleep again," replied Grace. "If you feel at all nervous, come and lie down here beside me, and I can rouse you at once if there seems any need."

"But you will want to go to sleep yourself," objected Bertha, to whom, however, the plan commended itself as the most reasonable thing to do.

"Oh, it does not matter when I sleep; I do not know that it would very much matter if I stayed awake all night," said Grace, "although, as a matter of fact, I am always as sleepy as if I worked hard all day. But, Bertha, I've got a piece of news for you, and I feel as if it will not keep until the morning. I have distinctly felt my big toe to-night."

"What do you mean?" asked Bertha, who was too sleepy to take in the full significance of this information.

Grace laughed softly. "Don't you understand that for all this time since my fall I have had no feet at all? When anything has touched my foot or feet I have not known it, unless I have seen it. Imagine, then, what it is to feel that one has suddenly acquired a big toe, even though all the parts in between are missing."

"Oh, my dear, how glad I am!" cried Bertha, leaning over to kiss Grace; and just at that moment Bouncer whined again, and then began scratching at the door in sign that he very badly wanted to get out.

"I guess that a friend of his has come for a stroll in this direction to-night. Let him out, Bertha; he is not likely to run away before morning, and you will get no more sleep if the creature is going to be restless," said Grace.

Bertha got up then and, feeling thankful that she had not undressed on the previous night, felt her way carefully across the outer room to the door, at which the dog was eagerly scratching to get out. There was no anger in the dog's manner, only joyful excitement, and the creature nearly knocked Bertha down as, with a chorus of joyful barks and whines, it burst out at the door and tore away across the dark paddock. But there was no more sleep for either Grace or Bertha that night, for from the distance Bouncer made night—or rather darkness, for it was really morning—hideous with his lamentations—whining, barking, howling in a passion of entreaty (so it seemed to those who listened from the inside).

Grace would not hear of Bertha going out to see what was wrong. "Time enough when daylight comes for investigations of that sort," she said, and

Bertha had not the least desire to withstand the mandate, for all her own feelings pointed to the desirability of staying where she was.

At last came the grey light of dawn, and Bertha sprang up, eager now to enquire into the disturbance of the night. The first thing she saw on opening the door was a good-sized packing case standing on the edge of the veranda, and all at once she realized that it must have been this being put down which had roused her from sleep so suddenly in the night; but Grace would not have heard it, because her room was on the other side of the house, and her window looked the other way. Farther away she could see Bouncer, tied in an ignominious fashion to one of the posts where the lines were stretched for drying clothes, and then she understood that the intruder, whoever he was, must have been known to the dog, which wanted to follow him, but got tied up instead.

"I wonder who sent the thing; I mean, I wonder who brought it," she said to herself, and then she walked round the box, which was a good big one, and looked heavy. But there was not much enlightenment to be got from an outside survey, for the box was merely labelled, "This side up, with care", and had "Mrs. Ellis" marked with a burnt stick in big letters at the side.

"Grace! Grace!" she cried, running back into the house. "Someone did come last night, and left a big case, directed to you, on the veranda. They must have put it down very softly, too, for it is just outside my window."

"What sort of a case?" asked Grace, in bewilderment.

"A big packing case, a deal box, you know, rather rough, and nailed down in all directions. I wonder what it is that has been sent in such a mysterious fashion?" Bertha was so excited, because it was such an unusual thing for anything unexpected to arrive, and this thing had come in the dead of night, too, which made it all the more remarkable.

"It is a box as big as a house," shrieked Molly, who had been out to investigate, clad only in her nightgown, and who was now prancing about with bare feet, while the twins, aroused by her shouting, came tumbling out of bed to see what was going on, and only Dicky and little Noll slept serenely on.

"Bertha, do make haste and get it open; I feel as curious as possible to know what is inside," said Grace, whose eyes were positively eager.

"I am afraid that I shall have to open it outside, but I will drag it along in front of the door, so that you can see me do it," said Bertha, and then she went off for a chisel and a hammer; for the person who had nailed the box up had plainly meant that it should not come undone in a hurry.

The children were rushing round and round like wild things, the twins had dragged Dicky and Noll out of bed, and the clamour was something tremendous, while Bouncer from the background kept putting in his ideas on the subject, only, as they were all set forth in dog language, no one was a whit the wiser.

By dint of much hard work with the chisel, a good bit of hammering, and some bashing of her fingers, Bertha finally succeeded in getting the cover off the box, revealing a layer of brown paper. But before this was lifted she managed to drag the thing over the threshold, so that Grace should share in the fun of the unpacking, and then, with a crowd of eager little ones pressing round, she lifted the brown paper, and then the white paper, which lay immediately underneath.

"Oh, oh, oh, oh!" burst in excited chorus from the children, while Grace exclaimed, "Bertha! Bertha! Who could have sent it?" as the lifting of the white paper revealed a whole stock of invalid comforts in the shape of bottles of meat juice, packets of nourishing soups, tins of cocoa, arrowroot, and biscuits, jellies in packets, custard powders, and so many other nice and nourishing things, that Bertha was fairly bewildered by their number and variety.

Underneath these was a thick layer of big juicy apples, at the sight of which the children set up a wild shout of joy, for apples were a luxury quite out of their reach under present circumstances, and the only approach to fruit they could get were melons and squashes.

Below the apples came household stores, currants and raisins, packets of tea, coffee, sugar, rice, and beans, a square tin box full of the most delicious cookies, and a great packet of candies, which could only be for the children; then right at the bottom of the box a layer of books, which looked as if they might have been bought from a secondhand bookstall, but that were none the worse for that.

"New books!" cried Grace, her voice almost a shout. "Oh, Bertha, what a winter we shall have!"

"It is the nice things for you that please me most," said Bertha, in an unsteady tone. "It makes me feel bad to see you trying to eat the rough stuff that the rest of us can enjoy, and now I shall be able to get you nice, dainty things for months to come. But oh, I do wonder who could have sent it? And oh, I wish that he or she could be here to see how delighted we are with it all!"

"So do I," replied Grace, and then she said, with a merry laugh, "What elaborate precautions the donor took to get his gift here unobserved! Fancy travelling to a lone house like this in the middle of the night for the sake of dumping a box unobserved upon the veranda."

"And incidentally scaring us all nearly out of our senses. I don't think that I will ever let myself be scared by a noise in the night again, only, as it happened last night, it was not so much a noise as a sensation," said Bertha, who sat on the floor surveying the riches contained in the packing case as if she did not know what to make of it all.

"I wonder who could have sent the things? Oh, how I would like to thank them!" said Grace.

"We can't have all we want in this world, and so I am afraid the knowledge will have to be one of the things that you will have to go without," Bertha answered, with a laugh, and then, springing to her feet, she began unpacking the things and putting them away.

"Bertha, suppose it is a mistake, and that they are not meant for us," objected Grace.

"There could not possibly be a mistake that I can see; the things were brought to the house, the case has Mrs. Ellis on it in big letters, and we are going to keep it," said Bertha decidedly; then she suddenly jerked out, "Don't you think that perhaps Tom sent it?"

"No, I don't, for the very good reason that the poor, dear fellow had no money to buy things with; indeed, Mr. Brown had to advance him the money for the journey when he went to join the party, and Tom had only one solitary half-dollar of his own in his possession," Grace answered.

"It would not be anyone at Pentland Broads, either, because, of course, they are all as poor as we are; indeed, some of them must be poorer," said Bertha musingly.

"Much poorer, I fear, especially the Longs, who have lost house, furniture, and everything else, and will not even get their insurance, because the destruction was from tempest and not mere carelessness," said Grace, with a fine edge of irony in her tone.

"Perhaps we shall never know, but we can be just as grateful, and time will show," answered Bertha.

CHAPTER XIX
A Disquieting Rumour

THE weeks of fall weather went swiftly on, the nights grew longer and colder and darker, save when there was a moon to shine with frosty brilliance from a sky that was studded with a myriad of stars. Bertha was very busy in those autumn days, for there was a bit of swamp two miles on beyond Duck Flats, on the wilderness side of them, and thither on fine afternoons she drove with the children to pick berries and gather in the little unconsidered harvest of the wilds. Always she left either Dick or Molly at home to look after Grace, and always her journey back was a progress of anxiety, lest anything had happened to the invalid in her absence.

But Grace declared herself to be only half an invalid now, because sensation had come back to the toes of both feet, and she had actually achieved the great feat of lifting one hand to touch her lips. The day when this took place they held as high festival, but as the time went on the pleasure for Grace of being able to feel her feet once more was tempered by the torture of cramp which she suffered. Vainly did Bertha beg to be allowed to send for Dr. Benson, but Grace declared that as they had no money to pay the bill, no doctor would she have.

"But you have eighty dollars a month coming in, or will have, which is the same thing. And think how dreadfully worried Tom would be to know how you were suffering, when perhaps the doctor could tell you of some simple remedy that would save you half the pain and perhaps quicken your recovery," said Bertha anxiously.

"I know what you shall do, Bertha—you shall write to him. You can tell him that we have no money, and so he must not come, but you can ask him if it is natural for anyone in my condition to suffer so much from cramp; and if he says yes, well, then, I will bear it cheerfully; for, after all, it is better to bear pain than to have no feeling at all," replied Grace, who had been the more willing to listen to Bertha, because of that suggestion that she might recover the more quickly if she had a doctor's advice at the present stage.

"I will write the letter, and get Mr. Smith to take it with him. I would go over to Pentland Broads myself to-day, only I can't leave you so long," said Bertha, who had been rubbing the tortured muscles, and doing everything in her power to stop the suffering.

"That will do quite well, and perhaps I shall be better as the day goes on," said Grace, whose face was pinched and drawn with the suffering.

Bertha sat down and wrote the letter, although her day's work lay all before her. She was seriously worried about Grace, and when she had written a letter to the doctor which Grace might read, she hastily scribbled a little private note, which she slipped inside the envelope, begging that the doctor would come over, if he thought it the least bit necessary, and that she herself would borrow the money from her sisters to pay the bill, if there was no other way. Then she threw a saddle on old Pucker and rode away across the ruined wheatfields to the quarter section where Mr. Smith was ploughing. It was quicker than walking, and more restful, also, and there was quite enough active exercise for her in every day to make her anxious to save her strength where she could.

The Smiths had been terribly hard hit in the harvest disaster, for they had taken up a mortgage on their land the year before, in order to have more money to invest in wheat-growing, and so they found themselves with interest on the mortgage to pay in hard cash, as well as to find means of a livelihood until harvest came again.

Mrs. Smith had drooped under the trouble until she was quite ill, and doubtless would have been worse if it had not been for the fact that Grace insisted on sharing some of the nourishing things with her which had come in that mysterious packing case.

This kindness of sharing was bringing its own reward in the neighbourly goodness of Mr. Smith, who did many things for them which were not in his ploughing contract. He was just starting a new furrow, but when he saw her coming he waited for her to come up, and, getting off his plough, stood holding his horses, which were in prime condition, and mettlesome from the amount of corn they managed to lick off the ground when they had scraped the battered straw away with their fore feet. They were doing it now, being as wise in their way as humans, and turning the brief resting-time to the best account they could.

"Good morning, Miss Bertha, nothing wrong, I hope?" he said, lifting his hat, as she came near enough for speech.

"I don't know whether it is wrong or right," said Bertha, in a worried tone, "and that is why I have ridden across to you instead of waiting until you came past the house at noon."

Then she told him about the pain which Grace was suffering, and asked him if it would be possible to get her letter to Pentland Broads that day.

"It will have to be possible," he said quietly. "I will unyoke and go at once. If the doctor is in, I will bring back an answer from him; but if you don't see anything of me, you will know that I have gone back home because the doctor was not at home, and that I will ride over again for you this evening."

"You will not need to go the second time, thank you," said Bertha, "because I have asked the doctor to come over. I think that it is necessary that he should see Mrs. Ellis, only she does not know that I have asked him to come."

"I see; very well, you will know that your errand has been done, even if you don't see the doctor or me either before to-morrow."

Mr. Smith was unhitching as he talked, and then he proceeded to tether one horse to the plough, while he rode away on the other. The tethered horse being fastened to the broadside of the plough, there was no danger of it running away, or even dragging its hobble far from the furrow. Bertha rode back to the house, satisfied that her errand would be done with dispatch. But she contrived that her work should not take her near enough to Grace for any sustained talk that morning, because Grace had such a way of getting out of her what was in her mind, and she wanted to keep to herself the fact that she had sent for a doctor until he really arrived.

The day wore on, as all their days did; it was the same unvarying monotony, which was so much more monotonous to them all, now that there was no cheery head of the house to come out and in. The children did their small tasks, and then gathered about their mother for the simple instruction in all kinds of things, which was all the education they had as yet.

It was late afternoon, and Bertha was in the barn milking the cow, when she heard the sound of a horse coming at a canter, and, going to the door, saw the doctor riding up the paddock. Knowing that he would be sure to bring his horse to the barn instead of stopping at the house door, she turned back to the cow, and by dint of working quickly managed to finish milking by the time he arrived. Then she fed his horse and took the doctor back to the house, where the children had already announced his arrival.

He had not seen Grace since the disaster of the harvest, and he announced himself amazed at the change in her. He even congratulated her on the pain she had to bear, and told her that it would probably get worse, but that it was a sign that Nature was working a more clever cure than any mere doctor might hope to accomplish. He showed Bertha how to relieve the distressing cramp, and then he went back to the barn to get his horse, and Bertha went with him. It was then that the pleasant professional manner dropped from him, and he turned sharply upon Bertha, whose heart quailed with a sudden fear; for there was that in his face which betokened tidings of evil.

"Is Mrs. Ellis worse?" she gasped, quite forgetting in that moment of dread how the doctor had told Grace she was going to get well.

"No, no; she is amazingly better. It will be months yet before she will even be able to sit up, for Nature is slow; but she will go on improving, and there is no need to worry about her, although for my own satisfaction I shall see her now about once a fortnight. There may come a time when Nature will need a little help, and although there was no sense in worrying her with visits when matters were at a standstill, it is altogether different now," said the doctor, whom Bertha shrewdly suspected to be talking for talking's sake.

"Then what is it?" she asked bluntly, and she clenched her hands tightly, so that she might bear without flinching whatever had to be borne.

"There is a rumour current at Rownton that Brown's Expedition is in difficulties. I can't trace its source, but the general opinion is that it was not adequately provisioned, that there was not enough capital behind the venture, and that the high wages to be paid to the men were existent only on the contracts."

Bertha drew a long breath of relief. Of course it was bad enough, but it might so easily have been worse, and to her at that moment the possible bankruptcy of the expedition was a mere trifle compared with what might have been.

"Is that all? Oh, I thought that it was something bad that you had to tell me," she said, then added, with a laugh, "Some of the wages are a solid reality, for a quarter of the amount due to Tom is paid every month to Grace through a Winnipeg Bank, and I believe that Eunice Long has something in the same way too."

"Well, I am thankful to hear it, for she needs it, poor thing; she is almost too ill to keep about now, and every day I am afraid that she will break down. I suppose you know that they will not get a penny of their insurance money, and now, to make matters worse, the postal orders and stamps that were destroyed have got to be made good," replied Dr. Benson, as he led his horse out of the stable.

"Poor Eunice, how I wish that I could help her!" exclaimed Bertha, and then she added, with a sigh, "But it seems to take all my time to help myself just now."

"I should think so; at any rate, you can't be dull for want of employment," returned the doctor, with a laugh. "Don't say anything about this rumour to Mrs. Ellis; she is not strong enough to bear worry very comfortably yet awhile. Of course, if the men hear that there is not enough money to carry the venture through, they will most likely throw up the job and return before the snow blocks them in."

"That also I must keep from Mrs. Ellis," said Bertha, whose heart had given a sudden throb of hope at hearing there was even a remote possibility of Tom returning before the winter.

"Of course; for if the poor thing even guessed that her husband might return, she would know no peace or rest, and her recovery would be put back in consequence," the doctor went on, his voice dropping into a graver key. "The trouble is that in matters like this the men most concerned are usually the last to know that there is anything wrong, and they may get too far to return before autumn, in which case they will have to wait until the snow will let them out."

Bertha nodded, and the hope that had sprung up that Tom would return died out again, for well she knew that he was not the sort of man to turn his back on a forlorn hope, nor would he be likely to leave his employers in the lurch, even though he knew that he would not get his money, and perhaps be half-starved into the bargain.

She watched the doctor ride away and then went into the house, her mind in a turmoil of mixed feelings—joy for Grace, anxiety for Tom, and for herself a determination to make the very best of the hard bit in front of her.

"Bertha, why did you send for the doctor?" Grace asked reproachfully, and then she went on, "My dear, it is no use for you to try to put me off, because you are so very transparent, that I always feel as if I can see right through you. I expect that you wrote a little private note when I was not looking, and asked him to come because you were anxious."

Bertha sat down and laughed. "It is really of no use to try any underhand performances with you; but that is just what I did, and I am so very glad, because now he will watch your case carefully, and be ready to help you when you need it."

"Yes, that is all very well, or would be, if we had any prospect of being able to pay the bill within a reasonable time," said Grace. "But oh, the worry of it is so hard to bear!"

"It need not be," replied Bertha calmly. "I told the doctor that I would pay it if you could not."

"And pray, where are you going to get the money from, seeing that you will take no money in salary this year?" asked Grace.

"Oh, I shall borrow it of Anne and her husband. They have not had me to keep, as they would have done if you had not spent so much energy in making me useful," said Bertha coolly.

"Perhaps it will not come to that, at least I hope not," Grace sighed, for she had always been very proud, and the thought of dependence on relatives for the paying of her doctor's bill was fearfully repugnant to her.

"Most likely it will not, but I always like to have another way out in the back of my mind; it helps one to have confidence in oneself. But I fancy that when the snow comes I ought to have time for a little writing, if the children keep well; and if I should chance to sell a story, why, that can go to help in paying the bill." Bertha spoke diffidently now, for she could never get away from the feeling that she was going to be laughed at when she spoke of her literary aspirations, although nothing could possibly be further away from the thoughts of Grace than any idea of throwing cold water on her desire to be a writer.

"I should not be surprised if you were to write some very good stories this winter, because you have had to live through so much since last year, and you have grown so much wiser. One must live through terror, suspense, and pain, you know, before one can really know quite how it all feels," said Grace.

"I suppose you are right; and perhaps if I could have had the easy, leisured life I have always longed for, I might never have been able to write of realities," said Bertha.

Grace laughed softly, and then replied: "But you are forgetting. You might have had the leisured life a few months ago, if only you had done as Anne wished and gone out to Australia."

"That may be, but I am very much afraid that I should not have done much good with it. Anyhow, I am very glad that I did not go," said Bertha, who was bustling round now preparing supper. The children were running in and out, each one endeavouring to be useful according to his or her ideas of usefulness, and although she could have done many of the things much quicker herself, Bertha accepted all the assistance she could get, and was thankful for it.

But the small people were mostly so sleepy by supper-time, that it was no uncommon thing for Noll or one of the twins to fall asleep before the meal was done, which was rather worrying, as it meant that there would be wailing instead of smiling during the necessary washing of dirty little bodies, which always had to finish each working day. But to-night they managed to keep awake, supper was dispatched, Molly and Dicky cleared away and washed the dishes, while Bertha bathed the three young ones. Then, when they were all in bed, there came an hour of delicious rest, when Bertha sat in the rocking-chair by the stove doing absolutely nothing at all, while Grace talked about the stories which were to be written when the snow came, and there should be time for all the things that had to be done.

"Summer is always such a fearful rush; it seems as if Nature hurries us all up after her own fashion," said Grace.

"Yes, and it is just that same rush which makes winter so welcome," answered Bertha, in a sleepy tone.

CHAPTER XX
An Impossible Favour

THE snow came down and hid the ruins of the ungathered harvest from sight. The nights were long, and on some days there seemed almost no daylight at all. It was so different from last winter, however, that Bertha was astonished at the lack of monotony in the days which, to an outsider, must have seemed so much alike. Nearly every day someone happened along, either in a sledge or on snow-shoes, and although these visitors never stayed long, it was something to see an outside face and to hear a different voice.

Just before Christmas another mysterious packing case arrived, and, like the previous one, it came in the night, but with this difference, that on the second time none of the lonely household was disturbed, or knew that anything out of the ordinary was happening. It was a bigger case than the last one had been, and there were toys for the children, which seemed to have been chosen by someone who had scanty knowledge of children and their ways. There was also a great store of good things for Christmas and the New Year, and because their neighbours had such a poor chance of anything approaching to a merry Christmas that year, Grace and Bertha put their heads together to see what they could do by way of sharing their good things with these less fortunate ones.

A Christmas party on quite a big scale was the first idea, but it had to be abandoned for several reasons. Nothing had been heard of Tom or of the expedition, and it would be impossible to get enough of a festive feeling to make a party enjoyable when, for all they knew to the contrary, the master of the house might be face to face with starvation, or suffering all sorts of hardships. Then, too, there was only one pair of hands to make all the necessary preparations, and, willing as Bertha was, Grace declared that she could not endure the thought of anything which would lay an extra burden on her shoulders.

"Why not make up a parcel of things for all the people we want to send to—I mean a parcel for each house?" said Bertha, waxing incoherent from sheer excitement. "Then I could hitch Pucker to the sledge and take them all round on Christmas Eve. I dare say Mrs. Smith would bring her children over and stay with you. If she did that, I could take Dicky and Molly with me, and the outing would be a festival to them."

"That is a simply lovely scheme!" exclaimed Grace. "But it won't do to put it off to Christmas Eve, for, if I know anything about prairie housekeeping, Mrs. Smith will be much too busy on that day to be willing to pay a visit of uncertain length here, and the more scanty the Christmas fare, the more careful the preparations will have to be in order to cover the gaps in the feast.

We must make our arrangements for the day before that, and then if we tell Mrs. Smith that the happiness of the community depends entirely on her coming here to stay with me, I am pretty sure that she will come."

"Then the day before Christmas Eve it shall be, and we shall just have to get to work at once to get everything arranged," Bertha replied; then followed an eager discussion as to the things to be sent to this one and to that.

From the time the big case arrived until the day of the distribution, Bertha gave up her room as a storeplace for the things, and slept on the couch by the kitchen stove, while the children were packed as thickly as sardines in a tin in the beds in their mother's room. But the festival feeling ran so high that week, that no one minded anything about such minor matters as overcrowding. The children lived in a continual whirl of paper and string, of carrying parcels from one room to the other, and of doing this and that towards helping forward the preparations for the great distribution, that Grace declared they would all be worn out with the dissipation.

At last the great day arrived—a fine morning, with a keen frost, and a temperature something below zero, but with a crisp quality in the air which made the youngsters positively hilarious, while Bertha darted to and fro, feeling that, in spite of very pronounced drawbacks, it was going to be a very nice Christmas indeed.

Mrs. Smith arrived in good time, a little anxious and concerned about the work which she ought to have done that day at home, but more resigned to the inevitable, because she had brought a great bundle of household mending with her, which she could get through while she talked to Grace. Her face changed, however, and a shower of tears seemed imminent, when she was told why she had been sent for, and was presented with her share of the contents of that wonderful packing case.

"There would have been no Christmas fare in our house this year," she said, her face working pitifully. "We shall have to be in debt for necessaries later on, so we dare not have the least thing that we can by any means do without."

"All the more reason why we should help each other," said Grace softly, and then with infinite tact she managed to keep Mrs. Smith from dissolving into tears, which would doubtless have induced a similar shower from some of the small people; and this was no day for tears.

Dicky and Molly, wrapped up until they looked like a couple of Eskimos, were in a state of uproarious delight. They laughed, sang, and shouted at such a rate that old Pucker nearly did a bolt on the outward journey, which would have been disastrous, seeing how heavily the sledge was laden. The old horse had done so little work for weeks past, that the outing must have been quite a pleasure trip.

Bertha herself was in a jubilant mood, and this was increased, on arrival at the post office, by finding a letter of acceptance from a New York editor of one of the stories she had sent to him a couple of months before.

"Oh, it is good to be alive!" she exclaimed, as she tied Pucker fast to the post outside the door and went in to see how it fared with Eunice.

Mrs. Humphries was doing the post-office work at the present, for Eunice was too ill to rise from her bed, and the elation in the heart of Bertha turned to dismay at the sight of the suffering on the face of the sick woman.

"Don't look like that, child," whispered Eunice. "Your face was like a picture with happiness when you walked in at the door, and then it changed into dreary melancholy, all because I carry my woes of body writ large outside for anyone to read."

"Oh, I had hoped to find you better, and now you look like this!" Bertha's tone was shocked, for no one had told her of the change in Eunice, and she had not seen here for weeks.

"The doctor says that I shall get better if I try hard enough; but I suppose it is the indolence of my nature revolting against hard work, for it seems too much trouble to struggle on trying to get better. Death looks so easy and pleasant, just getting a little weaker every day and then dropping to sleep at the last, like a child that is too tired to play any longer," said Eunice, and she looked so white and worn, that Bertha thought she was actually dying then.

But instead of words of grief, or even of resignation, a torrent of reproaches rose to the lips of Bertha, and were uttered through an irresistible impulse, cruel though they must have sounded at the time.

"Oh, you are selfish, most dreadfully selfish, to want to die and leave us all just when we need you so much! I have no friend outside my own people except you, and I cannot do without you!" she wailed. "And think how dreadful it will be for your brother when he comes home, to find no one to give him a welcome. Oh, it is not like you to think of yourself first and not to mind what becomes of other people!"

Great tears came into the eyes of Eunice and rolled unchecked down her face. "I don't want to be selfish," she said meekly, "but I am so tired, that I thought other people could get on without me somehow. And you could comfort my brother, Bertha, if you would, and make him the happiest man in the world."

"No, I couldn't, really, I couldn't—oh, don't speak of it!" cried Bertha distressfully, turning very red in the face.

"Are you sure?" asked Eunice, and there was such a world of wistful entreaty in the eyes of the sick woman, that Bertha turned her head away from a fear that she might be drawn into giving promises impossible to fulfil.

"I am quite, quite sure. Oh, please dear, do not ever speak of it to me again—it is too dreadful!" burst out Bertha, with tremendous emphasis.

"Is there anyone else?" persisted Eunice.

An indignant denial rose to the lips of Bertha and stopped there, for before her eyes rose the picture of a grey heaving sea, a rising tide, cruel black rocks, and a small boat so wedged that its occupant could not get it off the rocks. But she never could recall with any vividness the face of the man she had rescued, that is, she could not see it so clearly that she could be sure of knowing it again. At the time when the wheat fired, she had felt quite sure that the man who came along with the Smiths to help fight the fire had been the man whom she had helped, but many times since then she had told herself that there was no real certainty in her mind about the matter.

Of course, if she could have got hold of him afterwards, to have asked him if he had lost a coat and anything else, it would have been different. But Mrs. Smith, who did not know his name, had said that he was leaving the firm for whom he travelled on the next week, and one would want to be very sure indeed before making enquiries.

"Is there anyone else?" asked Eunice, and this time there was undisguised anxiety in her tone.

"Oh no, of course not—it is not possible!" exclaimed Bertha, coming out of her embarrassed reverie, and speaking in a great hurry, yet without any conviction whatever.

Eunice looked pained and disappointed, but said no more, and Bertha made haste to bring the uncomfortable interview to an end. It was certainly dreadful to have to disappoint a good friend such as Eunice had been to her, but not for forty friends could she consent to make that dreadful Mr. Long happy. Not that he had ever ventured to ask her; his plan of action had seemed to consist in paying her the most embarrassing sort of attentions, which rendered him the laughing-stock of the community, and made her simply furious with indignation. If he had asked her straight out to marry him, she would have been able to say, "No, thank you", and so have ended the miserable business. But it had never entered into Mr. Long's calculations to do anything so sensible, and so the discomfort for Bertha had gone on.

Somehow the flavour of the trip was spoiled for Bertha now. She was so terribly upset by the change in Eunice, and the fear that the poor thing would slip out of life. But she had to thrust the trouble into the background, and be as merry as she could for the sake of the good folk to whom she was playing an amateur Santa Claus.

It was quite late in the afternoon, the sledge was empty, and she had turned Pucker's head in the direction of Duck Flats, when she encountered the doctor. She pulled up in a great hurry then to ask him if he had been over to see Grace.

"No, not to-day. Did you want me to see her?" he asked.

"Oh no, there was no need, only, I have been away since the morning, and I did not know if you might have been coming anywhere near us, and so had dropped in," she answered.

"Duck Flats is not near to anywhere. It is the most out-of-the-way location that any man could ever have fixed upon for his home, I think," rejoined the doctor testily. "I can't think how ever you manage to endure life in such a place, Miss Bertha; but, upon my word, you seem to thrive on it, and so do the youngsters. Why, they grow like weeds!"

"I am used to the loneliness now. Of course it is awkward to be so far from civilization sometimes, but if one is very busy it does not matter much in an ordinary way," said Bertha, and then she asked anxiously, "Is Miss Long very dangerously ill? I was frightened to see her looking so badly."

"She is starved," said the doctor grimly.

"Oh, you cannot mean it!" cried Bertha, in a tone of protest, while her face went very white.

"I do mean it, or I should not have said it," said the doctor bluntly.

"But surely, surely that need not have been?" cried Bertha, who was dreadfully distressed. "We are all poor, of course, and dreadfully pushed for ready money, but so far as I know no one has had to go short of food yet. Besides, we understood that Eunice had money from the bank in Winnipeg, just the same as Mrs. Ellis does."

"Of course she has had it, and that is where the maddening part of it comes in," said the doctor crossly. "But instead of living on the money, as a sensible person would, and leaving her brother to make good the value of the postal orders which were destroyed on that black Sunday, the silly woman goes and simply starves herself to death in order that the loss may be made good the sooner."

"Oh, what shall I do? I have been saying the most dreadful things to her to-day, but I did not know all this!" exclaimed Bertha. "Oh, she must have thought me cruel, cruel! I would go back now and tell her how sorry I am, only I should be so late home, and Mrs. Smith will not want to stay with Mrs. Ellis much longer."

"And pray, what was it you said that needs so much repentance?" asked the doctor, a gleam of amusement showing on his face; for he had never found Bertha addicted to cutting speeches.

"She said that she did not want to get better, and I told her that it was miserably selfish of her to want to die when she was so useful, and everyone needed her friendship and advice so much. It was horrid of me, I know, but I felt as if I had to say it, and so out it came. Poor Eunice, she looked so startled and surprised; for I don't suppose that anyone ever dreamed of calling her selfish before."

The doctor burst into a shout of laughter. "Well done, Miss Bertha, I should not wonder if you have half-cured my patient for me, and if so you have earned my lasting gratitude. No one can even guess what a fight I have had for her life, and all because of this mistaken idea of self-sacrifice. Why, she had better have let the Government people send her to prison for embezzling moneys entrusted to her care; for at least she would have got enough to eat then, and this illness would have been averted."

But Bertha was almost reduced to tears by the thought of how disagreeable she had been, and was not even comforted by the doctor's congratulations on the drastic measures she had used to bring Eunice to a more reasonable frame of mind. The thought of the things she had said haunted her all the way home, making her silent and absorbed, instead of bright and merry from the pleasure of the gifts she had been out to bestow.

Grace believed that she was tired, and so refrained from asking her any questions. But after Mrs. Smith had gone home and the children had all been put to bed, Bertha plunged into the story of her trouble, and told Grace all that she had not been able to tell the doctor, of how Eunice had asked her to be kind to the brother so that the sister might die in peace. And then Grace did what the doctor had done, she laughed and laughed until Bertha began to feel afraid that she would do herself an injury.

"I can't see anything very funny in it myself, but that is because I lack a sense of humour, perhaps," Bertha remarked, almost disposed to feel affronted at having provoked so much mirth.

"Oh, my dear child, do forgive me!" cried Grace. "It is too bad to make fun of you. But the fancy picture of you attempting to console that dreadful Mr. Long for the loss of his sister was too much for me. Eunice must have been a little delirious, poor dear, or she would never have suggested such a thing."

"Then you don't think that it was wicked of me to refuse to make her happy, to let her die in peace?" said Bertha, drawing a long breath of relief, for it had been a real trial to her to refuse Eunice anything, and the pinched white face of the sick woman haunted her still.

"Why should you throw your life away at the whim of a sick woman who doubtless does not know what she wants?" said Grace, her voice unconsciously stern. "Do you know, I have been so afraid of asking rash things myself that one day, when I was fairly capable of knowing what I was about, I got Tom to draw up a sort of statement, in which I besought my friends to take no notice of silly favours which I might ask when body and mind were alike under the influence of sickness."

"But you have never asked for impossibilities," said Bertha.

"And I trust that I never shall. But I am thankful to hear you speak of it as an impossibility, Bertha; for I should never have forgiven myself, nor have been able to look Anne or Hilda in the face again, if that sort of settlement had been possible to you. Oh dear! oh dear! I think that poor Eunice must have been mad!" cried Grace.

"Well, it is settled once and for all, and there is no more need for you to think about it," Bertha replied soothingly, and then, in spite of herself, she found her thoughts back again with that stranger who had sat so helplessly in his boat, while she swam out to his rescue, and she wondered anew whether he would ever cross her path again, then grew angry with herself because her thoughts would wander so persistently in that direction.

CHAPTER XXI
Out of the Silence

THE new year was only a week old when there came a blizzard of such violence that for three days it could not be said to be light at all, and during all those hours it never ceased snowing. The little household at Duck Flats was entirely isolated, of course, and it would have gone hard with them in the matter of food if it had not been for the cow.

Fortunately, Bertha had some weeks before constructed a kind of tunnel between the house and the barn by walling up the snow on either side of the path, then laying some sticks of firewood across. On the sticks she had piled masses of the beaten, tangled straw from the ruined wheatfields, of which there was such a sad abundance everywhere, and then the snow had drifted on to the straw and completed the process of roofing in. So she was able to pass between house and barn in comfort, looking after the cow, the fowls, and old Pucker, which, with three lively pigs, made up the sum total of the livestock.

The great trouble in her mind was lest the kerosene barrel should run empty, because then they would be condemned to so many hours of doing nothing, and she wanted every moment of that mid-winter leisure for writing. It did not matter if the food was coarse and monotonous in kind, she and the children were hungry enough to eat almost anything that was eatable, and there had been sufficient saved from the big packing case of good things for Grace to have the variety of nourishment necessary for her.

The solitude of those days might well have driven anyone mad, but, strangely enough, Bertha minded it not at all this year, although last winter, when it was not nearly so bad, the isolation was almost more than she could bear. Grace was nervous and anxious on account of her husband, wondering and wondering, as she lay in her helplessness, where he was spending those blizzard days, and whether there was food to eat and fire to warm him.

The three days of storm were followed by two days of fog, so dense that the barn was not visible from the house, then came another day of heavy snow, which seemed to clear the air; for at night the barometer went up and the thermometer came down, until everything was crackling and sparkling with the frost. When the next morning came, the sun showed itself for the first time in a week, so, wrapping herself up warmly, Bertha went out for a breath of fresh air; for after a week of imprisonment between house and barn it was good to be outside once more.

What an awful desolation it was! As far as eye could reach on every side there was nothing but snow to be seen—snow, snow, snow—until sight grew dim and senses reeled before the glare of the unchanging whiteness.

She did not stay out long. It seemed better to bear the cramped confinement of the house than to face the dazzle of snow and sun outside. There was work to be done, too—the animals and the poultry had to be looked after, there was bread to be made, the house to be put tidy, and Bertha's time went by in a whirl of business. The short winter day began to draw in, and she was just going out to the barn to milk the cow and feed the stock for the night, when, chancing to look from the window, she was amazed to see a two-horse sledge approaching the house. It was not coming very fast, and it was so piled with things, that she supposed the horses must be tired.

A wild thought flashed into her mind that it must be Tom who was returning so suddenly, and she thought that he must have got some of the other members of the expedition to bring him over on their way to their own homes, or why this mountain of luggage? But she would not raise the hopes of Grace lest they might have to be dashed again later on; so merely saying that someone was coming, but she could not see who it was, she threw a shawl round her and ran out of the house.

The horses came at an easy walk right up to the door and stopped, then, to her dismay, she saw that there was no driver. What had happened? And where was the driver?

Bertha walked up to the horses, patted their heads, and fastened them to the veranda post pending enquiries, and then, dragging at the outer rug in order to cover them from the cold, she was appalled to see that there was a man lying underneath. A dead man he looked; but of course he might be only unconscious from the extreme cold. But what was she to do? And how could she, singlehanded, get a full-grown man out of the sledge and into the house in his dead or unconscious condition?

"But I must do it somehow; for he is a stranger, and we must know why he has come," she said to herself; then, stepping into the sledge, she took hold of the man by his shoulders and began to haul away at him with all her might.

His body was limp, and so she told herself that he could not be dead, but was probably only unconscious from the cold.

It was a matter calling for quick action, however; so she pulled and tugged with her utmost strength. It was a heavy task to get him out of the sledge, but when once that was accomplished the rest was easy enough, and in about five minutes she had flung open the door and dragged him across the threshold into the kitchen, which was so warm from the heat of the stove.

"Why, Bertha, what have you got there?" asked Grace in surprise, for she had heard nothing of the arrival, as the snow muffled all sounds.

"It is a man, and he seems in a very bad way. He is a stranger, too. Do you think I dare leave him while I go and put the horses in the barn?" asked Bertha anxiously. It did not seem right to leave the man in his unconscious condition, and yet it was downright cruel to leave the poor horses standing out in the bitter cold.

"Horses, are there? Did he come in a sledge?" asked Grace.

"A two-horse sledge, piled high with baggage of some description. I expect that I shall have a great difficulty to get the barn door open, so if I am rather long, don't be more worried than you can help. But if the man comes round before I get in, send Dicky to shout for me, will you, please?" said Bertha.

"Don't try to get the sledge into the barn; it won't snow again to-night, and if it does it will not matter. And can't you take the horses one at a time along your covered passage and into the barn by the little door?" Grace mostly saw the way out of a difficulty in a flash, and Bertha had often to be thankful for her quick grasp of a situation.

"Oh, I can do that, and it won't take me long, either. I was going to make a great effort to get the big doors open, and then I should have taken horses and sledge in that way. I won't be long, dear, and oh, I do hope the unknown will not bother you," said Bertha, departing in a great hurry to unhitch the two horses, which were getting restive with standing in the bitter cold. She had a horror of strange horses, and would never venture near them if she could help it. But to-night the situation was fairly desperate, and so she had to unharness the poor beasts, or leave them there to die.

They were very gentle and quiet, very eager for food and water, but never once showing the least symptom of a desire to kick or bite, and when they reached the barn they ranged up beside the manger as if they had been used to the place all their lives. She took care to tie them securely, so that there was no danger of their falling foul of old Pucker, which worthy animal had a rather disagreeable temper where strange horses were concerned.

Then Bertha hurried indoors again to see how it fared with the unconscious man who had been thrown so strangely on their care that night. "It will be horrid to have a stranger here to-night, and a man; a woman might have been bearable. Oh, dear, how awkward things can be!" she exclaimed, with a touch of impatience; for if she had to delay very long over trying to bring the senseless man round, she would have to do the milking by lantern light.

She found him lying on the floor near the stove just as she had left him, while Dicky industriously rubbed one hand, and Molly worked away at the other.

"Is his face frost-bitten?" asked Grace, as Bertha came to kneel down by the stranger.

"No, nor yet his hands; but he appears quite unconscious still. What shall I do? Do you think that I dare leave him lying here while I go and milk? I would not be long, and then I shall not have to leave you alone with him again," said Bertha.

"Yes, go and milk; he is quite harmless and inoffensive lying like that, but I shall want to have you here when he comes round again. Were the horses much trouble to you, dear?" asked Grace, as Bertha rapidly wound herself into her milking pinafore.

"None at all; they behaved like lambs, and walked to their places as if they were quite at home," Bertha replied.

"Did they? What colour are they?" asked Grace, with sudden interest.

"Oh, about the ordinary. They reminded me very much in build of the horses Tom sold in the summer, after we were hailed out, only they are not skittish, as our horses were, and they are so encrusted with frost that it is not easy to say what they are like." Bertha was moving off as she spoke, for she was in desperate haste to get her work done and reach the house again before the helpless man came to his senses.

The milking was put through at a rapid rate that night, and then, with a last look round to see that all the live creatures were comfortable for the night, she took up her pail of milk and went back to the house.

"Oh, Bertha, I am thankful that you have come!" exclaimed Grace, with a hysterical note in her voice. "That poor fellow gets on my nerves lying there, with no one but those children to look after him. I am so afraid that he will slip through our fingers."

"No fear of that," said Bertha cheerily, as she set the pail of milk aside and proceeded to give her very best attention to the stranger. "He is better than he was, there is more life and colour in his face; but oh, Grace, what an awful nuisance he will be, and what a pity it is that we cannot put him out in the barn to sleep with his horses!"

"I know, dear, but we must try to feel towards him as we should like anyone to feel towards Tom under like circumstances," said Grace softly, and then she went on, with a catch in her breath, "Do you know, when you came in at the door dragging that poor fellow with you, I really thought that it was Tom, and my heart came right up into my mouth; indeed, it was all that I could do to keep from screaming."

"I thought that it was Tom, too, when I saw the sledge come up to the door; but when I got outside I could see no driver at all, and then I was dreadfully frightened, for I thought that he must have fallen off. Then I pulled at the rug to cover the horses, and found that the man had fallen down in the sledge, and the rug had hid him from my sight."

Bertha was busy with the stranger while she talked. He was drawing deep, sobbing breaths, as if he were coming round, and the two children had got up, moving a little away, because they were rather shy and frightened, while the twins and Noll had fled to cover under their mother's couch, their three small heads peeping out from underneath like chickens looking out from under their mother's wing.

"Gee-up, and get along, can't you; gee-up, I say!" The man on the floor was plainly coming round, and his first thought was about his horses.

"Lie still for a little while, and then you will soon be better," said Bertha soothingly. She was relieved to find that the unknown spoke with the intonation of a man of education, and it was an unspeakable comfort to find that his voice was gentle and refined.

"I can't lie still. I'm to be paid according to the time it takes to get there, you know, and I have touched my last dollar; besides, the people at Pentland Broads are in sight of actual starvation—there was hardly any flour left in the place three days ago—and it was because no one else would face the journey that I got the job." As he spoke, the stranger tried to sit up, but he was so weak that he fell back on his pillows, which Bertha had piled under his head, and looked into her face with such a desperate eagerness, that she felt she must help him if she could.

"You can't get to Pentland Broads to-night, that is certain," she said briskly, "but you can start off at daybreak if you are well enough. I have put your horses in the barn and fed them, so though they are very worn out to-night, they will be quite rested by the morning."

"They must be hitched up again to-night, I tell you," said the stranger, with an imperative wave of his hand. "You have no idea how serious the need is over there. It is one of the places that were hailed out last harvest, and the poor things have been living from hand to mouth all the winter. Now their cupboards are bare—there is neither food nor fire nor light there by this time. I tell you I know, for there was a plucky chap—a doctor he was—got through to Hartley on snow-shoes to beg for supplies three days ago; but he was so near done that it is doubtful if he will recover. And I must go on; I tell you I must!"

The poor fellow's voice rose to a wavering shout, as he again made a frantic but ineffectual effort to rise. Dicky and Molly fled to cover in their mother's bedroom, and the three juniors under the couch burst into a united howl of terror.

"What is that noise?" asked the stranger, with a bewildered look coming into his eyes.

"There are little children here, and you have frightened them rather badly because you shouted so. I don't think that you are quite yourself yet," said Bertha. She was trembling so badly that she could hardly keep her voice steady, but for the sake of the others she must appear as brave and courageous as possible.

"Did I frighten the children? Oh, I am sorry, for I am downright fond of kiddies; but something has gone wrong in my head, I think; and, please, would you mind telling me whether there is one of you or whether sometimes you are two?"

Bertha gave a little jump of dismay. She really could not help it, for plainly the poor man was delirious, and whatever would she do if he became violent? She had heard that delirious people had very often the most tremendous strength, and whatever would happen if this man insisted on starting off for Pentland Broads in his present condition? But she need not have been afraid of any outburst of violence, for when her hand was off him and he attempted to rise, he dropped back again with a groan, and lay still, looking as if he were going to die.

"Give him some more milk, Bertha, quick, or he will faint!" said Grace urgently,

Bertha lifted up his head and managed to make him swallow some of the hot milk, and then he seemed to drop into a sleep of exhaustion.

"Is it not dreadful? Whatever shall we do?" asked Bertha, looking towards Grace, and feeling as if the situation were quite beyond her.

"We cannot do anything until morning, and then we shall have to be guided by circumstances," said Grace, who was thinking busily. "I am very much afraid that the poor fellow will not be fit to sit in the sledge and drive, so, unless it is blowing a blizzard, you will have to track out to Pentland Broads with the sledge; for it is too dreadful to think of the poor things being without food in this bitter weather."

"But that would mean that I should have to leave you alone," said Bertha, "and worse than alone, if I have to leave the man here also."

"It cannot be helped, and it will be daylight, although I would bear it all night, if necessary, rather than that those poor wretches should be without food. It is too awful to think of, and, of course, they do not know where it has gone astray," said Grace.

"You don't mean that you want me to go to-night, do you?" asked Bertha, with some alarm in her tone, for very much she doubted her ability to find her way across the waste of untrodden snow with only the stars for a guide.

"No, certainly you must not go to-night, but be ready to set off with the first gleam of daylight, and do not worry about me or the children while you are away. Divine Providence always takes care of those who cannot help themselves, and I am not afraid," replied Grace.

"He seems to have fallen asleep now," said Bertha. "Oh, Grace, whatever shall we do if the poor fellow is going to be ill on our hands?" and she bent over the figure on the floor with a keen anxiety in her heart.

"Don't worry about it yet, dear. After all, the worst troubles are often those that never come, you know. Get the children off to bed early to-night, so that you can have some sleep yourself, and then you will be more fit for whatever to-morrow may bring in the shape of care and toil."

Bertha sighed impatiently. She lacked the cheerful courage of Grace just then, and the condition of the man on the floor worried her dreadfully.

"THERE WAS A MAN LYING UNDERNEATH"

CHAPTER XXII
The Errand is Done

BERTHA had no chance of going to bed that night, and very little opportunity for lying down either. The stranger was very ill, and, although there was little that she could do to relieve him, she could not leave him tossing wildly to and fro; for he was only lying on a rug by the stove, and the night was so bitterly cold, that she was afraid that he would freeze if he became uncovered from his wrappings and the fire went down. So she stayed in the kitchen the long night through, sitting in the rocking chair and dozing fitfully, waking with a start each time the sick man's moans rose to cries of pain, and doing her best to soothe him by such ministrations as were possible.

She was very, very tired, and the cares of the morrow rose like an armed host to menace her peace, even when, but for disquieting thoughts, she might have slept. When she did fall into troubled slumber she would fall to dreaming of the hunger-stricken community at Pentland Broads, and then would wake in a perspiration of trouble and pray that morning might come quickly; so that she might set off to relieve the suffering by driving the load of foodstuff to the store.

There was no fear of her oversleeping when morning came. Long before daylight stole tardily over the white wastes, she was out in the barn with her lantern, feeding the horses and milking the cow; then, coming indoors, she gave the children their breakfast, made a pretence of a meal herself, and, attending to Grace, who could manage the business of putting the food in her mouth herself now, if it were only put quite ready for her, and stood within reach of her hand.

The sick man had sunk into a deeper slumber, and seemed to be out of pain. Bertha lifted his head and contrived to make him swallow half a cupful of hot milk, but when she put his head back on the pillow he seemed faster asleep than ever, and she could only hope that he would remain in that condition until she returned from Pentland Broads. Then she made up the fire, so that it would last without being touched, and fitted a wire guard right round the stove, so that there might be no danger of accidents. It was an awful trouble to her to go away and leave that helpless household of invalids and infants alone with a fire in the stove; but it would have been far worse to have left them without a fire in such severe weather, and so she had to face the risk and not worry about it more than she could help. Then she brought out the horses, hitched them to the sledge, put a saddle on Pucker and tied the old horse to the back of the sledge, slipped on a big coat, and, stepping into the sledge, set off on her journey.

There had been no more snow in the night, and for a while she followed the marks of the sledge which had been made when the horses brought their load to Duck Flats on the previous night. She did not have to break away from them until she was halfway to the end of her journey, and could see right away on the edge of the horizon a few hummocks and mounds in the snow, which stood for the cluster of houses at Pentland Broads.

"It is funny that he should have turned off here," she said to herself, as she left the trail made by the sledge runners and took a bee-line across the snow for the houses. "It really looks as if the theory of Grace must be right, and these are our horses which were sold in the summer. Oh, dear, I wish that I were not so stupid about recognizing things, and then I should have known whether these were the horses or not."

It was fine going this morning: the snow was frozen so hard, that the sledge skimmed the surface; the horses seemed very fresh, and galloped along at such a pace that ever so many times Bertha wondered whether they thought that they were doing a bolt; but it did not seem worth while to check them, as she was in such hot haste to get her journey done.

There was no chance of judging distance across that dazzling field of snow. The houses looked so close, that it seemed to Bertha as if she must be within shouting distance, while she was still some miles away.

Her coming had been observed, too, and she saw two men coming out to meet her, and then it was that she took a sudden resolve: "I need not go the whole distance; even ten minutes' gain is important in my case," she muttered, and, when the two men were within speaking distance, she tugged and tugged at the lines until she brought the horses to a standstill.

One of the men coming towards her was Dan Semple, the storekeeper's son, and the other was a lad with red hair whom she did not know.

"Dan," she called, "Dan, make haste, and help me on to my horse, will you, for you must take the sledge to your father, and I shall get back all the quicker."

"Why, it's our lot of goods out from Rownton that we expected last night, and Miss Doyne driving it!" exclaimed Dan, in amazement. He was not a very nimble-witted youth, and the situation was beyond him.

"The horses brought the sledge to Duck Flats last night just as it was getting dark. The driver was lying under the robes unconscious, and he has not come to his senses properly yet, though he managed to tell me last night how badly you wanted the goods," said Bertha. "So I have left Mrs. Ellis with only the children to look after her while I drove the sledge over. But I want to go back at top speed, for I am most dreadfully anxious about them."

"I should just think that you would be," said Dan, while the red-haired youth ran to assist Bertha in mounting on to Pucker. "It was downright good of you to come, Miss Doyne; but what will you do about the driver? You've got enough on your hands without having a sick man to look after."

"Indeed I have, and I was wondering whether someone from here would drive a sledge over presently and bring him back. I would keep him if I could, for he looks shockingly ill; but what could I do with a sick man at Duck Flats, now that Mr. Ellis is away?" Bertha paused in her mounting and looked wistfully at Dan, as if mutely pleading to be spared this extra burden.

And she did not ask in vain. "We'll be over for him in a few hours, Miss Doyne, and we'll bring him back with us, even if he pegs out on the journey," said Dan cheerfully.

With a nod of thanks, Bertha gave Pucker a slap on the side, just to show the old horse that she was in a hurry and that he had better be in a hurry too, and then away they went at a pelting gallop across the snow, and were very soon a vanishing speck in the distance.

She was in a wild heat of worry—a scorching anxiety on account of Grace was upon her—and she was questioning whether she had done right in leaving home to drive the sledge to Pentland Broads, even though the people there were in actual want of food. Home duties should come first, and she had a feeling that she would never be able to forgive herself if anything bad had happened in her absence.

She had reached the place almost where the trail from Rownton joined the one from Pentland Broads, when she saw a sledge with two men in it coming rapidly from the direction of Rownton, and as one of them waved his arm to her to stop, she drew rein, and waited in fuming impatience until they should overhaul her. Then she saw that they were police, and suddenly her heart gave a great throb of fear, and her thoughts flew to Tom. Something bad had happened, she told herself, and the police were coming to break the news to her. So she sat rigid, like a figure carved in stone, with all the fuming impatience dropped away from her, whilst the horses with the police sledge came nearer and nearer.

"Have you seen a man with a sledge piled high with packages that look like provisions, the sledge drawn by two powerful brown horses?" asked the man who was driving, while the man at his side lifted his helmet in respectful salutation to Bertha. "The sledge must have passed somewhere in this direction either last night or this morning, we think."

"A sledge came to our house at Duck Flats last evening. It was drawn by two powerful brown horses, but the driver was lying unconscious in the sledge," answered Bertha, telling the same story which she had told to Dan Semple a short time before, and explaining to the police how she herself had left her helpless household to drive the sledge to Pentland Broads because of the food famine there.

"And the man, where is he?" asked the policeman, whom, from his appearance, she judged to be an inspector.

"I left him at Duck Flats asleep. He has been very ill all night, and I am very anxious to get back," she said, and, in spite of herself, there was a quiver of breakdown in her voice, although she was hugely relieved to find that the business of the police was with the sick driver and not with herself.

"Will you ride on, then, and we will follow, if the man is at your place? We must go there first, although it would seem as if there is some mistake, and this cannot be the sledge that we are looking for," said the inspector.

Bertha set forward, then, at the very best pace that she could get out of old Pucker. The fact of having two other horses pounding along behind him seemed to exhilarate the old horse to an astonishing extent, and he raced across the snow at such a rate that the police sledge was some distance in the rear when the solitary little house at Duck Flats showed on the horizon.

A sob of relief came into Bertha's throat as she drew nearer and saw that it looked all right. It was fire that she had been afraid of all through that journey out and home again, so well she knew how easily an accident might happen with only little children, a delirious sick man, and poor helpless Grace at home, and the fire going in the stove. She had been strung up to bear all sorts of things, and when she found the outside looking quite peaceful and all right, a sudden weakness assailed her, and for a few moments it was all she could do to keep her hold of the saddle to which she was blindly clinging, while old Pucker raced along as merrily as if the journey had only just begun.

That ridge in the snow was the paddock fence. She would be home in a few moments now, and already the horrible feeling of faintness was passing. She sat straight up on her saddle, and wondered what had made her so silly, when a sound reached her ears which filled her with terror. The children were screaming; she could hear them as she approached the house.

Riding right up to the door, she slid off and burst in at the door, coming upon a scene of indescribable confusion. The table, which stood in the middle of the room, and upon which she had left the children's breakfast spread, was lying on its side, while the crockeryware and food lay more or less in ruins on the floor, where also lay the sick stranger, squirming feebly, as if he had been trying to pull himself up by the table, and found the effort too much for him.

But the children in their fear had flung themselves upon their mother, shrieking and screaming with terror, while Grace herself was trying to pierce the din with her voice in order to reassure them, but was in a fair way of being suffocated; for the twins had cast themselves upon her, while Noll was clinging with both chubby hands to her head, his deep boo-oo-ooing in sharp contrast to the shrill squeals of Molly.

With one bound Bertha had crossed the room, and, scattering the children to right and left, slipped her arm under the head of Grace, which she lifted up into the air. For one terrible moment she thought that the helpless woman was going to faint, and instinct told her that if Grace fainted it would be the end. But the long minute passed, and then Grace managed to say feebly: "It needs a really strong sense of humour to appreciate a scene such as we have had."

"You poor, poor darling, how awful it must have been for you!" cried Bertha, with actual tears of pity coming into her eyes as she gently fanned Grace, taking no notice at all of the sick man, who still lay, feebly struggling to rise from among the ruins he had caused by his ill-advised efforts to pull himself up by the aid of the table.

"Dear Noll was the worst," said Grace, and now there was a weak gurgle of laughter in her throat. "He thought that there was safety with me if he only hugged me tightly enough, poor little man; and I could not make Dicky understand that I must have air. But you came just in time, Bertha."

Just in time! Something came up in Bertha's throat and half-choked her, and at that moment the inspector came into the room, but paused just across the threshold as if he were fairly staggered at the scene upon which he had stumbled.

"You see, there was a need for me to ride so hard," said Bertha to him, as she swung out her hand to call attention to the ruin of the breakfast table.

"Steady, there! What is the matter?" asked the inspector, turning his attention to the man, who was again making feeble attempts to rise, and, stooping, he lifted the poor fellow in his strong arms, then sat him gently in the rocking chair, after which he shut the door; for more cold was coming in than was good for anyone.

"I must get on. Don't you see that I have work to do?" said the sick man urgently. "And if I don't give satisfaction on this trip I shall get turned off, and then it will be starvation."

"Steady, there, steady, your job is going on all right!" said the inspector soothingly, but keeping his hand on the man in order to prevent him from falling out of the chair. Then he said to Bertha, in a low tone: "We must have been at cross purposes, I think, for this is not the man we are after. There is not much of the rogue about him, I fancy. But would you mind just stepping to the door and asking my mate to come in, then we will help you to clear up a bit, while we make up our minds what is the best thing to do for you and this poor chap."

Bertha went to the door and called the other man in, and then was amazed at the manner in which the two set to work and tidied up the disordered room, while she made coffee and broiled bacon to make them a breakfast, for they had had nothing since the previous night.

The children, their terror all gone, were making friends with the police, and Dicky was telling the inspector how useful he was at helping Bertha in the barn, now that his father was away, and then Molly chimed in with the story of her achievements; but Noll and the twins had gone to their usual cover under their mother's couch, and were surveying the scene from that safe vantage-ground.

Bertha prepared a small cup of bread and milk and approached the stranger, asking him if he could feed himself, or whether he would like her to do it for him.

"I can manage, thank you," he said, looking up at her with his languid eyes, and then he asked, "Will you please tell me where it is that I have seen you before?"

Bertha looked at him in surprise, and then remembering how ill he had seemed all night, she said gently, "I do not think that you have ever seen me until last night, only you were so bad then, that I expect that it seems as if it were a week or two ago."

He shook his head a little doubtfully, then replied, "I am sure that I have seen you once or twice before, only to-day I am so stupid that I cannot remember where it was. Now, will you please ask those men if they will help me hitch my horses to, and then I will be pushing on; for I must get to Pentland Broads as soon as possible."

"But I have driven the sledge over for you; I went at dawn, and I have only just got back," she said gently, wondering if he were still a little off his head.

"You are very kind, but then you have always been kind, if I remember rightly," he answered, and then he frowned as if he were trying to recall that other time of which he had twice spoken.

"I think, Miss Doyne, that our best way will be to take the man with us," said the inspector, drawing Bertha out of earshot of the stranger. "If he is ill, we can take better care of him at our place than you can here, and I fear that it must have been very distressing to poor Mrs. Ellis to have had the worry of him here last night."

"It is very kind of you," said Bertha, looking up gratefully into the kindly face of the middle-aged inspector, and then she dropped her gaze suddenly, because her eyes had filled with tears of which she was ashamed.

"Oh, that is all in the way of duty, you know," he rejoined lightly, and then, going over to the stranger, he began to explain to him the advisability of getting on to Pentland Broads as soon as possible.

"You are the police, aren't you?" said the poor fellow, making as if he would rise to his feet, but falling back through sheer weakness. "Is it a warrant you have out for my arrest, or are you running me in on suspicion?"

"Neither; we are only trying to help you on your way, Mr.— Mr.—, by the way, you have not told us your name," said the inspector, in a tone of kindly forbearance.

"My name is Edgar Bradgate," replied the stranger, and again he tried to rise, but would have fallen if it had not been for the arm the inspector slipped round him.

"I think that we had better turn straight back to Rownton with Mr. Bradgate, and let the other business wait awhile," said the inspector to his subordinate, and then the two packed the sick man into the sledge and started off again, to the huge relief of Bertha.

CHAPTER XXIII
Something of a Mistake

"OH, GRACE, he has gone, really gone; now I shall be able to breathe freely again!" cried Bertha, skipping into the kitchen again after she had seen the sledge with the police and Edgar Bradgate disappear across the snow and vanish into the mist, which was beginning to obstruct the clear brilliance of the winter morning.

"Poor child, it has been bad for you," said Grace, "and yet, do you know, as the poor man sat in the rocking chair, I kept thinking what a nice strong face he had, and it was intellectual and good also. I should think that he was a man well worth knowing."

"Humph! Anyhow, I am thankful indeed to be spared his closer acquaintance," retorted Bertha, as she cleared away the breakfast which she had prepared so hastily for the police, and she was bustling to and fro, intent on getting the day's work through as quickly and as easily as she could make it go, when she heard a jingle of sledge bells, and a minute later up dashed a sledge drawn by two horses and driven by Bill Humphries, while Mr. Semple, the father of Dan, sat by his side, and appeared to fairly bristle with rage.

Bertha went out to meet them with a smile, and expected that Mr. Semple was at least going to be very grateful to her for having driven the sledge of goods over so early in the day; but, to her surprise, instead of the thanks she expected, and felt that she had honestly earned, Semple senior asked in a loud and angry tone:

"Where is that fellow who brought the sledge here?"

"Inspector Grant came over from Rownton, and finding how ill the poor man seemed, took him back to the barracks at Rownton, because he said that they could nurse him more easily than I could," said Bertha, and because she was offended at the lack of proper gratitude in Mr. Semple's manner, her tone was more cold and distant than her wont.

"I am downright disappointed to hear it," snorted the irate storekeeper, who seemed to be in a great state of indignation, "for I had promised myself the pleasure of punching the fellow's head and then rolling him in the snow, and if I could have added to that the chance of keeping him tied up in my barn for two or three days on short commons, I think that I should have been really happy, in spite of having had to go so short of food myself the last few days."

"The man could not help being unable to deliver the goods last night," Bertha reminded him, with considerable dignity in her tone. "He was quite unconscious from the cold when the horses reached here, and at first I thought that he was dead, as indeed he would have been but for the accident of his slipping down under the robes of the sledge, which luckily were most beautifully thick."

"Do you know what was in that sledge?" demanded the storekeeper, in a tone of extreme exasperation.

"Food supplies, so the driver said, when he came to himself a little last night. He told us how the doctor had made his way through to Rownton, and had said that Pentland Broads was hard pushed for food; so he had volunteered to drive a load through as quickly as possible, and when he found that he could not get on, he was in very great distress," Bertha replied, and her tone was offended still.

There was a cackle of unmirthful laughter from Mr. Semple, with a hoarse sort of explosion from Bill Humphries, and then the storekeeper said, "A regular first-of-April time we have had this morning, and no mistake about it. When Dan came driving that sledge to the door this morning we all swarmed about him like bees round a honey-barrel, and the women came running out of their houses for meal, and sugar, and tea, and all the other things we wanted so badly, but not a solitary eatable thing was there in the load anywhere, and all the packages that I have opened so far seem to consist of clocks, watches, cases of knives, dozens upon dozens of spoons, and a mess of cheap jewellery which would be dear at any price."

"But there must have been some mistake," protested Bertha, disposed to take the part of the stranger now, although she had been so very glad to get rid of him. "I know that the poor man thought that he was bringing food to you, because he was so pitifully anxious to get on, and he could not rest at all until I promised that I would drive it over this morning the very first thing. And I certainly should not have left Mrs. Ellis this morning as I did if it had not been that I was so anxious to bring food to you."

"Then, if it wasn't the chap who drove the stuff that blundered, I should like to get the one who did, and have him all to myself for about ten minutes. I fancy I could do a great deal towards curing shortness of memory or a taste for practical joking in that time," said the storekeeper grimly.

"It is a really dreadful business. Whatever will you do, Mr. Semple?" asked Bertha, who, although she did not much care for the storekeeper, was genuinely sorry for his present worry.

"My Dan and young Fricker, that red-headed chap, started for Rownton directly we found out how we had been had. The snow was hard this morning, you see, and would bear. It has been like walking through bran these last few days, and the trail hasn't got packed yet since the blizzard; but I doubt whether they will get back very easy, for this mist that is creeping over means a top thaw, if I know anything about it, with most likely some more downfall later on." Mr. Semple looked up at the sky as he spoke, or rather at the white mist which hid the sky from his sight.

"Is there anything that we can let you have, Mr. Semple?" asked Bertha. "We have enough flour for two or three weeks to come, and sugar and tea, also coffee. If any of it will be of any use to you, please take it."

"Very kind of you, I'm sure, and if Dan hadn't started for Rownton I don't say as I mightn't have taken some, just to keep matters going; but, as it is, why, we'll just go on eating corn porridge and molasses until the things turn up. It isn't very appetizing, but I dare say it is wholesome enough," said Mr. Semple, and then, refusing to come in, he was for turning round and driving back as fast as he could go, but Bertha stopped him, while she enquired of Bill Humphries how Eunice Long was getting on.

"She is picking up slowly. My wife says that she has been getting better ever since two days before Christmas, when you came to see her. She took a turn then, and she has really tried to get on a bit; so you did her a power of good, and if you don't take care you will be making the doctor jealous," said Bill Humphries, with his deep, rumbling laugh.

Bertha laughed also as she stood watching the two men driving away into the white mist. It was delightful to hear that Eunice was getting better, and that she herself had had some hand in it; although all that she had done was to scold the invalid for wanting to die. Then she went into the house and told Grace about the disappointing character of the goods in the sledge which she had driven to Pentland Broads that morning, and they laughed together over the absurdity of the blunder, although all the while they were genuinely sorry for the poor people who wanted stores so badly and still had to wait for them.

"Do you know, I should not be surprised if that is the sledge which the police were after," said Grace, with that swift putting of two and two together which was so characteristic of her. "I expect that somehow in the heavy weather the sledges must have got mixed, and the man that was here—Edgar Bradgate, I mean—hitched his horses to the wrong sledge at some stopping-place."

"But such a blunder would hardly be made by any man who had any sense at all," replied Bertha. "Why, he would see the difference in the sledge robes and the fittings generally. I told you that those were really beautiful sledge robes; they were lined throughout with wolf-skin, and were as warm as could be. I felt myself in the lap of luxury all the way to Pentland Broads this morning, only I couldn't enjoy it because of my worry about you. I wondered then that a mere freight sledge should be so well turned out."

"I fancy that the blunder was made because, poor fellow, his sense was so far gone. He looked to me like a person who was in for a very sharp attack of influenza, and as a rule people in that condition are not very discriminating," said Grace.

"Well, at least our part is done, and we are out of it, which is something to be grateful for," said Bertha, and then she had to hurry off to the barn and put in an hour and a half of work there, which should have been done much earlier, but for the enforced journey and all the other delays which had eaten into her day so far. She was most dreadfully tired, having had but so little sleep on the previous night; but there was so much work to do, that she had no time to give way to her feelings, until night came round again and ended the long day of toil.

But it was destined that she should have one more surprise before she went to sleep that night, only this was a wholly joyful one.

She had been in the farther bedroom, putting the twins and Noll to bed, when she heard a squeal of amazement from Molly, with a shout of "Mummy! Mummy!" from Dicky, and, thinking that something must have gone wrong, she ran back to the kitchen, and there, to her amazement, was Grace sitting erect on her couch, holding fast to the edge of the little bookshelf, by which she had contrived to pull herself erect.

"Bertha! Bertha! Look at me!" cried Grace, in an ecstasy of joy. "I did it myself, all myself; the children did not help me at all. And oh, I am so proud of it!"

"And so am I. Why, it is just splendid, and at this rate you may be able to stand on your feet by the time that Tom comes back," said Bertha, as she hastened to put a pillow behind Grace, which would allow her to sit without holding on to the shelf.

"It is lovely to survey the world from such a giddy height after having been on my back all these months," said Grace, and then her voice grew wistful as she went on, "I wonder where poor dear old Tom is to-night, and whether there is any instinct to tell him that I am so much better?"

"He may be home soon now, unless indeed they have a camp, which they cannot leave until the snow breaks," said Bertha. "But it is pretty certain that they cannot do much prospecting of any sort or kind in this weather."

"I do not think that he will be here until the snow is gone. I never seem able to see him coming before then," Grace replied, with the far-away look in her eyes which always came there when she spoke of her husband.

The next day it was blizzard again, and nearly another week wore itself out before news of the outside world reached the isolated household at Duck Flats.

Then it was Dan Semple and young Fricker who drove over with the mail, which had found its way, after many delays, to the post office at Pentland Broads. They had news also, and were eager to tell it as they sipped the hot coffee which Bertha insisted that they should come in and drink.

"I should just think that we did have a journey back from Rownton!" said Dan, in his jolly, boyish voice. "We should have been frozen to the sledge, I guess, if it hadn't been for Fricker's red hair; but, you know, they say that people with hair that colour never suffer from frostbite, so I kept as close to him as I could get, and that is how I escaped, and of course he was as warm as toast, lucky dog!"

"I hope that you won't believe all he says, Miss Doyne," said Fricker, blushing like a girl. "But it was really an awful journey, and it was next door to a miracle that we got back all right with the sledge."

"Did you ever find out how the mistake came about?" asked Bertha, as she plied the two boys with more hot coffee and oatmeal cakes.

"We have made a pretty good guess at it," said Dan, "but we shall have to wait until that chap Bradgate is on his feet before the mystery is cleared up, I suppose. When the police came over and took possession of that sledge which you drove to our place, they said that a sledge laden with foodstuffs had been found at old man Holman's place over beyond West Creek. Holman is rather a shady customer, and he does not always speak the truth either; so of course we don't know quite how much to believe of his story, and how much is merely trimming, so to speak. The old fellow says that on the night before Bradgate turned up here a man came to his place to put in for the night. The sledge was run back under the shanty—for it threatened more snow—and the man, who seemed very queer, came indoors, sat awhile by the stove, and then went to lie down on a lump of straw at the end of the shack, which is all the bed that old man Holman's lodgers ever get. Very soon afterwards another sledge came along, this time with two men, and it was run into the shanty in front of the first, and the horses being put in the barn, the men came indoors to supper."

"And a jolly good supper it was, too, according to old man Holman," broke in Fricker, who was not disposed to let Dan do all the talking. "The old fellow said that the two men had brought their supper with them, and there was potted beef and fowl, cheese, ham, canned tongues, and I don't know what besides, and drink enough to drown anyone. At any rate, it about drowned Holman's wits; for when they took to card-playing after supper they cleaned the old man out of every cent piece he had got. Then I suppose they all went to sleep, being thoroughly tipsy, and they slept longer than they meant to do, for it had been daylight a good long time when they woke up, only to find that the man who had got there first had hitched his horses to the wrong sledge and had gone off with it."

"Ah, that was because it stood first, I suppose," said Bertha, laughing at the discomfiture which must have overtaken the other men when they found their mistake out.

"Just so," said Dan, breaking in now, because Fricker was just then busy with his coffee-cup. "And the first man, who was Bradgate, was not over-clear in his head, poor chap; he evidently didn't know anything about the sledge which came after his, and so hitched on to the first one and started with it. The men were in a royal rage when they found their sledge was gone, and threatened to shoot old man Holman for not having guarded their property better. But he isn't the sort to take a thing of that kind in a very lamb-like spirit, so they got as good as they gave, and a little better; for the old fellow happened to have a shooting-iron handy, and he whipped it out and held up the pair of them. They climbed down a bit then, and said that they would ride after the sledge and make the other fellow give it up; but old man Holman, having got the drop on them, decided that he might as well get the money back which they had won from him overnight, so he told them that they might go when they had handed him over the money which they had won overnight by cheating. He had been wiser, though, if he had let well alone, for when he allowed them to put their hands in their pockets to get out the money, what they did was to pull out a couple of barkers, and then, of course, being two to one, old man Holman was done, and they rode off with his money in their pockets, and that is the last he has seen of them."

"What an extraordinary story!" exclaimed Grace, who was sitting up on the couch this morning, well backed up with pillows, but looking much more like herself. "I wonder the men have not tried to get their sledge again, for I suppose the contents must have been valuable."

"Very valuable," replied Dan. "Why, there was enough cutlery and clocks, watches and that sort of thing to have stocked two or three shops, and the marvel is where they could have got it from. It is supposed to have been stolen, and the police were on the trail after it, because their suspicions had been aroused. They have got it now at the Rownton Police Barracks, and are waiting for someone to come forward and claim it; and they are also waiting for Bradgate to be well enough to tell them what he knows, and if he should happen to peg out without getting better, they will have to go without knowing, I guess."

"Oh, I do hope he will get better, for I did like his face so much," said Grace, and then she asked Dan Semple about his mother, and charged him with a message for Eunice, while Bertha listened to young Fricker, who was telling her about his home in Halifax, and how he downright ached sometimes for a sight of the dear old folks down east, and a sniff of the wind from the sea or a fierce Atlantic gale.

"Why, I am from Nova Scotia too, and I am just horribly homesick for the dear old place sometimes!" said Bertha, with kindling interest in the red-haired boy, who had such pleasant manners and seemed so eager for friendship.

"Well, Fricker, my boy, I guess we must get, or the old man will think that we have started on a holiday tour," said Dan, reluctantly preparing to depart.

"May I come again, Miss Doyne, and talk about Nova Scotia?" asked Fricker eagerly, as Bertha came to the door to see them off.

"Of course you may come," she said, laughing at him in a cheerful elder-sisterly fashion. "Do you think that we have such an endless rush of visitors out here that we are simply sick of seeing fresh people?"

"No, I don't, but I do think that you are awfully brave to stick through a winter in such a place. Why, it would be more lively in prison!" exclaimed the boy from Nova Scotia.

CHAPTER XXIV
A Revelation for Bertha

THE weeks of winter dragged on; January wore itself out in fierce storms. February was a month of keen frost and bright sunshine, which reduced Bertha to the infliction of wearing coloured spectacles to keep from going blind, and then March came in with lengthening days and stormy winds which howled across the wastes, but bore on their gusty breath a welcome hint of the coming spring.

It had been a busy winter for Bertha. Time for writing had been made whenever other duties were not pressing, and her success had justified the time she had spent on the task. Four stories had been sold, and although three others had failed to find a market, she already knew enough about the literary life to feel sure that the setback of their rejection might be for her ultimate good. Meanwhile, she was intent on getting her first book into shape, although she guessed that it would be next winter before she could hope to finish it. All the same, it was something to work for and hope for, while already she was happy in thinking that she had really achieved something. The few dollars she had earned would keep her in pocket money until Tom would be able to pay her a salary again.

The joyfulness of feeling that she had found her work in the world and that she was of so much use, that one family, at least, would find it hard to do without her, was so great, that she was entirely content, and would not have changed places with anyone. Her letters to her sisters were so vigorous, bright, and breezy, that neither Anne nor Hilda could in the least understand the change in her, as their replies abundantly testified.

It was the last Sunday in March when Mrs. Smith drove her two children over to Duck Flats to spend the morning with Grace, so that Bertha might go to church. It was the first time since Christmas that Bertha had had a chance to go to meeting, and so the occasion was very much in the nature of a festival.

The morning was brilliantly fine, and on the south side of the house the icicles were melting in the sun, although when night came again it would most likely freeze as sharply as ever. Dicky and Molly were in wild spirits, for they were going to church with Bertha, and the three tucked themselves into the sledge and set off in good time, for they would not risk being late on an occasion like this. Somehow Bertha's thoughts kept going to that Sunday last summer when she had taken the children to church, and Eunice had been so sure that disaster was coming. How soon the storm had come after that, and how truly awful the disaster had been!

Bertha shivered as she looked at the gleaming white landscape and thought of the bright hopes which lay buried underneath the snow, and she found herself hoping that Eunice would have no forebodings of evil to spoil this Sunday as it had done the other. But when she reached Pentland Broads it was to find that Eunice had gone to a distant farm to spend the day, in order that the mother of a large family might be able to go to church with her husband.

"Some of us would hardly get a chance to put our heads outside our doors all the winter, if neighbours and friends were not kind to us," said Mrs. Jones to Bertha, in explaining the reason why Eunice was not at home.

"Everyone seems to be kind to each other here, I think," said Bertha, and was conscious of a huge relief, because there was no Eunice present to foretell disaster. Of course it was very silly of her to be afraid, and at any other time she would have been really glad to see Eunice, who was her only close friend at Pentland Broads among a large number of acquaintances.

The service was over, and Bertha was tucking the sledge robes round the two children, when young Fricker came rushing up to her in a great state of excitement.

"Oh, I say, Miss Doyne, I am glad to see you here this morning. I spotted you in meeting, and thought my eyes were playing me a trick. I should have come over to see you this week, but as you are here this morning, why, I can tell you now. You remember that poor chap Bradgate who was taken bad on the sledge?"

"Oh, is he dead?" cried Bertha, in a tone that was much more tragic that she knew.

"No, I should say that the fellow has as many lives as a cat; at any rate, he has not come to the end of them yet," returned Fricker, with a laugh, and then he pulled a thick letter out of his pocket, which he handed to Bertha. "But I want you to take this home with you and read it. You can return it at any time, only I think that it will interest you, because it turns out that Bradgate comes from Nova Scotia, and he has been about as all-round unfortunate as falls to the lot of most men."

"How funny that there should be three of us here so close together, and only to find it out by accident that we all hail from Arcadia!" said Bertha; and then she asked, with a little hesitation in her tone, "I hope that Mr. Bradgate is really better now?"

"He'll do, I fancy; but it beats me to think that he has been lying ill at Rownton all this time and I have never been near him, when, so to speak, he was one of my own people. I feel downright mean about it, though of course

I did not know. However, I shall go over and see him next week if I can get away, and then I can give him my mother's message that she sent in that letter," and Fricker nodded towards the letter which he had given to Bertha.

"But if this concerns Mr. Bradgate, would you not rather that he saw it first?" she asked.

"I should not show him the letter, and the message I know by heart. You keep it, Miss Doyne, until I come for it. Hullo! this old horse of yours wants to run over me, and I'm too valuable to be turned into road metal just yet, so good morning!" Fricker stood aside and raised his hat as old Pucker dashed ahead, kicking up the snow in a fashion suggestive of a five-year-old, and actually squealing with delight at being in motion again.

Bertha tucked the letter into the inside pocket of her coat, and thought no more about it just then. The sun beat down in dazzling brilliancy, and her eyes ached from the glare, despite her coloured spectacles. But it was good to be out in the keen fresh air, and to know that the long winter was nearly over.

Dicky and Molly chattered like two young magpies all the way home, and if Bertha answered them in an abstracted fashion they did not notice it, so there was no great harm done, and she was able to enjoy the peace and rest of the long, monotonous drive in her own fashion. Mrs. Smith would not stay for dinner because her husband would be expecting her home, and when she had gone, Bertha's first business was to get the midday meal ready, though by this time it was long past midday, and breakfast was a dim and distant memory.

Then came the delicious rest by the fire in the afternoon, while Grace told the children Bible stories, and Bertha had nothing to do but lean back in the rocking chair and think her own thoughts. The funny thing was that she did not then remember the letter which Fricker had given her; but then she was not thinking about him, or indeed anyone at Pentland Broads. It was later, when she had donned her working pinafore and gone out to the barn to milk the cow and feed the animals, that she suddenly remembered that the letter was still in the pocket of her coat.

"How stupid of me to forget! But then I have been stupid more or less all day to-day, I think," she said to herself, as she pulled down a great armful of swamp hay for the cow, saw that Pucker was getting a comfortable supper, and attended to the other things which had to be done on Sunday as well as every other day in the week.

"I have brought a letter home to read, and I am going to forget all about it again unless you help me to remember," she said to Grace, when she went in with the milk pail.

"I will not let you forget; and in return for my kindness in reminding you I shall want to see the letter, or at least to hear it read, unless indeed it is very particularly private," replied Grace.

"It cannot be that, or Mr. Fricker would not have given it to me to read," said Bertha. "I thought it was rather funny of him to bring it to me, but he seems to think that because we both come from Nova Scotia we ought to have a great deal in common. For my part, I don't see that it follows; but he is such a nice, friendly boy, that it is too bad to snub him. And I fancy that he is homesick too, poor lad, so I am obliged to have a soft corner in my heart for him."

"That is undoubtedly good for you. It makes your sympathies wider, and you can save the snubbing for Mr. Long when he comes home again. Fricker is happily too young to need it," laughed Grace.

It was not until the children were all in bed that Bertha fetched the letter from the pocket of her thick driving-coat and, sitting down by Grace, proceeded to read it aloud.

It was a long epistle in a woman's handwriting, signed Mary Fricker, and commencing "My dear son". The first page was devoted to small items of family interest, just those things which a homesick boy would love to hear about, and then Mrs. Fricker plunged into the chief interest of her letter.

> "I was very much interested by your letter telling us about the shortage of food at Pentland Broads in the blizzard. That girl Bertha Doyne was fine and courageous to leave such a helpless household to drive the sledge over for you, and it must have been maddening indeed to discover that it was not foodstuffs after all. I am glad to hear that she comes from Nova Scotia. It is fine to think that our little state can produce real live heroines as well as a fictitious Evangeline. Now, I am going to tell you something which will amaze you, and that is, the Edgar Bradgate who got so mixed as to the sledges is from Nova Scotia also, and, though not actually your kinsman, is so nearly connected with our family that we may almost consider him one of ourselves. He is stepson to Cousin Fanny's husband, whom you do not know, but who is a very good fellow. His name is Mallom, and he came over to see us yesterday, when he told us of Edgar's long illness at the police barracks at Rownton. He told us, too, of some of the things that unfortunate young man has battled through, and really it made my heart ache. It seems that, when Edgar was of age, there was a little money to come to him from his dead mother's estate. This he was induced to invest in a company which speculated in land and real estate of various kinds. They gave Edgar employment as

a travelling agent, and he was abroad a great deal in the interest of his firm. For a whole year he was in Peru, then he went to Australia, and afterwards he was for a long time in Prince Edward Island. But there was treachery somewhere; the promoters feathered their own nests at the cost of the agent and the shareholders. After the company was wound up there was a meeting of shareholders at Paston, at which Edgar was present, and he was set upon by the infuriated people, who would persist in believing that he was entirely to blame, although he was really innocent, and very much the victim of the rascally promoters. He would have been severely mauled, perhaps even killed, if he had not succeeded in slipping away in a boat, intending to row himself some distance along shore and then to strike inland to reach the rail. But he was always the most unfortunate of creatures. His boat got wedged in those Mestlebury rocks which they call the Shark's Teeth, and he himself would have been drowned if it had not been for the pluck of a girl—a poor fisher girl, I think she was—who swam out with a rope to his boat, and so he was towed to safety. It took almost his last cent to reward the girl for what she had done for him, and he had to walk seventy miles to Mr. Mallom's house, earning his food by doing chores, or going hungry when he could not get a job. I wish that you would cultivate his acquaintance, my dear boy, for he is the sort of man it is good for a fellow to know—undaunted in disaster, falling only to rise again, he is bound to succeed in the long run. It is easy to see how much Mr. Mallom thinks of him, and the pride he has in him. But Edgar Bradgate is proud, and rightly so. He will not live on his stepfather, but will make his own way in the world or starve, and that is the right spirit to show."

"Oh, Grace, what shall I do? To think that I have been keeping Mr. Bradgate's property from him for so many weeks, and he so poor; it makes me feel unutterably mean!" cried Bertha, with actual tears in her eyes, as she broke off from reading her letter. "But why, oh why did he not try to find me out to ask for his coat and what was in it?"

"I should not be surprised to know that in the trouble of having to escape in that fashion from the angry shareholders, he entirely forgot that he had left his valuables in an outside coat; it might even be that he forgot he had a coat with him at all. A man in peril of his life twice in one day might be forgiven a lapse of memory like that," replied Grace, whose face showed a little pucker of anxiety, although she tried to speak as cheerfully as usual.

"Then I must remind him of it as speedily as possible, for no one can even guess how utterly thankful I shall be to get the wretched things out of my possession. If I write a letter to him to-night, I may get a chance to post it before the week is out," said Bertha.

"But what can you say in your letter?" asked Grace, and now the pucker of anxiety showed more plainly than before.

"I think that I shall tell him straight out that I have valuable property belonging to him, and that the sooner he fetches it away the better I shall like it," Bertha answered shortly, for the whole thing got upon her nerves.

"Oh, don't do that!" cried Grace distressfully. "If you put a thing like that in black and white, I shall never dare to be left alone again, for I shall always be afraid that someone will come along to try and rob the house. As it is, there is no danger at all; for the most optimistic of thieves would hardly expect to find anything worth carrying away in the house of a hailed-out farmer."

"What can I say, then?" asked Bertha. "You see I must ask him to come and fetch his property away, as I could not possibly send valuables like that through the post."

"Could you not write to him and ask him if he would kindly come over to see you as soon as he is able to leave the police barracks? You might say that you had news of importance for him which you could not very well put in a letter. That would commit you to nothing, and if anyone else read it they would not be unduly enlightened," said Grace.

"I might do that, certainly, although I should think that he will be mightily amazed, and perhaps a little disgusted, at receiving a letter of that description from a girl he knows nothing about," said Bertha, shrugging her shoulders; for the letter written by Mrs. Fricker to her son had somehow left the impression that Mr. Bradgate was the sort of individual to be approached with respect.

"He will be surprised, probably; but as Mrs. Fricker speaks of him so highly, he is probably a gentleman, so he will do as you ask him, without unpleasant comment, and really I do not see how else you can hope to see him, unless you ask him to come here. Would you like to get Eunice to come and stay with me while someone drives you to Rownton?" asked Grace.

"That would certainly be simpler than dragging a man who is an invalid so many miles across the snow," said Bertha.

"Write your letter to Eunice instead, then." Grace had quite an eager note in her tone now, for in her way she was quite as eager as Bertha to get rid of that little case of dull-looking stones which had been in the house so long.

Bertha wrote the letter, but it was Wednesday before there was any chance of getting it sent to Pentland Broads, and it was the following Sunday before she received a reply, and then Eunice wrote that it would be a week before she could get away, as Mrs. Humphries was in bed with bronchitis, and there was no one else to take the post office from her shoulders.

"It seems as if I were fated to keep those wretched stones," said Bertha, when she had read the letter from Eunice.

"Only one more week to wait, dear, so have patience," replied Grace cheerfully, and neither she nor Bertha even dreamed of all that case was to cost in care and trouble before it reached its rightful owner.

CHAPTER XXV
Disappointment

BEFORE that week was out, a howling storm of wind and rain swept across the prairie, and for three whole days it raged without ceasing. There was discomfort in plenty for a little while in the small house at Duck Flats; for the melting snow, piled high against the sides of the house, found its way through various ill-stopped crevices, streaming through the walls in little trickles of wet, which in time became big puddles of water on the floor, despite the constant activity of Bertha in wiping them up. The children took bad thaw colds, which was not to be wondered at, seeing that from the time they dressed in the mornings until they went to bed at night they were damp-footed from running about in the half-melted snow. But this was a yearly occurrence, and Grace was not unduly worried by it all the time that the colds could be kept well in hand, although it added not a little to the daily burden of work and care which rested upon Bertha. However, the snow would soon be gone at this rate, and then the discomfort would be over.

Meanwhile, there was the smell of spring in the air, and that in itself was something of a compensation for the misery of the dampness, the dirt, and the dismal look of everything indoors and out. At last Eunice succeeded in getting away, and Bill Humphries drove her over to Duck Flats one mild afternoon, when the brown earth was showing in patches here and there.

"It was good of you to come to-day; now I can get away early to-morrow morning," said Bertha, and she was just going to turn from Eunice in order to arrange with Bill Humphries to come over in the morning and drive her to Rownton Police Barracks, when Eunice said to her, with a laugh:

"It is not to-morrow morning that you are going, but in about two hours, so you had better make haste and get ready, while I take hold of things here and get used to the babies. I expect that there will be sadness and sighing with the twins and Noll, but they will soon get used to me; and Dicky and Molly will be a great help in letting me down gently into the bosom of your big little family."

"But I can't go to-night; I cannot be spared for two nights away," objected Bertha.

"My dear, you can be spared for a week if it is necessary," replied Eunice quietly. "The fact is, Mr. Humphries has business of his own in Rownton to-morrow, only he must get there early, so he would rather take you back to-night, which will save him two hours, perhaps more, in the morning. And having business of his own, he will be able to take you to Rownton without charging you a cent, which is a consideration in these poverty-stricken days."

"It is, indeed," laughed Bertha, "although I feel quite rich just at the present moment; for a dear, kind editor has seen fit to pay me fifteen dollars for a story, and I feel about an inch taller in consequence."

"How delightful!" Eunice patted her on the back in kindly congratulation. "In your place, Bertha, I am afraid that I should be so tall as to topple over from sheer giddiness at having reached such a lofty height. But run away and make your preparations, child, while I go and explain the situation to Grace, and begin to take hold a bit."

Bertha was thankful that Eunice had not volunteered to come and assist her in dressing for the hasty journey, for it was necessary to hang the case of stones in a little bag round her neck under her clothes, and she did not want even the eyes of her friend to see that. The coat had been made into a bundle, which was rolled round with a piece of coarse canvas and securely tied with string.

"It will seem dreadful to be away from you, even for two nights, Grace," she murmured, when the time came to say goodbye.

"Don't worry, dear, it will do you good to be away, and you will come away with a load gone from your mind, and I shall have a load gone from mine also," answered Grace, who mostly contrived to put the best face possible upon any situation.

Bertha nodded; the relief would be tremendous. She had felt so much like a thief with regard to that case of stones, and she was always afraid lest in some way she might lose them, which would be disaster indeed, since in such a case she would never be able to make the rightful owner believe that her intentions had been all right.

"It is just about time that you had a holiday, I should say," remarked Bill Humphries, when at length they were really under way, and the two horses were floundering along through the soft mud of the trail. "You have shown real grit in the way you have stood by the Ellis lot, and if that poor woman ever gets better she will owe her life to you, for she has had more than nursing. She has had peace of mind, and I guess that beats doctor's stuff into fits."

A thrill of positive rapture swept over Bertha. It was beautiful to think that she had been able to do things. And there was not in all the wide west a happier girl than she was, as the wagon bumped and swayed through the slush of the surface thaw, and over the chunks of frozen earth which lay beneath. She would have been flung out of the wagon half a dozen times before Pentland Broads was reached if it had not been that she clung tightly to the side of the wagon. How Bill Humphries managed to keep his seat, seeing that he held on to nothing but the driving lines, was a problem, but he did it; and after being jolted, bumped, and shaken until she was sore all over, the end of the journey was finally reached in safety, and Bertha received a riotous welcome in the household of the Humphries.

Still she was too restless and anxious concerning the outcome of her visit to Edgar Bradgate to-morrow to be able to really enjoy the little change of spending an evening in the house of someone else. To her it was a dreadful ordeal to pay a visit to a man whom she scarcely knew, remind him that she had at one time saved his life, and that she had not received the money which he had emptied his purse to leave for her. How horrible it would be to be obliged to tell him that, and yet for her own sake she must do it, since not even to a stranger would she care to stand in such an ambiguous position.

It was freezing hard next morning when the start for Rownton was made in the faint light of dawn, and for the first few miles the horses could scarcely keep their feet at all, while Bill Humphries slid and slithered along at their heads, pulling them up when they went down, scolding and encouraging at the top of his voice, and guiding them on to the roughest part of the trail, so that they might have the better chance to keep their feet.

Bertha, sitting perched in the wagon, had more ado than ever to keep herself from being pitched out of the wagon. But it would never do to risk being damaged, seeing what she carried tied in the little bag round her neck, so she swayed and jolted with the wagon, determined that she would not go over unless the crazy old thing really capsized, which luckily it did not. Then, after a couple of hours of this sort of progress, the sun came out with dazzling brilliance, the top ice speedily became slush, and the worst of the journey was over.

Then Bill Humphries clambered into the wagon to ride, for there was no sense in using his own feet so long as his horses were able to stand on theirs, and the first question he asked Bertha, after he had taken his seat at her side, was the part of Rownton to which she wished to go.

"I've got to drive to the depot, but the stores are at the other end of the town mostly, so I can go in that way and drop you there before I go on to the depot," he said, puffing a great deal from his recent exertions.

"It is the police barracks that I want to go to. Do you know which part of the town that is?" asked Bertha, and then flushed hotly because of the surprise which came into the face of her companion.

"I can drive you to the door, and as it is close to the stores, you will be all right until I come back from the depot," said Bill. "I shall have to give these critters a couple of hours for rest, and then we'll be starting back bright and early; for I don't somehow fancy having to slip and slide on the way back same as I've had to do coming. It is a leetle bit too exciting for an old fellow like me."

"I don't think that you must call yourself old, for no one could have jumped about more briskly than you did," replied Bertha, laughing softly at the remembrance of his gymnastic performances, as he helped his horses along that dangerous bit of trail.

"Well, I guess I am fairly nimble, though it is nearer sixty than fifty I am, and I've worked as hard as most men ever since I have been able to work at all," he answered, with a sigh of satisfaction, and then he went on, "A good many men would have made their pile by this time, I reckon; but though I have earned a good bit of money, it has never seemed to stick to me, so I guess that I have got to be a poor man to the end of the chapter. But I don't know as I would have that altered, provided that I can always pay my way, for the life of a poor man suits me best. It is what I am used to, you see, and there is a mighty deal more in habit than you may think. Ah, there is Rownton showing up on the edge of the prairie! Can you see it?"

Bertha shook her head. Her eyes were still weak from the glare of the snow, and the sunshine was trying her very much, for she had forgotten to bring the coloured spectacles, which, by the way, she most cordially hated. But there was not much to see in the town—a couple of grain elevators, straggling groups of houses dotted over the level plain, and the railway track running at this point due east and west.

The sight of the railway brought a lump into the throat of Bertha. She had not been to Rownton since the day that Tom had met her on her arrival from the east. Her misery of homesickness had been so dreadful that day as to make even the remembrance of it a pain. There were even tears in her eyes, which she was trying hard not to shed, and Bill Humphries, seeing them, wondered mightily what cause she had to cry. In fact, he wondered about it so much, that he forgot to be curious as to her errand at the police barracks.

Bertha's courage failed her when at length she stood before the long, low framehouse which was the headquarters of the Rownton division of the police, and instead of asking to see Mr. Bradgate she asked for the superintendent, who fortunately chanced to be at home. He had to keep her waiting for a few minutes, and during that time Bertha's courage was oozing and oozing, until she felt fit to turn and run away, if only running had been possible, or there had been anywhere to run to.

Inspector Grant, who was superintendent of the division, was one of the kindliest men alive, but his sympathies had been taxed to the uttermost during that winter following on the disaster to the wheat. So when he heard that Miss Doyne of Duck Flats was waiting to see him, he promptly made up his mind that it was some story of destitution, or fierce struggle with hardship, which he had to hear; and if he sighed a trifle impatiently he was surely to be forgiven.

When he entered the bare room, with its uncovered deal table well splashed with ink, and seated with wooden benches all round the walls, his first glance at the white face and trembling lips of Bertha confirmed his fears about her errand, and unconsciously added a deeper gravity to his manner.

"I am very sorry to have troubled you," began Bertha, in a faltering tone.

"Do not mention the trouble, Miss Doyne; I shall be only too glad to serve you if I can. The worry of it all is that my powers are so limited in this respect," said Inspector Grant kindly.

"Oh, we are not in difficulties of that sort," said Bertha quickly, understanding all at once that this big burly superintendent supposed that she had come to beg for money or food. "I have come because I want to see Mr. Bradgate, only somehow my courage failed me, and so I asked to see you first. Mr. Bradgate does not know me, or at least he would not remember me, and it is so awkward to be obliged to recall one's self to a person, and I thought that perhaps you would help me."

"Mr. Bradgate has very good cause to remember you, anyway, seeing that but for your kindly offices he must have perished from cold," said the inspector genially. He was feeling immensely relieved because it was no trouble of straitened means which had brought Bertha to ask his help that day. He felt himself equal to most other situations, but this long winter of struggle, following on the disaster of the harvest, had seriously impoverished him; since it was not easy for him to bear the sight of suffering while he had money in his pocket to relieve it.

"Oh, that was nothing!" broke in Bertha hastily. "And my errand to Mr. Bradgate has nothing to do with that either, but I have found out by a strange accident that he is the man whose boat was caught on the rocks at Mestlebury, in Nova Scotia, a year ago last fall, and something of value was left behind in my keeping which I have never been able to restore, because I did not know his name or where he came from. So I have come over from Duck Flats to restore his property to him, and—and I thought perhaps that you would help me to do it."

"I would with pleasure if I could, but Mr. Bradgate is not here now; he went away three days ago," replied the inspector.

A blank look came into Bertha's face, and a horrible desire to cry assailed her. She had been so delighted at the thought of getting rid of the stones, and she had faced all the discomforts of that journey to Rownton with a cheerful courage, just because of the relief it was to bring her. Now it would all have to go on again, the waiting and the uncertainty, and, to make matters worse, she had those horrid stones on her person, and must of necessity carry them home with her again.

Pulling herself together with a tremendous effort, she managed to ask quietly, "Can you give me his address, then? It is very important that I should be put into communication with him as soon as possible, or I would not trouble you."

"I am only too anxious to serve you in any way that I can, but I am very much afraid that Mr. Bradgate's address is what they would call in some circles a negligible quantity. He has gone to railhead to work, and it is very difficult to make sure that a letter will reach him, although of course you can try. You will also have to take your chance of a reply being forthcoming, as pens, ink, and paper are almost unknown luxuries in a railway construction camp," said the inspector.

A cold despair gripped at Bertha, and then an indomitable determination seized her to get rid of those stones at all costs, and she asked abruptly, "Where is railhead?"

"A few days ago it was at Wastover, about a hundred miles from Rownton, but it will have pushed on since then, and I expect that it will have nearly reached Brocken Ridge; it will stop there for a week or two, for there are three bridges to be built within the space of two miles, and that will take a little while," answered Inspector Grant.

"Can you tell me how long it will take me to get there, and how much it will cost?" asked Bertha, thinking ruefully of the fifteen dollars which she had received for her last story, and deciding that if it all had to go, she would have to manage somehow to do without any new frocks next summer.

"Ah, you think of going to find Bradgate for yourself?" The inspector's tone was grave, and Bertha read into it strong disapproval, which caused her to flush distressfully right up to the roots of her hair.

"I am afraid that there is nothing for me to do but to go," she said faintly. "If I cannot reach Mr. Bradgate by a letter, I cannot let him know that I have something of his in my possession which he ought to have; and, you see, he does not even know that I have it, so I must find him somehow."

"What is it? Or would you rather not tell me?" asked the inspector, with the same interest he might have displayed if it had been his own daughter who was faced with a difficulty.

Again Bertha flushed hotly. How horrid it was that she could not speak right out and have done with this stupid mystery! She would have done it, if she had been quite sure that she would be able to reach Edgar Bradgate and restore the stones to his possession; but for the thought that in spite of her efforts she might be obliged to take the case back to Duck Flats, when poor Grace would have to bear the added burden of knowing that some outside person was aware of the exceedingly valuable property in their possession.

The inspector saw her hesitation, and hastened to reassure her. "Pray don't trouble to tell me, Miss Doyne. I assure you that there is no need, and my curiosity was quite unjustifiable; but I thought that I might help you more effectually, if I knew the nature of the property you had to restore."

"I can tell you part of it, anyhow," said Bertha, with a rather watery smile, "then you will better understand the difficulties of my position."

"That must be as you please, only do not feel bound to reveal more than is convenient," replied the inspector, with a considerable lightening of his gravity; for Bertha did not look the sort of girl who would be likely to embark on anything indiscreet, and he was only too eager to help her in any way he could.

She nodded her head in a queer, shaky fashion and plunged into rapid speech. "On the day when Mr. Bradgate's boat was caught on the rocks at Mestlebury he was in great danger of being drowned, and I swam out with a rope to be fastened to the boat, which was afterwards towed ashore. But when I reached him and he helped me into the boat, I shivered so badly that Mr. Bradgate pulled a coat out from under the seat and told me to put it on, which I did. We were capsized before we reached the shore, and he was unconscious when we were helped out of the water, so I left him to the care of the fisher people, while I ran home just as I was. Then I was ill for two or three weeks, and one day, when I was better, I found his coat lying wet and horrible in the corner of the room where I had dropped it before I was taken ill. I suppose that my sisters in their hard work and anxiety had been too busy to sort up the muddle in the little room where I slept when I was well. I picked up the coat to shake it out and dry it, but something dropped from the pocket which worried me a great deal. As soon as I could I went to the fisher folk who had taken care of the stranger and asked for his name and address, but I could never get either."

"And it is the something which you found in the pocket that you wish to restore, I take it?" said the inspector quickly.

"Yes, and I shall have no peace until it is safely in Mr. Bradgate's possession," said Bertha, with a distressful pant in her breath.

The inspector frowned. He understood to the full the difficulties of Bertha's position, and he was not disposed to be lenient to the man who had brought the trouble about.

"If the thing found in the coat were so valuable, why did not the man come to enquire for it, also for his coat?" he asked grimly.

"That is what has always puzzled me so greatly until the other Sunday evening, when I read the letter which Mrs. Fricker, of Halifax, wrote to her son; but since then I have thought that most likely Mr. Bradgate forgot that he had had his coat with him in the boat at all, in which case, although he might search for it in other directions, he would not think of approaching me on the subject," answered Bertha, and then she poured into the ears of the sympathetic inspector the story of how Edgar Bradgate had emptied his pockets to reward her for helping him, and how Mrs. Saunders had kept the money, refusing to let her know the name or abode of the man with whom she so earnestly wished to communicate.

"The old lady was afraid of being bowled out, I expect," said the inspector, with a laugh, and then he asked Bertha to let him have an hour in which to consider what was best to be done.

"If you have any business in the town, go and do that and be back here within the hour, by which time I may be able to tell you whether it is possible for you to be sent to railhead, and how long the journey will take," he said.

"Thank you, very much," replied Bertha, as she rose from the wooden bench on which she had been sitting, and then she said nervously, "You will not let anyone know what I have told you about the something being of value? Mrs. Ellis says that she would never dare to be left alone if anyone knew, and that kind of worry is so bad for her."

"Your confidence is quite safe with me, have no fear. The police have to keep almost as many secrets as a lawyer, and to their credit be it said they mostly do keep them," he answered, as he bowed her out of the bare room and reminded her to be back within an hour.

She had not gone the length of two blocks, when she met Bill Humphries coming to meet her with a very bothered look on his face, and at sight of her he cried out in great concern, "Here is a pretty business—a blockhead of a fellow hauling rails ran into me and smashed one of my hind wheels, and I can't get the wagon back to Pentland Broads to-day! Whatever shall I do with you?"

CHAPTER XXVI
En Route

BERTHA gave a little gasp of surprise. An hour ago she would have been most dreadfully dismayed at such a disaster, but now it seemed like a providential chance which would admit of her going to railhead without seriously upsetting the plans of anyone.

"It is not so much what shall I do, as what you can do yourself," she answered slowly. "I thought that you said you must get home to-night, because you had some work to do."

"So I must, even though I have to walk every step of the way, although luckily that is not necessary, as I can ride one of the horses," he answered.

"Would you like me to wait in the town and drive the wagon home when it is mended?" she asked. "I could stay at Mrs. Smith's boarding-place, where I stayed when I came west, until Tom could meet me."

"If you could do that I'd be more obliged than I could say. But wouldn't you be afraid to bring the horse and wagon all those miles alone?"

"Not if you will leave me Jupiter to drive," she said. "I should be afraid of the black horse because it does rear so, but I could manage the other very well indeed."

"You are a downright brick of a girl, and I'll send young Fricker over to Duck Flats to-morrow to tell Eunice that she will have to hang on at your job until you can get back. And we will manage the post office somehow; there is not much business doing these days, that is one comfort under present circumstances," said Bill Humphries, with an air of huge relief. "I wish that you would just come along with me to Luke Moulden's and arrange with him about what time he is to have the wagon ready for you the day after to-morrow. My word, but you have taken a load off my mind!" Bill Humphries gave vent to a windy, gasping sigh as he spoke, and hurried through the slush of the badly made sidewalk at such a rate, that Bertha had some difficulty in keeping up with him.

It was not the wheel only which had suffered from the collision, but one side of the wagon was stove in also; and Luke Moulden scratched his head in a dubious fashion when told that he must have it done by the day after to-morrow.

"It is sprung and it is ratched, the panel is broke right through, and, goodness gracious, man! do you think that I can mend your old wagon by steam?" demanded Luke, as he walked round the derelict, surveying the damages which he would have to put straight.

"You will have to this time, and if you have to charge a leetle extra for making haste, why, that is not my fault; and seeing that the railway people have got to pay the bill, because it was the carelessness of their man what did the mischief, why, I shan't be so much upset as if it had got to come out of my pocket," drawled Bill Humphries, winking in the direction of the depot yard, as if it were all a very good joke indeed.

"Needs must, I suppose, when the old 'un drives," rejoined Luke Moulden, with a slow, rumbling laugh. "You shall have the job finished to time, even if I have to sit up both nights to get it through, and I'll hitch up for the young lady smart and early; for she won't want to get benighted on the road."

"I thought that I should manage him if I just happened to say he could charge a trifle more for getting it done quick," chuckled Bill, as he went back with Bertha along the muddy road to the stores, where he spent half an hour with her, arranging for the lading of the wagon and the sort of goods he wanted her to bring back; and, when this was done, he had to mount his horse and ride off to Pentland Broads at the best pace he could make, while Bertha, left to her own devices, went slowly towards the police barracks to see what arrangements Inspector Grant had been able to make for her.

She did not have to wait for him this time, but found that he was waiting for her, and there was a smile on his face which seemed to indicate that he had been able to manage to his own satisfaction.

"Well, Miss Doyne, I have got on better than I expected," he said cheerfully. "The wife of one of our men stationed at Brocken Ridge wants to go through to her husband, and she will take care of you on the way out to railhead, look after you while you are there, and see you safely on the cars for the return. I have got to write a pass for her, and I will write one for you also, then the journey will cost you nothing beyond your food and the bodily discomfort which you are bound to endure; for I warn you that the journey will not be exactly a picnic, as you will have to travel out on a freighter."

"How very kind you are!" she exclaimed. "I don't in the least mind the discomfort, if only I can get my errand done."

"Very well, be at the depot by six o'clock this evening, and I will step along to introduce you to Mrs. Walford; she is a very respectable sort, and will take proper care of you. If I had had any doubt about her, I should not have allowed you to go; for railhead is not a nice place for a girl, despite the efforts of the contractors to keep the construction camps clean and wholesome."

"I am not afraid," said Bertha simply.

"I don't believe that you are," he answered, smiling at her in a kind, fatherly fashion, "but that is all the more reason why other people should be afraid for you when duty calls you into questionable places. Now, don't forget it is six o'clock sharp, and be sure that you are at the depot in good time."

Bertha thanked him, and then made her way to the boarding house kept by Mrs. Smith, a little Irishwoman who had arrived at Rownton with the railway and stayed there ever since.

She received Bertha with a great demonstration of welcome, for no one who had ever spent a night under her roof was forgotten, and she declared that the prairie life must have suited the girl from the east, who had been so homesick, because it had made her so good-looking.

"It is rale beautiful that you have grown, my dear. Sure, but there is nothing to equal these lonely places for making the roses bloom in the faces of girls like yourself!" she exclaimed, taking Bertha by the shoulders and turning her round to the light.

Bertha flushed, and a happy light stole into her eyes. It had always been a secret trouble to her that she should be so plain and uninteresting, when Anne and Hilda had been so pleasant to look upon; therefore the feeling that someone thought that she was nice-looking warmed her heart and sent a glow of happiness through every fibre of her being.

"The prairie is a wonderful place for bringing out what there is in one," she answered, laughing and flushing under the little woman's gaze. "I had no idea that I could work so hard until I came out west."

"And do you like it better than you thought that you would, or are you homesick still for the woods, the hills, and the seashore?" asked Mrs. Smith; and there was a wistfulness in her own eyes which seemed to point to the fact that she herself had unsatisfied longings for the land of her past.

"I believe that I long just as much as ever for the beautiful scenery, and especially for the sea. But one cannot have everything, you know, and I have so much more to fill my life now than I had in the past; so I am content," replied Bertha, smiling down into the wistful eyes of the little Irishwoman.

"Ah, and it is that which makes for your good looks, my dear! Sure, and there's nothing like contentment for making the roses bloom in the cheeks and the eyes to shine. How long have you come to stay with me, dear?" said Mrs. Smith, giving Bertha a gentle push into the big rocking chair which stood beside the stove.

"I am here for two nights, only I shall not be here," replied Bertha, in some confusion, and then broke into a laugh at her own foolishness in mixing her speech up in such a fashion. "I mean that I am not going back to my cousin's house until the day after to-morrow, but I have business which will take me to railhead, that is out beyond Wastover, and I am going out to-night in a freighter, and I suppose that I shall come back some time to-morrow night, only I can't be sure when."

"But you can't go to railhead alone; them construction camps ain't no place for a young girl like you," objected Mrs. Smith, uplifting her hands in horror at the bare idea of such a thing.

"I am not going alone," answered Bertha, with a reassuring smile. "Mrs. Walford, of the Mounted Police, is to take care of me, and Inspector Grant has written me a pass."

"Ah, then it is right you are if the inspector has had anything to do with it, for he is the most particular man, and as careful of women and children as if they was new-laid eggs!" said Mrs. Smith, and then she bustled about getting a meal for Bertha. The supper at her boarding house was always spread for half-past six o'clock, which, of course, would be too late for Bertha, who, therefore, had to be fed separately.

Having had no food since her early breakfast, Bertha was quite prepared to do justice to Mrs. Smith's providing, especially as it was exceedingly doubtful when and where she would obtain her next meal. There was time for a brief half-hour of rest after her early supper, but Bertha could not sleep, being too much oppressed by a dread of losing her train. A few minutes before six o'clock she walked across to the depot, and the first person she saw when she arrived was a stout, elderly woman, who promptly pounced upon her much as a hungry cat might spring for a young and tender mouse.

"Now, do say, are you Miss Doyne, the young lady that is going to railhead?" demanded the stout woman, with a blowing sort of gasp intended to relieve her feelings.

"Yes, that is my name, and I am going to railhead. Are you Mrs. Walford?" asked Bertha, smiling at the stout woman with great satisfaction, because she looked so comfortable and motherly a woman.

"That is my name, and I am not so old as I look. It is this dreadful stoutness that is so aging," said Mrs. Walford, with a second blowing gasp, which reminded Bertha of an engine letting off steam. "Forty-five, I am, and not a week more, for my birthday was the day before yesterday; and, I am sure, to look at, anyone might well take me for sixty. I tell Walford sometimes that I will go in for some of those patent medicines that are advertised for reducing the figure. Then he laughs at me, and offers to swop jobs for a few weeks; for, as he says, a mounted policeman has no use for fat, and certainly he can't keep it."

"What a good idea! Why don't you try it?" asked Bertha, laughing at the fancy picture her mind conjured up of plump Mrs. Walford in a policeman's uniform, seated upon a frisky horse.

The stout woman laughed too, as if the little joke tickled her, then she answered, in her gasping, jerky fashion, "I would swop jobs with him for a time if it wasn't for one thing, and that is, I would not dare to mount a horse. My own two legs are shaky, I know; but I do feel safe when I am on them, which is more than I should do if I were mounted on four legs. But though I can't take his job I can share his life, and now that they are going to have a police barracks at Brocken Ridge, I'm going to live there, to make some sort of a home for him and the other men stationed in that district, and it won't be my fault if I don't manage to run off a little of this fat of mine before I have done."

"I am sure I hope that you will be successful, if it is going to make you more comfortable," said Bertha, and then she asked, "Do you know if Inspector Grant is coming to the depot before we start?"

"He was coming, but just as we were moving out of the door a message came for him that he was wanted at Ardley Crossing as soon as he could get there, and so he had to go. He told me I was to find you, and I wasn't to go without you, even if I had to get the freighter kept waiting for half an hour, though I guess there would be a pretty row among the officials if I were to try on any games of that sort," said Mrs. Walford.

Bertha laughed, and then turned to follow her companion towards the door of a covered freight wagon (box car, as it was called), and of which there were only three in the long train of wagons, laden with railway construction stuff, which had drawn into the Rownton depot.

"Now, which of these cars have we got to ride in, I wonder?" said Mrs. Walford, in a puzzled tone, as the first car appeared to be fast locked, and there was no possibility of getting near the others save by wading or swimming, as the melted snow covered the track in pools of muddy water; then, seeing a man in the distance who appeared to be in some way connected with the train, she called out loudly, "Here! Hi! young man, can you tell me which of these cars has been reserved for Mrs. Walford, of the Mounted Police?"

"This ain't a passenger train, ma'am, but only a freighter going through to railhead loaded with construction stuff," said the young man, lifting his cap politely.

"I did not say it was, but it has got to carry a passenger, or rather two passengers, this trip, so just stir round, will you, please, and see where we are to be accommodated, for I don't want to stand in this cutting wind much longer," said Mrs. Walford impatiently.

"But there ain't anywhere for you to ride," objected the young man, looking so much worried by the stout woman's persistence, that Bertha had some difficulty in keeping from laughing.

"Well, all I have got to say about it is that you will have to make a place for us to ride, then, and that very quickly, too, for I'm not here to be kept waiting," rejoined Mrs. Walford, with a note of asperity creeping into her tone. "I have a pass from Inspector Grant to carry this young lady and myself to railhead, and we have got to be taken there, even if you have to unload one box car on purpose for us."

"I wish that we could be told when we have got to carry passengers, then we might be able to have proper accommodation for them," said the young man, whereupon he departed in all haste to find the brakeman, who was presently unearthed from the caboose of the engine, where he had been refreshing himself with a cup of hot coffee, and was only dragged forth by the importunities of the young man, who was really concerned on account of the stout woman and her companion.

"There is a lot of camp bedding in that first box car; we might make room for you in there. It will be rather close, I'm afraid, and you won't be able to have a fire, but it is the best that we can do for you," said the brakeman, when he had mentally figured out the different kinds of lading contained in the three box cars.

"We shan't need a fire if there is so much bedding. The nights are not as cold as they were, and, for my own part, I would rather not be shut up in a box car, with a red-hot stove, over a track that is not properly settled," said Mrs. Walford, who was an old hand at pioneer travelling, and knew to a nicety what it was best to avoid.

"Well, come along, and I will stow you away as comfortably as I can manage it. We are due to draw out of Rownton in less than half an hour, and we shall need much as that, I guess, to fix you up so that you won't fall out of bed," said the man, and, seizing a lantern which hung inside the depot shed, he fixed a short ladder to the opening high up on the side of the box car, and, running up it, he unlocked the doors and swung them back.

The car was packed from floor to ceiling with bundles of bedding fastened up in coarse canvas, and at first sight there did not appear to be an inch of space in which the two passengers could be stowed; but the brakeman called the young man to whom Mrs. Walford had at first applied, and the two worked with so much zeal and energy, that at the end of twenty minutes they had succeeded in clearing a little space which would enable Mrs. Walford and

Bertha to sit side by side, though they could not lie down. Then, ripping open a bundle of blankets, the brakeman spread them out for the comfort of the adventurous pair of travellers, and the preparations were complete.

"I'm sure I hope that you will be comfortable," said the brakeman, as he helped them to climb up the side into the car. "I remember taking a couple of men a night journey in a car of bedding five years ago, when I was braking down in Montana, and when we opened the car in the morning they was both as dead as door nails. Fact is, they was drunker than they should have been when we took them on board, and we found two empty whisky bottles lying beside them."

And with this cheery reminiscence, he locked the doors on Mrs. Walford and Bertha.

CHAPTER XXVII
A Weird Night

CLICKETY clack, rick rack! Clickety clack, rick rack!

It seemed to Bertha that the horrible noise and rattle had been going on for hours, and days, and weeks. Her head ached from the constant noise and the lack of ventilation, her arms ached, her back ached, and she ached in every bone in her body. A small, badly trimmed lamp swung from a hook above her head and occasionally dropped kerosene upon her; but she could not move away, because there was no room to move two inches in any direction. She was wedged in on one side by a great roll of bedding, while on the other the stout figure of Mrs. Walford crowded against her.

But, horrid as was the smell of the lamp, it would have been ten times worse to be without it; for they had not been half an hour on their journey before she had seen the inquisitive nose of a big rat peering down at them from a great pile of bedding. A jerk of her head had scared it away then, but she had not dared to say anything about it; for Mrs. Walford had confided to her only a few minutes before how much she feared and disliked rats.

That rat would come back again, Bertha was sure of it, and the fear kept her awake long after her companion had sunk into peaceful slumber. Bertha had no book, and the light would not have been good enough to read by in any case, so there was nothing for her to do while the long hours dragged wearily away but to think; and naturally enough her thoughts clung with maddening persistence to the interview that she was going to face when that nightmare journey should be at an end.

She thought of Edgar Bradgate as she had seen him first, sitting in his boat on the Shark's Teeth rocks at Mestlebury. The next time she had seen him was when the wheat fired, and he had come along with the Smiths to help put it out. She had not recognized him until afterwards, and even then she had not been sure who he was—indeed, it had seemed to be her fate not to know him when she encountered him. There was that other time, when the horses brought him unconscious and half-dead to Duck Flats. She had not known him then, otherwise this horrible journey need not have been undertaken, and she would have been safely at home in the humdrum isolation of the lonely prairie house, instead of riding through the black night cooped up in a box car of bedding on her way to railhead, a place where a girl very rarely ventured.

"Oh, I am stupid, I am sure of it!" she muttered to herself for about the hundredth time.

Clickety clack, rick rack! Clickety clack, rick rack!

"If only that fearful clatter would stop for half an hour, how thankful I would be!" she went on, talking to herself in whispers, because it somehow kept her from feeling so lonely, though she was careful not to disturb Mrs. Walford by speaking aloud. "But no, I don't want it to stop, because if it did it would mean that we were standing still, and that would lengthen the journey. I shall not mind anything when once I have got my errand done, and can turn my face towards home again."

There was a dismal fear at the back of her mind, lest the journey should take longer than she had expected and arranged for. A hundred miles on a well-made line would not be a very serious matter, but they might have to travel for miles and miles over a skeleton line, that is, a part of the track not yet finished, and then the pace would be of the slowest, certainly not faster than, probably not so fast as, an average horse would travel on trail. And suppose that she could not get back to Rownton in time to take the wagon back at the appointed time!

But there is no sense in meeting trouble halfway. By the watch on her wrist Bertha saw that it was a little past two o'clock, and they seemed to be going ahead at a fine rate, so there might be no delay after all. It might even be possible to get a little sleep. She had not seen the rat again, so it had most likely been effectually scared away. Mrs. Walford was still sleeping profoundly, and it seemed foolish to keep awake for nothing at all.

She was dozing from sheer exhaustion, and in a few minutes would probably have been fast asleep, when there came a fearful lurch, followed by a crash. The lamp swung violently and then went out, and for a moment Bertha thought the train must have been wrecked; but no, it was still going on, only now the pace was an absolute crawl, varied by so many bumps and such violent shaking, that even the profound repose of Mrs. Walford was not equal to the strain put upon it, and she awoke with a start, crying out at the darkness, and groping for something familiar to the touch in the dense gloom.

"Where am I? Where am I? And oh, what is happening?" she gasped, in accents of terror, as another violent lurch of the train sent her flying on to Bertha once more.

"I think we must have reached the skeleton line, because it is bumping and shaking so desperately," said Bertha, who was somewhat damaged, and decidedly out of breath, from the violent assaults of Mrs. Walford's bulky form.

"Oh dear! oh dear! And now we shall have to bear this kind of thing right up to the end of the journey," groaned Mrs. Walford, as the cars swayed and bumped along at a slow crawl, and they were shaken in a most wearing fashion.

"Do you know how long it is likely to take?" gasped Bertha, who began to feel most horribly sick from the swaying, although she had never suffered from train-sickness before.

"No, nor anyone else. We may be out of it in a couple of hours, or it may go on for goodness knows how long. It is one of those things that you can't reckon on at all. But oh, dear, how I wish that the lamp had not gone out! Do you happen to have any idea what the time is, my dear?" asked Mrs. Walford, with a windy sigh.

"It was a little past two o'clock when I looked at my watch, but I don't know how long ago that was, because I was nearly asleep when the first bump came," replied Bertha.

"That makes eight hours since we started, and if we haven't stopped anywhere in the night we must have passed Wastover and got a good way out on the skeleton line before the shaking began. Oh-h-h, ah-h-h!"

The exclamations were dragged from Mrs. Walford by the violence of the motion to which she was at that moment subjected; then came another violent lurch, and then the cars stopped.

"Oh, what a relief!" sighed Bertha, who had been battling with her bad feelings as best she could.

"You won't say that if we are stuck here for three or four solid hours. What I feel about it is that I would rather suffer and get it over; there is no sense in prolonging the misery," said the stout woman tartly; for the last shaking had banged her arm against the post of the door, and she felt very badly bruised indeed.

"But as the stopping is not our fault, there is no wrong in enjoying the relief of it," said Bertha, with a laugh.

Then they began to crawl forward again with much clanking and groaning of coupling-irons; but the whole train was scarcely in motion again before there was another pull-up, followed by another attempt at starting, and so on, for what seemed to be an interminable time. This was followed by quite a long wait, accompanied by much shouting from driver, stoker, and brakeman, then there was a terrific jolt which sent the two unfortunate passengers flying into each other's arms. The coupling-irons clanked again, and then they heard the whole train moving off, but they remained still.

"Now, what does that mean, I wonder?" said Mrs. Walford, in a tone of concern.

"Our car was the last on the train at Rownton, so it looks as if we have been left behind," said Bertha, straining her ears to catch the rumble of the train which was rapidly dying away in the distance.

"Ah, I expect that the couplers broke when that last jolt came, in which case here we shall be stuck until those precious train-men discover what has happened, and that may not be until they reach Brocken Ridge," groaned Mrs. Walford.

"But we cannot stay here indefinitely!" cried Bertha, in dismay. "Just think of our plight, shut in this stuffy place in the dark, and without a mouthful of food. We have been here eight hours already, and I do not know how you feel, but I am nearly starving."

"It is very bad, I know," admitted Mrs. Walford, "but I have been in tighter places myself and endured more discomfort, too. I don't say that I should not be glad of a little more fresh air, for this bedding does smell horribly fusty."

"I wonder if I could work the door unfastened. We should get air then, and if we have got to starve, there is no reason why we should suffer from poisoning by bad air also," said Bertha, getting on to her feet with some difficulty and beginning to grope for the fastening of the doors.

"Why, they are locked, of course. Don't you remember hearing the brakeman lock them before we left Rownton?" asked Mrs. Walford, wincing, as Bertha inadvertently trod on her foot.

"That is so much the better! If they had been fastened by a bar dropped into a socket, I could not have hoped to get them open. As it is, I may succeed if I try hard enough," Bertha replied, as she groped and fumbled with her naked fingers round the doors. "Ah, here is the lock! Now, I wonder if I can work it back with a hairpin. I have no pocket knife with me. Have you one that I can have?"

"Yes, I have a knife, and a bradawl too; or you can have a small nail. What are you going to do? Work the lock back?"

"Very likely; but if I cannot do that easily, I may be able to unscrew the lock and take it off, as you have a bradawl, which is just about as useful as a chisel, if only one knows how to use it," answered Bertha.

"A screwdriver you mean, I guess," laughed Mrs. Walford. "Well, this is an adventure for two lone women at dead of night on a skeleton railway! But it will do well to put in your next story, my dear," and the stout woman laughed in a cheerful fashion, which showed her in no way daunted by the situation.

"How did you know that I wrote stories?" demanded Bertha, in a tone of amazement, as she worked away at the lock with that very useful hairpin, prodding her fingers badly in the darkness, but caring very little about the pain, because she felt that the lock was giving, which meant that if only she were patient enough she would get it unfastened.

"Why, because I have read them, to be sure," replied the other, with a complacent chuckle. "That one which came out in last week's *Banner of Liberty* was fine; but I should not have known it was you that I'd got the pleasure of travelling with, if it had not been that Inspector Grant hadn't told me to take special care of you, because you were the young lady that wrote the stories about the prairies."

"I wonder how he knew?" said Bertha musingly; for although her work was all signed with her own name, it had never occurred to her that perhaps the people of the district would ever find out that they had an author living among them. Moreover, the papers for which she wrote would scarcely be likely to have much circulation through that impoverished district.

"I don't know, but the magazines were sent from somewhere down east to that poor man who was ill at the barracks so long, and as I have done the washing for the barracks all winter, ever since my husband was sent up to Brocken Ridge, they often used to let me see books and papers; for I'm downright fond of a bit of reading, and I liked your stories so much because they were so true to life. Why, dear me! you might have been talking about people and things that I have known, I mean writing about them; it was all so natural," said Mrs. Walford.

Bertha thrilled from head to foot. To her this was the sweetest commendation that she had ever had for her work, and it more than compensated for heaps of hard things which she had been called upon to endure. She suddenly realized that it would not have been possible for her to have written as she had done, but for the disasters which had overtaken the Ellis household.

There were tears of happiness in her eyes and such a radiant joy in her heart, that when once again she sent the sharp point of the hairpin right into her finger she did not even wince, and the next jab she gave the lock was successful in fetching it open.

"Hurrah!" she cried, as with a smart push she sent the two doors swinging outwards; then, after one startled glance into the blackness below, she dropped back upon Mrs. Walford, gasping and speechless from sheer terror.

"What is it, Miss Doyne? Good gracious! what is the matter?" asked the good woman, in great amazement, seizing Bertha and holding her fast, under the impression that she had had a bad scare.

"We are on a bridge or something. It almost seems as if we were suspended in mid air, and down below, oh, such a horrible, horrible way, I could see the stars reflected in the water!" said Bertha, with a shudder of horror.

"Is that all?" said Mrs. Walford, greatly relieved. "We have been left on a bridge, of course, a skeleton bridge like all the rest of this precious line; but if it would bear the whole train to pass over it safely, it will certainly bear the weight of this one car, so that you have nothing to be afraid of. But, my word, how bitterly cold it is!"

"I will shut the doors again. We have had enough fresh air to last us for a little while, and I do not want to look down there oftener than I can help," said Bertha faintly; then she gathered up her courage to reach outward for the purpose of drawing the doors towards her, although she was trembling in every limb from the shock of seeing that gleaming water so far below.

"Sit still; you are shaking like a leaf. If you get leaning out in this condition, the next thing will be that you will take a header into the water, and a pretty business that would be. I will shut the doors myself, for my head is steady enough," replied Mrs. Walford sharply; for she guessed that Bertha's trembling was largely hysterical, the result of overwrought nerves and want of food.

"The wind will shut them for you if you will wait a minute. Oh, how it roars!" exclaimed Bertha, as a trumpet blast of wind rushed up the river valley and shook the car so much, that it moved forward on the rails, then slid back again, as if the gradient were against it.

A shudder shook Mrs. Walford then, for she was a sufficiently experienced traveller to know that there was grave danger in a car which could be moved backwards and forwards at the mercy of the wind.

Bang came one door, and she reached out her arm to seize it and hold it fast, until she could bolt it to the floor.

But somehow neither she nor Bertha could ever quite tell how it came about. A gust of wind jerked the door outwards again, and she was carried with it. But she was not even clinging with all her might, so when the strain of her heavy weight came upon her arms she could not keep her hold; and with a scream of terror she dropped downward into the blackness below.

A wild shriek broke from Bertha, although she was not conscious of it, and, clutching at the door-frame with both hands, she peered down into that awful void which showed below the swaying car. It was getting lighter, dawn was not very far away; and the clouds drifting just then from the face of the waning moon, lighted up the trestle framework of the bridge, which looked so slender and cobwebby in the gloom, but that was in reality so strong.

At first Bertha could see nothing but the framework, and she strained her ears to catch the splash from far down below which would tell her that poor Mrs. Walford had fallen into the water, but none came; and then, after what seemed an interminable agony of waiting, she thought that she heard a faint groan or cry from somewhere down below, but the wind bowled so loudly through the trestling that at first she could not be sure. When she heard it again she was quite sure, and, raising her voice to a joyful shout, she cried: "Mrs. Walford, where are you?"

"Down here," cried a voice faintly; and to Bertha it seemed to come from beneath her, although she still could not see whence it came.

"Hold on tightly! I will come and help you," she called back, making her voice sound as courageous as possible; for well she guessed that even a small gleam of hope might make all the difference between life and death to the unfortunate woman at this juncture.

"Stay where you are, child; it is an awful risk to climb down here," cried Mrs. Walford; but Bertha shouted back that she was coming and would soon reach her.

Winding a blanket round her neck for use in case Mrs. Walford was unable to climb back to the car, Bertha began to creep out slowly from the door of the car down on to the ties which carried the rails across the void. The door swung back with the wind, and only escaped crushing her by a margin so narrow that it seemed almost like a miracle, and the wheel on which she had placed her foot jerked round as the force of the wind moved the car along the rails, causing her to drop on to the ties, where she clung for a long moment, too sick to move backward or forward.

"I cannot get down—oh, I cannot!" she moaned to herself, as the force of the wind, rapidly rising to a gale, nearly tore her from her hold. Then the thought of Mrs. Walford's peril stirred her to fresh courage, so cautiously lowering herself through the ties, she got a foothold on the trestling and began to climb down.

The light was stronger now, and she could see Mrs. Walford lying on a sort of trellis-work platform, but though she called loudly to her there was no response that she could hear. Either the poor woman had fainted from fright, or else the wind carried the sound of her voice away.

Down, down, down went Bertha, her head clear and her courage steady now; for the danger was so great that in some strange way it had taken away her fear.

"I wonder however I shall get her to climb up here," she said to herself, as she paused, breathless, to get a little rest before going lower. There was only one more section now between her and Mrs. Walford; but her hands and arms were aching so much from the continual strain, that she was forced to wait a few minutes before finishing her perilous journey.

At last she had reached the spot where Mrs. Walford lay.

Then, as she stooped and laid her hand on the huddled figure, a dreadful fear assailed her, lest the poor woman had died from the shock of her fall.

"Mrs. Walford, are you hurt?" she cried anxiously.

Mrs. Walford gave a great start and looked up, then gasped in amazement, as if unable to believe the evidence of her eyes. "Miss Doyne, is it really you?"

"Yes, yes, and I have come to help you climb back again. You would never have fallen, if it had not been for my cowardice in being afraid to shut the door. I am so very, very sorry," said Bertha, with a sob coming up in her throat.

"You need not be; for you could not help the wind catching me in that fashion. Oh, the wonder is that I was saved from an awful death! It was a simply miraculous escape!" exclaimed Mrs. Walford, as she scrambled to a sitting position and, woman-like, began to arrange her disordered hair.

"Are you hurt?" asked Bertha, greatly relieved to find that her companion could sit up; but hardly able to believe even yet that there was no serious damage.

"I don't think so. I may be bruised a bit, and certainly I have had the wind pretty well knocked out of me, but one soon gets over these things. I feel horribly sick and giddy, though. I am afraid to stay here, and I dare not attempt to move. Whatever shall we do?"

"Oh, I will help you climb up to the railway track, then we will get into the car again," said Bertha confidently, although privately she very much feared that Mrs. Walford's courage would give out under the strain.

"I can't climb up there—I dare not—I would rather die!" cried Mrs. Walford, with a sob, as she cast a fearful glance upward at the network of trestling, on the top of which she could see the car moving to and fro on the track under the influence of the wind.

"But if you don't climb back, what will you do?" asked Bertha, in dismay. But part of her trouble was because she had seen how the car was sliding to and fro, and she wondered however they would be able to climb into it, even if they succeeded in reaching the track.

"I don't know, and I don't care. I feel as if I would like to drop down the rest of the way and end it all. Oh, it is dreadful, dreadful to be in a place like this! Whatever shall I do?" wailed the poor frightened woman.

Bertha tried to comfort her, pointing out if she had fallen so far without receiving serious hurt, she would certainly be able to manage the journey upward with help.

"No, no; I tell you I cannot get up there!" cried Mrs. Walford, with hysterical violence; then suddenly Bertha caught a glimpse of something which seemed to fairly make her heart stand still.

The wind was blowing a gale now, and roaring up the river valley with a noise like thunder. The car, perched up so high, and with nothing to steady it, was oscillating violently, and, the momentum increasing, it presently went over with a crash, falling into the river with a terrific splash. A groan broke from Mrs. Walford and a sharp cry came from Bertha's dry lips. What would have been their fate but for the accident to the former, which had sent the latter to her rescue, and so saved the lives of both of them. For a time they crouched close together, unable to move or to speak, dumb from the mercy of their great deliverance, and trembling before the dangers which might yet be in store for them.

But the thunder of the wind roared on, filling their ears with sound and their hearts with awe. They were in the grip of Nature in her wildest mood, and it was small wonder that they were afraid.

CHAPTER XXVIII
Consternation

THE end of steel, as railhead is called, on this particular bit of track, was at the junction of a small river with a large one, which necessitated the building of an extra long bridge to take the track across the river valley into the country of low rolling hills which lay beyond.

The building of the bridge naturally delayed progress, so, meantime, quite a considerable town had grown up. There were stores of sorts, and a hotel, so-called, which was kept by a dour-faced Scot and his smiling Irish wife.

The huts of the construction workers were made of any odd materials that came handy; indeed, some of them were mere holes scraped from the face of the cliff-like banks of the river and fronted with boards, sheets of tin, or any other building material which came to hand. But the whole place hummed with work and endeavour; there was no room for idleness or even leisure. From dawn to dark, or, to use a colloquialism, from kin to k'int, everyone toiled to the utmost of their strength; since the more work they did the more money they earned, and to earn money was with most of them the sole end and aim of their existence.

The place was all astir when, in the first faint light of dawn, the long freight train from Rownton rolled and rocked over the last half-mile of unfinished track, finally coming to a stand in the middle of the crazy collection of dwellings which, after the manner of such places, had the impudence to consider itself a full-fledged town.

It had been expected from the previous evening, and quite a crowd had gathered, since it would bring a mail bag, newspapers, and all those other attributes of civilization for which the dweller in the wilderness hungers; so when the engine was sighted coming round a bend in the track, there was something like a rush to be the first to greet the arrivals. Foremost among these was a big man wearing the uniform of the Mounted Police. Mike Walford was a splendid specimen of a man, and he towered over his fellows like a pine tree of the forest might tower above the scrub growing at its base.

"Hulloa! Here, I say, have you got my wife on board?" he shouted, in a voice that matched the rest of him, as with much squealing and groaning of couplings the long freighter came to a standstill.

"We've got two passengers on board this trip. At this rate we shall soon need to hitch a pullman on at the end of every freighter," said the brakeman, with a pretended groan of dismay at this addition to his work.

There was an instant rush to follow the brakeman along to the rear of the train, which, owing to the curve in the track, was not visible from the engine;

but, sweeping the others to the right and left of him, Mike Walford strode to the side of the brakeman and led the way.

"My word, what a train! The last car, did you say? Why, man, it is a wagon loaded with ties! You surely did not put a couple of women to ride all night in a place like that!" exclaimed Mike, with anger in his tone.

"They are in a box car of bedding—a little stuffy, but downright warm and comfortable," explained the brakeman, and then suddenly he stopped, and a cold horror crept into his eyes. "The car is gone—broke away it must have done; and yet I know that it was safe when we cleared out of Wastover."

Mike Walford turned on him savagely. "How was it that you didn't take more care? And I thought that it was the place of the brakeman to ride in the rear of his train?"

"It ain't no use to do that when there are as many cars as we have got here, so I ride in the middle, then I can see her tail as she twists round the curves, and yet I'm not too far away to call to the driver if I want to," said the brakeman, on the defensive now, for it was a serious thing to drop a wagon *en route* and not to know that it was gone. Then he started to run back towards the engine, while Mike Walford, with dismay in his heart, started to run by his side, and the crowd coming along in the rear ran also.

If the brakeman had looked dismayed, it was nothing to the consternation displayed by the engine driver, who was prompt to locate the place at which the disaster must have occurred.

"You remember the job we had with her when we came over the Wastover bridge?" he said, with a jerk of his head towards the long train of freight wagons that comprised the "her" of which he spoke. "I thought at one time that we should have had to leave half the train behind and come on with the first part, for there is a bit of up-grade directly the bridge is past, and this old puffer had its work cut out to pull her along; so it must have been when we were starting and stopping, starting and stopping, that the couplers of the last car broke. How many wagons is missing, Jim?"

But Jim, who was the brakeman, declared that he had been too scared to count. The thing which mattered most was that the box car with the passengers was not there.

"Uncouple that old engine of yours and set off back as hard as you can go, and don't waste any more time in talking about it," said Mike Walford sternly. "You'll take me with you too, if you please."

"That is what we are going to do, just as soon as we can get her unhooked from the wagons; but we shall have to break up a bit before the engine can get past," answered the driver, as he began to shout to the brakeman, who in his turn shouted back, while the stoker had to turn shunter for the time being; so half an hour was wasted in endless starting and stopping, pulling up and setting back, in order that the wagons might be out of the way, to allow the engine to slip back on to the main rails.

If Mike Walford raged up and down silently abusing the men for their slowness, he might surely be forgiven, since he knew the country so well, and all his fears pointed to the car having broken away on the bridge; and Wastover bridge was not a very safe place to be stranded upon with the wind blowing a gale as it was this morning.

The crowd looked on for the most part with a sort of fascinated curiosity. No one could quite make up his mind to go back to work while the engine was puffing and panting to and fro, and Mike Walford was raging up and down like a wild beast escaped from his cage. There was an element of tragedy peeping through his unrestrained anxiety, for, as a rule, he was one of the most unemotional sort of men, as some of them knew to their cost.

At last the engine had a clear track, and was able to slide out backwards on to the main track, to go in search of the car that had broken away. But before he boarded her to go with the train-men, Mike Walford held up his hand and called for volunteers.

"I want half a dozen men who are prepared to risk their lives, and to lose them, if need be," he said, his strong voice echoing clear and steady over the silent crowd. "I know what that bridge at Wastover is like when the wind is blowing only half a gale, and this morning it is more than that. If the car broke away on the bridge, something will have happened to it before we can get back there; so I want six men who can dig, and who are willing to risk their lives for the sake of saving life."

Thirty men rushed forward. Thirty more would have followed, if there had been the slightest chance of their being able to go. But of the first lot Mike hastily chose six who happened to have shovels in their hands, and the last man thus picked was Edgar Bradgate.

"Hold, Bradgate, you mustn't go; remember, man, how long you have been ill, and you can't swim, either," objected a clerk of works, as Bradgate swung himself aboard the crazy tender, which rocked behind the locomotive.

"There are other things to do besides swimming, and I'm not afraid to risk my life, or to lose it either, if need should be. Besides, Mike is my friend, and I'm proud to be chosen to help him now," replied Edgar Bradgate, with a haughty upward fling of his head, which might have gone against him with the clerk had the fellow not been sufficiently a gentleman to recognize another gentleman when he saw one.

"Well, go along with you then; all the luck comes to some people!" growled the clerk, in such deep chagrin at not having been chosen for the purpose of risking his life, that it would have been comic if only it had not been so intensely tragic.

Directly the engine and tender had slid out of sight round the bend, everyone hurried off to work again, for they could do no good by hanging about there staring at the empty track; while the need to earn money was acute, and the necessity to toil so urgent, that nothing in the nature of delay could be excused.

The volunteers rode on the tender with the brakeman, but Mike Walford was on the engine itself, prepared to help stoke if need be, and also determined to see that the driver got every ounce of speed possible out of the crazy old engine.

The rocking was truly awful as the engine tore its way along the half-made track, and the marvel was that those men, who had come out to risk their lives if it were necessary, did not lose them on the way to the scene of action.

It was fifteen miles to Wastover bridge, and the engine did it in something over an hour, though it had taken the train more than three hours to crawl its weary way up to Brocken Ridge. But every minute of that backward journey was a peril so great, that nothing but the danger of the two in the box car could have justified the risk being taken.

"There is no car on the bridge," said Mike, as they came in sight of the towering trestles which carried the railway track across the Wastover river.

"Then it's below the bridge that we'll have to look for it!" groaned the driver, "for I'm sure that is the only place where it could have broken away. Jim went the length of the train before we cleared out of Wastover town, and the car was all right then, and being downgrade until the bridge, there would be no pull on the couplers, can't you see?"

Mike nodded, and now his gaze went searching along that bewildering network of bars and crossbars, almost as if he expected to find the missing car stuck somewhere halfway down. In reality he was trying to see the water, but could not as yet, because the valley was so narrow and deep that the river was not visible until they were close on to the bridge.

"What is that?" cried Mike, in a tone of horror, as with slackened speed the engine went slowly out on to the bridge, and every man of them all was craning his head downwards to get a better view of the river, swollen now with melting snows.

"It is the car! Holy Mary, have mercy on the women!" groaned the driver, who was a good Catholic when he remembered to be anything at all, and then he put his head down on the side of the cab and burst into tears like a woman. But Mike Walford gave him a fierce push and bade him reverse his engine.

"Slip back to the bank, man, and stop. I'm going down there to find my wife, and you can do your howling while I am gone," he said, with brutal sternness, which was the only way he had of hiding his own pain.

"You'll never be for swimming out in such a current?" objected the driver. "It will be murder and sooicide all in one, for where you go the boys will be sure to follow."

"If my wife is down there I am going to get her out, dead or alive," replied Mike; and there was that in his tone which made the other feel that he dared say no more.

The engine retreated slowly to where the land, rising in an embankment, gave it a little shelter from the wind. There it stopped, and the little band of volunteers scrambled down and, falling into line behind their leader, made their way down the steep slope to the water's edge.

"I will swim out first with a rope," said Mike, who had a serviceable hatchet slung at his waist; "then one of you can follow when I've got the rope fixed, and we will chop an opening at the end of the car that is out of water, and pray God we are not too late!"

There was a murmur which sounded like "Amen", and then the men scrambled downwards for a few moments in silence.

"Help! Help! Help!" It was a girl's voice, hoarse and strained, shrieking against the roaring of the wind. The heads of the men jerked upwards with a sudden flash of hope, for the sound had come from above.

"There they are—two of them!" yelled out one of the volunteers. "Hurrah!"

"Hurrah! Hurrah!" chorused the others, as, breaking into a run, they scrambled across the rough slope to the trestling, up which they swarmed like a set of monkeys.

CHAPTER XXIX
A Great Embarrassment

THE men had seen the two huddled figures high up in the trestling, and were climbing as fast as they could go to reach them. Bertha ceased to shout when she saw them coming. Her voice was strained, and her throat was sore from the efforts she had made to attract attention, ever since she had first heard the engine coming on to the bridge. But the wind roared so loudly, and the engine was noisy too, that it was little wonder she could make no headway against it, and when the engine went slowly back again she had almost given up hope of getting help.

Then she saw the men go scrambling down the bank towards the water, and guessed that they were making for the box car, which just showed sticking up in the bed of the river, and the sight had given her courage to shout her loudest, and so she had made them hear at last. But she was dreadfully spent and almost perished with cold, for the raging wind seemed to blow right through her; moreover it had required every atom of will power that she possessed to prevent poor Mrs. Walford from flinging herself headlong from the trestling into the river down below.

The trouble was that although it would have been quite possible for them to have climbed upward on to the track, after the manner in which Bertha had climbed down from the platform where they were, it was not possible to get lower save by a drop of four or five feet, and that Mrs. Walford could not face. Equally she declared that she could not climb higher—her head would not stand it—so, seeing the dangerous state of excitement under which she laboured, Bertha dared not urge her to move, being afraid that if she were to get any higher she would lose self-control entirely.

She had wrapped the poor woman in a blanket and urged her to shut her eyes, even to sleep, if she could, knowing that sleep, more than anything else, would rest the nerves and quiet down the wild agitation. But sleep was impossible to Mrs. Walford just then, and every time a blast of wind roared down the valley, she shrieked out that they would be blown away.

It was a terrible experience for Bertha. Never, never had she faced a situation calling for more strength of mind and quiet self-control. She was sick and giddy herself with all she had gone through, and from the awful height at which they were perched. She was faint, too, from want of food, and so thoroughly chilled that she could scarcely keep her hold on the timber against which she leaned for shelter. By drawing Mrs. Walford close to one of the uprights on the windward side, she had sheltered her a little from the force of the wind; but it was necessary to hold her there, or the poor woman, in her excitement, might easily have made an incautious move which would have sent her hurtling downwards through the network of crossbeams into the muddy water of the river.

It was that four or five feet of distance from the last crossbars on to the platform where the two were crouching which proved a serious obstacle to the men who were climbing up to the rescue, and for a few minutes it looked almost as if they might have to climb down again, then scramble up the bank, and come down from above. But after a moment spent in silently surveying the situation, Edgar Bradgate solved it for the others by flinging his arms round a bit of the trestling and calling out to Mike Walford to step on to him, and so mount upward to the crossbar immediately above.

"It is to be hoped that you have something extra tough in the way of a backbone, then, for I'm rather more than feather-weight," said Mike grimly; but he sprang up without a moment's delay, and, letting down the rope he carried, fastened it so that the others could climb up in that fashion.

When they were all up, there was still another section of the bridge to be mounted in the same fashion, and again Edgar offered himself as a human step-ladder, but this time he was good-humouredly pushed aside by one of the others, who said that it was share and share alike on that venture. Mike was the first up again; but this time, instead of stopping to fix the rope for the next man, he hurried along the open planking, walking with the fearlessness of a cat on a roof ridge to the place where Bertha knelt with her arms round Mrs. Walford.

"The Good Lord be praised that you are safe, wife!" he exclaimed, his voice breaking unsteadily now for the first time since the knowledge of his wife's danger had come to him.

"Mike! Mike! is it really and truly you?" cried the poor woman, lifting her head and gazing at her husband with a yearning light in her eyes, as if even now she could scarcely believe the good news true, despite the evidence of eyes and ears.

"Yes, yes, I'm here right enough; but how you two got up here is more than I can think. Why, it is nothing short of a miracle. Were you flung out of the car when it fell, or what happened to you?"

"We were not in the car when it toppled over, or it is a widower that you would have been at this moment," said Mrs. Walford, with a shudder. "I was flung out of the car in trying to shut the door, and I was caught on this platform as I fell; then Miss Doyne crawled out after me, and climbed down to help me up to the track again. But, bless you! I couldn't do that; my head was not strong enough. Indeed, my senses would have left me altogether, and I should have flung myself down into the river long ago, if she had not stopped me."

"Poor soul! you have had a bad scare, and no mistake. But the fall saved your life, and Miss Doyne (God bless her!) saved hers when she came to your help," said Mike, bowing low to Bertha, as if she were a royal princess. Then he went on, and the grim note came back to his tone: "But you've got to buck up, wife, for we shall have to haul you up on to the track somehow, and it rests with you whether you will climb up on your own two feet, like a decent Christian woman, or whether we have got to tie you like a calf and swing you out, to be dragged up hand over hand by sheer strength of arm. The rope is fairly strong, I know, but then you are not a light weight. There are only seven of us and the young lady, and it will be a tight job and a risky one to get you up that way."

"I can't go up, I can't! I feel just like a fly walking on a ceiling, and my head gets lighter than a feather," moaned the poor woman, hiding her head against her husband's shoulder and sobbing like a baby.

"Funny creatures women are," said Mike, in a tone of rueful apology, as he looked across at Bertha. "To see my wife going on like this, you might think her an awful coward; but she ain't, not a bit of it. Why, when we were living at Denver, just after we were married, a hut caught fire, and there was a baby inside. Its own father and mother stood shrieking outside, but my wife, she dashed right in and fetched the poor mite out, though the gown was burnt off her back, and she hadn't a hair on her head for six months afterwards. Then, five years ago, when I first joined the police, and we was stationed wide of Edmonton, there was a poor fellow down with smallpox; she nursed him through it all, and saved his life, too, though grown men were scared to fits at the thought of going near him."

"There, do be quiet, Mike. I wonder what you will be saying next?" cried Mrs. Walford, but with a thrill of so much gratification in her tone, that Mike looked across at Bertha, and was actually guilty of something approaching a wink, for which indiscretion he promptly apologized by coughing violently.

"I was only telling the truth. Women are most dreadfully one-sided creatures; ready to go through fire and water one minute, the next afraid of their own shadows, and screaming at the sight of a mouse," he answered, following up his advantage with a skill that was the result of long practice.

"I'm not to say really afraid of a mouse, though I will admit that I do go queer if I know that there is a rat anywhere about," said Mrs. Walford, with a flash of her old spirit; and then she said, "I'll have a try at climbing, if you will tie a rope to me, but I simply can't do it on my own."

"We wouldn't trust you to do it on your own; there isn't enough ballast in your head for it," replied her husband, as he slipped a rope round her without a moment's loss of time, one end of which he fastened to himself and one to another man.

Then he ordered Bertha to be fastened in a similar fashion, and when she was roped to Edgar Bradgate and a fair-haired young Swede, whose mastery of the English tongue was, so far, limited to "T'ank you", the upward climb was begun.

Oh, the horror of it! As she was pulled, almost without effort of her own, from point to point on the trestling, sometimes swinging right out over space, Bertha wondered more than ever how it was she had managed to get down to where Mrs. Walford had fallen without breaking her neck.

And in all that dreadful upward way Edgar Bradgate never spoke to her, save when she hesitated once just before they had to make the last bit of climb up on to the ties, and, chancing to look down, she turned so giddy that, if she had not been securely roped, she must have fallen, and then he said sternly: "Shut your eyes, and do not open them until I give you permission, or you may drag us both down with you."

She writhed under the words, and did not even guess that he had spoken like that on purpose to sting her pride into doing her very best. He knew very well that it was as much as they could do to mount the trestling with any chance of safety in such an awful gale, and every possible precaution had been taken. Bertha's skirt had been roped so tightly round her that she could only move her feet a few inches, and when it came to climbing up the last bit of the way, she had to be lifted from point to point, and only the gasping breath of the two men who helped her betrayed to her how heavy their task must be. Then a fiercer blast of wind took her, and she thought she would have been torn from the grip of the two who held her so firmly. But no; foot by foot she was guided along the stretch of railway track until the shelter of the embankment was reached, where the engine was waiting for them.

Mike Walford and the other men were behind, although they had started first. Mrs. Walford's nerves had been unequal to the strain of that fearful climb, and she had fainted, having to be borne to the top in a state of limp unconsciousness. Her husband was in a state of acute worry about her; for it is sometimes very dangerous to a person in a fainting condition to be hauled about like a bale of dry goods. But as there was a fearful risk in her remaining where she was, he had to choose between two evils, and so he decided to take the risk and get her to the top as soon as possible.

So she was hauled and swung from point to point, the efforts of five men being necessary to the task, and when at length they reached the shelter of the embankment, where Bertha and the other two men were awaiting them, there was not a man of the five who was not dripping with perspiration.

Bertha, who by this time was unroped and able to move freely once more, at once went to the aid of Mrs. Walford, and, thanks to the knowledge she had gained in taking care of Grace, was soon able to bring the poor woman round again.

"Are we still on that dreadful trestling?" asked Mrs. Walford, with a shudder.

"No, no; we are safely on the track now, and the bridge is behind us. Look down at your feet and see the good honest dirt and stones on which they are resting," said Bertha, in a cheery tone, forcing herself to make light of what they had gone through, just because the horror of it would have entirely unnerved her if she had let herself dwell upon it.

Mrs. Walford burst into tears of sheer thankfulness, and the men stood round in miserable embarrassment, not liking to disturb her, and yet feeling that something ought to be done.

Then Bertha ventured a remonstrance. "Don't you think that it is a pity to cry now that all the danger is over? It looks a little ungrateful, too, when these kind people have worked so hard to save us."

"Of course it is dreadfully silly, and I would not have done it if I had not been all of a twitter with what we have gone through," said Mrs. Walford, giving herself a shake, and wiping her eyes in token that she was restored to normal. "I am more obliged to everybody than I can say for helping us up from that awful trestling, and no one can guess what we have been through since I fell out of the car."

"It was falling out of the car that saved your lives, anyhow, so you have reason to be grateful for it," said her husband; then he hurried them into the tender, the men climbed in after, and the engine started on its way back to Brocken Ridge.

Very little was said on the way there. Neither Mrs. Walford nor Bertha was fit to discuss their adventures; indeed, it took every scrap of endurance that Bertha possessed to sit that dreadful ride out. But there was one thing about which she had to make sure before she allowed herself to be carried off for rest and refreshment at the end of the journey, and that was, she had to know at what time the long train of empty wagons would start back to Rownton, for it would never do for her to be left behind, seeing that it might be two or even three days before another train came through.

"We can't possibly get off much before midnight, miss, and it may be later than that," said the brakeman to whom she had put her question. "But we will not forget to call for you, never fear, and you shan't ride in the last car next time, I will see to that."

Mike Walford looked at Bertha in surprise, and he wondered more than ever who she was, and why she had come up to Brocken Ridge in a freight car just to return by the same train. It was certainly no pleasure trip under the best of circumstances, and, as things had turned out, it had been an experience of dire peril. But he was so grateful to her for the way in which she had helped his wife, that he felt he must do as much as he possibly could to further whatever business she might have on hand.

"Is there anything that I can do for you, Miss Doyne?" he asked, as he piloted her and his wife across to the hotel.

Bertha turned a grateful face towards him. His uniform was comforting, and then Mrs. Walford had said so much in his praise during the long and weary journey, that she knew he was to be trusted apart from his official position.

"Oh, could you manage that I have a chance to see Mr. Edgar Bradgate alone for ten minutes as soon as possible?" she asked, turning her white, weary face eagerly towards him.

Mike Walford stared at her in blank amazement. "Mr. Bradgate, did you say? Why, it was he who helped you up the trestling. Didn't you know him then?"

A wave of hot, distressful colour swept over Bertha's face. Surely no girl was ever forced into a position so strange and horrid as this in which she found herself! But she took the shortest way out, by speaking with direct simplicity.

"Mr. Bradgate does not remember me, and he has no idea that there is any reason why I should come so far to see him on business which could not be settled otherwise than by a personal interview, and although I tried I simply could not get up enough courage to ask him to let me see him alone, and so I thought that I would ask you to manage it for me."

"I'll do it; you trust me. If there is no other way, I will arrest him and run him in," said Mike, with a jolly laugh at his own joke, and then he stalked into the hotel and ordered the very best meal obtainable for his wife and Bertha. But he would not stay to share the meal, for he had promised to get Bertha the interview she wanted, and he guessed that there might be difficulties if he let the matter wait, for the workers at Brocken Ridge had scanty leisure, and the work of rescue had already made serious inroads into the day of toil.

It was nearly an hour before he appeared again, and then he was smiling and victorious, and he did not choose to tell Bertha how near it had come to his being compelled to resort to force to induce Edgar Bradgate to come back to the hotel for an interview with a girl who had come all the way from Rownton, no, thirty miles wide of Rownton, for the sole purpose of interviewing him in private.

"Miss Doyne, did you say? I don't seem to remember having heard the name before, and if she wanted to see me, why couldn't she have said so when I was helping her up the framework of the bridge," he had said, when Mike told him what Bertha had come for. "The private interview could even have taken place then, seeing that Jan has next to no English, and then my time need not have been wasted."

"Oh, if it is a question of a dollar or so, the time you lose can be put down to me," said Mike Walford. "I'm too grateful to Miss Doyne for standing by my wife to begrudge that much in her service."

So Edgar Bradgate had been forced to come, and because he was a gentleman first and a workman second, he even washed his hands and face before appearing at the hotel.

There was some little difficulty about a private room for the interview, but even this was secured, thanks to the good offices of Mike Walford, who took refuge with his wife in the bedroom of the proprietor, so that Bertha might have the room known as the "parlour" free for her interview with Edgar Bradgate, which she waited with a breathless impatience.

She was fumbling with a little calico bag, which she had pulled from the front of her blouse when he entered the room, and it was immediately evident to him that she was most painfully nervous, although when she spoke her voice was quiet and steady.

"I am sorry to have given you so much trouble and to seem so mysterious withal, but it was better for you that no one else should have any knowledge of what I have to give you. Of course you will remember your own property," she said, as she slipped the little morocco case from the calico bag and laid it in his hand.

She had expected to see his face light up and to hear him exclaim: "Where did you get this from?" but, to her utter surprise and dismay, he only shook his head as he surveyed the case with mild curiosity, saying, in an indifferent tone:

"I think that you must have made a mistake. I don't smoke, and I have never possessed a cigar case."

"Look inside and then you will remember!" she cried, in a perfect agony of impatience. "It is not a cigar case—I mean, there are no cigars inside. No, that is not the way to open it. You press the spring like this. There! Now, do you remember it?" she asked, as the case flew open, revealing the stones inside.

"What are they?" he asked, looking at her now with such a genuine bewilderment in his face, that Bertha's dismay rose almost to the point of actual panic.

"They are diamonds, your diamonds that you lost at Mestlebury in Nova Scotia," she said, with a little catch coming into her voice.

"Ah, pardon, they are not mine, for I have never possessed a diamond, never even seen one in this state. If you had not told me they were diamonds, I should not have known them from pebbles," he said, touching them now with a cautious forefinger, as if the thought of their value interested him.

Bertha drew her breath in a gasp of dismay and asked abruptly: "But are you not that Mr. Bradgate who nearly lost his life on the Shark's Teeth rocks at Mestlebury, and was saved by a girl swimming out to him with a rope?"

"That is my name, and the drowning would have been an accomplished fact if it had not been for the extraordinary pluck of a girl," he said, with a keen look at her distressed face. "Is it possible that you——"

But Bertha had reached the end of her power of endurance, and, overcome by the disappointment and perplexity of it all, she put down her head and burst into miserable tears.

CHAPTER XXX
Bad News

A CURIOUS change came over Edgar Bradgate at the sight of Bertha's breakdown, and, leaning forward, he gently touched the bowed shoulder that was nearest to him and asked, in a sympathetic tone: "Won't you tell me all about it, and why you are so upset because the things are not mine?"

"But they must be yours. The case dropped out of your coat, the coat which you wrapped round me because I shivered so badly," she said, with a little gasping sob, as she strove to get calm again and to argue the matter out on common-sense lines. She was fighting against the possibility of having to retain the stones longer in her own keeping; for, bad as it had been before, it would be much worse now, because the knowledge was shared by at least one more person.

"Then you are the girl who saved me, and you must have thought me worse than a heathen because I never stopped to thank you for your bravery," he said, with such a thrill of genuine admiration in his tone, that Bertha felt the hot colour sweeping up over her face right up to the roots of her hair; then he went on in apology for his neglect: "But I was hard pressed. It meant everything to me to get clear away, so I did what I could and went. I did not remember the coat until the middle of the night, when I was far away from Mestlebury and, truth to tell, miserably cold; but there was no help for it, and it was rather an aged garment also, that is to say, it had seen considerable wear and tear of one sort and another."

"It was a very good coat, indeed," said Bertha, "and I brought it with me to restore it to you, only it was in the car, and is, of course, at the bottom of the river now. But as the diamonds fell out of your pocket, they must be your property. Perhaps being ill has made you forget all about it."

He smiled and shook his head. "That does not follow, since someone may have put them in my pocket without my knowledge, unlikely though it seems."

"But they fell out of the inside pocket, so they could hardly have been put there without your knowledge," she objected.

"You are sure that it was my coat?" he asked quickly.

"I am quite sure that it was the coat which you wrapped round me in the boat," she replied—"a dark-brown coat with a black velvet collar and the top button missing, it having been torn out by the roots."

"The description is exact, even to the pulling off of the button," he said, with a laugh, and then, becoming suddenly grave again, he asked, "But what are you going to do about these stones, which are certainly not mine, nor have I the remotest idea of where they came from. You will carry them back with you, of course?"

"Oh, will you not keep them?" she cried imploringly. "I am so tired of having to guard what is not my own, and they have cost me so much trouble and disappointment, that I should be only too thankful to be rid of them. Moreover, I am downright afraid for it to be known that I have such valuable things in my possession."

Edgar Bradgate stiffened unconsciously, and his manner was suddenly cold and repellent when he replied: "I shall certainly not touch them. They came by accident into your possession, and you must keep them until time or chance reveals the rightful owner to you. There can scarcely be any danger to you from having them in your keeping, if no one knows of their existence."

Bertha looked as she felt, utterly wretched, and as she thought of all that she had endured in her attempts to restore the stones to their rightful owner, the tears brimmed up in her eyes again, and it was only with great difficulty that she kept them from falling. It was silly to care so much, of course; but then she simply could not help it.

There was a long minute of strained silence which she was too miserable to break, then Edgar Bradgate spoke again, his tone being more masterful than she had heard it before.

"Mike Walford says that you are going back on the cars to Rownton to-night, and I shall go with you myself to see that no harm comes to you. And I shall go right through with you to Duck Flats; that is the very least that I can do for you after all the time and trouble you have spent in trying to restore to me what you supposed to be my own."

"Pray, do not trouble," cried Bertha, stung by what she deemed the disapproval of herself and her conduct expressed in his tone. "I can manage quite well, I assure you."

"I do not doubt your power to take care of yourself, but all the same I am going, and I shall not leave you until I see you safe in the hands of your natural protectors," he said, in that same tone of grave disapproval which had made her wince so badly only a few minutes before.

But at his mention of her natural protectors the comic side of the matter struck her, and she burst out laughing, then, seeing the look of offence on his face, made haste to explain her untimely merriment.

"Oh, please forgive me for being so rude as to laugh! But it really does seem strange for anyone to talk of taking care of me, seeing that all through this winter I have been in charge of my invalid cousin and her family. I have been the man of the house, you understand, and the woman too, for the matter of that, and when I reach Rownton to-morrow I have to drive a horse that I know very little of, for thirty miles."

"If you are so valuable in ordinary life, that is all the more reason why you must be taken care of when you set forth on such adventurous journeys," he said, smiling himself now; and his face softened so much that Bertha's self-respect came back to her again.

It had been the most humiliating part of her experience that the man whom she had come so far to serve should receive her with such evident disapproval, and she had suffered acutely during that most disappointing interview.

"I must go now," he said presently, when Bertha had told him all the story of how she had gone to Mrs. Saunders to find out where he lived, and how the old woman had refused to tell her anything, and how the fat German had given the key to her reticence. "I shall be back in good time, though, to start with you, and I will see that you are not allowed to ride in the rear car while you are in my care."

A glow of happiness warmed Bertha's heart. It was good to be cared for, though she did not think that it was right or even proper that this masterful man should be permitted to go such a long journey on her account, and she meant to consult Mrs. Walford on the subject the very first minute that she could get the stout woman alone. In the end, however, it was Mrs. Walford who broached the subject to her, speaking in a tone of great distress.

"Oh, my dear Miss Doyne, are you obliged to go back to Rownton to-night? Or could you manage to put in a few days with us until the cars come up next time? Mike and me would be most proud and glad to have you, and this hilly country would be a nice change after the flats round Pentland Broads."

"You are very kind, and I would love to stay if only it were possible," said Bertha, smiling into the face of the stout woman, and thinking how extraordinarily kind everyone was to her. "But it will be nothing short of a disaster if I cannot get through to-night, because I am wanted at home so badly."

"I am afraid that you will have a dreadful journey; Mike says that there are a lot of rough fellows going out by the cars, and he is sure that it is not right for you, a young girl, to travel alone with such a lot, for they are safe to find something strong to drink, even if it is only perfumes or cough mixture; and when a crowd of that sort are tipsy, it is no place for a girl like you," said Mrs. Walford anxiously.

"Shall I have to ride in the same car?" demanded Bertha, in dismay. "But I will not; I will travel in one of the open wagons first, and on such a long train I can be far enough away to be out of earshot of anything that they may say. But Mr. Bradgate said that he meant to take me back to Rownton himself, or all the way to Duck Flats, if necessary, and I wanted to ask you if I should be doing right to allow him to go with me. You see, I came up here on his business, or what I thought was his business, and he thinks that it is his duty to take me home."

"What a mercy!" ejaculated Mrs. Walford fervently. "If you must go, there is no one to whom you could better trust yourself than Mr. Bradgate, who is a Christian and a gentleman, though a bit cold and stern—stand-offish, I call it—but it is easy to see that he is a down-east aristocrat."

"Then you do not think that it would be imposing on his good nature to let him come with me?" asked Bertha, who knew too much about the value of time and the importance of sticking at daily toil, not to have some qualms of conscience about accepting such a sacrifice from a stranger, or almost a stranger.

"I think that, seeing you came up here on his account, the only thing that he can do is to take you safely back home again," said Mrs. Walford, with decision. "Oh, it has taken a load off my mind, for I'd been seriously wondering whether I ought to go back with you myself, though at this minute I feel as if I would rather lie straight down and die than have to go through another night like the last."

"Oh, it will not be as bad as that, I hope!" said Bertha, although she could not repress a little shudder at the remembrance of her climb down the trestling when she went to the help of Mrs. Walford.

"I should hope not too, but in these wild parts you can never tell what is going to happen next," said the stout woman, with a windy sigh, and then she bundled Bertha off to get a sleep which would fit her for the long journey she would have to take in the night.

The bed was not a very clean one, the room was a little corner boarded off from one end of the bar, while the noise of coming and going was incessant; but as there was nothing in the shape of alcohol sold in the place, in accordance with Government regulations, there was no disorder, only the hum and clatter of ordinary business. But Bertha slept through it all as peacefully as an infant, and had to be awakened so that she might get some supper before the cars started back for Rownton.

The place was bright with electric light, the power for which was obtained from a waterfall close at hand, and the crowd of people coming and going was so great, that Bertha was fairly bewildered when she came out into the public room, and she marvelled that she could have slept through such a hubbub.

She was eating her supper—and a very good supper it was—at a little side table in company with Mrs. Walford, who was staying at the hotel until the cars left, in order to keep her company, when she heard a man behind her talking excitedly about Brown's Expedition.

"Every man of the lot was dead, so Alf said, and it was evident that they must have died weeks, perhaps months ago, poor fellows!" said the man, with a ring of genuine pity in his tone.

Bertha dropped her knife and fork with a clatter, and suddenly stood straight up in her place and turned round.

The man who had been speaking became as suddenly silent. A girl of any kind was something of a rarity in a railhead hotel, and this one had a look on her face which fairly frightened him, and he shrank away as she approached, feeling as if he had been guilty of some crime against her.

"You were speaking of Brown's Expedition," she said, in a curiously still voice, while a hush dropped upon that part of the room and spread rapidly, until everyone ceased talking and listened eagerly to what the pale-faced girl was saying. "Do you mean the expedition which Mr. Brown of Winnipeg commissioned and sent off last August?"

"Yes, miss, that is the one, for it ain't likely that there would be two Mr. Browns doing the same thing, both starting at the same time, and both hailing from Winnipeg," he answered, talking as if he were trying to gain time.

Bertha caught her breath in a little gasp, but her voice was quiet and steady when she said, "Will you tell me, please, exactly what has happened, and how the news came? I have a right to know, for my cousin, Tom Ellis, is with them."

There was a strained moment of utter silence, as if the man could not get out the tidings which were so evil in the presence of this girl to whom they meant so much, then he jerked out, unwillingly enough: "They are dead, miss, every man of the lot, Brown himself amongst them. An Indian brought the news to White Fox Creek last week telling how he had stumbled, with his tribe, on a white man's camp, with dead white men sitting in the snow huts, frozen solid, and he brought a packet of papers which he found on the bodies."

"Why did they die?" she asked, her voice ringing sharply through the hush of the room.

"Their provisions must have given out. There was a letter among the papers which stated that they had finished their survey and were coming back, but they had somehow failed to find the provisions which they had cached on the outward journey, and so they were dying of cold and starvation," replied the man, talking as if the words were being dragged out of him.

Someone moved forward from among the group by the door and quietly took his place beside Bertha. She did not look round, but some instinct told her that it was Edgar Bradgate, and she was dumbly grateful to the man who had thus constituted himself her friend and champion. It took away something of the awful sense of desolation which had been upon her ever since she had started on her momentous journey.

Then she thought of poor Grace, and the helpless little ones, and of Eunice Long. Suppose this dreadful news were to reach Duck Flats while she herself was away! The misery of the thought was too great to be borne, and she faced quickly round upon Edgar Bradgate, who was standing close beside her. "Oh, can you tell me how soon we can start?" she cried distressfully. "I do not know what will happen if this bad news reaches home before I can get there."

"I came to tell you that your car is ready, and we start in about twenty minutes," he answered quietly, and with never a word about the tragic news which she had just heard; for he guessed that she had enough to bear, and that even a word of sympathy might prove the last straw in the burden of her endurance at that moment.

The groups of men parted silently to let her pass out, and talk was not resumed until it was made certain that she was out of hearing.

The best had been done for her comfort that could be done, and an empty box car close to the one occupied by the brakeman had been set aside for her use through the kindly offices of Mike Walford, who had done his very best for her, because of the manner in which she had helped his wife. There was a fresh-trimmed lamp in the car, and a hammock had been slung across one end to mitigate the shaking and jolting as much as possible.

"Are you not coming in this car too?" Bertha asked a little timidly, as, having seen her comfortably settled, Edgar Bradgate turned to leave the car.

"No, but I shall be in the next car with the brakeman, and if anything frightens you, pull this cord. I have fastened it through into our car, and if you give a good tug at it there will be a fine commotion in our car, and I will be with you inside of one minute. Now, I am going to lock you in, unless you have any serious objection. There are a rough lot on the cars to-night, and some of them are getting unpleasantly intoxicated."

"Thank you; I would rather be locked in," replied Bertha, and then she added, with a laugh, "But I dare say that I could pick the lock if I wanted to do so just as I picked the one in the other car."

"I hope that you will not have the same reason for doing it," he replied gravely, and then he bade her goodnight and shut the door.

It was something of a comfort to hear the lock shot and to know that whatever larking the half-drunken men on the cars might indulge in, they could not annoy her, and she swung herself into the hammock with a feeling of blessed security, which certainly would not have been hers, had it not been for the presence of Edgar Bradgate in the train.

Of course it was horrible that she must still carry those wretched diamonds about with her, and with no hope of getting rid of them either now or in the immediate future. But at least she was no worse off than she had been before, for although Mr. Bradgate knew that she had them in her possession, there was no danger that he would speak of the matter, and he was entirely to be trusted himself, seeing that he would have nothing whatever to do with them.

The hammock was a great comfort in saving her from the awful jolting of the car as it rolled and bumped over the unfinished track, and Bertha felt as if she could have been quite at ease about the journey, if it had not been for her dread of crossing the bridge on the Brocken Ridge side of Wastover, and the trouble of the rumour of Tom's death.

At first she had not doubted the truth of the report, but Mrs. Walford at parting had told her not to take the news too seriously, for the Indians often grossly exaggerated ill news of this sort, and had been known to declare that a whole party had perished, when perhaps it was only one man who had died. Even the fact of the letters might have been coloured up too, and, as the stout woman had said with much kindly emphasis, it did not do to take a trouble seriously, until it was proved beyond a doubt that there was no other way out of it.

"At any rate, I cannot do anything until I get back, and if it is true that poor Tom did really die in the snow, why, I must just do the best that I can to earn a living for Grace and the children. I can manage it easily if I can only sell my stories as fast as I write them," she murmured to herself, as she swayed gently to and fro in her hammock, and the clattering racket of the empty wagons rolling over the ill-made track lulled her into forgetfulness and slumber.

CHAPTER XXXI
The Tidings Confirmed

ROWNTON was not reached until nearly noon on the following morning, and Bertha's first care was to discover if the wagon which Bill Humphries had left for repair was finished and ready for her. She must get to Pentland Broads before dark if possible, and when she reached that place she would know whether the bad news had got before her. But Edgar Bradgate, who seemed uncommonly good at getting his own way, told her to go straight to Mrs. Smith's and get a meal, while he went to see about the wagon, which should be ready at the door of Mrs. Smith's boarding-house in half an hour if he could compass it.

"You have had no food yourself. Won't you come to Mrs. Smith's also?" asked Bertha, who was rather disposed to revolt at having herself arranged for in this summary fashion.

"A cup of coffee, which I can swallow while you are tucking yourself into the wagon, and a piece of bread in my hand, which I can eat *en route*, will do quite well for me, thank you," he answered, and then hurried away, leaving her undecided whether to be most relieved or most vexed at being looked after so thoroughly.

However, she was thankful not to be obliged to pick her way along the muddy sidewalks, or rather apologies for sidewalks, in search of her wagon, and as she was desperately hungry, she made the best of her way to Mrs. Smith's, where she was able to pay some very needful attention to her toilet, while a hasty but substantial meal was prepared for her.

"You are surely not thinking of driving all the way to Pentland Broads to-day!" exclaimed Mrs. Smith, her hands uplifted in horror at the bare idea. "You will get benighted, and then you will have to put up at the halfway house, and that is certainly no place for a girl."

Bertha smiled happily—she was thinking of the long journey down from Brocken Ridge with that lot of rough and mostly intoxicated men. Not a hint of vexation had been allowed to come near her, thanks to the quiet intervention of Edgar Bradgate, and she knew that she could trust to him to shield her still, if such shielding were necessary.

"I don't think that there will be any need to put in at the halfway house on this trip," she replied. "You see, the horse did no work yesterday. Mr. Bradgate is driving over with me too, so if it is nearly dark before I get in it will not matter so much, and I am anxious to get back as quickly as I can."

"I am sure that you must be," answered Mrs. Smith, with quiet sympathy in her tone. "I was sure that it must be very uncommonly serious business which took you on a journey to Brocken Ridge, but when I heard about Brown's Expedition having come to grief, of course I guessed directly that you had gone up there to verify the rumours."

Bertha turned pale, and a cold chill crept into her heart; but she had the good sense to keep quiet, for she had heard that Mrs. Smith was one of those women who simply cannot help gossiping, and it was something of a comfort to know that for once she had got hold of an entirely wrong impression, and could talk it out to her heart's content without doing anyone the least harm.

"I declare that it knocked me all of a heap when Inspector Grant came back here from Ardley End and told me of the tragedy which had overtaken Brown's Expedition," went on Mrs. Smith. "It seems to bring things so close home to one when it is people that you know who are mixed up in a disaster of that sort. And there is your cousin, as well as poor Miss Long's brother, and oh! how she will feel it, for she thought the world of him, though somehow I never could see where his perfections lay; but there they say that love is blind, and perhaps it is just as well, or some folks would get no love at all."

"Here is the wagon!" exclaimed Bertha, with secret relief. She was finding the conversation of Mrs. Smith very wearying, and was in fear as to the good woman's next move from a talking point of view, for well she knew that she was no match for her if she began to ask questions.

"And there is Inspector Grant talking to the driver. Who did you say it was, my dear? Oh, I remember, that Mr. Bradgate who was ill so long at the police barracks. How dreadfully shabby his clothes are! and yet, in spite of it, he looks a gentleman, every inch of him. Ah! I have always maintained that you can tell the real thing at a glance," said Mrs. Smith, who had so much to say upon every subject, that the marvel was she ever got through between dawn and dark.

"I must speak to the Inspector," said Bertha, jumping up in a great hurry, and then, as she hurried out of the house, she said to her hostess, "Will you please give Mr. Bradgate a cup of coffee and something to eat as quickly as you can, because we want to start."

This request had the effect of keeping Mrs. Smith indoors and busy at the stove, so that Bertha had a moment alone with Inspector Grant when Edgar went into the house to get his coffee.

"Is it really true about the Expedition?" she asked, with quivering lips. "I heard the rumour just before I left Brocken Ridge, but Mrs. Walford told me not to put too much faith in hearsay."

"I am afraid that there is no room for doubt this time," replied the Inspector. "I have seen the papers which the Indian brought down, and they were plainly genuine documents. A very hard time the poor fellows had, and they bore it to the end like heroes."

"But I cannot understand why they sat there and waited for death to take them when they knew that they had no provisions," said Bertha. "Why did they not set out to try and reach civilization, or even an Indian encampment, where food might be obtained?"

"Well, it seems there was food somewhere near them, only they did not know where to find it. There had been some ghastly blundering somewhere, only just at present we cannot put our finger on the spot. However, we have sent two of our best men to investigate the story of the Indian and to bury the bodies, and when they return we shall know more about it," said the Inspector.

"How long will that be?" asked Bertha, who was sick at heart at the thought of the waiting which must ensue for Grace, who would know no rest or peace until the details of the tragedy were to hand.

"Say it takes them three weeks to reach the place, they must be there at least a week, perhaps ten days, and then the journey back—well, it must be seven weeks or two months before anything can be known for a certainty. It is a case for long patience, Miss Doyne, and it will need every ounce of fortitude that you possess to weather through this hard time and to help Mrs. Ellis to bear up in the face of her heavy bereavement."

Bertha nodded; she had no words with which to reply to the kindly inspector, and then, as Edgar came out of the house at this moment with a great wedge of oatcake in his hand, she clambered into the wagon and waited for him to take the driving lines in his own hands.

"I think that you will have to do the driving this trip," he said, with a smile. "I am merely escort to the expedition, not the expedition itself."

"I shall hate to drive while you sit and look on. I shall feel as if you are criticizing my way of doing it, and I do not want to be made nervous," she said, hesitating still, as if she thought that he would immediately take the lines if he saw that she did not want to do it.

"Oh, I will do my criticizing aloud, and so it will have all the effect of a lesson in driving," he answered easily; and she had to take the lines, which he handed to her, and then, as he climbed into the wagon after her, he asked a question of the Inspector, who was waiting to see them start. "Do you think that we should be wise in driving straight to Duck Flats, instead of turning off to Pentland Broads? Miss Doyne is very anxious to reach home before this bad news about the Brown Expedition, especially as Miss Long is there looking after Mrs. Ellis."

"That is a very good idea, and by taking the cross-trail through Benson's wheat you will save at least three miles; at the worst, Bill Humphries will only think that the repairs to his wagon took a little longer than he bargained for, unless, indeed, he thinks that Miss Doyne has run away with his wagon," said the Inspector; and then the black horse, refusing to be held in any longer, dashed away down the street and out along the muddy trail, ploughing through soft places and pounding along at such a wild rate, that Bertha was thankful, indeed, to have someone with her to whom she could turn if the task of driving became more than she could manage.

Her companion munched his oatcake in silence until it was gone, and even then he did not speak, leaving it to her to talk if she wished, or to sit in silence if that was what she preferred. Meanwhile, he had letters to read which had come to the police barracks for him, and had been given to him by Inspector Grant. Presently he jerked up his head and spoke with so much brisk energy in his tone, that Bertha, who had been very much absorbed, gave a little jump of astonishment.

"Do you care to hear some good news? At least, it is news that is very good for me."

"Yes, indeed, I care, and good news will be a treat, seeing how rare it has been of late," she replied wearily.

He gave her a keen glance, but made no comment on her words, only asked a question. "How much do you know of the disasters which have driven me into doing navvy work, or anything else which gave promise of an honest dollar?"

Bertha flushed, but looked steadily at him. "I do not know anything except what Mrs. Fricker said in her letter to her son, that you had been manager or agent to a company which failed, and the shareholders believed you to be guilty of deceiving them, and treated you accordingly."

"Then Mrs. Fricker let me down very gently, which is like her, for she is a kind and very noble woman," he said, smiling, although his eyes were sad. "However, it seems that I am to be cleared at last, after having lain under a cloud for more than two years. I have a letter here from Mr. Mallom, my stepfather, who tells me that one of the directors has just died, and, at the end, confessed to having thrown the entire blame on me for making certain investments, when all the time I was only working under orders, and very stringent orders at that. I came very near having to stand my trial for embezzlement also. Indeed, seeing the charges against me, I never quite understood how it was that I was not arrested; but this confession, of course, explains that the real culprits feared to go quite so far, lest a criminal enquiry might reveal that I was only the scapegoat. So they stopped at taking away my character, making me a byword among honest men, so that I have found it impossible to get work of a responsible sort. It has been a bitter experience, and I have been an Ishmael among my kind, until I have almost forgotten what it feels like to be able to hold up my head in public, or to walk abroad without having the finger of scorn pointed at me."

"But some people have always believed in you," she reminded him gently.

"Thank God, yes; and first among these has always been my stepfather, who offered to spend every dollar he possessed in the attempt to clear me. But I would not have it, for I knew that the people who were shielding themselves behind me had longer purses than we had, and so it would be victory to those who could hold out longest, and my good stepfather would have been left penniless in his old age. Moreover, I have always believed in the ultimate triumph of right, and this result proves my belief to be justified."

"What will you do now?" asked Bertha, expecting to hear him say that as soon as he had seen her safe at Duck Flats he should go east as fast as steam could get him there.

But he only gave a low, quiet laugh of intense satisfaction as he replied, "Why, just at first I shall do nothing at all, save enjoy the fact that no one any longer will call me thief, swindler, and the like. Then I shall look round for the most responsible post that I can find, and boldly ask for it. I find that really to appreciate the fact of having a good name, one needs to live under a cloud for a while."

Bertha was silent for a little time, and then she said, "I suppose that you will not go back to work on the railway again?"

"No; but that settled itself yesterday when the contractor's man told me that if I was not at my work this morning I need not trouble to come again. Kind man, he has saved me the trouble of sending him a civil resignation!"

"Oh, and it was on my account that you lost your work. I was afraid that you would have to suffer for doing so much for me," said Bertha, in distress.

Edgar laughed again. It was impossible not to feel light-hearted when such a cloud had been lifted from him.

"You did me a real kindness in coming up to Brocken Ridge to fetch me away, for otherwise I might have had to wait at least another week for this news, and think what that means to a man in my position," he said earnestly.

But Bertha was not disposed to sit passive under an imputation of such a kind, and so she said spiritedly: "You are quite wrong in thinking that I came so far to fetch you away. Nothing was further from my thoughts than that you would take the trouble to come back with me. Indeed, I would not have permitted it in any case, had it not been for Mrs. Walford's trouble about me. She had got it into her head that she would have to come back as far as Rownton with me herself, and the mere prospect of another railway journey, after her experience on the bridge, was more than she could stand, poor thing."

"All the same, it was manifestly my duty to do what I could for you, seeing how carefully you had guarded what you deemed to be my property, and it was a pleasure also," he answered, with such a sudden softening in his tone, that Bertha coloured hotly in spite of herself, and then was intensely ashamed because of her silliness.

The horse had its own notions of what was required of it in the matter of pace, and went ahead in a fashion that was so satisfactory as to leave Bertha but little to do in the way of driving. The halfway house was passed, and they just stopped to leave a message which might be given to anyone from Pentland Broads, to the effect that the wagon belonging to Bill Humphries was returning by way of Duck Flats instead of by the direct trail, and then the horse went on again with unabated vigour, until the place was reached where the cross-trail forked through Benson's wheat.

Then, indeed, the horse did object, and was disposed to fight for its own ideas in the matter of route. But Bertha had not been compelled to bear with old Pucker's obstinacy so long without learning a good deal about the whims and fancies to which horseflesh is liable, so she humoured and coaxed the big creature, even getting down from the wagon, and with her arms round its neck talked to it as if it had been a troublesome child, until it was soothed and convinced that one way would do as well as another; then she clambered back into the wagon again, and the animal went forward at its old eager pace, while the number of miles to be travelled grew speedily less and less.

Edgar had watched the little tussle without offering to interfere. It was easy to see that the girl was not in difficulties, or he would have come to her assistance at once. As it was, the incident was interesting, revealing as it did the force of character which could influence by persuasion, when no amount of scolding or whip could possibly have been so effectual. But he was very silent afterwards, and Bertha, supposing him to be absorbed in thoughts about his own affairs, was very careful not to disturb him by any attempt at conversation, and so she was considerably surprised when he asked an abrupt question about a matter which concerned herself.

"How will Mrs. Ellis and her children be supported, now that her husband is dead?"

"We shall manage somehow," said Bertha rather vaguely, for she could not tell this man, who was almost a stranger, that she deemed it her duty to be breadwinner for the family as far as she could.

"That means, I suppose, that you intend to work yourself to a skeleton in order to provide for them," he said, with that curious directness which characterized him.

Bertha coloured, and replied with a nervous laugh: "And if I do, it will be no more than paying back an old debt which my sisters and I owe to Mrs. Ellis, who gave up a good position to come and take care of us when our mother died, and one good turn deserves another, you know."

"I thought that was what you would say," he remarked, with an air of great satisfaction, and then he relapsed into a silence which lasted almost until they reached the ugly little framehouse, which stood solitary in the wide brown wilderness.

"Why, there is someone here; look at that wagon drawn up by the veranda post!" said Bertha, in surprise, pointing to a wagon standing before the house. The horses were still hitched to it, but covered with red blankets to keep them from being chilled by the cold wind drawing across the prairie, for night was coming down, and winter had as yet been pushed but a very little way into the background.

"A visitor, most likely," answered Edgar, and then he looked grave, guessing what the visitor's errand most likely amounted to, for ill news flies fast, and people are uncommonly keen in spreading the tidings of disaster.

"Why could they not have waited until I got home? It will be enough to kill poor Grace to have such tidings blurted out to her!" cried Bertha.

"Run in and do your best to stave off the telling until you can do it in your own way—you may be in time. I will see to the horse," he said, taking the lines from her hands as she sprang down without waiting for the creature to stop.

"Thanks!" she murmured, and then she ran up the steps and opened the house door, to be confronted by an amazing sight.

CHAPTER XXXII
The Man at Last

GRACE was not on the couch where she had lain so long, but was sitting in a chair by the stove. Her face was hidden in her hands, and she appeared to be weeping bitterly. Plainly the bad news had already been told to her, and Bertha clenched her hands hard at the thought of the pain she must be suffering. But the amazing thing was that a frail old man knelt at her feet, his straggling white hair hanging down on the collar of his coat, his hands clasped in entreaty, while he was speaking in a high-pitched wavering voice, pleading as if his life depended on his gaining the thing for which he asked.

"Say, is there enough goodness and charity in your heart to enable you to forgive an old man who has sinned so sorely, that if you will not forgive him, perchance he will lack forgiveness from heaven also? I was mad with jealousy that Tom should prefer an invalid wife and a houseful of little helpless children to me and the power my money could give him. I have had so little love in my life, and by my folly I have flung away what I might have had. But now, if you will forgive me for the sake of the holy dead, I promise you that want shall never touch you nor those children who call him father. Ah, I would not help him when I could, and now it is my punishment that he will not know how sorely I have repented my hardness towards him." The old man's white head dropped lower on his upraised hands, and a choking sob broke from him which was echoed by Grace.

Eunice and the children were not to be seen, but from the sounds which came to the ears of Bertha, as she stood hesitating on the threshold, she guessed that Eunice was trying to keep them quiet in the bedrooms until the visitor had had his interview with their mother.

But who could this old man be? Then at the same moment she recognized him as the old man whom she had taken care of when he was ill on the train during her journey out west, and at once she knew that he must be Tom's Uncle Joe, the queer old man who had cast his nephew off, yet who seemed to be always hanging round on the offchance of making up with him again.

Grace must be comforted. That was the one thought in Bertha's mind, as she stepped quickly across the floor and, pushing the old man to one side with very little ceremony, knelt down and wound her arms with a loving pressure about Grace.

"Oh, my dear! my dear! I have tried so hard to get home to tell you all about it myself, and it is dreadful to think that you should have had to hear it from someone else! But, Grace, dear Grace, don't believe it all just at the first, because it might not be true, you know," said Bertha, bringing her words out in a great hurry, and speaking of the hope to which she herself clung, yet without any previous intention of doing so; for both she and Edgar Bradgate had decided that it was not kind to let Grace indulge in any hope which had no chance of proving true.

"Bertha, Bertha, it can't surely be true! It is too ghastly and horrible! Why, I have been expecting Tom every day since the snow went away, and now to be told that he will never come home at all—oh, it is too hard to bear!" wailed the invalid, clinging to the girl's slight figure with the desperation of despair.

"Then keep on expecting him until we are quite sure," whispered Bertha, in loving encouragement. "There can be no harm in hoping until there is no longer anything to hope for. Of course it was a kind thought of this—this gentleman to come and tell you the bad news, but on the whole it will be kinder not to insist on your believing it just yet."

"I did not come solely to tell the bad news, but to assure the widow of my dear nephew that I would take care of her and her helpless children for the sake of the dear dead," said the old man, with trembling tones, it is true, but with so much arrogance of manner, because of the favour he had it in his power to bestow, that Bertha was stung into impetuous speech.

"Grace will not be an object of charity, nor will she need that you should take care of her for the sake of her husband. I shall take care of her for her own sweet sake, and because, when my mother died, she came and took care of me," she said, tumbling her words out in a great hurry, and getting very red in the face from indignation at what she deemed the horrible patronage in the old man's manner.

He held up his hands in a meekly protesting fashion.

"Oh, my dear, you have a long life before you in which you may do kind acts to anyone you please, and lay up for yourself a harvest of blessedness for the years to come. But I have only a few years to live at the most, and there is no time for me to make amends for all the wrong things that I have done, but I want to gather just a little love for myself before my barren life comes to an end, so do not refuse to let me help at least in providing the necessary money to keep the home going."

The note of wistful pleading in the old man's tone at once melted Bertha's resentment against him, and she gently guided him to a chair on the other side of the stove. "Sit down and rest a little; there will be plenty of time in which to decide what it is best to do when we are quite sure that Tom really died in that frozen-out camp. But just now Grace is tired, and must stay quiet for a while."

"Thank you, yes; and I will rest too, for I also am tired," he answered, submitting to be put into the chair as if he were a child, and then he sat leaning back with his eyes closed, and looking so frail that Bertha became suddenly anxious on his account; for this was just how he had looked that day when he was taken ill on the train.

"Oh, Bertha, what a comfort it is to have you back again!" cried Grace; and then she said anxiously, "But poor Eunice is in there with the children. I asked her to take them out of the way when Uncle Joe first began to speak, and I do not think that she heard anything about it. But she must be told. Can you tell her, dear?"

Bertha nodded, and, crossing the room, opened the bedroom door, where Eunice was doing her best to keep the children from making a forcible rush out upon the visitor who was talking to their mother.

"Dicky, there is a gentleman out in the barn trying to unhitch that black horse which Bill Humphries drives over here sometimes. I wish that you would go and help him. Take Molly with you, and ask the gentleman if he will unhitch the pair as well," said Bertha, and, nothing loath, the two eldest dashed straight through the kitchen and out-of-doors without staying to bestow a single glance upon their mother or the frail old man who sat in the chair on the far side of the stove. They were followed by the twins and sturdy little Noll, so Bertha and Eunice were left alone.

"Bertha, what has that old man come to tell Mrs. Ellis? Is it anything about the Expedition?" asked Eunice, her face sharpened into anxious lines.

"Yes, there is news, and bad news, but Inspector Grant is sending reliable men to investigate, and it will be seven weeks, or perhaps two months, before we can know for certain," said Bertha, coming to the point without any delay, because she realized that it was the kindest thing to do.

Eunice shivered and turned white, but she did not faint or give way to hysterical ravings. Those women of the west had to face grave issues too often to be strangers to death or disaster, so she was silent for a little time, and then she said: "I am so thankful that you have come home, because now I can go back to Pentland Broads to—to be ready for anything that may come."

"Yes, you will be able to go back now, that is, to-morrow morning; but, unless I am much mistaken, you and I shall have our hands full to-night with that poor old man out yonder. He is an old uncle of Tom's. He is nearly frantic about this bad news, and I have seen him like this before, for he is the old man who was so ill on the train when we were snowed up on my journey out west."

Bertha had struck a right note when she spoke of the need there might be for the help of Eunice in taking care of Uncle Joe; for it seemed to quiet her directly and to take away the eager desire to be gone which had come to her on hearing the evil tidings.

"I was just beginning to get supper ready when he came, and oh, Bertha, he behaved like a man distraught," said Eunice, in a whisper, and then she followed Bertha back to the outer room, where the two of them laid Grace back on her couch, and then began active preparations for supper, for with extra people to feed it was necessary to set about preparing the meal for them.

"How did you come?" asked Eunice, putting aside her own pain and anxiety, which must perforce wait for seven or eight weeks before it could be made into certainty of any kind. It was there all the time, but was pushed into the background for the sake of other people.

The old man took no notice of either of them, but sat with his eyes shut, while they moved softly to and fro between the stove and the table, until the daylight began to merge into the shades of night. Then the door burst open and the children trooped in, dragging Edgar Bradgate with them.

"I have unhitched all the horses, and, if you will permit me to shake down in the barn, I think it will be better for me not to attempt the journey on to Pentland Broads to-night," he said, addressing himself in courteous tones to Bertha, after he had been duly presented to Eunice. "That horse of Mr. Humphries has done a heavy day's work, and is rather the worse for it, and the pair are just about spun out. Where have they been driven from, do you know?"

But Bertha only shook her head with a warning glance at the old man, who seemed to be dozing in the corner, and then she said that she feared Mr. Bradgate would find it very uncomfortable in the barn.

"It is a decidedly more palatial lodging than I had at Brocken Ridge," he answered cheerfully. "Why, the men in the State prisons are far more comfortably lodged than we were. Now, if you will give me the pail, I will go and milk. I have already fed the pigs and the poultry under the guidance of Dicky."

"It is very kind of you," said Bertha, but she accepted his services without any protest; for where there was so much to be done it was only fair that each one should take his or her part, and she was anxious to spare Eunice as much as she possibly could.

It was not until supper was ready on the table that the old man roused himself, and then he appealed to Grace, as the head of the household, to know whether he might stay there all night, because he felt too ill and worn out to go any farther.

Grace gave one swift, imploring look at Bertha, and, reading what she wanted there, answered, with sweet cordiality: "Why, yes, Uncle Joe, of course we shall be very glad to have you, and I hope that you will not find the children too noisy for your comfort."

"Thank you, my dear niece, thank you," he said, then sat with his head drooped forward as before, while Bertha watched him uneasily, for just so had he sat on that day in the train before he had been taken ill.

Then Edgar Bradgate came in, carrying the pail with the evening's milk, and she went with him into the little pantry, which was also storeroom, to put it away, then when he came back with her they sat down to supper.

"Don't trouble; Noll and I can share chairs," said Edgar, with a laugh, as he lifted the youngest of the Ellis children on to his knee, to save Eunice the trouble of fetching another chair from the bedroom.

It was then that the old man lifted his head, opened his eyes, and looked straight at Edgar. A curious change came over him then, and Bertha, who was looking at him, thought that he was going to have a fit.

For a moment he sat speechless, his face working strangely, then he sprang to his feet and hurled himself upon the astonished young man, who was nursing Noll, crying out in incoherent rage: "You—you thief, you thief! What have you done with my property, which you stole before my very eyes?"

Bertha sprang up also, her face very white. "Hush, hush, you will feel better soon!" she said soothingly.

But he pushed her aside with an impatient hand and, gripping Edgar by the coat, shook him savagely, as a dog shakes a rat which he is worrying to death.

"Where is my case of diamonds that you stole?" he shouted, his voice rising to a shriek of fury. "I say, what have you done with my diamonds? Worth two hundred thousand dollars they were, and you walked off with them as calmly as if they were your own, though I shouted and yelled until I was hoarse! What have you done with them? I say, what have you done with them?"

"Look here, try to be a little quieter, if you can, and tell me what you mean," said Edgar, standing quite still and speaking in a soothing tone, for it was easy to see that the old man was in a state of dangerous excitement.

"Haven't I told you already?" shrieked Uncle Joe, more furious than before. "I have searched for you everywhere! Your description has been posted up in every police barracks between here and Nova Scotia, and I knew that I should run you to earth at last, and you cannot escape me now!"

CHAPTER XXXIII
The Mystery Clears

WAS there ever such a scene of confusion?

Noll burst into howls of terror, and the twins speedily followed suit, the three of them scuttling away to their mother's sofa, under which they bolted like rabbits to their burrow. Dicky and Molly cast themselves upon Bertha, loudly demanding protection from the naughty old man, who had grumbled at their mother until she cried, and then had attacked the nice kind man who had unhitched the horses and milked the cow; and for a few moments, despite the best endeavours of Bertha and Eunice towards peace and quiet, the turmoil was so great that it was impossible for anyone's voice to pierce the din of screaming and crying which arose from the excited old man and the badly scared children.

But Edgar Bradgate stood perfectly quiet, and it was his calmness which finally soothed the old man into something like self-control again. Then he addressed himself to Grace in a tone of apology, even looking a little ashamed of his outburst.

"I crave your pardon, my dear niece, for making such an unseemly riot in your quiet home, and my excuse must be the extreme provocation that I have received. For two long years I have been tracking this man from the description which I could give of him, but I did not even know his name, and I have often despaired of bringing him to justice or getting my stolen property back again; so when I saw him calmly sitting on the other side of the table and nursing your child as if he were quite at home in the house, I will admit that I permitted my temper to run away with my discretion."

"But won't you tell us what it is that he has done, Uncle Joe, and then we shall be better able to understand things?" asked Grace, in a persuasive tone, and casting such a look of kindly encouragement at the accused as rendered the old man almost incoherent from indignation again.

"What he has done! What he has done! Why, it was the most barefaced robbery that I have ever heard of, and why he was not taken at the time with the stones upon him I could never understand; for I raised outcry enough. Indeed, I have often thought that the police must have been in league with him, and so they connived at his escape," raved Uncle Joe, shaking his prisoner again with a savage air; but Edgar bore it with perfect patience, waiting quietly for explanations.

"What did he steal?" asked Grace again, while, as before, she sent a kindly glance towards the accused.

"Diamonds, magnificent uncut diamonds!" shouted the excited old man, with another fierce shake of his passive prisoner. "I had just taken a case of diamonds from a man, and I had lent him two hundred thousand dollars on them. I stuffed the case into the breast pocket of my overcoat—a brown cloth coat it was, with one top button missing, which a tipsy man had dragged off the day before, pulled it out by the roots, in fact—and I got into the cars, for I was off to Paston to attend a meeting of shareholders of a company which had gone wrong. I stood to lose five hundred thousand dollars over that business, so I was feeling pretty sore all round, or perhaps I might have taken more care of my diamonds. I was late in reaching the meeting, and I went into a dressing-room to leave my coat, which I took off and tossed on to a heap of others, quite forgetting that I had left the case of diamonds there. But I remembered it before I reached the room of the hotel where the meeting was being held, and I was turning back as quickly as I could move, when the door opened and an excited young man dashed out. He rushed past me and hurried into the waiting-room, picked up a coat, and dashed off again by another door; and it was not until he had gone that I saw it was my coat he had taken with him. I think something gave way inside my head at that moment, for I seemed to go quite mad when I rushed after him screaming and shouting at the top of my voice. But I did not catch him, and from that day to this I have only seen him once."

"When was that?" demanded Grace; but into the face of Bertha there had come the light of a great relief, and, turning a little aside, her hands were busy fumbling at the front of her blouse to reach the little bag which she wore strapped round her neck.

"It was just before harvest in the very next year—indeed, it was that day when I came to borrow some money from Tom, and you told me that he was too poor to lend it to me—I was driving back to Pentland Broads by a cross-trail through the wheat, when a man passed me driving a wagon, smothered in dirt and dust he was, but I knew him again. It was the man who had run away with my coat and the case of diamonds—this man who stands here, and let him deny it if he can!" cried the old man, as his lean fingers took a firmer grip of his prisoner.

"I don't even want to deny it," said Edgar Bradgate quietly, and then he looked across at Bertha, saying, with a smile, "The explanation lies with you, Miss Doyne."

And Bertha was quick to respond. Giving a final tug to the bag at her neck, she pulled it out, and, drawing the case from it, she laid it in the hand of the angry old man, saying quietly: "Can you tell me if those are the stones which you lost? Because, if they are, they have been in my possession ever since the day when you lost them, and Mr. Bradgate has known nothing whatever about them."

"They are mine! They are mine!" shrieked the old man, and the shock of recovering them so suddenly being quite too much for him, he dropped where he stood in a faint on the floor.

Edgar Bradgate stooped to lift him. "I was afraid so much excitement must have been bad for the poor old fellow," he said, in a pitying tone, and then he handed back the case of diamonds to Bertha, for they had dropped from the old man's nerveless hand, "You will have to take care of this case again, Miss Doyne. It seems to be your fate to have those stones in your custody."

"Take care of them, Grace, they are more your business than mine, now that we know to whom they belong," said Bertha, tossing the case on to her cousin's couch, and then she went to help Edgar and Eunice restore the old man to consciousness again.

But that was what their combined efforts could not do. For a long time they worked, doing their utmost, but the frail old body had been quite unfit to bear the strain of such fierce excitement, coming, as it probably did, upon a long fast, and at length Eunice desisted from her task and said to the others:

"We can do no more, and I think that the poor old man is dying. We ought to have the doctor."

"I will go for him," said Edgar, without hesitation. "The moon should be thinking of showing pretty soon now, and I shall be able to find my way along the trail all right."

"But the horse—you said that it was dead beat," said Bertha.

"Can't I have your old horse?" he asked. "That, at any rate, is fresh enough by the way it squealed and kicked when I fed it this evening."

"Oh, I had forgotten Pucker," Bertha said, with a great relief in her tone. "I will go and hitch up while you get some supper. No, it is of no use to protest, because you have not had one proper meal to-day, and I can feed when you are gone. Then, too, I can harness old Pucker quicker than you could hope to do it; for the old horse has a rather queer temper, and simply loves to show off to strangers."

Edgar gave way then, since there was so much truth in what Bertha said about being able to hitch up more quickly than he could do it; so he went back to the kitchen, where the neglected supper was spread upon the table, then he coaxed the children out from their hiding-place about the sofa and fed them while he got his own meal. Of course the coffee was cold, but even cold coffee is satisfying to a man who has not had a proper meal for twenty-four hours, and when one is very hungry, anything in the way of food becomes absolutely appetizing.

The children were also very hungry, and so they were the more easily consoled, although, it is sad to relate, they could not hide their elation when they knew that the cross old man was very ill, and Molly voiced the general opinion when she said that she hoped that he would stay so.

"Can I bring you anything, Mrs. Ellis, or do anything for you?" Edgar asked, when he had the children all happily employed at the table.

"Thank you, no. I shall do very well until Bertha or Eunice has time to attend to me," Grace answered, and then, a thought coming into her mind, she asked quickly, "Will you tell me quite candidly whether you think that I have any reason to keep on hoping that my husband is alive? I know that Bertha would bid me hope, from the very best of motives, just to keep me from giving way to despair; but what do you think?"

What could he say? Previously he had not had the slightest doubt that the whole of the Expedition had shared the same fate, but, to his own surprise, he suddenly found himself doubting. Why should everyone be so ready to believe that they had all perished? Was it likely that a score or more of able-bodied men would tamely sit down for death to claim them when the stores gave out? It was much more likely that they would make an attempt to reach some place where food could be found, and so, although they might have to suffer great hardships, they might yet win through.

"What do you think?" persisted Grace, her wistful eyes scanning his face to see if haply she could glean a little hope from its expression.

He hesitated a moment, then answered frankly, "Five minutes ago I did not think it possible for there to be any more hope that they have any of them survived, but now I am disposed to think that perhaps we may hear of some of them having got through; only, it will take some time for that, you know, and we cannot be sure of anything for weeks and weeks yet to come. Don't give up hope all the time that there is the barest shred of hope to cling to."

"Thank you," she answered softly, and he went out of the house with a pang at his heart, because he had no better comfort to give to her.

"It is so cold to-night, that you will need to wrap up well. Have you no other coat?" asked Bertha, when she led old Pucker up to the door.

"No; you see my entire wardrobe," he said, with a laugh which was quite free from embarrassment. His poverty was owing to no fault of his own, so there was no need to be ashamed of it; then he asked, "Could you lend me a sack or an old rug to wrap round me? It will never do to let the influenza fiend find me out again, or I shall be a nuisance to somebody as I was before."

Bertha darted into the house and returned in a moment with a shabby brown coat that had a well-worn black velvet collar, and this she held out for his use.

"Most likely it is your own coat, the one which you left behind when you picked up the poor old man's by mistake," she said, with a nervous laugh. "At any rate, it is as much like the one in which I found the diamonds as it is possible for one coat to be like another."

"Wait a moment, I will just run through the pockets before I put it on, in case there should be anything valuable there," he said, taking the coat from her and feeling in all the pockets, turning out gloves, handkerchief, and a bulky woollen scarf.

"Oh, there is the old neck-wrap that I gave him that cold day when we were snowed up on the rail!" she cried, picking it up and holding it out for inspection.

"May I borrow that also?" Edgar held out his hand for it, and she gave it to him with a sudden sense of embarrassment not to be accounted for by any laws of reason or logic.

Even the touch of their hands as they met added to her unexplained confusion, and she was glad that it was so dark out on the veranda that he could not possibly see how violently she was blushing about nothing at all.

But was it nothing at all? Something like panic set up in Bertha's heart as she went back into the house, where Eunice was still busy with the poor old man. It was of no use for her to try and blind herself to what that sudden confusion meant, and her fear was lest someone else should read on her face the very same tidings that her heart was telling her in such unmistakable language just then.

"Oh, I should die of shame if anyone were to guess that I cared for him!" she said to herself, with a little gasping sob, then she plunged into the confusion of things waiting to be done, and losing some of her miserable self-consciousness as she darted to and fro, clearing the table, putting the children to bed, and comforting Grace between whiles.

She dared not trust herself to think how she would manage to meet Edgar Bradgate when he came back with the doctor. She would have to thrust this new knowledge of her own heart far into the background, lest haply it should be seen by the very eyes from which she was most concerned to hide it.

Meanwhile Pucker was tearing along the lonely trail to Pentland Broads, with the wagon swaying and bumping in the rear.

The man who was driving was trying hard not to go to sleep, but he was so tired that wakefulness was almost beyond him. He had hardly dared to close his eyes on the long journey down from Brocken Ridge in the empty freighter, for he had been so afraid that Bertha might want him, and that he should not hear her, and it would not have fitted his ideas of what was right and proper to fail the girl, who had gone through so much to serve him.

He had been looking forward to a night's rest in the barn, and to be forced to turn out and drive so many miles through the dark, cold night was by no means a pleasant experience. But it had to be done, and so he sat huddled on the wagon seat, dozing fitfully, and comforting himself that the old horse knew the way much better than he knew it himself, when suddenly Pucker stopped dead, almost flinging Edgar from the driving seat, and arousing him from his dozing with a jerk.

"Steady, old man, steady!" he muttered, in that tone which is usually supposed to restore confidence to a horse troubled with nerves. But on Pucker this advice seemed a little thrown away and entirely unnecessary, as the creature was standing as if it had been planted there.

"What is up? Go on, can't you," said the driver, wondering if the horse were a jibber, and, if so, whether it would be his unfortunate lot to sit there for hours until it seemed good to Pucker to proceed.

But Pucker paid no heed to the admonition, and a jerk of the reins producing no other effect than to make him toss his head, Edgar decided that he would have to get down and investigate the business at close quarters.

"Steady, there!" he murmured encouragingly, as he unrolled himself from his various rugs and wrappings and then got slowly out of the wagon.

He was so stiff and cramped, that he stumbled and nearly fell, but, recovering himself with an effort, he went to the horse's head, and by the light of the rising moon saw that a dark object was lying in the soft mud of the trail.

"A man! And if it had not been for the horse, I should have run over him!" he exclaimed aloud; and now there was a thrill of horror in his tone, for he had been far too sleepy to notice whether or not the trail was clear.

Leaving the horse, which had been too wise to trample on that prostrate figure, Edgar stooped over the man to investigate his condition.

"Tipsy? Hardly likely, for if he had been intoxicated when he left Pentland Broads, he would be sober by this time, or at least I think that I should be if I had managed to walk so far. He looks like a dead-beat, poor chap, and what on earth shall I do with him?"

Edgar stood straight up and gazed round in the darkness, as if in search of inspiration.

"Well, I'm going for the doctor, so the best thing I can do is to take the poor chap along too, if I can get him up in the wagon, that is. I must get him into the wagon, for it is certain that I cannot leave him lying out here while I go to get help."

Stripping off his coat, and then peeling off the jacket which he wore below, Edgar set to work upon his task. And a frightfully hard task it was, too, for the unknown was bigger than he was himself, and it is likely that he never would have succeeded in getting him into the wagon at all, but for the fact that the man was wasted to a mere bag of bones, and so was the easier to haul about.

Once or twice the poor fellow groaned, as if in protest at the rough treatment which he was receiving, so Edgar knew that there was still life left in the man and persevered in his task, determined to get the poor fellow up somehow. Pucker stood like a post. Perhaps the old horse understood that there was life to be saved, and certain it was that Edgar's task would have been much harder, and perhaps impossible, if the horse had been restive and anxious to get on; for there was not a post, or a stump, or indeed anything to tie an animal to, so that standing still was an act of grace on the part of the horse, and it helped to save a man's life.

As soon as he had managed to get his unconscious passenger on board, Edgar slipped on his jacket, but took the brown coat to wrap round the unknown. Bertha's scarf, however, he kept for himself, and the feel of it about his neck seemed to keep his heart warm. It was ugly, ragged, and old, but it had a magic property in it on this cold spring night, when the light of the moon came faintly through dense masses of clouds, which meant rain next day.

Would the man live until Pentland Broads was reached? The question beat itself out to a monotonous, dirge-like tune in the brain of Edgar as he drove along, and the clop, clop, clop of Pucker's feet was the only sound that broke the stillness.

Night in the forest is rarely entirely quiet; there is sound and movement all the time, faint whisperings, stealthy creakings, and a suggestion of hidden life on every side. But on the open prairie there is none of this; it is a dense, brooding quiet, which may be literally felt, and it lay upon Edgar as a burden that was too heavy to be borne. Pentland Broads at last! The moon came out from behind the clouds to throw a flood of silvery radiance down upon the ugly houses which were grouped about the store, and the horse quickened its pace, as if understanding the need there was of haste in reaching the end of the journey.

One solitary light gleamed amid the cluster of sleeping dwellings, and that was at the house of the doctor, for which Edgar made a bee line, although he nearly upset the wagon, and must have given his unconscious passenger a cruel shaking, for he drove across a piece of ground which was being trenched for building purposes, and never realized that he was off the trail until he was so nearly upset. However, he got through safely, and, as he saved about ten minutes, the short cut had been well worth taking.

To spring down from the wagon and to bang at the doctor's door was the work of a minute only, then came a brief period of acute anxiety lest the doctor should not be at home.

"Who is there? What do you want?" shouted a voice from the window hastily thrust open, and Edgar found to his great disgust that his own voice was not entirely steady when he answered:

"I want you to come out to Duck Flats to see an old man who seems to be dying, but as I was coming for you I nearly drove over another man, a deadbeat apparently, and I brought him along with me. You will have to look after him first, for he seems in a bad way, I can tell you."

"I'll be out in three minutes," growled the doctor, in no very pleased tone, then he banged the window, and Edgar was left to wait through an interminable three minutes, which seemed to him to be at least half an hour, so impatient was he about the condition of the man in the wagon.

Then the door opened, and the doctor bustled out, as neat and trim of appearance as if he had been sitting up waiting for patients to come, instead of having been in bed sound asleep less than five minutes before.

"Now, then, what is wrong?" he said, bustling round to the end of the wagon, and peering at the figure which lay wrapped in the brown topcoat. "You are right, he does look in need of some attention. We shall have to carry him indoors. My word, but he is a fine lump of a man, though he is only a bag of bones. How did you manage to get him into the wagon, if he was senseless when you picked him up?"

"I dragged him up somehow. I could not have done it if the horse had not stood, as it were, planted in the ground and had taken root there. As it was, I had my work cut out, for the poor fellow is bigger than I am," panted Edgar, as he and the doctor lifted the man from the wagon and carried him indoors to the light.

"Well, I never!" exclaimed the doctor, in a tone of pure amazement, as he surveyed his new patient by the light of the lamp.

"Is he dead?" asked Edgar, in a tone of deep disappointment, for it seemed too bad to have had to work so hard and then not be able to save the man after all.

"Dead! Good gracious, I hope not!" cried the doctor, beginning to work at the poor fellow in feverish haste. "Why, man, it is Tom Ellis himself, the owner of Duck Flats, and there are women and children there who will love you all your life for what you have done to-night!"

CHAPTER XXXIV
The End

IT was more than a week later before Tom Ellis was well enough to be carried to his home at Duck Flats, and by that time everyone knew all that there was to be known of his wonderful escape from death.

When the supplies ran short, and the Expedition, unable to find their cache, were faced with starvation, the members drew lots for two of them to take the risk of working their way back, through the constantly recurring blizzards and over the wide stretches of trackless country, to the nearest point of civilization, whence help could be obtained. The lots fell to Tom Ellis and the brother of Eunice Long, and when they started they believed that they were going to certain death, but the lot had fallen to them and it was their duty to go.

So many times death stared them in the face, that it was like a miracle they did not perish on the way. The poor man Long had to be left at the first Indian encampment upon which they chanced, for he was so badly frostbitten that he could not stand upon his feet. From that time Tom Ellis had to press on alone; then he fell into a wolf trap set by an Indian, from which he was fished out more dead than alive, and he lay for weeks too ill to remember the errand on which he set out, and he must have died but for the kindness and the care of the wild people, who were hard pressed themselves for food.

As soon as he was able to walk he set out again, but the very first point of civilization which he reached was an outlying settlement, where the news had been first carried of the disaster which had overtaken the Expedition, and then he knew that he had failed. The knowledge was so bitter, that at the first he was ready to lie down and die from sheer despair at having failed. But the thought of his helpless wife and the little children waiting for him at home spurred him on to make the final effort necessary to get home, and when he had rested a little he set forth again; but it is certain that he would never have reached home alive, had it not been for Edgar Bradgate having to fetch the doctor in the middle of the night, when the horse found his prostrate body lying in the middle of the trail.

Great was the rejoicing at Pentland Broads when it was found that both Tom Ellis and the brother of Eunice Long were alive. Young Semple and the redhaired Fricker set off for the Indian encampment to bring home Mr. Long; but for the present Eunice stayed on at Duck Flats, and left the nursing of Tom Ellis to the doctor's housekeeper, for death had come to the solitary little house in the wheatfields, and Bertha could not be left alone at such a time.

Uncle Joe had never recovered consciousness, but had slipped out of life immediately after the doctor's arrival, so he never knew the joyful news of which the doctor was the bearer on that bright spring morning.

If there was no real grief, but only gentle regret for the old man who had hastened his own end by the violence of his passions, that was surely more his own fault than that of anyone else, since it is open to everyone who comes into this world to earn love and to keep it. They were sorry for him, but there was no sense of loss—the bitter feeling of emptiness which constitutes real grief.

He was laid to rest in the bare little burying ground at the back of the meeting house, while Edgar Bradgate and Bertha were the chief mourners, because there was no one else to stand in that position. Poor Tom was too ill to be told anything about it, and Grace, of course, was not fit for the exertion of following anyone to the grave, because she could not as yet stand upon her feet. One thing, however, she insisted upon, and that was that she should be carried over to Pentland Broads to see her husband, and although the journey must have shaken her very much, the joy of being with him again was so great that it did her more good than harm.

It was Edgar Bradgate who drove the pair of them back over the rough trail to their home as soon as the doctor would allow Tom to be moved, and, as the long miles had to be covered at a pace which would not shake the two invalids unduly, it was not wonderful that the talk which was indulged in grew very intimate and confidential before the end of the journey was reached.

Edgar told them that he wanted to marry Bertha, but that he dared not ask her because he had discovered the fact of her writing, and he feared that a girl with a literary future before her would not care to tie herself to a poor man.

"Still it is not fair to Bertha that she should not have the chance of doing what she pleased," said Grace, while a flush of colour rose in her pale cheeks.

"What do you mean?" asked Edgar, leaning down a little nearer to Grace, who sat propped up in a funny, old easy chair behind the driving seat.

"I mean that if Bertha happens to care for you, it is rather hard on her that she should never have a chance of choosing happiness with you, and all because she has made the very best use of the gift that was in her," Grace answered, in a spirited tone.

"Do you think——?" began Edgar, with a gleam of hope lighting up his eyes, which were apt to look a little sombre.

"I don't think anything, and I would not tell you if I did," Grace replied crossly. "I only say that if you care for Bertha, as you say that you do, it is your duty to tell her so."

"And to get flouted for my pains, maybe," said Edgar moodily.

"If you have such a poor opinion of Bertha as to think that she could be guilty of such meanness, your love cannot be worth much," retorted Grace.

"Don't be too hard on him, wife. I have felt very much the same myself in days gone by," said Tom, with a laugh, and then he began to talk of the advisability of sowing oats and potatoes, as well as wheat, for the next harvest, and the conversation did not come near matters purely personal again during the remainder of that long, slow drive.

It was a week later still when a letter came from Hilda which contained tidings of importance for Bertha. Hilda was intending to sail for Australia, where, with her European training fresh upon her, she intended setting up for herself in Adelaide. She wanted to have a home of her own, and she was quite positive that she could soon get a teaching connection large enough to support herself and Bertha, and with Anne only fifty miles away, it would be almost like the old days at Mestlebury over again. So she begged that Bertha would give up her position as hired girl in Cousin Tom's household and come to Australia without delay.

"What cool impudence, to call you a hired girl!" growled Tom, who had long ago taken quite an unreasonable prejudice against bright, capable Hilda.

"Bertha would certainly have more time for her own work, and an easier life altogether, in living with Hilda," put in Grace; but to this Bertha made no reply, as she took the pail and went out to milk the cow.

She was feeling miserably depressed, although in reality she ought to have been very happy indeed, seeing that some, at least, of the tangles had been smoothed out of her path.

By the very same mail which had brought Hilda's letter, a communication had been received from the lawyer engaged in winding up the estate of Tom's Uncle Joe, stating that the old man had left a brief will behind him, in which everything he possessed was left to his dear nephew, Thomas Ellis; so there would be no more straitened means for the household at Duck Flats, and it was very certain that they would not forget their past indebtedness to her for standing by them so bravely in their troubles.

"Bah! As if money were everything!" she exclaimed, with almost spiteful emphasis, as she rose from her stool, and then she blushed a furious red as Edgar Bradgate entered the barn.

"Where have you sprung from? I thought that you were at Rownton," she said, in surprise.

"I have been even farther than that, for I have just come from Gilbert Plains," he answered, and then he went on, "And I have had some work offered to me at last, really responsible work, I mean, which is one of the good things resulting from having a character once more."

"Are you going to take it?" she asked.

"That is what I was coming to ask you," he replied. "Having a prospect at last of being able to keep a wife makes me bold enough to ask for what I want, and as I would rather marry you than be President of the United States, or any equally exalted office, it is for you to say whether I can take this post and be happy."

The colour went flaming over Bertha's face as she placed the milk-pail on the ground and stood looking at him, as if in actual doubt of his meaning, although his words had been plain enough. Then a light of dancing mischief came in her eyes, and she asked demurely—

"And if I say no?"

His face fell, and he winced visibly, though his voice was very quiet as he replied: "In that case I must be outcast again, but with this difference, that now I shall have no hope left, and in the worst of my troubles hope never failed me before."

But Bertha had already repented of her teasing, and, slipping her hand into his, murmured softly—

"And it need not fail you now."

Hilda was dreadfully disappointed to find that Bertha was not coming to keep house for her in Adelaide, while Anne wrote long letters protesting that Bertha was too much of a baby to think of getting married yet for years to come. But when Tom, at the instigation of Grace, wrote to them of the tremendous changes which had taken place in Bertha, and the capable manner in which she had borne herself through crises which might well have tried the nerves of a much older person, the elder sisters decided that she was at last able to take her own way, and to choose her own lot for herself.

The case of diamonds, which had given so much trouble and anxiety to Bertha, was sold to an American millionaire, something in shoe blacking he was, and they realized the two hundred thousand dollars which the old man had said that they were worth. Some of the money went to provide Grace with the best medical skill the Dominion could supply, another portion was set aside as a wedding gift to Bertha, and some of the remainder went in building a more commodious house at Duck Flats; for nothing would induce Tom Ellis to leave the prairie which he so dearly loved.

Bertha protested at the size of the gift which was to be hers when she married, but Grace stopped her, saying, with a laugh which bordered closely on tears—

"But for you, dear, there had been no money at all, for Uncle Joe's affairs are so hopelessly involved, and he has muddled so much money away in foolish speculation, that when it is wound up his estate will only just about clear itself."

"That is all the more reason why you should keep the money, and it is no virtue of mine that I took care of the stones, seeing that I supposed them to be another man's, and only waited for the chance of restoring them to him. It is not a virtue to be honest," Bertha repeated, with emphasis.

"I think that it must be, seeing that it is a vice to be dishonest," said Grace, as she leaned her head against Bertha's shoulder. "But if it had not been for you and your brave doing of hard and unpleasant duty, I should not have been here at all. I could not have struggled through all that long, hard time of helplessness if it had not been for you. It was because of you, and what you did for me, that I kept my hold on hope, and it was hope that saved my life."

"And if it had not been for you I should never have had the courage to do anything at all," replied Bertha. "And, Grace, that Boston firm has written to say that they will undertake my book and bring it out next fall, and that would certainly never have been written if it had not been for you, so the burden of indebtedness is about even."

Then Grace quoted softly the words from Holy Writ—

"For none of us liveth to himself."